SEA-BORN WOMEN

John F. Blair, Publisher · Winston-Salem, North Carolina

SEA-BORN WOMEN

BJ MOUNTFORD

Published by John F. Blair, Publisher

The paper in this book meets the guidelines
for permanence and durability of the
Committee on Production Guidelines for
Book Longevity of the Council on Library Resources.

Library of Congress Cataloging-in-Publication Data

Mountford, B J
  Sea-born women / by B J Mountford.
    p.   cm.
  ISBN 0-89587-265-X (alk.paper)
    1. Volunteer workers in parks—Fiction. 2. Portsmouth Island (N.C.)—Fiction. 3.
Archaeological thefts—Fiction. 4. Women detectives—Fiction. 5. Serial murders—
Fiction. 6. Hurricanes—Fiction. I. Title.

PS3613.O86 S43 2002
813'.6—dc21

                                                              2002016300

Background image on front cover by Pat Deshinsky
Design by Debra Long Hampton
Composition by The Roberts Group

To the memory of my husband, Ed, who was
always there when I needed him

To my daughters, Pat and Linnette, who have almost
as much time and creative effort in this novel as I do;
to the Carteret Writers' genre group, without whose
help this book would not exist; and
to publisher Carolyn Sakowski and editor in chief
Steve Kirk, who made me rewrite until it was right

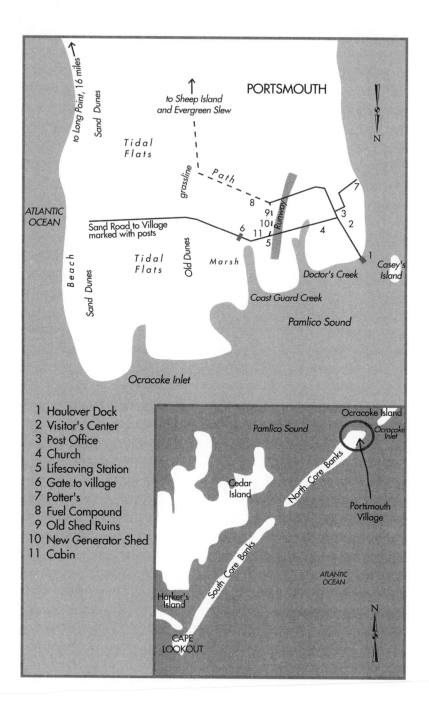

PORTSMOUTH

to Long Point, 16 miles

to Sheep Island
and Evergreen Slew

Sand Dunes

Tidal
Flats

grassline

Path

ATLANTIC
OCEAN

Sand Road to Village
marked with posts

Beach

Tidal
Flats

Old Dunes

Marsh

Sand Dunes

8

Runway

9
10
11
5

7

3 2
4

6

1

Doctor's Creek

Casey's
Island

Coast Guard Creek

Pamlico Sound

N

Ocracoke Inlet

1 Haulover Dock
2 Visitor's Center
3 Post Office
4 Church
5 Lifesaving Station
6 Gate to village
7 Potter's
8 Fuel Compound
9 Old Shed Ruins
10 New Generator Shed
11 Cabin

Ocracoke Island

Pamlico Sound

Ocracoke
Inlet

Cedar
Island

North Core Banks

Portsmouth
Village

South Core Banks

Harker's
Island

CAPE
LOOKOUT

ATLANTIC
OCEAN

N

Author's Note

Of all Charles Harry Whedbee's stories, "Sea-born Woman" from *The Flaming Ship of Ocracoke & Other Tales of the Outer Banks* is my favorite. Who murdered the ex-pirate Spriggs on Portsmouth Island, and why? And why did his housekeeper, Jerushia, whose birth saved a shipload of emigrants, haunt the house? The tale seems unfinished.

Then I had occasion to serve as volunteer resident for the National Park Service at Portsmouth Village, North Carolina, four years in a row. If there are any ghosts in the village, they're friendly. The abandoned Coastal Heritage Site sparked my interest in history. During my research, I discovered there really was a pirate by the name of Spriggs, who served under Ned Low and vanished after an encounter with the British navy. As per Whedbee, lots were sold at Portsmouth by Councilman Michael Coutanch of Bath Town, but there is no record that Spriggs bought property or settled in Portsmouth Village, nor have I been able to find any evidence that Jerushia Spriggs O'Hagan ever existed. There is a large marble sarcophagus at Portsmouth like the one in the story. However, it marks the tomb of "Governor" John Wallace, not Francis Spriggs.

Taking Whedbee's tale as a jumping-off point, I fabricated my own story and characters, using details from the islands I've grown to love. Jerushia and Spriggs are borrowed, but all the other characters, both from the eighteenth century and the twentieth century, are figments of my imagination.

Cape Lookout National Seashore is very much in existence, as is Portsmouth Village. The lifesaving station, the church, and the Piggott and Salter-Dixon Houses are real places, but there is no blue cottage belonging to Luna Mae, and the screened porch on the summer kitchen is wishful thinking. Although a fuel compound and generator shed exist, there are no old shed ruins, nor is there a cart path to the generator. Little is left of the marsh and creek that originally filled the area.

Prologue

THE WOMAN FELL, pitching to her knees, the pain stabbing violently. Even as she fell, she pushed herself forward over the reeds, struggling to continue her flight, each breath a moaning wail. Fear tore at her throat and constricted her chest. She was so stupid. First, she forgot to charge the inverter. Then she came out in the marsh alone. Stupid, stupid. He'd be angry again. He was angry all the time now. It was this cursed place. No, not truly the place, it was the hate that lurked here, leaking up from the ground like the ever-present water beneath the sand. She'd tried to warn him, but he wouldn't . . . Oh, Lord Jesus, the path was vanishing. The fog was in front of her now.

She lurched to a stop, her hand to her throat. Even from here, she could feel the beginning of the cold.

"No," she whimpered. "Please."

Her hand stretched out, trying to ward it off, but the dark mist advanced. This was no ordinary mist rolling in from the ocean. This was a dank, cold fog that came from God knows where.

Slowly, inexorably, it covered her feet like a lapping wave, icy, darker than the salt marsh around it.

Eyes wide, frozen, she watched it rise over her knees and reach her thighs, trapping her lower body in a pool of liquid ice. Now, it reached her waist. Soon, it would swallow her, choke her with that cloying breath. Already, she could feel the moisture crystallizing inside her nose. The evil would take her—and keep her forever.

Sheer terror broke through her catatonic state, driving her forward, deeper into the icy darkness. Her feet were numb, dragging, catching in the rushes. The cold mist clutched at her arms, pulling, sucking. Ever so slowly, she plowed on, only her head and shoulders above the morass, her arms flailing as if against a current, her head back like a swimmer gasping for air, chest tight, eyes blind and staring.

Have to reach the shed, she told herself. Fight. Just a little farther.

Suddenly, a peaked roof thrust above the swirling, opaque mass—the shed. She threw herself against the door, praying it was open. The knob would not turn.

"No, no!" she wept, hands fumbling frantically. The keys, where were the keys? Oh, Jesus, please let them be here. Yes, in the bottom of her pocket. She mustn't drop them. If she bent down, it would get her. This was an old evil, as old as the world itself, and as strong. There would be no escape once it possessed her. Better to die than be swallowed by the evil. Fight for your soul. Fight the Being. There, the door was open.

She fell into the room, but it was too late. The cold came in, too, slithering over the black floor, shimmering obscenely. It began to wind up her legs, like a snake to the kill.

There was no escape. It would take her this time. Wait, it didn't like heat. The kerosene, on the shelf.

Her arms were like wooden blocks, awkward and stiff. Tight bands circled her chest, and pain stabbed her spine. The jug crashed down, tipping, spilling. No matter. All that mattered now was to light it quickly. The barnburners—there, in the can. She fought to strike one in the dark, but the mist was faster. Wind brushed her cheek as the mass heaved up in a violent wave, lapping over her hands, wetting them. She grabbed a fistful of matches, striking them hard, wildly, against the side of the box.

Sparks flew, and the blessed scent of phosphorus rose to her nostrils. Screeching in triumph, she flung the matches down at the gray being.

Flames flashed at her feet, rising, searing the thing.

It writhed, hissing as the fire roared. Flames shot across the room, spreading in fat, hot tongues, climbing her gown, melting away the ice. Her mouth broke open in a macabre grin, perfect teeth glimmering bloodily in the dancing flames. Her hair torched and flared madly for a moment, then withered into wormy black ash, but she felt only warmth as the flames enveloped her, lighting the whole building, bringing her back to the world of the sun.

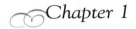Chapter 1

A FLOCK OF SEABIRDS FOLLOWED the ferry across the sound, swooping and diving for morsels churned up by the big engines. Ahead, a row of peach roofs began to appear, protruding starkly above the low line of dunes and green marsh grasses.

That must be the fishing camp. Bert leaned over the rail, fighting not to grin like an idiot. This twenty-two-mile-long strip of sand was to be her home for the next three months—three whole months in one of the most beautiful spots on the Carolina coast.

Don't expect too much, she warned herself. She had a job to do, mostly maintenance, and she'd be living in the abandoned village site, not on the beach. It would be hot here, and buggy.

Yes, but I'll be all alone, her heart sang. Most of the people coming to the island stayed at the south end, at the fishing camp at Long Point. She would be stationed at the north end, sixteen miles away.

The ferry slowed, running the channel between two rows of vertically driven white plastic pipes. To either side, Bert could see the sandy bottom less than a foot underwater. A truck was parked by the plank dock. That would be Hunter O'Hagan,

National Park ranger temporarily assigned to island management. She'd met him at the park office earlier—average-sized man, average everything, except for all that hair.

Behind the Long Point landing were the rental cabins, most of them brand-new, thanks to a frontal northeaster two years ago. Behind them was the Atlantic Ocean. That surprised Bert. She hadn't realized North Core Banks was so narrow, just a long ribbon of sand.

What a campsite! A person could see both the sound and the ocean from one spot. She knew that wouldn't be true at Portsmouth, a modern-day ghost town inhabited only by a succession of National Park volunteers like herself. The land was much wider—and marshier—there. The colonists had built the once-booming port on the sound side of the island, where it was protected by high dunes that had never been overwashed. It was a place unlike this windblown, vulnerable strip pounded by both ocean and sound.

The ferry captain put one engine in reverse, which swung the cumbersome boat around in the channel and let it back into the ramp area.

Another truck came bouncing into view from the ocean, its occupants hooting, obviously pleased they'd made the ferry. The ranger, dressed in park green and gray, ambled over. An overblown blonde on the back of the truck reached out and fluffed his full mane of russet curls. Big breasts swung under the woman's ragged white tank top as she bent over. Girlfriend? Bert wondered. On the heavy side, but nice tan, and cleavage. How old was Hunter, anyway? Mid-forties? Hard to tell. Beards tended to age a man—especially bushy, grizzled ones like his.

Two marines and an old fisherman had ridden on the ferry with Bert. They'd fallen into easy conversation. The fisherman was bringing his camper over for the season. "I pay the park five dollars a week to keep my truck in that lot." The old man pointed to an open field. "Cheaper that way. Costs seventy-five dollars to bring a vehicle on the ferry, you know."

Yes, it was both expensive and difficult to get here. There

were no bridges. The only way to Cape Lookout was by boat. North Core Banks was the most remote of the three islands. It was two hours by water from the park's visitor center at Harkers Island, and even longer by a combination of car and ferry. That was part of its attraction.

"My daddy had a cabin down by Old Drum Inlet. That's south of here. It weren't nothing fancy." The old man's hand made a wide swath. "Park set them all on fire when they took over." He clucked his tongue. "There was more than four hundred camps here once."

Bert was unsure how to respond. She'd been warned there were some hard feelings about the annexation twenty-five years ago.

To her relief, the old fisherman grinned toothlessly. "I still miss that old cabin, but I don't miss all them wrecked cars none, that's for sure. Reckon you take the good with the bad."

Wrecked cars? Bert struggled to remember what the park had said about that.

Just then, one of the marines joined them, eyeing her khaki T-shirt and volunteer park insignia. "You a ranger?"

Relieved to change the subject, Bert was quick to answer. "No way. I'm just the new volunteer caretaker for Portsmouth. Roberta Lenehan, but everyone calls me Bert."

The three chatted while the ferry tied up to the dock.

The marines returned to their Jeep. "Hey, Bert!" they called in parting.

"You have a good summer, now, you hear, gal?" the old man shouted from his camper.

The ramp in place, the vehicles were off-loaded first, but not before greetings and a good bit of banter passed between the fishermen and those collected at the dock. Bert watched from the boat, enjoying the casual, unhurried atmosphere. A heron hunted in the tall reeds, and minnows lazed in the shallows. Behind the fishing camp, the Atlantic shimmered blue. The sky was clear of clouds.

When the cars were off the deck, Hunter came aboard and reached for Bert's government-issue bag, a huge waterproof duffel. Bert grabbed the smaller duffel, her fishing pole, and a bag of groceries.

"Anything else?" Hunter slung the big duffel over one shoulder and picked up the cooler loaded with a week's supply of food and beer.

"This is it," Bert gasped, carefully stepping over the plank to the wharf. "For this trip, anyway. I'll probably be hauling in stuff all summer."

Hunter didn't respond, tossing her bag and cooler into the well of the truck.

Bert leaned over and deposited the rest of her luggage, sticking her pole in the bumper rack. "It wouldn't be so bad if it wasn't for the food," she apologized.

He was probably cussing his luck at getting stuck with a single, middle-aged female. She slapped at a fly digging into her calf and was climbing into the passenger seat when the blonde ambled over.

"Hey, I'm Lettie." She stuck out her hand. "You on your way to the village?"

Hunter came from the back of the truck and put an easy arm around the woman's shoulder. "How you doing? Behaving?" He hugged her, glancing toward Bert. "You'll probably be seeing a lot of this girl. She waits tables at Morris Marina, but she's over here whenever she's off. Can't keep away from us."

Bert shook hands, trying to keep from staring. Lettie's nipples showed clearly through the thin top, while below, a sagging stomach hung over abbreviated cutoffs. "Nice to meet you. I'm Bert. Do you ever come up to Portsmouth?"

The woman grinned, her eyes lighting up. "Bless you, gal. Used to go up all the time. Before the accident, that is. Ain't been up for a spell now." She turned back to Hunter. "Stop by later, why don't you? You coming back this way, ain't you?" Someone shouted from the ferry. Lettie waved without looking up. "Harry brung fresh barbecue this morning."

"We'll see." Hunter pushed her toward the dock. "Best get moving. Miss Mary'll be on your tail if you miss that ferry."

Lettie chuckled as she ran across the sand, her breasts and belly jiggling. "You take care, Bert, and don't listen to nothing he tells you about me. I'll be up to see you soon."

Hunter was already in the truck, so Bert hurried to get in, shoving aside her backpack. "She seems nice. Is she from around here?"

"Lettie? She's a Jones from Atlantic, related to most people in these parts." He started the motor, then added, "Those she's not related to by blood, she's related to by marriage."

"She's married?"

"Not now she's not, but she's been married more times than I can keep track." He handed Bert the backpack, which had slipped over the gearshift. "You'll probably be seeing a lot of her. Got real friendly with the other caretakers."

Bert shoved the pack down over her feet, on top of the bags of groceries. "Were you here when Anne Source had her accident?" Bert was Anne and Olin Source's replacement, coming in a month earlier than planned.

Hunter ignored her to point out two tiny cabins side by side. "You can keep your ATV in the shed when you come off. The key will be in the ranger cabin." He pointed. "Up yonder's the caretaker's house and all. You can phone from there, if you can't reach the park from the village. Over here," he swung the truck around the sandy ruts to some fuel pumps, "is where you can gas up. Saves paperwork if you fuel up in the village, but don't worry. Justin'll take good care of you if you forget."

Bert listened intently. Justin? Must be the caretaker for Long Point. She was having difficulty understanding Hunter's drawl. Had trouble with Lettie's, too. It was what they called "Outer Banks brogue"—cockney English with a Southern overlay.

Driving past the fuel pumps, the ranger entered an area half hidden by dunes and low shrubs—the parking lot she'd glimpsed from the ferry. It contained a rusty assortment of campers, trucks, and all-terrain vehicles.

"That's the park ATV." He pointed. "If you want, you can ride it up now. Save you coming for it later."

Bert hesitated. She'd driven an ATV only once, and that was during her training. She'd planned to practice when no one was around. On the other hand, it was sixteen miles up the beach to

Portsmouth. At twenty-five miles per hour, it would take a big chunk out of what was left of the day to come all the way back with Hunter, then return with the ATV.

"That's probably what I should do. You don't mind?" Thank God she'd worn her leather Nikes. Her worst problem during training had been changing the foot-activated gears with the top of a soft-toed sneaker.

A green Gator—similar to a golf cart—pulled up beside them. Hunter introduced her to the caretaker, who was indeed named Justin. He was a young, bearded man with an enormous gut and an easygoing manner.

"Call in iffen you need any stuff from over the mainland," he said as he helped her get the ATV started. "Ferry come by two, three times a day. Just so it's something they keep in the store. Have water, too, if you run out." The well at Portsmouth was brackish. All drinking water had to be carried in.

Hunter waited until she mounted the bike, then drove over the dune ramp to the beach. He kept the truck on the damp sand between the high-water line and the ocean. Bert followed on the ATV, dropping back far enough to avoid the sand Hunter's wheels were spraying. There were no roads. The beach was the only way from Long Point to Portsmouth Village, and she'd been warned it could be a miserable trip at high tide with a northeast wind.

She'd lucked out today. There was no wind, and the tide was on its way out. At first, Bert concentrated on steering the four-wheeler and feeding the gas smoothly with the thumb throttle, letting the truck lead from a distance. It was hard for her to see the dips and rolls in the bright sunlight, but she learned quickly to watch for the pale streaks of sand that indicated a tooth-rattling bump. After a while, Bert relaxed, sneaking glances at the ocean and the island. This was incredible, to be driving mile after mile on a totally deserted beach, not a building or person in sight. Small dunes lined with immature sea oats bordered the white beach. Between the dunes, she had occasional glimpses of thickets and of the sound a short distance away. To her right, the sky was a clear, soft blue, the ocean deeper shades of aquamarine and cobalt. Rolling breakers lazily swept up the shore. The huge whelks and other shells dotting the sand tempted her to stop. Not today, but surely sometime over the next three months, she promised herself.

As they approached the north end, the island widened and flattened out. There was sand as far as Bert could see to her left. Ahead, a promontory of weathered dunes curved down to the sea. Behind the dunes was open water. In the distance, Bert could see a low skyline—Ocracoke, she assumed. Hunter veered left, heading inland over the rut-marked sand, past a redwood sign carved with the words *Portsmouth Village*. He followed a row of posts to a narrow trail over worn dunes and pulled up at a wide expanse of shallow water. Car tracks led directly into it. Before he said a word, Bert knew this must be the tidal plain that extended from the swash to the inlet. An area of sandy mud flats often covered by anywhere from two inches to a foot of water, it separated the sound-side marshes and the village from the beach.

Leaning out the truck window, Hunter pointed at two rows of poles lining the crossing. "Just keep between those poles and you'll do all right. Unless the water gets too high, that is."

Bert cut her engine, grateful for the break. "What's too high?"

"When the ATV floats on you."

Bert laughed. "Does it rise with the tide? How do you figure the time difference?"

Her question seemed to surprise him. "Don't have much to do with tide tables," he drawled. "How high the tide gets has more to do with the wind. A good northeaster can push a mess of water through here." Sunshine flashed on his white teeth and highlighted his bushy beard with red. "Gonna cut the island off again at Swash Inlet one of these days." With that cheerful observation, he put the truck in gear and began the crossing.

Bert hung back far enough so as not to get splashed. It wasn't as bad as she expected, the water clear, the bottom firm and sandy. It was not the murky, muddy swamp she'd conjured in her mind, although it did have a funky smell.

Then they were there at last—in Portsmouth. A gate guarded

the entrance. As Bert dismounted to close it behind them, a shell caught her eye. Stooping, she plucked it from the saw grass. "Oh," she exhaled, staring at the delicately whorled, helmet-shaped shell, cream with gold and brown markings. "A perfect Scotch bonnet." She held it up to Hunter. "Look."

He took the translucent, paper-thin shell and examined it carefully. "It be a good one, all right." He handed it back, "I reckon you just got welcomed to the village."

She smiled at him shyly. "Couldn't be a nicer gift."

The trees dropped away as she followed him around the next curve, and Bert glimpsed brown buildings and open water. Hunter pulled up by a small cabin the size of a garage. Across the mowed grass was the lifesaving station, a rambling clapboard structure with a square tower typical of old Coast Guard stations in North Carolina. Beyond the buildings stretched a wide expanse of green marsh and blue water. The lifesaving station had no power, plumbing, or water. It was the cabin that would serve as her home for the next three months. Entering it, Bert took a quick look around: high ceilings and plenty of windows, thank goodness. It was bigger than it looked from outside.

Her bags deposited, Bert followed Hunter back outside for a tour of the surroundings. They crossed the sand road and walked up a short path to the generator shed, her power source. There were no electrical lines—or telephone lines either—to the island.

"You got your keys?"

She had been formally issued keys just that morning. Bert pulled the ring from her pocket.

Hunter picked one out. "Try it."

Bert opened the padlock to the brand-new building. She looked around surreptitiously for signs of fire but couldn't see a thing. "Where was it?" she asked. "The old shed?" She'd been told the original generator, powered by kerosene, had been destroyed.

Hunter frowned, hesitating before he motioned farther up the path they had taken. "This side of the creek, back of that big hummock and brick cistern." As Bert stretched to peer, he added,

"Can't see it from here. Never understood why they set it such a distance from the station."

Slowly and precisely, he showed her how to turn the generator on, after checking the oil and coolant, and how to throw the switches so it recharged the storage batteries. Then he had her close it down, read the battery power levels, and record the procedure in the log. "It's easier to work than the old one. Reckon some good comes from trouble."

This was the first time he had referred to the accident in any way. Bert was quick to take advantage. "She died in the fire, didn't she? When the old shed burnt up. Were you here?"

"No. Didn't they tell you? I'm filling in on account of Ben Willis—he's the chief—pulling a groin muscle two days before Miss Anne's accident. Just my luck." Moving faster than he had since she'd met him, he was out the door and striding back toward the lifesaving station.

Bert ran to catch up, hoping she hadn't irritated him with her questions, but he was still talking: "Airlifted her out before any of the Park Service got here. Still, Jimmy and I had a mess of fixing to do." They passed Bert's cabin, then reached the sand road and turned toward the village, away from the closed and padlocked lifesaving station. "Took the best part of three weeks and four men till we hauled in all the machinery and got the new generator working right. Camped out here the last few days. Rough work, all right. Didn't get around to cleaning out the cabin till yesterday." He glanced back at her. "We got the job done, though. Her husband, he flat out refused to come in. Made us pack up all their belongings." He continued at a fast pace down an overgrown lane. "I'll show you around the visitor center. You can explore the historic sites later."

Bert ran behind him. "You mean Olin Source came back yesterday to get his things but didn't want to go inside the cabin?"

Hunter shook his head. "It's a hard thing, losing your woman."

Something about the way he said it made Bert wonder if he spoke from experience. "I met them, you know, when we went through orientation and training. Olin was the one who really wanted to do it. She was sort of strange." Bert hesitated. "You know how the wind whistles around the restrooms at Harkers Island? Mrs. Source said that was spirits talking, that she could feel them. In fact . . ." She trailed off, afraid she was talking too much.

"Yes?" Hunter slowed, looking at her now as if she was an individual, rather than a job to get done.

"I didn't really know them, but from the questions they asked during orientation, I didn't think she'd last." Bert hoped she wasn't saying the wrong thing. She'd actually bet herself Anne Source wouldn't last a month—not with her belief in ghosts, and not with that pasty white skin that had never seen the sun, much less a mosquito or green-headed fly. They'd been a strange couple. Anne Source was a retired nurse and the main breadwinner. Ten years older than her husband, she was thick through the middle, with a cobweb of fine hair and a mouth that resembled a squashed violet. Olin Source had weathered better—or exercised more. Tall and graceful, he showed no sign of a paunch. His youthful face had a dark, Mediterranean look. "I kind of expected to be called in early, but not like this," she added.

"Worst accident since I been around. No one knows exactly what she was—" Hunter cut himself off to show her a white house with a widow's walk. "That's the visitor center. You open it every morning, after you check in with me." He eyed her solemnly. "I'd be much obliged if you call in by eight. If I don't hear from you, I'll have to boat over. Every morning, you got that?"

As they made their way back to his truck, Bert remarked, almost to herself, "I hope she didn't suffer."

Hunter said nothing until he was in his truck. Then he leaned out the open window. "Don't know if it's something that happens when you get burnt bad, but the medevac pilot told us she had this crazy grin on her face. Seems the fire got so hot it melted her caps away. All that was left of her teeth was little black fangs. Burnt right to a crisp, she was, but smiling, like she thought it was funny."

Bert stared after him until the truck disappeared around a stand of yaupon. "Thanks a lot, buddy," she said aloud. "That's just the image I need for my first night alone." ⌒

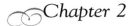

Chapter 2

BERT STARED AFTER HUNTER'S TRUCK until even the sound of the motor faded. Then, savoring her solitude, she slowly surveyed her new domain. It was more open than she expected. Creamy sand flats stretched out toward the dunes. Coast Guard Creek—a bay, really—was right at her front door, and she had a good view of Ocracoke Inlet behind the salt marsh lining the shore. It shouldn't have surprised her, she knew. That's why they built the lifesaving station here, so they could access the ocean quickly. She could visualize the wooden surfboats on the bank of the creek, ready for instant launching.

The cabin was dark and musty. Bert lost no time pulling up the blinds and opening all the doors and windows. But the place still wasn't bright enough to suit her. She dragged the kitchen table so it sat between the window and door, giving her a good view of the sunlit water in the sound, about a mile away. As she unpacked, she grew more enthusiastic. The cabin consisted of two big rooms and a small bath with a discolored metal shower. The propane refrigerator and stove were new and clean, thank God. Not so the cupboards, especially under the ancient sink. In addition to the dozens of empty or almost empty containers of soap and cleansers, she spotted dark pellets and shredded paper and smelled the telltale odors of mice and moisture. Oh, well, so she'd have some cleaning to do. The dishes and glasses were on the grimy side also. The queen-sized bed, dresser, television, and armchair seemed lost in the huge bedroom. The cabin had no air conditioning—she hadn't really expected it—but there was a ceiling fan, and the placement of doors and windows allowed for a good cross draft. Yes, she'd be comfortable enough here.

An hour later, the toilet, sink, shower, and bathroom floor scrubbed, the counters wiped off, and her food in the fridge, Bert decided to reward herself with a walk around the village. It shouldn't be hard to find her way. There was just the one main road that ran from the beach across the flats, then through the village to the pier on the sound.

It wasn't just the housecleaning that had her sweating. It was definitely a lot warmer here than on the beach. After showering and changing into shorts, Bert loaded her pockets with bug spray, sun lotion, and the ring of keys. Then she belted on her radio, as she'd been told to do anytime she left the cabin. Pausing long enough to scribble down the call numbers for the radio, she took off across the grassy, abandoned landing strip that separated the lifesaving station and her cabin from the village.

Her plan was to find Haulover Point and the dock used by the boats. It was the main way into Portsmouth, other than driving the sixteen miles up the beach from Long Point. It was also where the road ended. She laughed at herself. Not here two hours and already she was heading toward the water. The heat wasn't really oppressive in the village. Two blackbirds called raucously from a wind-swept juniper. Bees buzzed around a patch of wild roses climbing a peeling yellow house. A couple of green-headed flies bombarded her. One of her chores would be to mow the grass in the main areas, but did they expect her to trim, too? As Bert ambled the sandy lanes, she decided that the contrast was what gave the place its strange appearance. The main part of the village was pristine, but the edges—where the grass was uncut, where a screen had been left ripped and rusty, where shutters hung loose and porch boards were missing—lent a touch of sadness. That and the total lack of people clutter—no cars or toys or mowers or even shrubs and gardens.

One little cottage had recently been painted a bright blue and stood out among its battered brothers. The bushes were neatly trimmed, and late-blooming orange irises brightened the yard. There were even two molded plastic chairs on the new porch.

Bert stared at a dishtowel flapping in the breeze. Must belong to one of the lessees, she thought. Were they here often? Her sole day of training, part of it spent with the Maritime Museum historian, had left many questions unanswered. The park's interpretation ranger, a younger woman by the name of Christine Wright, had said that some of the cottages were let out on long-term leases for use as vacation homes. In return, the lessees agreed to undertake extensive restorations. The ranger had shaken her head. "With all the cuts in federal funding, this seemed like a great way to save a lot of the houses, but sometimes the lease program causes as many problems as it solves." She went on to say that lessees often ignored the park rules, riding their ATVs over lawns and mooring boats where it interfered with visitor access. "Another big problem is artifact hunting. They dig for old bottles and jewelry. There's a woman by the name of Luna Mae Harris. Let the rangers know anytime she's on the island."

Unconsciously, Bert hurried her pace until she came from the shadow of the huge myrtles to the open water of Haulover Point. She heaved a sigh of relief as she reached the long dock. What was it about an expanse of open water and sky that so lifted her spirits? She definitely was not a child of the dark.

It wasn't far to Ocracoke Island, she decided, staring northeast across the blue-green water. But Ocracoke wasn't part of this park. Portsmouth was at the northernmost end of Cape Lookout National Seashore, more than fifty miles by water from the park headquarters on Harkers Island. Ocracoke, six miles north, was part of Cape Hatteras National Seashore. Jimmy Range, seasonal employee with the park's maintenance staff, would be over in the morning to show her how to run the mower. She was to meet him here.

Bert strolled out the long dock, peering over the sides. The bottom was quite visible, only about two feet down. She even saw a couple of blue crabs scuttling along. Over there was a hermit hiding in a whelk shell. Small fish darted about the eelgrass. This might be a good place for flounder.

As she came to the cross arm and deeper water, Bert noticed a small boat tied up behind the ladder. It hadn't been visible from the road. She glanced back toward land. There was no one in sight. Who was it? One of the lessees, or just a visitor? Were they watching her now? Though she'd planned to stay and see the setting sun color the horizon, she suddenly felt self-conscious, the casual ease gone.

As she strode back down the road to her cabin, she told herself not to be silly. This was not her private domain. It was a park, and there would be lots of visitors popping up in unexpected locations. It came with the job.

An old building deep in the woods caught her eye. Bert made herself stop. The idea had been to explore. Still, she hesitated. It didn't look as if anyone had cleared around it for a while, and the last thing she wanted to do was get into trouble her first day. Funny how vulnerable one felt when there was no one around to help. Don't be such a wimp, she told herself. If the going proved too rough or she saw any weird people or snakes, all she had to do was return to the road.

Careful where she put her feet, Bert made her way through the coarse grass and small shrubs, picking the most open areas. It was an old plank house. The entire structure was in poor condition, the wood totally devoid of paint, the walls cockeyed, the roof missing in places and looking as if it might fall in at any moment. The museum historian had told them that some properties were too far-gone to save.

Bert continued around the building. The bugs were thicker here, but that was to be expected. In a way, this place was more fun than the renovated homes. She peered in through a grime-covered window, half expecting someone to yell at her for trespassing. The glass was old, the type with bubbles and streaks that distorted vision. Inside, things lay scattered about. It was hard to make out what they had once been—a piece of broken wood furniture that was perhaps a table or chair leg, a filthy old bucket on its side, and a heap of what were probably old rags. Bert grinned as she made out the inevitable Mountain Dew bottle, dusty, old, but evidence of more recent visitation. She drew away, wiping her hands on her pants. The whole building was filthy and decaying, particularly the long extension to the side. Perhaps it had been an old Coast Guard station before they built the one near her cabin, or quarters for the slaves who worked the lightering ships. Suddenly, a picture came to her head—slaves crowded together in a hot, airless barracks night after night, sleeping on the floor in rows, naked except for a few rags. . . .

A woman moaned.

Bert whirled around so fast she hit her head on an overhanging branch. Another cry came from the woods toward the marsh.

"Something wrong?" she yelled, pushing her way through the tangle of myrtles and briars, careless of the prickers. "What is it? I'm over here." The brush was too thick. She couldn't get through. She stopped, listening.

Not a sound.

Was it someone from the boat she'd just seen? A visitor? Kids? Some lessees having sex—or a nightmare?

"Is someone there? This is the caretaker," Bert called, brushing off some mosquitoes she'd disturbed.

She heard nothing save the lap of the water through the trees. Then came a soft rustling, like a bird in the grass or someone moving very slowly.

Poised on the balls of her feet, hand on her radio, Bert called out, "Hello. Anybody there?"

An egret took to wing. Nearby, something splashed.

Maybe it wasn't a person. Maybe it was an animal. Cold prickles ran up Bert's spine. What kind of animals lived here? Raccoons, nutria—what was that, some kind of feral cat? Suddenly, the woods were threatening. There were bear on the mainland, and she knew they could swim. And who had been on that boat?

Looking over her shoulder, Bert hurried back through the scrub and briars to the road. Even that did not seem safe. Was something stalking her from behind the cedars and myrtles?

She walked rapidly back to the blue house. No one seemed to be around. It wasn't much farther to what a sign proclaimed was the Dixon House. There, back among the green lawns, with the Wedgwood-blue church nearby, Bert's fears of stalkers and bear seemed ridiculous. Above the clapboard spire, a pink-tinged vapor trail cut the sky, a reminder of man's presence in this isolation.

It would be dark soon, and there might be a visitor injured in the woods.

Bert pulled out her radio. She tried Hunter first, not really expecting to get him. He'd be on the ferry by now. She fumbled for her call numbers. It was after five. Better try KID 745, park headquarters. She'd been told someone was on call at all times.

The response was immediate: "This is 422. Come in, 543."

Bert peered at the list she held. Who was 422? Oh, good, Rudy. He was the ranger who had given her the ATV training, a big man with a round face and a light beard who looked like Santa Claus in uniform. "Rudy, this is Bert," she whispered inanely.

Rudy was polite about it. "Hear you loud and clear. What's the problem?"

"I, um, thought I heard a woman cry out, but there's no one around. I don't know what I should do. And there's a boat tied up at the dock."

"What kind of boat?"

"Seventeen-foot white boat, skiff, outboard motor." Good thing she knew a little about boats.

"What did Hunter say about it?"

"Hunter? Oh, I'm not sure he saw it. I didn't see it until I walked out on the dock just now. Do you know whose it is?"

"Hundred and twenty-five Johnson? Sort of a homemade cabin, plastic and Plexiglas?"

"I didn't notice the horsepower. I'm sorry. It did have a funny-looking cabin."

"Donny Southard." The disgust in his tone came through clearly. "He knows he's not supposed to tie up to the dock. Is J. J. there? That's the lessee in the Grace House."

"The white one? All the houses looked closed, but I didn't knock." She was beginning to get the hang of the radio.

"You'd know it if they was there. Those fellows act like this is Club Med, not a National Park. Besides, his boat would be around. Donny's probably out catching some clams. Seen anyone in the water?"

"No, but I didn't really look. You catch clams? I dig them."

"Come again? I didn't copy the first part. You holding that mike down before you start talking?"

So much for her radio expertise and feeble joke. Bert lifted the radio to her mouth, squeezed the mike, and counted to three before she spoke. "I didn't see anyone clamming, but I might have missed him. Do you think that woman I heard is with him? She sounded, um, funny."

"Like she just got punched in the belly and might be enjoying it?" came the easy reply.

"I guess." More like a woman having an orgasm, but Bert wasn't going to say that over the radio.

There was a long silence. For a minute, Bert thought she'd cut him off. When he came back, he was talking more slowly. "That wasn't a . . . ." He hesitated. "Donny doesn't usually travel with a woman, unless it's Lettie, and she's at Morris's. Anyhow, they're cousins. But those nutria, sometimes they cry out, moan just like a woman, they do," he snickered into her horrified ear.

Idiot, Bert told herself back at the cabin as she stirred a pitcher of instant iced tea. She knew she'd made their day. The story would be all over the park by morning—maybe sooner, depending on who was listening in. Dammit anyhow. Why hadn't she just waited to ask Hunter in the morning, or at least used the cell phone? Bert sighed.

Putting off a promised call to her daughter, she finished

unpacking and ran the grimy dishes and silver through some hot, sudsy water. She'd do the glasses tomorrow. All desire to do any more exploring had vanished. Anticipation had made her sleep poorly the night before. Now, she was not only annoyed with herself but also tired to the point of flakiness. Down with the sun would suit her fine. Besides, the mosquitoes would be out in droves come dusk.

Bert turned off the generator, which she'd run for the required hour, and locked the shed. Then she made herself walk back to Haulover. It wasn't far to the church and village, which lay just two blocks the other side of the airstrip, but it was another half-mile to the dock. She found no boat, no sign of any visitors. She shrugged. It would have salvaged her ego if she'd been able to produce a woman in peril, but it looked as if Rudy was right. Moaning nutria. What other surprises did the island boast?

It was getting dark. Dragging, Bert returned to the cabin and finished her evening chores. The radio had to be turned off and placed on its base to charge, the cellular plugged in and turned on, all the doors latched. "Not against people," Hunter had told her. "To keep the coons out. You take care and latch the doors, even if you're only going to the generator. Don't take them long to wreck a camp."

Feeling a little more cheerful, she unwrapped a pastrami-and-cheese submarine she'd brought over with her for dinner. Sandwich in hand, she inspected the bookcase. As Christine had said, there was a great collection of local history books in the cabin—park books, personal histories, old manuscripts, even someone's thesis and three handwritten logs. Plucking out *Survey of Portsmouth*, Bert flipped through until she found the lifesaving station. As she suspected, her cabin had been the summer kitchen for the station. Both had been built in 1894, the same year the hospital burned down.

Bert rinsed out a glass and poured herself some milk. That must have been the hospital Hunter mentioned, the one that used to be near the old generator shed. But two fires in one spot? Coincidences always intrigued her. The book went on to say that the maritime hospital had been built in 1846 to replace another facility constructed twenty years earlier.

She was deep into a complicated recitation of deeds and separation of land parcels when there was a tap outside.

Bert froze.

The tap repeated.

She peered around the partially open kitchen door, straining to see into the dark porch. Thank goodness she'd latched the screen.

"You wasn't asleep, was you?"

Someone was out there. "Something wrong?" She clung to the kitchen door so she could close it quickly.

"No, ma'am. I come by to leave you a mess of clams. You want them anyplace special?" He rattled something.

Now, she could see his outline. A slight man—or boy—carrying one of those five-gallon plastic buckets all the fishermen used. He didn't look threatening. Bert was already unlatching the screen door. "Come in."

He kicked off a pair of ragged beach shoes and placed an open can of beer on the stoop. His hair, fair to the point of being colorless, swung in a ponytail over his back. "Didn't mean to disturb you none." He edged past her on to the porch.

"Not at all," Bert lied, hoping he wasn't drunk. At any rate, he was no threat, standing even shorter than her five-five. But as she followed his muscular butt into the kitchen, she decided he was more powerful than her first impression. Older, too—in his twenties. "You J. J.?"

He was already at the sink, apparently familiar with the cabin. Swinging around, he gave her a grin marred by nicotine-stained teeth. "I reckon I should have introduced myself. I'm Donny Southard." He extended a dirty, callused hand.

Oh, shit, what had she done? Let in the enemy? Well, he seemed sober. She shook his hand, finding it surprisingly warm and dry.

"I reckon someone's been circulating the word about me already."

Apparently, her face had given her away, as usual.

Lifting the full bucket with ease, he began pouring clams into the sink. "Don't know what I done to rile them so," he continued over the clatter of shells against metal. "I leave my bike at the gate, just like I been told. I don't tie up the boat more than fifteen minutes. How'd you like to go through life with someone like Hunter hating you?"

Burt hurried to defend Hunter. "You were more than fifteen minutes today."

He lifted his big blue eyes to hers. "To catch these for you. You eat clams, don't you?" At her nod, he began running water into the sink. "Didn't disturb no one. That's a big dock. Plenty of room for folks to tie up. I just don't understand why the park got to make everything so hard." He turned off the water and leaned against the counter. "You want to leave them set in the water a spell. Clean the sand out good."

She didn't want to spoil his fun, but the Chinese had been using that method to clean the intestinal tracts of clams for centuries. "Interesting."

"You know how to open them?" He picked up a clam and took a knife from the jar of utensils on the sink. Holding the clam upright, the hinge against the counter, he placed the knife's edge parallel with the meeting of the two shells and banged down hard with his other hand. The clam split apart, shell and juice spraying over Bert's clean dishes.

Bert stopped him before he could open another. "Yes, that's great. But I'd rather freeze them. They open right up when they defrost."

His eyes crinkled. "You know about seafood?"

"That's what I do. I'm in the restaurant business."

"Where abouts you work?"

She really didn't want to get into that. "I had a restaurant in Swansboro that I just sold. I'll be opening another one, but not until January." That was why she was here, because she was waiting out a covenant not to compete. She had room and board for the summer and a chance to get a rest. Besides, it wouldn't cost her anything. She needed her capital for the new restaurant.

He was talking again. "Didn't reckon a gal like you'd know about clams." He picked up the bucket, still more than half full. "Best be on my way. You is probably all give out, this being your first day and all."

"I am tired," Bert admitted.

Still, he made no move to leave. Instead, he motioned toward her bathroom. "All right if I use the john?"

She nodded, surprised. The bath was anything but private, right off the kitchen and with a poorly fitted door. So as not to have to listen to him, she wiped up the clam bits and juice and filled the coffee pot in preparation for morning. Still, he did not emerge. This was unbelievable. She'd never have the nerve to walk into a strange house and use the bathroom for something serious.

Finally, the toilet flushed. He came out to the porch, where she had retreated. "Hunter be after me to put in one of them. Sent me a letter and all." He plunked himself down on a bench and leaned toward her. "Says I got to do it according to specs. Going to run over six thousand, what with the pumps and all, even if I do all the digging."

Even though all she wanted to do was go to bed, she couldn't help asking, "You don't have a septic? I thought all the cabins in the village had bathrooms or composters. The occupied ones, I mean."

"I got me a camp in Evergreen Slew, yonder the other side of Sheep Island." He leaned back. "Been in the family long as I can remember. Caught my first mess of fish off Haulover Dock, when I was a bitsy youngun. Shot my first pheasant here, too." His voice was low and pleasant. "My daddy was the gamekeeper. There ain't nothing about this here island I don't know." His eyes smiled, showing a fan of sun wrinkles. "Why, just this evening, I seen a bunch of quail nests the other side of High Hill, and you might want to let Hunter know they is some piping plover eggs by Captain Jane's." Relaxed as he was, he looked like a little boy in the dim light. "I can tell you where all the wrecks in the inlet is, and where there is some old cannons and crockery. I don't want to sound swell-headed or anything, but ain't no one in these parts can out-fish me." Clapping both palms to his knees, he sighed deeply. "I don't let myself think about what would happen if they took my camp away."

Bert refused to bite again. She rose to her feet.

He took the hint and stood. "Guess I run my mouth enough for one night." He waited hopefully.

She didn't know what he wanted and was too tired to care. "I'm sorry, but I'm whipped. Thanks for the clams."

She listened for his footsteps as he left but heard nothing. She hadn't heard him arrive either. Surely, he wasn't going back out in the boat at this hour. Bert glanced at the clock. Only nine? No matter. She was going to bed.

As she snuggled between the sheets, pulling the light cover up around her head, she heard a motor start up nearby. So that was it. He'd come by ATV from Evergreen Slew. Didn't he say something about leaving the bike at the gate? Must have taken his boat back to his cabin earlier. Oh, well, at least he was gone. And there was no one else around to bother her. No one to know she was going to bed so early. No way for some salesman to give her a late call about the restaurant either. No more restaurant. It was a pity, in a way. She'd never have sold the place if the building hadn't belonged to Larry. It was just too awkward not to be living with him but to have him as a landlord. Even though they'd remained good friends, he was still possessive about her. To be honest, she'd be damned if she'd see him with his arm around some other . . . It was all water under the bridge. Time to go to sleep.

Something woke her abruptly a couple of hours later.

Now what?

Unmoving, she rolled her eyes, trying to see what had disturbed her sleep. It was so dark. She'd left the light on in the bathroom but couldn't see it now. Had the door blown closed? No, there'd still be some light around the edges. Generator problems? Damn.

She leaned out of bed, fumbling for the flashlight. Had she latched the porch door behind Donny? Suppose some animal crawled in. Bert stiffened and forced herself to continue groping. She'd die if she touched something alive!

It was with relief that her hand found the cold metal of the flashlight on the night table. For a moment, the light flickered, sending panic back to her throat. Then the beam took hold. She flashed it around the room. The shadows were deep in the corners, but nothing moved. Swinging out of bed, she slipped her feet into her sneakers. No way was she going to tramp on a roach or something worse. She reached for the table lamp. Just because the bathroom light was out didn't mean the power was off.

None of the lights worked.

Bert peered out the window toward the shed. She couldn't even see it—just the outline of the scrub and, in the distance, water reflecting through the reeds. The stars overhead were amazingly vivid. Was that because it was so dark inside, or was it always that way here?

Damned if she was going out there in the middle of the night to figure out what was wrong. She was still half asleep. This was no time to be poking around wires and fuses. Besides, she'd have to cover herself with repellent, and then she'd stink all night. She didn't need lights now, anyhow. The best thing was to go back to sleep and work with the generator in the morning, when she was fresh. Machines weren't her strong point.

Bert couldn't help wondering, just before she fell back asleep, if it was something like this that got Anne Source out of the cabin in the middle of the night.

Chapter 3

NOT SURPRISINGLY, BERT DREAMT about Anne Source. They were back at the park building, and Anne was half running, half walking down a long, dark corridor. Behind her, the wind was howling, and Bert could feel the ice in its touch.

Head down, pushing against the powerful wind, Bert struggled to get closer. "Anne, stop. What's the matter?"

To her astonishment, Anne reacted violently, backing away, one manicured hand raised to ward her off. "No, please," she sobbed, purple lips stretching in terror.

Oh, God, her teeth were gone. A row of widely separated black fangs gleamed in the ruined mouth. Terrified, Bert tried to slink away, but the terrible mouth came closer and closer, the woman's wails reaching a crescendo.

The sound shook the bed. Bert sat up. Loud wails blasted her ears. Another one of her all-too-vivid dreams? She turned her head, listening. Anne Source might have been a dream, but those wails were real. What the hell was going on?

Her feet fumbled into her shoes again. For a moment, Bert couldn't identify the sound. Then she realized it was some kind of loud music. Had someone left a radio on, and when the power came back . . . ? Wait a minute. The power was on. The bath was lit again, the radio charger running. She tried the overhead light. Yes, it worked.

You're not on commercial power, she told herself. It can't just come back. You either didn't charge the generator properly or there's a short.

So what was making the noise? It was like a piano but not a piano. It was more like . . . Yes, that was it. Suddenly, she was a child again, bellowing out one of her favorite hymns. It was church music.

It must be some fishermen with a radio.

A hymn-playing fisherman? You'd think he'd have more sense than to turn it up so loud. Probably figured there was no one here. What was the rule on camping? Bert vaguely remembered one of the rangers mentioning a policy manual. She'd seen No Camping signs in the village, but not on the beaches. National Parks were usually pretty liberal about letting people do their own thing. Oh, well, she'd check in the morning.

Bert started to go back to bed, then hesitated. She'd never be able to sleep with that racket. It sounded so close—across the landing strip, maybe. The church? Suddenly, she was on her feet. That was it. It wasn't a radio but the church organ. Someone was in the church.

Cursing, conscious of a cold weight in the pit of her stomach, she pulled her jeans and T-shirt over her short camisole and again slipped into her sneakers. She hesitated, then grabbed the radio, wishing she had some kind of weapon. It wasn't her job to act as a policeman, but damned if she wanted to cry wolf to Rudy again. Better find out what was going on before she called. Could be Donny drunk and partying, or teenagers on a harmless prank, or even some other lessee with a touch of insomnia and unaware of Bert's presence.

Turning on the porch light, she took a deep breath and stepped out.

Immediately, the music stopped, leaving only an echo in the air.

Suddenly, Bert was angry. What was going on? First, someone fiddled around with the power. Now this. She jogged toward the church, sorry she'd advertised her presence.

By the time she arrived, there was no sign of life. The church was dark. The village, what she could see of it from here, was dark, too. She stood motionless, listening, but heard nothing except the distant crash of waves, an occasional leaf rustling—birds or nutria—and the whine of mosquitoes circling above her head.

Man, it was cold. Bert shuddered. There must be some kind of inversion by the church. The temperature had suddenly dropped about twenty degrees. Doctor's Creek was nearby, the ground around it low and marshy. Was it cold sea air? She glanced toward the ocean. The sky was very clear, Venus low on the horizon. It must be close to five, she decided. What was it they said about it being the coldest just before dawn?

The whine of mosquitoes increased. She felt one brush her cheek, then another. Damn, they were closing in. Much as she hated to, she dug in her pocket for the bottle of spray. None too soon, she thought as more descended. Dear God, she must be in some sort of cloud of bugs. Now, they were all about her, flying against her face, tiny wings soft as a breeze. She'd be bitten to shreds.

Both hands waving over her head, she ducked and began a fast jog back to the cabin. Oh, no, they were all over her, up her nose, in her eyes. Frantically, she brushed them off her face, feeling her fingers grow wet. She moaned, running now.

The whine rose to a roar. They were crawling in her hair, down her neck, over her lips. Her eyes were almost closed, but they were clustered on her lashes. One was inside her lid; she could feel it burn. Her arms were on fire. So was the back of her neck. She opened her mouth to scream and inhaled a mouthful, which made her double over and choke. Her stomach churned. Somebody, help! she screamed silently, afraid to open her mouth again.

She burst into the cabin, sobbing, coughing. In the light, she could see the black, wriggling layer practically solid on her arms. Could you die of mosquito bites? Frantically, she scraped them off with her hands and a towel, then grabbed the can of Raid. Eyes closed, she sprayed herself directly, right on the face, arms, and legs, then squirted most of the rest of the can up at the ceiling to kill those still flying around. The spray choked her, but she didn't care. "Die, you beasts, die," she said aloud.

She was having trouble breathing. Was it the Raid or a reaction to the bites? Benadryl, in the medicine cabinet—that was good for allergic reactions. The mirror reflected a mask of red-and-black gore; only the whites of her eyes showed. Dead mosquitoes full of her own blood were smeared all over her face.

She shook, staring at the reflected horror. Her mouth opened in a wail. She almost expected to see that her teeth had turned to fangs. Strangely, that thought made her giggle hysterically, which in turn had a calming effect. Still shaking, Bert swallowed two Benadryl capsules, then read the directions, wondering if she should take more. She was beginning to break out in welts. Shedding her clothes as fast she could, she stepped into the shower. The luke-warm water washed away the bugs and blood and helped calm the sting. But as she dried off, the itching started full force. Frantically, she searched for something to soothe the bites. Seawater was best, but no way was she going outside again. As she rummaged around the kitchen, she saw something on the shelf she hadn't noticed before. It was a plain glass jar with an old label, the ink faded to the point of barely being legible. "Infus--- of Bayber-ies for Bites of Fly--ng Pests," she read. So I'm not the first to be attacked, Bert thought, somewhat relieved. Was it a local remedy? Looked homemade. Had it been left by the Sources or some other occupant? Hesitantly, she tried a little on her hand. The relief was instantaneous. Bert splashed it on liberally and in-spected herself in the mirror. There were not as many welts as she'd expected from all those mosquitoes. Luckily, her pants and T-shirt had been sprayed with Permethrin, a long-lasting repel-lent. Did those mosquitoes carry any diseases? She shuddered. She'd never go out again at night, not unless she was covered from head to foot and lathered with bug spray to boot.

Carefully, she checked the room for live bugs. Strange, but

now that they were all dead, she could barely make out any mosquitoes—just some wispy remains on the pine boards.

The Benadryl was making her drowsy. It was just as well. She'd probably never be able to go back to sleep otherwise. Still trembling, she pulled the covers over her head in case there were any more bugs around. The intruders could play the organ or do whatever they wanted. She wasn't going out again until light of day. Her last thought, before she dozed off, was to wonder how the intruders, whoever they were, dealt with all the mosquitoes.

She woke in a sweat, the covers still over her head, the bed sticky and rumpled. Already, the sun was bright in the sky. Not a mosquito was in sight. In fact, if not for the dark smears on her clothes, she would have wondered if she'd dreamt it.

She'd planned to fish this morning. Forget that.

Coffee, toast, and another shower brought her back to nearly normal. To her relief, most of the welts were gone. There was just one on her cheekbone and a couple on her neck and the backs of her hands. That was the one saving grace of mosquitoes—unless you were allergic, the bites disappeared almost immediately. She'd have to get some more of that lotion, though.

An hour later, carefully sprayed down, Bert opened the porch door.

Something heaved at her feet.

Shrieking, she leapt back. What on earth? She peered through the screen. There was a sack, and something was alive inside it. Oh, God. Her hand went to her throat. A baby, a raccoon, something horribly mutilated? Adrenaline shot through her body as she retreated to the kitchen. What was she supposed to do now? No way was she opening that sack.

She pulled out the radio. Just then, it coughed static and voices. Headquarters acknowledged the caller in a bored tone. The person designated 211, whoever that was, was on his way to the lighthouse.

Bert took a deep breath. She'd better calm down before she called. Still clutching the radio, she peered at the sack again. Something was making a scratching noise. She sniffed—no rot or other nasty smell. What was she going to do, let the poor thing sit in the sun until Jimmy Range got here?

Getting the broom, she opened the door a crack and poked gently at the sack. There was no shriek of protest. She poked a little harder. Whatever it was, it wasn't in one piece.

As Bert maneuvered the sack down the steps to the lawn, her mind worked furiously. It hadn't been here last night or at five this morning, so either the jokers at the church were playing another trick or someone else left it. She'd slept late. Had Donny or that other lessee been here? She went back inside and put on her work gloves. Somewhere, she'd seen a hammer. She needed that for protection, and a pair of scissors to cut the tie, and something to close the bag up quickly, if necessary.

Heart pumping furiously, Bert cut the drawstring.

Nothing flew out.

Carefully, she hooked the edge with the broom handle and lifted the sack.

Something scuttled forward and shot out the opening.

Bert yelped, backing away, then began to laugh. She was looking at a very frightened blue crab waving its huge claws as it retreated over the grass. Two more crabs followed it out.

Damn that Donny. What was he trying to do, ingratiate himself with the park through her? He wasn't going to get very far this way.

Bert folded the top of the sack over before more crabs escaped. Then she sank down on the stoop and stared at the heaving mass. What on earth was she going to do with a sackful of crabs? She was supposed to call Hunter at eight and meet Jimmy Range around nine, so there was no time to cook them now. But it was not only that. She really didn't care for the idea that Donny had been prowling around her cabin while she was still in bed. Angrily, she hauled the sack to the sea wall at the lifesaving station and shook the crabs out into the water, turning the bag inside out to disengage the stubborn ones.

It was quarter of eight by the time Bert finally set out for Haulover. At first, she marched rapidly, unseeingly, but it was impossible to stay unaware of her surroundings for long. A blue heron perched precariously atop a juniper by the lifesaving station, while pink-beaked ibises waded in the sun-dappled creek. A cardinal crowning a prickly ash chirped a cheery greeting. Laughing gulls mewed.

"Birds to the right, birds to the left, on marched the Five Hundred," Bert muttered, striding down the winding road. Between the organ and the bugs, she'd really panicked last night, hadn't she? And then the damned crabs today. Thank God there had been no witnesses.

She was at the church already. It was one of the more imposing—and newer—buildings on the island. The old church had been destroyed by a hurricane in the not-so-distant past. This was the only building kept unlocked all the time, so anyone could be inside. Bert opened one of the doors quietly. She wouldn't have been surprised to find some strange woman in flowing robes asleep on the floor, or perhaps a whole family of raccoons, but there was nothing in the church. There was also no sign of recent entry—no sandy tracks, no bottles, no butts, no damage of any kind, thank goodness.

Her inspection of the generator shed was equally unrevealing. The switch was on, just the way she'd left it the night before. The inverter read a normal charge for the usage.

Promptly at eight, she called Hunter on the cell phone she'd brought along for privacy. The last thing she needed was some bunch of kids on Cedar Island rolling on the floor because they had succeeded in frightening the new caretaker.

"No, I didn't hear any more women moaning," Bert snapped, "but someone was playing the organ last night, unless those nutria can resonate, too." Damn. Rudy had told Hunter about her call.

"Donny Southard, probably drunk," came the laconic reply. "Didn't happen to see if his boat's still down by the dock?"

"It wasn't there at six last night. I went back and looked." But it hadn't occurred to her to check after she met up with the mosquitoes. Of course, she wouldn't have done it at that point anyway.

"The mosquitoes attacked me. I've never seen so many. It was worse than the organ."

There was silence on the phone. "Thought you didn't mind bugs. That's what it said in your application. You use the net over your hat?"

He'd read her resume that carefully? "Do these kinds of things happen a lot?"

"I reckon." His tone was grim. "Last time was when Crissie stayed for the night. Donny and J. J. were all over Coast Guard Creek, hooting and yelling. Kept her up all hours, they did."

Who was Crissie? She was confused. Besides having a drawl, Hunter and Donny used old-fashioned expressions and words she knew only from historical novels. It was a holdover from the old days, when island people had been isolated from the rest of the world. Their speech still contained many of the cockney inflections and idioms of their ancestors. Some even theorized they were descendants of the Lost Colony.

"You all right?" he asked. "They didn't give you too much of a turn, did they?"

The bugs or the intruders? she wondered. "I'm fine now." If Donny was drunk and playing the organ at five in the morning, when did he take the boat out and empty his traps? Those crabs were very fresh. She hesitated, hating to tell him how stupid she'd been. "Donny was here last night. He came back on his ATV."

"You saw him?" There was triumph in Hunter's voice.

She hurried to correct him. "Not when the organ was playing. Earlier."

"Didn't bother you, did he?"

"No. Actually, he gave me some clams. Said that was why he tied up to the dock."

"He's good with excuses." Bert was going to tell him about the crabs when Hunter added quietly, "Like to catch him at it, I would. Just once."

"You think he did it?"

"Yep, but in all fairness, it could have been anyone."

"What should I do if they try it again?"

"Same as you just did. Let people know you're about. If that doesn't stop them, call me anytime, you hear?"

"Thanks." Over her dead body.

He must have read her thoughts, because his response was fast and to the point. "And don't be a hero, you understand? That's not your job. You be sure to inform Jimmy. Should be along anytime now."

Bert reached the dock just before nine. She had on her khaki shorts, her khaki shirt with the volunteer patch and nametag, and her cap. She'd resolved to wear her full uniform until everyone got used to her.

She expected Jimmy to come across from Ocracoke, but to her surprise, an old boat with a high prow and squat cabin suddenly appeared from behind a small island to her north. Casey's Island, they called it. The driver wore park green and gray. Must be Jimmy.

As soon as he'd fastened the mooring lines, he strode over, extending his hand and confirming her guess. "I'm Jimmy Range. They told you about me?"

Bert nodded. "Bert Lenehan. Pleased to meet you," she mumbled idiotically, trying to hide her surprise. She'd expected a college kid. Instead, Jimmy Range was one of those men who could be anywhere from forty-five to sixty-five. He was gorgeous—tiger-shaped face with bright green eyes under a full head of tawny hair. His nose was straight, his mouth cleanly sculpted, his teeth strong, his skin a smooth gold. All that and he stood a head over her, and had a powerful build to boot. This job might be more fun than she thought. A little romantic interest—nothing serious— would be a hoot out here. Down, girl, he's probably married or gay, she warned herself, suddenly feeling shy. "Can I help you with something?"

"I'm here to help you, and I can tell it's going to be a pleasure," he responded almost too suavely. "I have a carton of toilet paper, a case of bug spray, and fifteen gallons of drinking water all for you, and I brought the clam rake back." He turned toward the shore. "We'll just load the stuff on to the cart."

Bert followed his line of sight. A four-wheeler with a utility cart attached was parked in a shed. "You want me to bring it over?" she asked.

"Sure, if you will." He dug into his pocket and tossed her a key. Bert liked it that he assumed she could be of use.

After they loaded the water, he glanced around. "You didn't bring your ATV?"

"Nope. Should I have?"

"Up to you." He patted the back of the ATV seat. "Hop on. This'll give us a chance to know each other."

When he put it that way, she couldn't very well refuse. She climbed on awkwardly, trying not to touch him.

Throwing a mischievous look over his shoulder, he pulled her hands around his waist. "This is the only way to ride double, you should know that."

They were definitely getting to know each other quickly. Bert gave up all thoughts of professional behavior and leaned comfortably against his back. He smelled fresh, spicy. Expensive aftershave. Probably wouldn't smell so sweet after a day's work.

"So how did you enjoy your first night?" he yelled over the motor.

"It was lively," Bert admitted. It was easier to talk to him like this, when she wasn't intimidated by his looks.

He slowed, glancing back. "Lively?"

"Someone was in the church playing the organ about five this morning. You didn't hear about it?" It must be that Cedar Island, where Jimmy lived, wasn't on the Portsmouth grapevine. Did that mean Jimmy didn't know about the nutria either?

They were close to the center of the village now. He stopped at the post office, turned off the engine, then swung around to face her. "Tell me again. Someone was in the church playing the organ? Were you scared?" He tried to catch her eyes, but Bert turned away.

"I was at first. Then I got mad." She wasn't going to admit her panicked flight.

He shook his head when she told him about going to the

church. "You shouldn't have done that. Next time, just turn on the porch lights. Lights up the whole station. I'll show you how."

"I figured it was kids. Hunter thinks it was Donny Southard."

"Most likely. You've got some rough characters around here. If they've been drinking, pretty gal like you . . ." His voice trailed off. "Turn on the lights and carry your radio." He grinned, showing those beautiful white teeth again. "Make like you're calling. They know the Coast Guard can intercept a boat pretty quick."

Bert nodded. "Yeah, I've done that before. Used my cellular when someone was playing games with me on I-95."

His eyes did a quick sweep over her. "You married?"

The question took her by surprise. "No. Yes. That is, I was. I'm divorced." Divorced ten years ago, but that was none of his business.

"That's good. Any boyfriends?" He kicked the pedal, starting up the bike.

Bert clutched his waist without answering. Damned if she was going to let him get that personal or encourage him by asking about his marital status. But she didn't have to. The next moment, he yelled back at her, "Just in case you're wondering, which I hope you are, I've been married twice. Currently single and unattached, but not for long, I hope. You have a boyfriend or someone I should be aware of?"

Bert gave up. "No. We just broke up, which is one of the reasons I'm here."

"Good for me, bad for him." He grinned as they bounced into the boat storage building that was part of the lifesaving station. "What do you think of O'Hagan?" he asked as he unloaded the cartons. "You know he's not the regular island manager? He's just filling in for Ben Willis." A huge riding mower was parked in the boathouse, plus a Gator like Justin's and several utility trailers in various stages of repair. Rusty metal cabinets lined the walls, and cans were stacked along shelves.

"He's nice." She really didn't want to start gossiping about their bosses—not until she knew Jimmy better, at any rate. "You worked here long?"

"This is my second year. I'm seasonal, summers."

The park hired a lot of seasonal help, from interpretation and protection rangers to maintenance personnel. Most permanent employees had gotten their start as seasonals. But what was he doing mowing lawns? "You're not from around here," she said.

"Yuh mean Ah didn't fool y'all none with my Southern drawl? Columbus, Ohio, originally. Also Pittsburgh and Tucson." Again, he anticipated her question. "I'm a dentist, or I was. Now, I'm semi-retired. I like to keep busy, work outside. And I'm crazy about water. This job was made for me." He took her arm after he locked the boathouse. "I'll drop the water jugs off to your place."

Suddenly, her whole attention was focused where his fingers met her flesh. Thoroughly rattled, Bert said the first thing that came to her head: "The power went out last night."

He swung around. "The power went out? What time?"

"I'm not sure. The clock was out, too. Early, I think. Midnight?" She was sorry she'd mentioned it.

He frowned. Pinching his lips together made him look older. "Was it the same time as when the organ went off?"

"No. I probably did something wrong with the generator."

Jimmy took her to the shed and watched silently as she went through the routine of turning the generator on and then back off again. "You didn't do anything wrong." He was still frowning. "But if you forget to throw that main switch, she won't charge. Here, I'll show you how to read the voltage meter. Then we'll take a look at the fuse box."

Once they reached her cabin, Jimmy turned on all the lights and fans one by one, then the marine radio's battery charger and the television. At one point, he lit everything simultaneously, but the circuits appeared adequate. Not a bulb flickered.

"Coffee?" Bert offered as he unloaded her drinking water.

"Can't understand it," he said, pulling up a chair. "Hunter and I ran all new wiring, buried every foot. There's been no rain, and that's a new box—well, not new, but a lot better than what was here before." He stared out the window toward the church, his lips tight. "What music were they playing?"

"Huh?" What did that have to do with anything?

"Did you recognize the tune?" he enunciated slowly, bringing his gaze back to her.

He was probably wondering if she was all there. She rushed to answer, the words tumbling over each other. "A hymn. Used to sing it when I was a little girl. Something about restless waves."

Jimmy hummed a couple of bars, his brows questioning.

Bert leaned forward, nodding. " 'Eternal Father, Strong to Save.' "

Jimmy's brows rose even higher as he nodded slightly.

"What's the hymn got to do with it?" Bert asked.

Pushing himself back in his chair, he explained: "That's a British hymn that was popular in Portsmouth during colonial times. The people were Church of England then." His tone was casual, almost too casual. "Not a tune I'd expect Donny to know."

Did this mean Jimmy didn't think it was a drunken lessee?

"I'm surprised you recognized it," he went on. "It's an old sea-faring song."

What did he think she was, some city gal? And what was this all about, ghosts? "I was born at sea," she snapped, "and that hymn's popular in any port. We used to sing it all the time."

"Not in Methodist ports, you didn't," he said mildly, stirring some sugar and a lot of milk into his coffee. "Never heard of anyone being born at sea—not these days, anyhow."

Bert sighed. Usually, this came up when someone asked where she was from. "My father was stationed in Chile, enlarging the port to accommodate aircraft carriers during the Second World War. He was merchant marine," she explained almost by rote. "My mother was pregnant, and in those days, you had to be American-born to be president of the United States. So when it was time for her to have the baby, he sent her back to San Francisco on a company ship. Only—"

"You came early."

His interest mollified her. "Yup."

"So now, I know your age. You sure don't look any fifty-some. Know how old I am?" He didn't wait for her to answer. "Sixty-two. Not bad, hey?" He flexed a bicep. "I'm in good shape in all the ways that count," he insinuated, eyes dancing.

"No demonstrations, please," Bert said, laughing. She pushed back from the table and rinsed out her coffee cup. "I think it's time we earned our keep."

"Can we do this again? I'll bring donuts."

"Instant cholesterol, at our advanced age?" she teased.

At one-thirty, Elbert, the concessionaire from Ocracoke, arrived with a load of visitors. Jimmy was getting ready to return to Harkers Island, the park headquarters. That was where he'd come from that morning.

"Takes over an hour and a half to get there," he explained. "I have to unload, hose down the boat, and report in, then it's an hour's drive back to Cedar Island. I wish they'd let me keep the boat at Cedar. Halve my time." He checked his watch. "I'll try to stay longer tomorrow. Besides, you'll have your hands full." He indicated the people from Elbert's boat, who had already spread over the village. "Meanwhile, don't go investigating any power outages or strange noises. Promise?" The smile was still on his lips, but his eyes were serious as they met hers.

Bert lifted her hand. "I promise. Honest. The last thing I want to do is lock horns with a bunch of drunks, or ghosts."

The smile faded from Jimmy's face. "What made you say that?"

"What? You mean there really are supposed to be ghosts?"

His face relaxed again. He shot her a mischievous glance as they started down the dock. "Haven't you read any of the books, woman? There's ghosts all over the Outer Banks—Indian maidens, burning ships, wailing spirits. Blackbeard's body still swims around looking for its head, and Spriggs guards his tomb. Then there's Sea-born Woman and . . ." He fixed her with his jade green gaze. "Sea-born Woman—why, you're a sea-born woman, too."

The phrase echoed in her ears long after his boat was a dot on the sunlit waves.

41

Chapter 4

SEA-BORN WOMAN. Bert liked the label. She rolled it around her tongue once or twice, tasting it. It was romantic, exotic, but did it apply to her? She hoped so. She'd have to find out more about this woman. Hunter would know; he seemed to know everything. Whether or not he'd tell her was another story. He didn't seem particularly forthcoming—probably just didn't like Northerners. There was a lot of that around. Or maybe he didn't like volunteers, especially female ones.

Bert shrugged and steeled herself to greet the visitors.

"In its heyday, it was a lightering port," she told a sweet old man wearing knee socks. "Ships would offload in Portsmouth, then the cargo was taken to the mainland by smaller boats that could negotiate the shallow waters of the sound."

"Beaufort take their business?"

"No. A big storm in the 1840s opened up Hatteras Inlet and changed the shipping lanes. Ships could go directly to the North Carolina mainland through the inlet without having to offload. To make it worse, that's when the waters around Portsmouth began to shoal up. About then, the railroads were getting into the action, taking goods to big ports like Norfolk."

"How did the people live after that?" a young mother asked.

"Fishing and oystering." Bert was surprised by how much she knew. That half-day with the museum historian had paid off. It reinforced some of the reading she'd done. "But the oyster beds were in trouble by 1890. The villagers also acted as hosts and guides for tourists—duck hunters, mostly."

"When did the last family leave?"

"About twenty-five years ago."

" 'Scuse me, miss." A small hand tugged at her shirt. "These tracks over here, they're unreal, like . . ."

It was a small boy with an Oriental cast to his eyes and a thick New Jersey accent. He was pointing to some nearby dunes.

"Like an animal dragging its tail?" Bert asked, walking over with him. He was adorable—skin like silk, bright, dark eyes. He nodded. "That was pretty sharp of you to notice." The boy grinned toothlessly at her compliment. "It's a nutria track. You know what they are?" When he shook his head, she went on. "Back when this was a big port, rats kept jumping the ships. Some say they imported the nutria to control the rats. Others say they were brought in for their fur. They're related to muskrats, I think."

"Do they bite?"

"Only if you corner them. That's why they won't let you bring dogs over. They tell me they have real big, sharp teeth."

He glanced around.

"They're shy. I've never even seen one," Bert was quick to assure him. Just heard one, she thought wryly. And now, she could hear something else, a car engine. Was it Hunter or a fisherman? Maybe it was just Elbert coming back for the visitors. Returning the boy to his family, she pointed toward the lifesaving station. "You'll find me over there on the mower if you need anything else. Enjoy your stay."

It was Hunter in the white truck. "Came to bring you these." He pointed at two Coleman lanterns. "In case you have more trouble with the power."

"Jimmy called you," she accused.

"He reports to me every day, same as you. How did you two get along?" He turned with the lanterns toward the cabin, but there was something about him that told Bert he was waiting for her answer.

"I expected a college kid."

Hunter hesitated, then said carefully, "Jimmy's a good man. It's just sometimes . . ."

Bert deliberately said nothing. Was he trying to warn her off Jimmy?

"He'd never hurt anyone on purpose," Hunter finished.

"Yes, well . . . Do you want me to take those inside?" She reached for the lanterns. It was none of his business, or the park's, how she handled Jimmy. And damned if she felt like inviting Hunter in right now. "I still haven't done the mowing."

"Don't you worry about that." He set the lanterns on her steps. "Just take things slow, explore, get comfortable around here. Jimmy told me he's fixing to mow tomorrow." Hunter hesitated, staring at the ground as one shoe etched a circle in the sand. "Would you mind going over what took place last night again? I'm not certain I caught it all." He shrugged. "Can't understand so good over that phone."

Bert fought a grin, her momentary annoyance forgotten. Apparently, he was having the same trouble with her accent that she was with his.

He listened intently to her recital of last night's events as he led her to an old log that overlooked Doctor's Creek. A couple of bugs circled overhead but kept their distance. The sun was warm, the ocean silver behind the silhouette of the Piggott House. Through the marsh grass, Bert could see visitors wandering the garden. It wasn't hard to imagine them as past residents come to life on this beautiful day.

"Both you and Jimmy seem more concerned about the power failure than the organ. Why?" she asked after she finished.

He scowled, sitting down on the log. "We thought we fixed it."

"Oh. You mean it's happened before?" Suddenly, Bert knew.

"Is that why Anne Source left the house the night she died?"

"Can't say for sure," Hunter was quick to reply.

"But you think it was?"

He nodded, his eyes swinging away from hers.

Bert stood. "Why didn't you tell me?"

"We knew they weren't powering the generator right. Couldn't get a handle on the phones either." He smiled up at her. "Seems they didn't take to machines."

He should smile like that more often, Bert thought, sitting back down. He really was an attractive man under all that bushy, dark red hair. She could have drawn some mean-tempered old coot or, worse, some fat slob who couldn't keep his hands to himself. Of course, Jimmy was kind of touchy-feely, but she could control his type, if she wanted to.

"Did you notice anything when you went out to the church?" Hunter asked slowly, staring at his feet again.

"What do you mean? I told you, I didn't see anyone."

"Not like that. Like, um, fog? Wind?"

"Nothing." Suddenly, she remembered the cold. "Except . . ."

"Yes?" He was looking directly at her now.

"There was, like, a cold spot around the church."

"Ah."

"That was right before the mosquitoes. I don't know how the people could stand it here. That was the worst . . ." She shuddered, rubbing her arms.

"You get used to them, you know."

"Never."

He waved a hand at the nearby cedars. "Bugs weren't so thick then either. All this was open in the old days. Wind blew from the sea to the sound. Kept things nice."

"You're from around here, aren't you?"

"I reckon. With a name like O'Hagan . . ." At Bert's blank look, he explained. "One of the villagers was an O'Hagan."

"Really? Which house?"

"Now, that's a good question. Folks been trying to find it since day one. House was swept away in the storm of 1899, along with a mess of others." He stood. "Crissie asked me to take you on a tour of the village. We'll use the ATVs."

This time, she asked. "Crissie?"

"You know, your trainer."

"Oh, Christine Wright." The interpretation ranger, a young, energetic woman with a figure that was Bert's idea of perfection, slim and long-waisted.

It was almost five when they returned.

"You have a park boat here?" Bert asked. The last ferry from the island left at four.

"I'm fixing to bunk at the ranger station tonight, at Long Point."

"You're not doing that because of me, are you?" A caretaker to take care of the caretaker. She wouldn't have a job long.

He ignored her question. "It'll only take me twenty minutes to get back here."

Twenty minutes if he did fifty over the sand—at night. Better him than her. She shrugged. "I'm so tired I don't think I'd hear a whole choir tonight." Something about the expression on his face made her stop. "What's the matter?"

For a moment, she didn't think he was going to answer. Then he said slowly, "I was fixing to take you fishing. Seen you brought your rod." He lifted his head, and for the first time, Bert noticed his eyes. They were a strange color contrasting with his olive skin—slate gray like a winter ocean, a deep ocean.

"I'm never too tried to fish," Bert said, her energy returning. "I was hoping someone would show me the good holes."

They took Hunter's truck. However, as they crossed the dunes that separated the mud flats from the ocean, he skidded to a stop. With just a brief "Wait here," he was out and striding rapidly up the dunes. As Bert squinted into the sun, she noticed a second set of tire tracks. Hunter followed them up the dunes and sighted across. Then, scowling, he hiked back to the truck. "You had any visitors in from Long Point today?"

"Not that I know of. Why, is that their tracks?"

"ATV, four-wheeler. I'd lay good money it's Donny's." He cocked his head and was silent. He apparently heard something because, without saying a word, he started the truck just as an ATV emerged from the dunes.

The truck's horn blasted Bert's ears. The ATV sped up momentarily, then came to a halt. Hunter's face was stern as he pulled up behind it. Picking up a pad, he motioned her to remain in the vehicle.

It was Donny, wearing ragged shorts and an even more ragged tank top, both stained dark by mud and oil. He fished in a pocket for his license. Hunter accepted it and jotted down the information.

Bert heard Donny protesting. "I come up on a cat, was just fixing to catch it, that's God's truth. Just trying to help out. I care about them birds as much as you-all."

"You were riding an all-terrain vehicle in a posted area. You been warned. I'm writing you up this time."

Donny sagged. "I didn't mean no harm. It were that black cat with the white lighting marks. I knowed you been trying to catch it."

Hunter went on writing in silence.

Donny tried again. "My lease come up next year. They's saying they might not renew—you know, on account of them pound nets."

"More than that," Hunter grunted, not lifting his eyes. "Fish and Game got you for illegal pheasant this spring. Rudy saw you riding in the village. The worst violation is your outhouse. It's supposed to be a composter, not a hole in the ground."

"I'm fixing to do it. Trust me, I have it all planned out."

Hunter didn't even look up. He handed the ticket to Donny. "Want to tell me where you were at five o'clock this morning?"

Donny's head jerked around. "I didn't do nothing. I was sleeping." He stopped, scratching his belly. "Now, that ain't exactly true. At sunup, I was out netting baitfish for my pots. I'm fixing to go to Atlantic tonight." He looked up at Hunter, the anxious expression still on his face. "I got it all planned. Iffen I run fifty pots this summer, I can buy a tank and dig me a septic. That would make them happy, right?" He gave Hunter a tentative smile.

Hunter stared back, unbending. "Know anything about the church organ going off? Were you in the village last night?"

"That what this be about?" Donny straightened. "I ain't been in the church since the reunion. She knowed I were there last night." He pointed at Bert. "Tell him. I give her some clams. Then I come right back to my camp."

"I did hear his ATV leave," Bert told Hunter when they resumed their trip to the beach. "And I didn't hear him come back." She twisted around to look back toward Donny. "Darn, I meant to ask if he left the crabs."

"What crabs?"

Bert told Hunter about her morning surprise. "See, it couldn't have been him at the church," she added. "There wasn't enough time."

"He could have left the crabs last night."

"Why would he? He said he baited the traps this morning. Must have emptied them then, too. Besides, they weren't there when the organ was playing."

Hunter shrugged. "Could have had them in a box at his place."

She obviously wasn't going to argue him out of thinking the worst. "You know, I feel sorry for him. He seems to be trying."

Hunter was curled over the steering wheel. "Trying to get in good with you, that's what he's doing," he growled. "Never saw a man come up with so many excuses."

"He said his place belonged to his father. Is the park really going to take it away?"

They had reached the beach now. Hunter turned toward Ocracoke and the dunes. "This has been coming for a long time, and Donny knows it. He just doesn't want to think about it." He exhaled. "They were supposed to go over all this with you at headquarters."

"They did, but we only had the one day. It was information overload."

"Yeah. Well, back in the sixties, Portsmouth was just about dying. That's when developers started buying up tax deeds and doing surveys. The last three residents got scared. They didn't want to see the village torn down, so they lobbied to have the state take it over, and the state got together with the Park Service. Piggott, that was the last man, and the two women, Miss Elma and Miss Marion, deeded their houses to the park. Then, after they all died, the park put some of the houses out on restoration leases, like they are now."

A lot of it came back to Bert as he spoke, but she was going to have to do some more reading.

"The rest of Core Banks was different," Hunter continued. "Nothing but fishing shacks, shanties, and lean-tos. People would boat over and set up camp anyplace they fancied. The park burned all of those. The owners that had title were told they could sell to the park and take the houses with them, or they could take a twenty-five-year lease. At the end of that time, the property reverted to the park." Hunter slapped the wheel. "Those leases are about up."

"You mean they're not going to renew? Does Donny know?" Bert stared at the blue-green ocean. How horrible to have to leave.

"Can't say for sure. There's a movement afoot to extend the leases. Got themselves a big lawyer from Beaufort."

"What will the park do with the houses?"

"Same thing they did with the ones that sold out—burn the trash and use the better ones as public buildings. Donny's will burn, if I get my say."

Bert didn't care for this side of him at all. "If my family had a place out here, I'd sure hate to give it up."

Hunter backed the truck down to the water's edge. He turned off the ignition but made no move to get out. Instead, he swung his arm over the seat, facing her. "Don't know if Crissie went over this with you already, but I'm gonna go over it again. If you're gonna do good for the park, you can't be getting too friendly with the lessees. They'll be looking to use you."

"You mean I shouldn't have taken those clams from Donny," she said, staring straight ahead. It had been dumb, but she wasn't going to admit it.

"Don't you be putting words into my mouth." He rapped the

back of the seat impatiently. "They'll drop by, invite you to eat, bring you fish and other things. No cause to be rude. J. J. puts on a fine feed. Just remember, you're working for the park. Take care they remember, too." He eyed her window. "Best to close it. Keep the flies out."

If there was anything she hated, it was being reproved. She rolled up the window as fast as she could. He must have gotten the idea, as he added softly, "Now, I'm fixing to forget all this shop talk and catch myself a mess of fish. What you say, gal?" He touched her shoulder tentatively.

His tone was gentle, and something in the way he smiled made her feel better. He had a job to do, and it was too nice a day to begrudge him the lecture. She forced herself to return his smile as she slid out of the truck. "Dollar on first fish, dollar for biggest."

They stood on the wide beach just above the surf, close to a ridge of dunes. The tide had turned about an hour earlier. The waves were moderate, the wind just ruffling the surface. "Big slough here," Hunter explained. "Other side of Swash Inlet is a good hole, too. If you want trout, go down to the airplane wheel by the fishing camp, although it's past time now."

"What should I use?" Rig in hand, Bert stood near the open tailgate of the truck next to the cooler they'd packed.

"Let's see what you got." Hunter sorted through the zip-lock bags and picked out a pack of bait Bert had put up herself. "Spot. Good thinking."

As they cut the fish into strips, Bert asked Hunter a question that had been running through her mind: "Are we allowed to use park stuff like this?" She indicated the truck.

He pulled out several weights and handed her one. "Depends on a lot of things. Here, it's not an eight-to-five job. You're on duty even when your work's done, so it's all right to use the park equipment."

"You're on duty now? You're getting paid for this?"

"I get paid to keep the volunteers happy and . . . comfortable."

Bert caught his hesitation. Had he meant to say *safe*?

"And relaxation is part of it," he continued. "You just have to be careful around visitors. They don't always understand."

Hunter caught an eighteen-inch flounder with his first cast. Over the next hour, Bert picked up two blues that she released, and Hunter threw back a small sea mullet.

The sun, low in the sky, was already casting pink light on the beach. There was no one around to disturb the scene, just miles of glistening sand and wavelets gleaming like lavender jewels. "Unbelievable," Bert breathed dreamily. Just then, something hit her line so hard she staggered trying to recover her balance.

Hunter grinned. "Good one?"

Off balance or not, Bert managed to snap the rod, although she figured the hook was already set. She definitely had something. "Ooh, biggest fish I ever hooked," she gasped, adjusting the drag. Please let me bring it in, she prayed silently. She reeled steadily, trying to keep the line taut, but the fish was strong. She kept reeling and backed up slightly when it swam toward her. Don't give him any slack or he'll break free, she warned herself.

Hunter had put his rod in the holder and was already standing in the surf, ready to help.

Suddenly, the fish broke water. It was huge. Hunter yelled something, but she missed it. She was too busy watching the surf, lowering the tip of the rod when the waves retreated, using their forward surge to haul the fish into the shallows.

Hunter ran forward as Bert used a breaker to bring the fish onto the sand. He expertly tucked his hand under the gills and lifted. "Red drum!" he howled, dancing up the beach. "Eight pounds at least. I reckon we got us a fish fry."

Bert stared at the fish. It was beautiful—silver graduated to orange-red scales down its back, a big spot at the base of its tail. "I never got one anywhere near this big. They're good eating, aren't they?"

"The best, gal, the best."

Bert grinned back at him. This was nice, especially after the earlier lecture.

Later, after both the fish had been reduced to fillets that fit Bert's fridge, she and Hunter sat on the porch steps having a beer.

Bert had hesitated offering him some of her smuggled stock, not sure if it was legal in the National Park or if he was allowed to drink. But the red drum seemed worthy of celebration. Hunter hadn't batted an eye.

"Do you get a lot of drum here?"

"Not that many, though I thought I seen a couple scratching when I come by in the truck earlier."

"Scratching?"

"They come in real close. Sometimes, half their backs are out of the water. Some say they're looking for sand moles."

"Hope you like your fish fried." She made her voice casual. An invitation to dinner seemed mandatory, but at the same time, she didn't want to make him feel obligated to hang around entertaining her.

"Don't want to put you out none." His eyes smiled shyly.

Maybe he didn't have anything better to do. "You can't leave me with all that fish, especially after you practically caught it for me."

"No, you did all the catching. Do a lot of fishing?"

"Not surf fishing. I like it."

Hunter nodded. "It's cleaner."

"And it gives me an excuse to be near the ocean."

"That why you took this job?"

"That and living on an island."

"It can get old pretty fast, being alone."

"I wish I was alone. Not you, but it would be nice if no visitors came over for a couple of days. Give me a chance to read and do some exploring." In a moment, she'd get up and begin cooking the fish, Bert thought lazily. Later, a shower and bed. She didn't care if all the ghosts in Portsmouth rose. Tonight, she'd sleep. That reminded her. "Hunter, tell me about Sea-born Woman."

He'd been sitting propped against the porch post, head resting on the rail. At her question, he sat up and swung his legs over the steps, his face an angry scowl. "You making fun?"

What on earth was his problem? "Fun of what?"

"I don't believe in ghosts, and my family don't care none for that story." He was on his feet. "Guess it's time I was getting back."

Bert almost let him go. There was no reason for him to get pissed like that. Oh, shit. She ran after him. "Hunter, Hunter, wait a minute." She reached out.

He stopped.

Bert realized she had her hand on his arm. Oh, God, she hoped he didn't think she was hitting on him. He was at least ten years younger. She started to pull away, then sort of slithered her hand off, patting as she went. Now, she'd almost forgotten why he got mad in the first place. Oh, yes, Sea-born Woman. "I wasn't making fun of you," she told him, speaking much too fast. "I was born at sea, and Jimmy said there was a local legend. I just thought you'd—"

"You were born at sea?" Now, his hands came up, grabbing her shoulders. "You sure? That would explain . . ."

Bert shook his hands off, backing away. "What's wrong with that? What's wrong with you?"

He turned back to the steps. "Come here." He sat and patted the stoop next to him. "I'm acting like a fool. You've no cause to know about Sea-born Woman."

Bert said nothing. No way was she falling into that trap again.

"Remember how I told you my people came from these parts? O'Hagan?"

"Yeah?"

"Sea-born Woman's name was Jerushia Spriggs O'Hagan."

"Oh."

He laughed. It was a good laugh, from deep inside. "Not *Oh. O'Hagan*. Family took a lot of momicking—hassling—about her being a haunt. Guess I'm too sensitive about it. Come on, I'll tell you some of the story while we fry that fish.

"John and Mary O'Hagan were Irish emigrants," he began as he rinsed and salted the fillets. "They left Belfast in 1720 on a clumsy old sloop, good for nothing except to transport emigrants. She had a right fancy name, though, to lure poor Irish to ship out on her. The ship's name was *Celestial Harp*." ∽

Chapter 5

"SAIL AHOY, TO THE PORT REACH!"

At last, the long-awaited cry. With studied disdain, Captain Francis Spriggs strolled to the port rail, careful not to betray his triumph. He'd taken a gamble, a bigger gamble than when he'd first gone to sea, and he'd won.

"Well done, Jody, m'boy! The finest pistol aboard is yours!" he shouted to the sailor in the shrouds. Then he turned to the main deck. "Haul sheets, men. Give me full sail now."

As the pirate watched his ship leap ahead before the freshening morning breeze, he thought back on the day five years ago when he'd first shipped out to sea. Francis Harrington Spriggs was born the fourth son of a "planter," as his father preferred to call himself. The family farm was too small to be divided, and the prospect of working the land for his brothers had filled Spriggs with dismay. Then, one day, a gaudily dressed stranger arrived at the nearby settlement. For a fortnight, the taps at the tavern flowed free to all comers. "There are fortunes to be made at sea," the flamboyant officer told the bevy of admiring young men, Spriggs among them. "England is at war with Spain, and the queen, God bless her soul, needs our help subjugating Spanish ships. And be it a Frenchy or Portuguese—who is to tell?—there be enough gold on one merchantman to build a house for every man jack here." He paused to let his words sink in. "And to keep several wenches in comfort for the rest o' your natural life."

The officer was canny. Besides having a fascination for the sea, Spriggs was above all a practical young man. The idea of making his fortune in a couple of short years appealed to him, as did the women. Over his father's halfhearted protests, the youth took himself to nearby Hongry Town, and from there to New Providence in the Bahamas to ship out with Captain Ned Low.

When the war ended, pickings became slim for privateers turned pirates. Forced out of the Caribbean by English men-of-war, Low's fleet retreated to the shores of North America. Competition with other buccaneers for the few prizes that dared sail these waters was fierce. But now, here at last was the long-promised merchantman. Spriggs smiled grimly. He needed this prize if he was to keep his ship and his men.

"Ready about." Worry creased his brow as they sped in pursuit. There was something about the way the vessel pitched . . . .

Spriggs's ship, the *Delight*, was a small, fast sloop carrying eighteen men. She had no trouble catching up to the larger vessel, which was now running before the wind. As they closed in, Spriggs's concern deepened. This was no merchantman. He doubted it was even a cargo ship—too slow and clumsy. Probably a passenger vessel bringing emigrants to the colonies—the New World, as they called it.

The men had come to the same conclusion. He could tell by the quiet that spread as they all stared at the dreary sails. Damn and blast them all to hell! This was not his doing. Nevertheless, the grumbling would begin, hidden and deadly.

Spriggs had to act quickly, before the men lost heart, if he still planned to take the sloop. And take the sloop he would. The devil willing, this might be a ship of rich colonists with ample supplies.

The danger lay in letting the crew become despondent.

Captain Spriggs was only twenty-three, but life as a younger brother in a large family had prepared him well in the art of handling men. The Royal Navy enforced discipline by brute force, so that even grossly incompetent officers had a degree of control, but a pirate captain had to be a true leader. Some built themselves a reputation for fierceness, as had Teach, others, like Low, for barbaric acts and random murder. Like his mentor, Spriggs planned to become renowned for innovative cruelty.

"Mister Holmes," he called to the bosun. "Fetch me the pennant. Fast, man, fast." The newly designed flag had been intended for their return to New Providence. "Must be providence indeed that guided my fingers—or rather those of my sailmaker—to prepare it."

"Yes, captain." Holmes disappeared down a hatch and re-emerged shortly. At a nod from his captain, he hoisted the flag.

The pirates roared their appreciation. Some of the younger crew broke into a hornpipe jig. Flying atop the main trunk, silhouetted by the clear blue September sky, were the pirate colors. Only this was not the usual skull and crossbones or the skeleton used by Ned Low. Spriggs had gone a step farther. His flag boasted a dancing skeleton holding an hourglass, a warning that the time to surrender was limited, and a bleeding heart rent by an arrow, the penalty if surrender was not prompt.

Donning his battle dress—a velvet tricorn and a blue damask waistcoat with a red silk sling about his waist—Captain Spriggs gave the orders all awaited: "Gunner, issue the pistols. Every man ready to fight." Besides his cutlass, Spriggs carried a brace of pistols slung in his bandoleer. They were not yet loaded, as the devilish things had a nasty habit of misfiring.

The other ship, close-hauled, pitched heavily in the light sea. Her crew worked frantically to add sail. As the *Delight* closed, Spriggs saw the ship was indeed poorly designed and probably foul with barnacles. Moreover, her sails were patched and gray with age. Her name was *Celestial Harp*. Spriggs stifled a curse. She was not a vessel to carry noble passengers, he feared.

"Ready to drop sails. Hard a-lee." To his relief, no quick gust interfered with his maneuver, and the *Delight* came broadside to the other vessel with impressive smartness. On Spriggs's deck were six cannons, three of which were aimed at the sloop.

"Ready grapples. Set to, you maggots!" the pirate captain roared at the top of his lungs, so he could be heard across the water. His goal was to demoralize the other ship to such an extent that not a shot need be fired.

The pirates shouted. Cutlasses flashed. Smoky torches and barrels of punk burned, ready to fire. Several trigger-happy men let loose volleys.

The captain of the *Celestial Harp* had no intention of putting up a fight, nor had he the means to do so. This was to be his last voyage, and now he doubted he would live to return home. "Damn you for villains!" he shouted back. "Send your men. We cannot stop you."

Grapples flew and caught. Amid a welter of smoke, shots, curses, and clanging of metal, the pirates swarmed aboard.

Captain Spriggs's fears were all too correct. It was an Irishman carrying the poorest sort of passengers. As he had the emigrants rounded up and brought to the deck, Spriggs grew angrier and angrier. "My cabin boy, Goree, wears better clothes than this." He raked apart a man's ragged shirt with his cutlass, then pointed at one of the younger women. "Search her, Mister Holmes."

Hoots of delight rose from the men as Holmes proceeded to disrobe the poor woman. But even this yielded little. The woman had no valuables. Her body was rail-thin, her breasts sagging to her navel. Worse, boils in various stages of suppuration lined her scrawny buttocks and underarms. His men had no use for such as this. They liked their women healthy and buxom.

Captain Spriggs's mood darkened. By jove, was there not a silver coin or a gold ring among them? Even the ship was worthless, a rotting old scow. He would be the laughingstock of New Providence, if he dared return. And if he did not return, then he was a dead man, for the ship he commanded was under the grace of Captain Low, and one third of the bounty belonged to him.

As Spriggs deliberated, one of the pirates, a gross man who

cared little where he took his pleasure, approached the naked woman, his intent quite apparent. Catcalls rose as he thrust himself upon the unfortunate female. At this, the woman's husband became frantic, downing one of the pirates in his attempt to reach her. With casual ease, Spriggs leapt forth and dealt the husband a head blow with the flat of his cutlass. The man dropped insensible. "Chain the swine to the yardarm, head down, Mister Everhart," he commanded. The Irish crew and male passengers outnumbered the men of the *Delight* two to one. Insurrection could not be tolerated. "Tie them all to the masts, every last man, woman, and child." Spriggs was so angry he trembled. Scurvy lot of filthy bastards! he thought. "We'll send them to the Promised Land, that we shall, with a fanfare that has never been heard before." Then, delighted by the bloody coup he had just devised, he threw back his head and roared. He had a deep, throaty laugh that proved as effective as the most dire threats on occasion.

Confusion reigned on deck as the men followed his orders, chaining the poor souls to the stanchions and even the rail when the masts were filled.

"Mister Green, Mister Wills, take three men and search below."

The search revealed little of use to the pirates. Her voyage almost over, the *Celestial Harp* had few supplies left. What live sheep and goats had survived the journey were readied for transport to the *Delight*. There was not even a keg of spirits on board. These were not passengers—these were paupers!

"Mister Everhart." Spriggs leaned over the rail to hail the dinghy that was leaving with the livestock. "Fetch me four cases of gunpowder. Hurry, lad. We'll give them a parting they'll never forget."

The mood of the crew lifted as the men realized what savagery their captain planned. It was with laughter that they brought the barrels on board, setting them about in strategic spots close to the waterline. Under Spriggs's direction, they began to lay the fuses. He would blow up the *Celestial Harp*. Those who did not die in the explosions would die chained to the ship as she sank.

As the horror of his plan became obvious to the doomed passengers, they began to cry and moan.

"Nay, have mercy. My babe, she be only four winters."

"Oh, Lord God, hear our prayers."

"You wretched, woebegone, miserable bastard, may your balls wither and drop off. May worms eat your bowels."

Their cries grew louder, infecting the children. One lass with deep red hair begged piteously, "Dada, Dada, can ye not do something? Please, Dada, I'm frighted."

Finally, Spriggs's mate said quietly, "Captain, is it not better to throw back the first fish, that others may follow?"

Then a woman's voice started singing "Eternal Father, Strong to Save." Others joined in. Their voices rose above the tumult, clear and sweet.

Slowly, his men stopped laughing. They looked to Spriggs.

Damn blast these swinish emigrants to Hades! They were spoiling his innovative sport. Spriggs strolled disdainfully closer to the prisoners, cutlass unsheathed, head churning. However, as he raised his arm to the first singer, the muttering in the ranks grew louder. Damnation. The men's thirst for blood had turned to piss.

In battle, a man had to make instantaneous decisions. But now, at least, he had the luxury of time. "Is this the whole sorry lot, then?" he asked Mister Green, temporizing.

"There be three women yet, captain, in the aft deck."

"Three more of the bitches free?" This was too much. "I ordered all tied to the masts!" he roared.

His mate cut in quickly. "Begging your pardon, captain, but they are birthing."

"What? All three?"

"Nay, captain." Mister Green stood his ground. "Just one. The other two be midwives."

Spriggs began to see a way out. Perhaps . . . He sheathed his sword. "A birth at sea?" he mumbled loudly, so all could hear. Then he made a show of glancing toward the pirate flag and the fork of Poseidon. With a grand flourish, he whirled around. "Take me below, Mister Green."

The wail of a newborn floated up the dark passageway.

Hastily, Spriggs entered the aft compartment just as one of the midwives lifted the child to the light. It was a beautiful, plump girl, strong of limb and lung. Suddenly, it all came clear to Captain Spriggs, who was a practical man. He needed an excuse to back away, and this child would provide it.

Accompanied by one of the midwives, an old crone in black rags who carried the infant, he marched back to where they'd tied the *Harp*'s captain. "Which is the father of this babe?" Spriggs demanded. When the captain pointed him out, Spriggs shouted, "Find also the mate of this sorry scow!"

Then he had the chains struck from all three men. By now, the singing had stopped. Even the children quieted.

He waited until the only sounds were the slap of the waves against the hull and the creak of the mast as the slow rolls passed beneath them. This bargain had to be struck perfectly and with a flourish or it would not work.

"I have a proposition for you." He paced back and forth before the three men—the old captain in stained breeches and faded jacket, the sullen mate, the young father, tattered homespun on his back and hope in his eyes. Spriggs whirled to face them, legs spread, hands behind his back, the sun glinting on the emerald cross he wore about his neck. " 'Tis bad luck to kill a sea-born woman," he said slowly, distinctly. "She commands the sea creatures and brings good fortune to mariners. Therefore, ye have only to name the girl for my dear mother, Jerushia Spriggs, and I will let your ship go, and all her passengers."

The captain gaped. The mate exclaimed. In unison, the three men sank to their knees, kissing the deck and calling blessings upon Captain Spriggs. Behind, he could hear a murmur of approbation from the men.

He feigned impatience, waving his cutlass. "Well, men, what say ye?" This had gone as he'd planned—nay, even better. This tale would live among the annals of New Providence.

It was John O'Hagan, a simple carpenter, who found his voice first and stood before the captain. "Aye, sir. 'Tis proud I'll be to name my sea-born babe after your old ma. Jerushia Spriggs O'Hagan it'll be. And may she live to save as many souls as you have on this day of her birth."

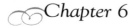

Chapter 6

AS THE SILENCE LENGTHENED and the slap of water grew fainter, Bert slowly came out of her reverie. "Don't stop," she whispered, not wanting to break the enchantment. But even as she said it, she knew it was time for him to leave.

Hunter rose and took their plates to the sink.

"Did he really exist?" she asked.

"Spriggs?" He washed both dishes carefully before he answered. "I took some liberties. Not exactly sure about his childhood, but he existed, all right. He's buried right over yonder."

"On the island?"

He nodded.

"Where? What happened to the baby?" Bert began putting away the food.

Hunter smiled, leaning back against the sink. "Took to my story, did you?"

"I love the way you told it," she said sincerely.

He didn't answer. Lifting his backpack from the chair, he started toward the door, then paused to cuff her shoulder. " 'Tis sea-born women that have the gift, don't you know?"

Hunter's words echoed in her mind as she prepared for the

night. What gift, bringing luck to sailors? Like Scheherazade, he was obviously planning to prolong the tale. Did that mean he liked her company? He was nicer than he'd seemed at first. She was such a bad judge of character. That's why she hated hiring. People who made a favorable first impression on her always turned out to be no good, and vice versa. Bert went to sleep smiling.

Rising early, she filled her travel mug with coffee and packed her fishing gear. The air was cool on her cheeks, the trees barely moving in the dawn's hush. This time, she took her four-wheeler. She hated to spoil the early-morning tranquillity with the roar of the ATV's engine, but she was not going to ride behind Jimmy again. As she chugged past the Dixon House, she had to admit it was fun to roll down the road through the village. Ahead, like light at the end of a tunnel, the open sky and water of the sound gleamed brightly. Overhanging branches shadowed the road, and the scent of pine and myrtle filled the air.

However, before she even emerged from the trees, the first whiffs of a dank rot merged with the pine, growing stronger as she neared Haulover Dock. She half expected to find a decomposing shark or pelican, but to her relief, no carcass lay on the mud banks. The stench must be coming from whatever was strewn all over the high-water line—seaweed and what else, whelks? No, too round. Parking her bike, she picked her way through the reeds to see what the tide had brought in.

Jellyfish—hundreds of clear, mushroom-shaped jellyfish—and fat clumps of seaweed lay on the shore of the inlet and in the black rush grass. God, what a mess. She hoped the next tide would take them right back out again.

There was no sign of Jimmy's boat. Good, she'd have time for some fishing. She walked to the end of the wharf, her pole in one hand, coffee in the other. Casting deep into the current to avoid the jellyfish, she propped the rod on her hip, sipping coffee and taking in the morning. To her left lay the still water of Pamlico Sound, the distant islands a white smear on the surface. Closer in was Casey's Island, a few bushes and a rusty fisherman's shack starkly outlined against the blue-green sea. Across the inlet was

Ocracoke, only the blue water tower and the lighthouse visible from here. Hundreds of birds of every possible size and shape stood on an emerging sand bar, and more circled overhead. A large flock of terns whirled and dipped, now flashing the white of their backs, now banking to show their dark sides.

She put her travel mug down on a piling and began to bring her line in slowly; flounder liked moving bait. The line moved sluggishly. Bert gave a quick jerk to free it—a jellyfish, no doubt.

The current must be bringing them in, but the tide was going out. No, they were swimming this way, using their pulsing mode of jet propulsion, their streamers trailing like hair in the wind. They were schooling, congregating about the pier.

What was attracting them? Algae, seaweed, some sort of bug hatching? Wouldn't it be great if scientists could genetically alter jellyfish to eat mosquito larvae? One nuisance to cancel another.

Shoot, there were just too many. Now, beds of eelgrass were drifting in, too. She wasn't going to catch anything with all this junk in the water. Bert brought in her line heavy with grass and the translucent blobs. As the rig came close, she saw that jellyfish were not only impaled on the hook but had also wrapped themselves around the weight and up the line past the swivel. Her rod was bent over farther than with the drum last night. Ugh. She knocked them off against the pilings, watching the pieces vanish among the stroking clouds of pale mushrooms.

Well, so much for fishing. There was no sense going back, since it was almost time for Jimmy. That white line of foam might be a boat heading her way. She took her coffee to the end of the pier and sat down, her feet dangling safely above the jellyfish. Such strange creatures: blobs of colorless protoplasm ashore, but in the water as delicately hued as a rainbow. She watched, mesmerized, as they floated by like fat glass dinner plates just under the surface. She couldn't even see the bottom anymore, they were so thick, one on top of the other, some as big as basketballs. There were so many that the water itself seemed to be pulsating.

Bert drew away from the edge of the pier.

The mushrooms darkened to shades of purple, chartreuse, and sienna—giant, throbbing bruises. The surface of the water, solid with the creatures, heaved rhythmically. The stench of rot thickened. It caught in her throat and made her eyes water. The sun was too bright, the light too white, too cold. Bert climbed awkwardly to her feet, her body stiff.

Don't stumble, don't fall. They'll get you. She knew they wanted her. She could feel them calling to her, motioning.

No, no! her mind cried.

But it's beautiful here, they whispered silently, slapping the sides of the dock. Come and see, they said. You don't have to stay.

No, never. She tried to put her hands to her ears but was rooted, unable to move. She wanted to get off the pier, away from this spot, but she was frozen in place.

Just then, a line of pelicans swooped down, skimming right over her head, so close she could see separate feathers. The breeze generated by their gliding bodies brushed her face, breaking the spell. The jellyfish retreated; the sun lost its glare.

She ran off the pier gasping, sweat pouring down her body, the fishing pole and mug still in her hands. Then she was back on the hot, sandy road away from the water—and those things.

As she stood by the ATV panting like a dog in the sun, the panic loosed its hold so she could think again. How could this have happened? Was it hypnosis brought on by the sun reflecting off all those jellyfish? Or was she having a breakdown? But why? She'd suffered no trauma, no particular stress.

She took a deep breath and let it out slowly. Perhaps she really wasn't suited to being alone like this, not if her imagination took over with so little provocation. The Chesapeake was infested with jellyfish. Everyone knew that. So it figured Pamlico Sound would have its share, too. Maybe she ought to call it quits and go home.

Yeah, sure. Her lease didn't begin until September, and this was the height of the tourist season. She'd have to move in with her daughter. Besides, when would she ever again be able to take a whole summer off and bum around a deserted island? No, she wasn't about to let bugs or jellyfish spoil this for her.

By the time Jimmy's boat rounded Casey's Island, Bert had decided she'd let her imagination get out of hand. Still, she kept her distance from the water.

Then, as she watched, the boat come to a halt so fast it reared up in the waves. Maybe she wasn't such a wimp after all.

Jimmy hung over the side, peering into the water. His boat veered and began to run parallel to the land. Now, she spotted another man on board. Too tall for Hunter—must be another ranger. Bert jumped on her four-wheeler and followed the boat down the shoreline. Three times they tried to put in, and three times they turned back.

At first, she didn't understand. Surely, the jellyfish wouldn't bother a big boat like that. The props would tear them to shreds. Then she understood. Just as birds could foul air intakes on jets, eelgrass and jellyfish could foul water intakes on boat engines.

Jimmy was standing, yelling at her, but she couldn't hear him. She plucked the radio from her belt and waved it. He knew her frequency. Sure enough, in a moment, he was on the air.

"You copy, Bert?"

"Hi, Jimmy. Jellyfish trouble?" Now that the problem was his, Bert suddenly felt comfortable again. She had overreacted. It was the newness, and being alone.

"Go to two."

Bert switched over. The park used channel two for local conversations, as the repeater didn't pick it up. This limited the range and gave more privacy. Plus, channel two didn't interfere with other transmissions. She glanced up to see another boat drawing near Jimmy's.

"Here's Elbert. What do you think, Elbert?" Jimmy yelled, his mike still on.

"I never seen anything like it," Elbert's drawled. "It do rightly make a man stand up and take notice."

The radio fell silent as the men engaged in animated conversation, hands flying.

Finally, Jimmy came back on. "Bert, sweetie. Elbert doesn't want to come through this either. Afraid they'll do something to his motor. Weather's closing in, anyhow."

Oh, damn, she thought. It was one thing to fantasize about being alone and another to have them take off and leave her here.

"Gonna miss me, huh?" She could hear the smile in his voice. "Hang on, I just had a thought."

Both he and Elbert leaned over the sides of their boats, Jimmy's hand flashing as he pointed toward the beach. His passenger remained seated inside the cabin. Elbert had about six people on board. They edged around to the stern, peering curiously at the water and at Bert.

Finally, Jimmy came back on the air. "I was thinking I could wade over. It's not all that deep, but Elbert doesn't like the idea. They don't sting bad, but with this many . . . Besides, I can't really leave my boat anchored out here."

"No, no, don't try it." Just the thought of anyone sliding into that throbbing water put her teeth on edge. "I'll be fine. Good time to get that mowing done." She hoped the radio distorted her voice sufficiently so they wouldn't hear the quaver deep in her throat.

Elbert had already started his engine when Bert realized she hadn't asked Jimmy about his passenger.

Jimmy came back on. "Call Hunter, will you? I'll check in as soon as I get back."

Elbert roared off in a rush of white foam. Jimmy waved at her and entered the cabin.

"Who's your passenger?" Bert yelled into her mike.

"Plumb forgot . . . Blow coming . . . Take care, now." Static masked the transmission. His boat powered up and roared off.

Belatedly, Bert studied the sky. It was still clear and blue over the inlet and Ocracoke. But hanging low over the sound farther north was a line of clouds dark as Hunter's eyes.

She flushed, embarrassed by the unbidden comparison. Don't get any ideas about him, she warned herself as she started the bike. Flashes of lightning ran from the clouds to the water. She was looking at a fast-approaching thundershower. Losing no time, Bert drove past the visitor center to the village.

To her surprise, the church door was open. Now what? She had closed it this morning, she was sure. Cautiously, she pulled up, walked over, and peeked around the door just as the first raindrops began to fall. The church was empty.

"Whatever are you doing?" said a voice from behind.

Bert screamed, dropping her keys. She whirled around, her back to the church door. In front of her, clutching a large purse, stood a diminutive old woman. She wore a straw hat covered by a mosquito veil over tightly curled hair. A print silk dress and short, black ankle boots completed the ensemble. Bert blinked, expecting her to disappear, but instead the apparition cackled merrily.

"Don't tell me you thought I was a ghost." She picked up Bert's keys, tipping her head like a sparrow and hopping about. "Didn't mean to give you a fright. Pull yourself together. Are you over here with the boat? Seems like I heard a motor a piece ago."

Bert nodded. "Yes. That is, no. I'm the new caretaker."

"Are you, now?" The old lady tipped her head again, studying Bert through the protective netting. "I suppose they told you all about me. Probably told you what a wicked old lady I am. How I'm stealing Blackbeard's treasure and all that."

Oh, shit, this was Luna Mae? Bert had been warned about her during her training and again by Hunter just yesterday. "There's a woman by the name of Luna Mae Harris," Christine Wright had said. "Let the rangers know anytime she's on the island."

"What does she do?" Bert had asked.

"Takes things. Luna Mae's picked up a lot of old jewelry." The ranger shook her head. "Her latest is some silver plate. We think she dug it up from a ruin."

But what if it was her family's silver?

As if reading Bert's mind, Miss Wright fixed the three of them—Olin and Anne Source and Bert—with a solemn stare. "That silver might have been hidden when Federal forces invaded Portsmouth. If we'd known about it, it could have been properly excavated. That's the problem. They dig up artifacts, and we lose a piece of history forever."

Bert had been conscious of a slight disappointment. Christine Wright seemed so nice, but that complaint smelled of pettiness.

And now, here was Luna Mae in person. Today was fast turning into a nightmare.

Just then, the sky rumbled loudly, opening up in earnest. The old lady grabbed Bert's arm and pointed toward the electric blue house. "Come quick. The rain brings out the mosquitoes."

It was the threat of mosquitoes that got Bert into the house. She was still wiping the rain from her face and arms when Luna Mae filled two mugs with hot tea and handed her one. "Just getting ready to have me a cup when I heard you roar into the village. Iffen I had my way, I'd take all them things and throw them into the sea."

"Thank you," said Bert, taking a page from Hunter and ignoring the comment about the ATV. She took a sip of the tea, then another. This was the best tea she'd ever had.

"Good, you think? Leave it steep for five minutes. Heat the pot first. Use one of them big iced-tea bags." The old lady was shaking some Oreos out of a coffee can.

"Please, don't bother," Bert protested vainly before accepting one. "Were you in the church this morning?"

The woman nodded. "I always check it out. We're going to be renovating it soon. They tell you?" She set the plate down near Bert. "Can't do much baking." Luna Mae motioned toward an ancient stove. "Takes too much kerosene."

Bert gaped. "You use—"

"Have to carry in every drop, don't you know. Getting too old to do all that lugging."

"When did you get in? Did you play the organ last night?"

"Me, play the organ?" Luna Mae cackled merrily. "Why, gal, I only got here this morning. My nephew Henry bring me across at sunup, he did, on his way to set his traps, you know."

"But all—"

"The jellyfish?" The little old lady hopped right in again. "Ain't that something?"

"What did you do?" Bert persisted. "Elbert couldn't—"

"Why, bless your soul, Henry done poled me ashore. Has a skiff, you know. Not like them big boats. They is worthless if the engines shut off. Not to change the subject or anything, but what days you be taking off?"

Bert blinked. Before she could respond, the old lady continued. "Them other ones," she began, wrinkling her nose. "That Olin Source, he were a bad one. Why, if I was to give out what I know . . ." She took a quick peek at Bert. "They was gone from Sunday to Wednesday. Miss Anne were telling me it took them one whole day to get from here to Havelock. You be doing the same, I reckon?" She looked at Bert for agreement. Bert shook her head, stifling a giggle. "You ain't?" The old lady stared, shocked into silence.

"This is my home for the summer. I'll be going off to shop and get my laundry and that sort of thing, but not overnight." She bet the old lady had been counting on having the place to herself three days a week.

Bert was right. Luna Mae's face was no longer jovial. "You ain't taking no time off? Why, they got no call to work you like that." She wagged a finger. "Ain't good for a body to work all the time. Ain't good to be alone too long neither. You needs to get among people, you do." Her chin bobbed up and down in emphasis. "If you want, I can put you in touch with a good lawyer, Julius Harrington. He's talking to the park now about the leases. J. J., you met J. J. yet?" Again, Bert shook her head. "We's lucky to have him here. Owns two car dealerships, you know. Hired attorney Harrington to speak for us. He's costly, but still, considering what all's at stake, it's justified. Though some don't see it that way." Luna Mae's voice softened. "J. J.'s a good man, he is, even though him and that Donny tear up something fierce when they's liquored up. But they be good to me. Not like that Jimmy Range." She shot Bert a glance. "Got a silver tongue, that man do, and a heart of stone. He don't care for a thing except himself. I warned

Ben. You know the chief, Ben Willis?"

Bert nodded.

"There's something strange about that man, I told him."

Bert wasn't sure whether she meant Ben or Jimmy, but Luna Mae's next sentence cleared that up. "Always sneaking around when he's supposed to be working. Body can't go about her business than he's there, hiding in the brush. Says he's picking up trash. How can you pick up trash when you ain't got nothing to put it in?"

What could she say? Jimmy was probably spying on the old lady, just like the park had asked Bert to do.

"He don't fool me none," Luna Mae said. "I know Christine thinks I'm digging up silver." She reached over and patted Bert's hand. "I ain't the one that's taking things, but I can't speak for some others. No, sir. You keep a pair of eyes in your head, you learn a lot while you here, that's for sure."

This was what Hunter had warned her about. She wasn't going to listen to gossip about park people. "I'm sure Jimmy's just doing his job," Bert murmured, standing up. "Thanks for the tea, but it's time for me to get back."

Luna Mae's face showed disappointment and concern. She might be a nonstop talker, but she was no fool.

Bert relented. "Come and see me sometime. How long will you be here?" The park would want to know. One thing was for sure: there was no way Bert was going to sneak around spying on the old lady. Jimmy could keep that job.

"Can't rightly say." Luna Mae followed her out the door. "Depends on how many traps Henry sets. Why, with all them critters about . . ." She shook her head. "Make a person think an O'Hagan was back on the island."

That stopped Bert. "What do you mean?" Sea-born women were supposed to have some kind of affinity with ocean life—like mermaids or Selkies. But what would Hunter's being here have to do with the jellyfish?

"Don't you know? 'Tis said Sea-born Woman's man will come for her when an O'Hagan returns to the island." With that solemn pronouncement, Luna Mae stepped back into her house.

Bert turned down the path. Neat legend. Did it apply to her, too? Would her man be coming for her soon?

Grinning at that fanciful thought, Bert started the bike and roared noisily—and guiltily—back to her cabin. ∞

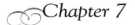

Chapter 7

BERT HADN'T EVEN REACHED HER CABIN when Hunter's truck skidded to a stop next to her. "You didn't call," he accused, sliding out. "You all right?"

"Oh, God." Bert's hand leapt to her mouth. "Oh, Hunter, I'm sorry. It was the jellyfish. I forgot."

"I was fixing to catch the nine o'clock ferry." There was nothing friendly about his eyes now. "If I didn't get hold of Jimmy, I'd have torn up the truck getting here. He told you to call."

"He did, but the rain . . . Then I ran into . . ." Bert pointed. "Luna Mae's here."

His voice was icy. "That don't make no matter. You want to tell me why your radio wasn't on?"

Bert was ready to cry. "It isn't? Oh, I must have turned it off without thinking. There was lightning, making all this static. I couldn't hear Jimmy."

He reached over, jerking it out of her belt. His arm brushed her side, sending tingles up her spine. Damn it anyhow, why him?

He clicked it on. A series of squawks came from the radio. "It's supposed to make static. That's how you know it's receiving."

Hunter leaned against the side of the truck. "You know, you aren't going to be much use if we have to keep checking on you."

He didn't have to be nasty about it. "Look, I'm sorry. I forgot. I won't do it again, believe me." Her voice trembled. "Hunter, there's something terribly wrong here."

"You mean the jellyfish?" He got back into the truck. "The park wants a report."

"So you would have had to drive up here anyhow?" That made her feel better.

"That don't take away none from you forgetting." He reached over and opened the passenger door. "Come along, now."

A dismal cold settled over her. She felt bad enough already. He didn't have to treat her like a three-year-old. They drove silently to the pier.

Hunter climbed on top of the cab to sight. Bert followed. If anything, there were more of the jellyfish than before, extending deep into the sound and the inlet. He took several pictures, then, kneeling on the dock, scooped some jellyfish into the white, lidded bucket he kept in his truck. It was the same bucket they'd used for the drum just last night—a million years ago.

"We'll get the lab at Radio Island to check these out." He poked one of the blobs. "Don't look any different than any jellyfish I've ever seen. Just more of them."

After stowing the bucket in the truck, he headed out to the end of the dock. Bert didn't follow. All she had to do was start talking to the damned things again and he'd send her back for sure.

Hunter didn't stay long. Loping back, he pulled out a handkerchief and wiped his face. "Makes you right dizzy when you look down at them, doesn't it?" He wiped his face. "Let's get out of here. That stink's getting to me."

The stench—was that the answer? Maybe it was slightly hallucinogenic. Suddenly, Bert's world was all right again. She wasn't nuts or hearing things; they'd made Hunter sweat, too.

She waited until they were back in the truck before speaking. "Luna Mae said something about Sea-born Woman being alive again. Did she mean the jellyfish?"

Apparently, he'd forgiven Bert. He chuckled, slapping the wheel. "Now, she could have something there."

He didn't speak again until they were back at the cabin. He leaned across Bert to open the truck door, filling her nostrils with his fresh, male scent. If he wasn't careful, she was going to do something stupid.

"Don't quite fit," he said. "She used it for good."

"You're not making a bit of sense." Bert slid out and closed the door. She needed that barrier between them.

"Sea-born Woman. That's part of the gift."

"The gift again. You going to tell me about it?"

"You wouldn't want to spoil my story, would you?" The smile in his voice eased what was left of her guilt for not checking in on schedule. "I made arrangements to bunk at the Long Point ranger station this weekend. You plan on being about, don't you?"

Bert nodded, surprised.

"All right. Have a good one, now. And don't forget to call." With a farewell blast of his horn, Hunter was gone.

Hmm. Maybe he wasn't totally oblivious. She knew he enjoyed her company, but she didn't think he was interested in her as a woman. After all, she was old enough to be his mother. Well, not exactly, but . . .

Oh, shit, she thought. You total idiot. Bert stopped in her tracks. He wasn't interested in her. Neither he nor Jimmy had left her alone except that first night. It wasn't sex that had Hunter coming around. It was something else—something to do with what was going on. They were protecting her, but from what? Something connected to the accident?

Bert's thoughts—and feet—had unconsciously taken her up Coast Guard Creek to the site of Anne Source's death. Although the park had removed the machinery and fuel tanks, the ruins of the shed were still quite obvious: charred boards, wires, and hunks of rusty metal strewn about a pile of dirty sand and broken rocks. The creek was nothing more than a ditch. Back in the heyday of Portsmouth, Coast Guard Creek had been much deeper and longer, extending far into the marsh. The marine hospital had been fully accessible by boat then. However, the barrier islands were in a constant state of movement, the northern and ocean shores eroding, the southern and sound-side shores filling in and growing as the islands migrated southwest.

By noon, the sky cleared up enough to let Bert do some mowing. Worried that she would stir up the sleeping bugs, she sprayed herself liberally. However, she soon discovered that something about the big mower kept both mosquitoes and flies away. She found herself enjoying the might of the machine, doing little wheelies around trees, cutting tight to the corners, leaving long, neat tracks in the grass. After several hours, her teeth on edge from the vibration, she called it quits. A swim right now, then a shower and a beer were what the occasion called for. Surely, those jellyfish weren't in the ocean, too.

Bert rode the ATV over to the beach. The sky was still partly cloudy, the humidity high. A couple of jellyfish had washed up on the sand close to the inlet, but the water was clear a mile farther south.

Still wary, Bert waded in. The water was warm and refreshing, so clear she could see the sandy bottom and even a small school of minnows darting away. There was no sign of jellyfish. Walking out just past the breakers, still in waist-deep water, Bert plunged in, doing a slow crawl parallel to the beach. Then she rolled over on her back, floating with her feet pointed to the ocean so she could spot any big wave before it dunked her. Not a soul in sight, not even a plane in the sky. Unbelievable. She unhooked her top and pushed it down to her hips. It wouldn't be a problem to run around here stark naked, she thought, practically dozing off in the warm water.

She braved the bugs and rode back to her cabin in her wet bathing suit. An hour later, fresh from the shower, Bert was deciding what to make for dinner when she heard the grind of an engine. Damn. She'd been looking forward to a quiet meal, then bed. Visitors or park people? She threw a park shirt on over her tank top and stepped outside.

Two men on an ATV were headed right toward her cabin.

One was Jimmy. Now, why didn't that surprise her? But who was the other man? It wasn't until they pulled up that she recognized Olin Source. Double damn. Now, she wouldn't be able to quiz Jimmy about what was going on. She was sure it was no coincidence he'd shown up.

"You didn't eat yet, did you?" Jimmy called as he pulled two crumpled and stained pizza boxes from the carrier. "Brought you a treat. If you don't mind warming it in the oven, that is." He bounced up the porch. Olin waved vigorously at Bert but stayed back on the bike.

Motioning Jimmy to go in, she made herself walk down to Olin. "I'm so sorry about your wife," she began. She never knew what to say in situations like this. "Would you like to come up?" For all she knew, he might have gotten over his thing about the cabin.

"No. Thank you. I appreciate the invite, but I have other things to do right now." He began unloading the ATV's carrier, which bulged with sleeping bags. "We'll be staying at the lifesaving station tonight. Orders from the supervisor."

Orders from the supervisor, her aunt's ass. Why did Olin always have to put on the dog? Bert helped him unload, then returned to the cabin to find Jimmy cramming the pizzas on one rack.

"So, what's going on?" she asked once dinner was safely in the oven. Bert hated pizza but wasn't about to tell him that.

"Surprised to see me, huh? Pleasantly surprised, I hope."

She was not going to be put off. Through the window, she could see Olin on the porch unlocking the front door of the station. "Level with me, okay? Were you sent here? Why are you guys sticking to me like this?"

Jimmy was poking around inside the refrigerator. "I could make us up a salad real quick, if you have any lettuce."

"Jimmy?"

He turned around, a head of lettuce in his hand. "You don't mind, do you? I figured you could join us for dinner—over there. He won't come in here."

Bert glared.

"There's nothing going on, I swear."

"Then what are you doing here?"

He gave a suggestive leer. "Do I have to explain?"

"Don't give me any shit, Romeo. Why?"

"Seriously, Source wanted to come over, and Hunter didn't want him coming alone. He's been pestering us for a week now. Says he lost something."

"Lost something, like what?"

"That's the funny part. He won't say. Something to do with his wife, I guess. Made me take him all the way to Atlantic when we couldn't land at Haulover this morning."

So that was the mysterious passenger. "What's to stop him from hiring a boat and coming over anytime he wants?"

"Nothing, if it comes to that. I think the park's afraid he'll complain to his congressman or start a lawsuit. Anyhow, we were told to bring him over and help him. Whatever he needs."

"You're not here to keep an eye on me?"

"No way, I'm sorry to say. You're much prettier than he is."

Luna Mae was right, Jimmy was quick with the blarney. Was she right about the self-centered part, too? Bert began tossing the salad. She would also pack some paper plates, napkins, and plastic forks. "Is there a table at the station?" So much for her peaceful evening.

"Two."

She handed Jimmy the bag. "Why don't you go ahead with this stuff? I promised my daughter I'd call when I got settled, and it's been too long already. I'll bring the pizza soon as it's ready."

She was longer on the phone with Belinda than she'd planned. By the time Bert got to the station, Jimmy had the tables wiped off, their places set. The two men quickly demolished the rather dry pizza and salad. Then Olin produced several packs of cheese and crackers. The men munched on those.

Bert had been in the lifesaving station before but hadn't really noticed this room. "Nice view," she said.

Olin acknowledged her comment with an approving nod. "This

room was used by the surfmen." He pointed to a black-and-white photo on the wall. "The keeper and eight surfmen were stationed here. This room was where they relaxed and played cards. Not that they had much leisure time. You worked for your keep in those days." He tipped his head as he spoke, glancing at them from the corners of his eyes. "Anne liked this room. She'd bring her knitting over, or read a book. I took care of all the visitors and the mowing for her. Anne did the cooking. She was a great cook."

Afraid he was about to get emotional, Bert changed the subject. After all, it was only a month since the woman died. "Jimmy said you lost something."

Again, he gave her that sideways glance, peering from under his hood of curly brown hair. "I wonder if I could ask you to do something for me. I'm trying to find a logbook. It's light brown—"

"Not that again," Jimmy cut in sharply. "Must have burnt with the shed. We told you it wasn't in the cabin."

Olin said nothing, lips tightening slightly. Bert jumped in. Jimmy didn't have to be rude. "There are a couple of logs in the cabin. You know, the ones kept by the caretakers. You wrote in one—"

Olin cut her off impatiently. "The one I want is a private journal, a tan notebook, bound and lined." He looked up, spreading his hands. "About this big. It could have fallen behind a dresser or bed."

Bert shook her head. "If it's not with the books, then it's not in the cabin. I moved all the furniture and swept out the dust balls and dead bugs before I unpacked."

"Hmm." Olin glanced at Jimmy. "I guess I didn't really expect it to turn up. Just had to give it one last try."

Something in his voice alerted Bert. "Did Anne keep the log?"

He nodded, eyes downcast. "Unfortunately, I didn't get around to reading it before, well, you know . . . The thought crossed my mind there might be something . . ."

No one said anything for a couple of minutes. Then Olin stood and began gathering the remnants of the meal. "Did I hear you say you were in the village earlier?"

He had his back to them, but Bert assumed Olin was talking to her. "I mowed the church, Dixon's, and Mason's this afternoon. There was no one over today, so it was the perfect time to get used to the mower."

Jimmy grinned at her. "See, I told you there was nothing to it."

Olin turned toward Bert. "I wonder if you happened to notice if any of the lessees were there."

"Luna Mae's here. I met her this morning. And Donny's at Evergreen."

Both heads jerked up, frowning.

"Just my lousy luck," Jimmy said. "Anyone warn you about them?"

Bert nodded.

Olin sat casually on the edge of the table, his long legs extended. He wore a pair of well-cut blue trousers and a navy knit shirt that hugged his long, slim waist. "I'm the one that reported Luna Mae for artifact hunting, you know. I happened to be on my way to the schoolhouse. Ran into her probing the Gilgo outhouse with one of those red flounder gigs. Caught her red-handed, you might say."

Had there really been a twinkle in his eye? Olin was so schoolteacher pedantic most of the time that Bert was shocked to think he might have a sense of humor, however poor. "I did get the impression she didn't care much for either of you. Now, I understand why," she teased.

"That woman is a menace." Jimmy wadded up his cup and tossed it in the garbage bag. "Never know where she's going to turn up. Sneaks around."

That's what Luna Mae had said about Jimmy. Bert was about to point it out when Olin cut in. "Sometimes, I wonder about the value of the lease program. It seems to create as many problems as it solves. What do you think?" His remark was directed at Jimmy, as were most of his comments. Bert suspected that was Olin's attitude toward women, yet he was quoting Christine.

Jimmy tipped his chair back against the table. "I think they should drown all the lessees and turn this into an R and R camp for volunteers and seasonal help. What do you say, Bert?"

"There you go."

"This could be the clubhouse," Jimmy continued. "Open up the airstrip again. Hire Lettie to tend the bar." Olin's lips tightened. Jimmy caught his expression. "Just kidding. Frankly, I agree with you. Three lessees in residence make more problems than seventy visitors, but there's nothing we can do about it."

"That's nonsense. There's always something you can do."

"You're right, Olin," Bert said. "One person can make a difference."

Olin ignored her remark to address Jimmy again. "I tell you, there are plenty of ways to teach people proper behavior."

"What do you have in mind, Olin? Prod Luna Mae in the ass—'scuse me, Bert—with one of her gigs?"

Olin actually smiled. "I remember when I was in college, there was a situation in the dorm. We had a Vietnamese student—that was before the war, you understand. He considered himself superior to the rest of us. You know how they are. After putting up with him for a month, a couple of us decided to teach him a lesson. We waited until he went to shower, then we jumped him and threw him outside, buck naked. It was winter." Bert shifted uneasily in her chair, but Olin paid no attention, enjoyment in his modulated voice. "Long as I live, I'll never forget him running around, hiding behind bushes, begging us to let him back in."

"Bet you didn't have any trouble with him after that," Jimmy said, bringing his chair upright.

Bert was shocked by Jimmy's approval. "He was a foreign student. Didn't you try to explain things to him first?" she protested.

"Come on, Bert," Jimmy said. "You have to be able to get along with others. Ever live in one of the park dorms?"

"No. Christine said I could have a room if I really needed it, but I got the feeling she'd rather I didn't."

Jimmy snorted. "Because she'd have to pay Ben Willis for it, that's why. They all have budgets."

"I didn't know that. Anyhow, I'm very comfortable in the cabin. For one person, it's great."

At the word *cabin*, Olin swung around. "By the way, did you by any chance find something in the cabin that didn't seem to belong there?"

"I told you already, there was no log." What was with him and that log, anyhow?

He seemed oblivious to her annoyance. "There weren't any strange flowers or herbs?"

"Herbs?" Memory flashed. "I found a jar of astringent, looked homemade. Is that what you wanted?"

He didn't look up, but his hands stopped moving. "Did you happen to notice what kind of a jar?"

"Old jar, old label. It isn't yours, then?"

"No, I'm quite certain it wasn't."

"It's way up on the shelf toward the back. Wait, I'll go get it." She needed an excuse to get out of the lifesaving station and back to the cabin anyway.

But the jar was no longer on the shelf in her kitchen. Dragging up a chair, Bert searched behind the supplies, thinking it might have gotten pushed to the rear or tipped over. Nothing.

"What's the matter?" Jimmy stuck his head in the front door.

"I can't find it." Bert opened the medicine cabinet, then checked her dresser in the bedroom. "That's so weird. I had it right here."

"He said you wouldn't find it."

A sudden cold invaded Bert's stomach. "Source said it would be gone? Why?" She walked out of the bedroom. "What did he mean by that?"

Jimmy shrugged. "Let's go ask him."

However, Olin was gone from the station. They spotted him walking toward the ruins of the old generator shed, head bent. Like a man visiting a grave, Bert thought as she waited, hoping he'd turn back. But Olin kept ambling up the path until he was lost in the tall grass.

"The bugs are going to eat him alive," Bert said, gathering up her salad bowl. "I'll make us coffee in the morning, about half-past six, okay?"

Jimmy walked her back to the cabin. After she washed the dishes, they sat for a minute on the stoop, much as she'd sat there the night before with Hunter. It was almost eight o'clock, and the sun was only now beginning to fade.

"Wish I wasn't so tired," Bert said. "I bet it's going to be a pretty sunset."

"I don't know." Jimmy glanced toward the west. "Supposed to be some weather coming. Got a big low over Texas headed this way." He grinned. "We could be stranded here."

"You think it's going to be that bad?"

"Not really. I'm more concerned about those jellyfish. When we started over, there wasn't one to be seen, but by the time we put in to Long Point, they were rolling in by the thousand." He laughed, casually putting his arm around her. "You should have seen that ferry move. Wasted no time getting back out."

His skin was warm and dry, and he smelled faintly of cologne. Bert didn't lean into him, nor did she move away. Such a good-looking devil, she thought. He was the right age, and he'd probably be fun, but not now. After a moment, she shook off his arm, rising. Must be getting old, she thought. "I'm afraid that mowing did me in. Is there anything you need?"

"Just something I don't think I can have."

Her fault. She should have watched her wording. "See you for breakfast, then."

The bed felt good under her aching back. Outside, she heard a door slam. She'd left the porch lights on to help the fellows see outside, and they shone in through the window. Bert tossed restlessly for a while and finally got up to turn on the fan. It wasn't hot as much as it was muggy. Besides, the hum of the fan would drown out the male voices drifting in from the lifesaving station.

Well, at least she wasn't alone here with Source. Did Hunter suspect him of something? Those jellyfish sure had done everything possible to stop him from landing, hadn't they?

Bert sat upright in bed. What a weird thing to think—or was it? ∞

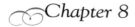Chapter 8

BERT DREAMT ABOUT THE OCEAN. She was caught in the surf, dragged into the water. Time after time, she fought her way up the steep beach, just to be sucked in deeper by the next breaker. As the last wave pulled her under, she woke up.

She'd had the dream before, many times. It had to be some kind of childhood memory. The waves and the beach were always huge, as if seen through the eyes of a two-year-old. She always saved herself by waking up just in time.

It was dark and hot in the bedroom. The fan was out. The porch lights, too. Oh, shit, the power must be out again. Bert hitched up on an elbow and peered at the lifesaving station through the bedroom window. No lights were showing. The building had no electricity unless the generator was on, but they'd borrowed her lanterns. Must have turned them off.

Should she wake Jimmy?

Bert listened. It sounded as if the men were already up. Footsteps thudded in the sand, and wood scraped against something.

She dropped back on the pillow. Damn, she didn't feel like getting up. She knew nothing about wiring. She'd be of no help.

She'd just end up wide awake and not be able to go back to sleep. Guiltily, Bert fluffed up her sweaty pillow and found a cool spot on the sheet. She'd pretend she never woke up.

She was just dozing off when a choking cry jolted her to her feet. Dammit anyhow, was someone hurt?

She yanked on her jeans. It was probably just another nutria. The beasts were worse than alley cats. What did a person have to do to get some sleep on this bloody island?

Bert balanced her flashlight on end so it reflected off the ceiling while she flung open drawers and found her long-sleeved shirt and mosquito hood. Jamming the hat on her head, she grabbed the can of bug spray and carried it to the porch. Where was Jimmy? He must have heard the cry.

Something rustled nearby.

"What's going on? Jimmy?" There was no glimmer of light anywhere. In fact, she could barely make out the roof of the lifesaving station. No stars were visible either. Must be clouded over.

Why wasn't he answering? She called again, "Jimmy? It's me."

Still no answer.

Maybe it hadn't been Jimmy's footsteps. Maybe the men were still asleep in the station. Adrenaline shot through her system.

After belting on the park radio, she sprayed herself from hood to sneakers. Bert checked the porch steps, then flashed the light around the yard. No red eyes stared back; no shadow moved. Swinging the beam back and forth in a wide arc, she followed the concrete walk to the lifesaving station, yelling as she went. Damned if she wanted to surprise an intruder—or a nocturnal nutria munching on the grass.

It seemed a long way over in the dark, but finally she was banging at the door.

No one answered.

Her skin prickled. Suppose it wasn't the men she heard by the shed? Suppose there was something else out here?

Bert burst into the station, shining her flashlight before her as if it were a weapon. The beam revealed only bulky wood furniture.

Dodging the two tables, she hurried up to the second-floor dormitory, shouting all the way.

There were four beds on each wall. Packs and clothes were strewn over them. Two of the beds were draped with open and very empty sleeping bags.

Holding her breath, Bert backed out of the room. Where were they? Why didn't they answer? "Jimmy!" she yelled as she went back down toward the door. "Jimmy Range!"

The nutria screamed again, as if in answer to her shouts—a high, prolonged wail that set her teeth on edge. Half in, half out the screen door, Bert stood motionless. She tried to tell herself it was just animals mating, but she couldn't make herself believe it. It was more than that, she was sure. Was it one of the men, in pain?

There was only one way to find out. She forced herself out of the station and cut a swath through the dark with her flashlight. Again, she shouted for Jimmy. Again, there was no answer, just the whine of mosquitoes and the distant lap of water.

The flashlight helped her see the ground immediately in front of her, but it also ruined her night vision and made her a target for intruders. It took all her courage to switch it off, as if by doing so she was opening the door to the devils of the night. Bert willed her eyes to hurry and adjust. There, she could see the outline of the cedars behind the station and the glimmer of water by Coast Guard Bay. Not a star was visible. It was a new moon, anyhow. She listened for the sound she'd heard before. Nothing. The sea would be like glass. She wished she were on the beach instead of here, wished she were home in Swansboro, safe in bed.

Slowly, Bert picked her way past her cabin, across the sand road, and up the path to the new generator shed. Hating to disturb her night vision but needing to see inside, she aimed the flashlight at the dark shed. The light bounced off the gray door. She picked out the padlock hooked over the hasp. It was hanging open.

"Jimmy?" she said tentatively.

Standing back, she nudged the door with her foot. It swung in, banging against a metal tank. Nerves screaming, she braced for something to come crashing out at her.

She swung the flashlight around. The generator stood at the center of the wall. Water softeners and equipment were stored on the sides. No people, no animals. Bert didn't know whether to be relieved or not. At least no one was lying there hurt.

Just as she switched off the light, another wail—almost a shriek—came from behind the shed. Bert moaned. Something or someone was hurt.

"Is anyone there? Jimmy, Olin. Where are you?"

There was no answer, just the sound of her frightened voice. She was not going down that horrible dark path into the deep marsh. She wasn't that stupid. There might be all sorts of creatures in the reeds, not to mention mosquitoes and whoever was behind all these tricks. Or whatever, she corrected herself.

She hesitated. What should she do? Sit on her butt in her dark cabin until someone arrived? She could call Hunter, but he wasn't even on the island. Besides, she wasn't sure Jimmy was in trouble. For all she knew, he and Olin were skinny-dipping in the ocean.

Her eyes were now totally adjusted to the dark. She could even make out the dunes and trees behind the generator shed. Again, she shouted for Jimmy and Olin, neither expecting nor getting an answer. Head whipping from side to side, ready to turn on her flashlight if necessary, Bert edged down the path past the generator toward the ruins of the old, burnt-out shed. The pale light that filtered through the clouds cast no shadows, making the dips in the path invisible. Bert staggered about like an old woman unsteady on her feet.

Cordgrass, black rush, and sage lined both sides of the raised path. Behind her was the lifesaving station, to her right the hospital cistern. To her left, over the marsh and dunes, lost somewhere in the dark sky, were the mud flats and the Atlantic. Even now, she could hear the distant sound of an engine. A shrimper? Or was it an ATV? She hadn't checked to see if the ATVs were still parked at the station.

Of course. That's where Jimmy and Olin were, on the flats with the bike. She sighed with relief and turned to go back.

The path had vanished, swallowed by a swirling, dark fog that billowed toward her.

Oh, no, she thought. Her lungs emptied in fright. She knew she shouldn't have come out here.

She shone her light at it, which only made visibility worse. Already, she could feel the cold. Instinctively, Bert backed away. Must be some kind of weather front. Damn, what was she going to do? It wouldn't be smart to try to get back through the mist. She might lose her way. She had no idea if there was quicksand in the marsh, but this was no time to find out. If she had to, she'd just wait here until the men found her or daylight came—couldn't be too long.

The mass rolled toward her, silent.

Right now, she could easily believe in ghosts. No way was she letting that cold fog engulf her. Bert turned down the path and fled.

The fog followed faster than she could move in the dark. A stream of mist snaked up the path in front of her, rising to her ankles.

As if feeling her panic, the nutria yowled again, a high-pitched call off to her left. Wait. The fog didn't seem as thick down there by the ditch. Maybe she could cut across and follow the creek back home.

The minute she left the path, she was sorry. The reeds were past her knees, thick and stiff. They caught her clothes. Crickets and other insects, flushed out by her stampede, flew up in panic. The ground sucked at her shoes, and huge roots blocked her course. Stumbling, she forced herself forward, straining to see.

The fog thinned. Ahead, water glimmered. Just as she reached the creek, she tripped over a log half in the ditch and put out her hands to save herself. Water splashed. Her hand sunk into the soft mud. Ugh. It stunk like sewage. She rolled away, scrambling to her knees. Oh, God, what was she on? It wasn't a log. It was soft, wet, and clammy, like an old sack. Storm wrack, garbage, a bag of offal? Campers were supposed to collect their leavings and take them out.

Bert stumbled away, but the reeds were thick. She put her

foot into the creek to save herself from falling and felt something give under it. She sprawled in the reeds, choked with fear.

Take it easy, she tried to tell herself. You're not hurt. Whatever it is, it's not alive. You just fell down, that's all. You're by the creek. It's not far to the road. Use your flashlight.

Of course, the flashlight. Bert was surprised to find it still clutched in her hand. Had it gotten wet when she fell? Scrambling backward, trying to edge away from the sack, she turned it on.

It was garbage: an old black boot and some wadded-up cloth partly in the water. She shone her light on the ditch. Something floated on the water. A clump of grass, another piece of garbage, a straw hat?

Oh, no. Bert blinked, not believing what she saw. She backed away, her light outlining what lay there in the water: a bare arm, thin and bony. Dear Lord, that was Luna Mae's hat.

The next second, Bert was back in the water, trying to jam the flashlight into its holder with one hand while she pulled at the woman with the other. Maybe it wasn't too late.

Luna Mae's body was so limp that Bert couldn't get a good grip. She straddled her, yanking her up the bank an inch at a time. Then she climbed up and grabbed Luna Mae by the arm. It was cold and flabby. Gritting her teeth, Bert hauled. There, she had most of her out. She tried to straighten Luna Mae out. Thank God the fog was lifting.

Give her mouth-to-mouth, she told herself. First, she had to open Luna Mae's mouth and clean it out.

No, she couldn't do it.

Bert turned her flashlight on the woman's face. She recoiled, gasping. Luna Mae was covered, dripping with mud, but the real horror lay in her eyes. They were wide open and had bits of dirt and grass pressed right into the eyeballs.

Moaning, Bert heaved her pizza.

She felt a faint vibration in the ground, rhythmic thuds. On her knees over the dead woman, Bert stared into the dark. Now, she heard the swish of grass. Someone was coming.

She stumbled to her feet, waving the flashlight. "Help! Over here!" The footsteps stopped. She strained to see into the dark. "It's Luna Mae. She's dead."

"Hello, Bert?" The answering hail came from the far side of the shed. That's funny, she could have sworn the footsteps were coming from the cabin side. Was someone else here, too?

"Is that you, Bert? What's wrong?" the voice called. She could hear him running down the path.

Jimmy? She waited, frozen in place. Brush crashed. A figure loomed, large and dark. Bert's mouth opened, but she couldn't make a sound. The light shone down on Luna Mae. She retched again.

The shape fell on its knees beside her. "What the hell, Bert?" It was Jimmy.

"She's dead," Bert whimpered. "In the ditch. There's something in the marsh."

"Did you try CPR?" Jimmy's hand went to Luna Mae's face, then down her neck, feeling for a pulse.

"No." Her voice was a husky whisper.

Jimmy seemed to know what to do. "Help me," he ordered, showing her where to put her hands as he tried to breathe life into the woman.

The flesh was rubbery and cold. It was like holding a dead chicken, Bert thought as she pushed and Jimmy blew into Luna Mae's mouth.

Cursing, he tilted her head back, wiped out her mouth, and tried again. "Can't get any air in. Water, I think." Pushing Bert aside, he straddled Luna Mae, put his hands on her middle, and made several firm upward thrusts. Then he bent to give her breath again.

"If she was killed, we're destroying all the evidence," Bert whispered inanely.

Jimmy just grunted and continued his efforts.

How long they remained there, Bert could only guess. Jimmy finally sat back on his heels, panting.

"How long? Do you know?"

"No, but she was cold and real . . ." Bert's stomach started to rise again. She made herself finish. "She was cold and limp. It was hard getting her out."

"I mean, how long were you here before I got here?"

Bert shook her head numbly.

"Five minutes? An hour?" he persisted.

"Five, ten minutes, I don't know. There was something else here."

"When you got here?"

"I don't know. I yelled, and you answered."

He stood and panned his flashlight around, listening. "Whatever it was, it's gone now. You have your radio? Let me have it."

Jimmy called the park, then the sheriff.

Huddled as far as she could get from Luna Mae, Bert heard him indistinctly. She was cold, wet, and crawly. Mosquitoes, maybe ticks or even—oh, God!—leeches. Bert moaned. Would Jimmy mind if she left? She'd never wanted a hot bath as much as she did right now.

"The woman's been dead several hours, not that I'm any expert," he said into the radio.

A static-ridden voice asked if he had worked emergencies before.

"No. Had some time in Korea." Now, he was asking whoever it was if he should bring Luna Mae in. "If I leave her here, the fiddlers will be at her by morning. She's been moved already, to give her CPR."

Then came coughing static. "Can you take pictures?"

"No way," Jimmy snapped. "Don't have a camera or a flash."

The man on the other end launched into an involved explanation broken by static. Bert got the idea he was consulting with someone.

Jimmy grunted. "Makes more sense. I'm guessing a heart attack."

Bert staggered to her feet. The sky seemed a little lighter now. Must be almost morning.

For the first time, Jimmy seemed to take her in. "Go on back."

He pointed toward the lifesaving station. "They have to get permission from the medical examiner before I can move her."

Bert wavered, hating to leave him alone. "I'm all right," she lied.

Jimmy fanned the air. "I'm not sitting around here all night, I'll tell you that."

Just then, the radio blared out, clearly this time: "Come in, 328. Party has been contacted. Permission received to remove code 13 to the village. Repeat. Go ahead and transport into the village. Contact us by phone when you get in."

Jimmy stood. "Copy. Three twenty-eight clear." He bent to pick up Luna Mae. "Guess the doctor didn't feel like going for a night boat ride. Smart fellow."

It took both of them to lift her over Jimmy's shoulder. Bert saw him turn his face away as the smell caught in both their throats. She gagged. Luna Mae had evacuated at the moment of death. Scuttling to the side, Bert heaved again.

Then she felt Jimmy's hand on her shoulder. "Is there anything else here that belongs to her?" he asked gently.

"Her hat." Bert waded over and picked it up. "She had a purse, too." She couldn't see it anywhere.

"They'll be over in the morning," Jimmy said. "They can look for it then."

They took Luna Mae to the boathouse at the lifesaving station, where Jimmy had a tarp. Bert spread it out, and he laid Luna Mae down carefully. Then Jimmy got on the cell phone to the park. Soon, he was deep in a conversation about transporting the body. Bert was about to leave when he stopped her. "I hate to lay this on you, but they want me to do an inventory search with a witness. It won't take long."

Bert jotted down the items on a sheet of lined paper used to tally the generator hours. The inventory was pitiful: a cheap cameo brooch, gold wedding band, gold guard band with three diamond chips, gold ring with small ruby, Timex watch with synthetic band. No pockets in the flimsy dress, and no purse or wallet. Bert turned away as Jimmy folded the plastic over the body and tied it securely.

It didn't seem right to leave her all muddy and dirty like that. She'd been such a nice old lady.

As if he heard her thoughts, Jimmy came over, putting an arm around her shoulder. "We can't clean her up, but we can do us." He led Bert outside to the hose. "It's best if we rinse off out here."

The mud was unbelievably sticky. By the time they scraped it off and hosed their clothes, shoes, and even their hair, Bert was feeling almost normal, her brain beginning to function again.

"Where's Olin?" she suddenly asked, surprising herself. She hadn't even noticed his absence until now.

Jimmy picked up his pack. "Good question." He led the way into the station and up the steps, Bert close behind.

A sleepy-looking Olin, wearing checkered pajamas, of all things, sat up in his sleeping bag. "Hi, Bert." He gave her a puzzled smile, leaning over to turn on the Coleman lantern. "You-all been swimming?" He fumbled for something on a nearby footlocker. They stared at him. He rubbed his ear. "What's going on?"

"There's been another incident," Jimmy said grimly. "One of the lessees, Luna Mae, is dead."

Olin blinked, putting his hand back up to his ear. "Another woman dead?" He broke into a fit of coughing. "Sorry," he choked between paroxysms, "the shock. I'd better get some clothes on." He reached for his pants.

"Find out where he was," Bert hissed at Jimmy, her teeth chattering. "I've got to get something dry on."

To her relief, the lights came back on while she was in the shower. She plugged in the coffeepot when she got out. Jimmy must have located the problem.

By the time Bert emerged from her cabin carrying coffee and a box of grahams, the wind was rising. Dark clouds, starkly backlit by the eerie light of the coming dawn, towered over the lifesaving station. That's all they needed right now, a damned storm.

Jimmy was on the cell phone when she arrived. From what Bert could hear, they were discussing the best way to move Luna Mae. When he was done, he explained: "They're going to send a plane as soon as it lightens up, unless the pilot decides it's too windy. If they can't get a plane in, Elbert will bring them."

"What about Hunter? Did you speak to him?"

"The only ones I've spoken to are Rudy and the sheriff. Hunter will probably come over with Rudy. Rudy wants to talk to all of us."

"No more than I do. Where the hell were you, Olin?" Bert turned to him, both angry and expectant.

"Right here. I was sleeping," Olin answered slowly. "All except for a very short period. Not more than fifteen minutes, I'd say."

He'd changed into shorts and a plaid shirt. How much did he carry in that pack, anyhow? Bert waited, tapping her foot.

For a moment, she thought that was all he was going to say. Then he continued with a petulant sigh. "I've been over this already with him." He inclined his head toward Jimmy. "I woke up about three. That's not unusual for me. I've been having trouble sleeping since my wife's, um, accident. Jimmy was gone, and the lights were out. I assumed we'd had another power failure and that he'd gone to fix it. I went after him to lend a hand, whatever that's worth." He attempted a smile. "As you've probably heard, I'm not mechanically inclined."

Bert stared at the man. His hair was matted. Dark creases showed under his eyes, and lines ran from his mouth to his sagging chin. His jaw was covered with gray stubble. For the first time, she wondered if he really was younger than Anne.

Olin darted a sideways look at Jimmy. "Think she was already dead then?"

Jimmy shrugged, motioning him to continue.

"Someone left the shed door unlocked. Jimmy wasn't there. I thought he might be at your cabin." He glanced at Bert, expressionless. "There wasn't anyone there either, so I went back to bed."

"You went back to bed?" Bert repeated, incredulous. "With the power out and everyone missing, you went to sleep?"

Olin hesitated as his eyes went from one to the other. "After dinner, I saw you on the steps." Bert remembered Jimmy's arm about her shoulder. "Then, tonight, when you both vanished, I assumed . . . You know." He looked helplessly at Bert. "I didn't want to be in the way."

It was possible, Bert thought. "But I shouted, all over the place. You must have heard me."

Olin put his hand to his ear and removed a very small hearing aid. She'd never noticed it. "I'm a little deaf. I take it out when I go to bed. Guess I forgot to put it in when I got up."

"How deaf are you? You had to hear those nutria. I went in after them." A terrible thought hit Bert. Swinging around to Jimmy, she asked, "It couldn't have been her screaming, could it?"

"I didn't hear anything." Jimmy shrugged. "Besides, she had to be dead awhile to be that cold."

"You must have heard something."

"Nope. Seems like you're the only one that hears animals screaming," Jimmy said.

Suddenly, Bert remembered. He'd arrived not from the life-saving station but from behind the hospital site, deep in the marsh. Maybe it wasn't Olin she should be quizzing. She fixed Jimmy with a stare. "What the hell were you doing in the marsh?"

Jimmy leaned back in his chair, grinning. "I've been waiting for you to ask." With deliberate indolence, he refilled his coffee cup. "You'll never believe what happened."

"This is not funny," Bert snapped.

Jimmy pointed his thumb at Olin. "I went to check on the power, like he said. He was snoring like a pig. I think that's what woke me in the first place." Olin was staring at Jimmy from under his brows, an unreadable expression on his face. "I had just opened up the shed when I saw someone sneaking across the marsh."

"Do you think it was Luna Mae?" Had she been digging up relics? Bert was about to repeat her question when Jimmy answered.

"Hard to tell size in the reeds. Could have been Luna Mae or Donny—or anyone, frankly. Figured I could catch whoever's been fooling with the generator, so I went after him—or her." He looked at Bert. "You didn't even notice that I turned the power back on when you left to shower."

Bert blinked. "I meant to say something. What was wrong?"

"Someone threw the main switch. Wasn't you, was it?"

"Don't be stupid. Why would anyone want to . . . ?" Her brain was too tired. "You were telling us about the intruder. Where did he—or she—go?"

"There's a road from the gas pumps to the flats. I thought I saw whoever it was coming from there."

"From Sheep Island?" Olin asked.

Jimmy nodded. "I figured it had to be Donny Southard."

"He was here last night." Bert frowned. "But he told Hunter and me he was on his way to Atlantic. Even if he came back, why would he turn the power off?"

"Maybe he's the artifact hunter," Jimmy said. "In any case, I can't be sure it was him. He vanished before I got close."

"In the fog?" Bert asked.

"What fog? No fog around me. He just disappeared."

"There was fog down by the old shed. A strange, cold fog." Bert didn't want to think about it.

Olin moaned. "I tell you, that's what killed her."

"Luna Mae?"

"No, Anne. She said it was the spawn of the devil. Spriggs guarding his tomb." He glanced at them from under his brows. "I hate to admit it, but I'm afraid I didn't pay much attention."

Bert's stomach dropped, and cold spread up her back. "It scared me, too," she said slowly. "That's why I got off the path. I would never have found Luna Mae otherwise."

"Don't get carried away, you two," Jimmy said. "Fog can hide things, but it's not alive. It can't think, and it's not a manifestation of long-dead pirates. Besides, I thought you said you went in after the nutria."

He's right, Bert thought. The nutria had lured her in there. No, that was impossible. ᏟᏅ

Chapter 9

BY SUNRISE, IT WAS CLEAR NO PLANE WAS COMING. The wind had picked up, and low thunderheads were rolling in from the north.

"As they say around here, looks like a mullet blow," Jimmy told Bert.

They stood by the pier at Haulover watching the two fronts meet. The higher layer of clouds flowed toward Ocracoke, the lower in the opposite direction, rolling over and under each other in synchronized perfection. The growing wind had whipped the sound into long rivers of spume, the waters dark beneath—dark not only from the cloud cover but also because of the jellyfish that swarmed just beneath the surface.

"At least it'll blow those damn things out of here," Jimmy said.

He made some calls on the radio while Bert checked to be sure the visitor center was tightly closed.

"Looks like you're going to have company," Jimmy told Bert in the Gator on their way back to the lifesaving station. "Plane's definitely canceled. The eelgrass is still too thick to put in at Haulover. Hunter's on his way, with Rudy. You know him?"

"He gave me my ATV training. He's nice."

"He's all right. You can stuff most protection officers, as far as I'm concerned."

"Really, why?"

"You'll find out," he said, laughing. He pulled up in front of the station. "I'm supposed to have the body at Long Point when they arrive. I'm not sure how long the weather will hold." He dropped his voice. "Source wants to stay here."

"Don't leave me with him, please." Bert followed Jimmy around to the front of the building.

"You weren't planning to stay, were you?" Jimmy frowned. "They want you down there, too—off the island. Better start packing up."

"You mean leave? No way." Damn, damn, damn, she cursed under her breath.

"It's only for a couple of days. Crissie can put you up in the dorm. I'll call." He lifted his brows and bared his teeth. "Pack something sexy."

"How are they going to know where we found Luna Mae?" Even as Bert said it, she knew they could flag the spot.

Jimmy tapped his palm in rhythm to his words. "Hunter wants you off the island. That's it, period."

"Okay, okay, but why so quick?"

Scowling, Jimmy checked his watch. "I'm going to have to haul ass to make that ferry as it is. Call Hunter and argue with him." Yelling for Olin, he started toward the boathouse.

Bert made the call from her cabin. The ranger told her what she expected to hear—that Hunter was not at Harkers Island. There was no reason to call Long Point and leave a message with Justin. By the time Hunter reached the fishing camp and called her, it would be too late to catch the morning ferry anyway. There'd be other ferries today, she rationalized. After all, Hunter and Rudy had to get back off the island, too. Having satisfied her conscience, Bert went to help Olin and Jimmy load Luna Mae into the ATV trailer and close up the lifesaving station.

"Hunter said not to let anyone into Luna Mae's house until

they get here," Jimmy told her. "No relatives, or J. J. or Donny."

"It's open? You want me to lock it up?"

"I closed it a bit ago." Jimmy wedged Olin's sleeping bag under the sky-blue tarp. "So, what are your plans?"

"I'll wait here for them. No reason I can't catch a later ferry if I have to," she answered casually, glad he'd worded his question the way he did.

He glanced up, face expressionless. This, Bert had already learned, meant he was not pleased. "Source is coming with me," he said after a pause. "Figured you'd be glad to hear that."

"Oh, how come?"

"I told him you were leaving. I don't think he liked the idea of being here alone." He dropped a kiss on the top of her head. "Buy you dinner if you come off."

Jimmy's mind worked quickly at times, Bert thought as she watched the ATV depart with its gruesome burden. But why was he so determined she go back to Harkers? Was he really that interested in her, or was it something else?

When the sound of the ATV and the protesting squeal of the metal trailer faded into the distance, Bert turned back to the village with a sigh of relief. At least those two were gone.

To her surprise, the hours went by with no sign of Hunter and Rudy. What if they never showed at all? The idea of spending the night alone here gave her goose bumps.

Don't be silly, she told herself as she swept out the lifesaving station. She could move down to the fishing camp anytime she wanted. She didn't have to worry about becoming the third dead woman.

The thought made her shiver. Two deaths in a small place like this, both by weird accidents, were too coincidental for her. And the way that nutria wailed, as if it were calling for someone to come help Luna Mae. That was not so far-fetched. Animals had more sense than most people believed. She remembered the time a flock of birds had flown frantically about her deck until she came out. Then a robin had led her to its nest, where a snake was swallowing its last chick, only the legs sticking out of the snake's mouth.

Bert pressed her lips together grimly. She'd been too late that time, too. Could she have saved Luna Mae if she'd gone out right away? She'd know when they found out what killed her, and how long she'd been dead.

She mowed for a while, then swept out the toilets and added water to the composter. She probably should be packing, but that was like agreeing to leave, and she didn't want to, not yet.

Finally, she heard a motor. There was no way to tell if it was a truck or an ATV—not from this distance, at any rate. She ran out of the cabin. It was the truck.

Hunter jumped out. "You all right? You were supposed to meet us at Long Point."

"I tried to get you on the phone. Figured I could go back with you this afternoon."

"Don't look like anyone's going back today." He turned toward Rudy, his passenger. "Headstrong woman. She don't listen to orders."

"You're staying over?" Bert asked Rudy as he climbed out of the truck. "Why?"

"Ferry struck a log making the crossing, ma'am. Trashed both props," Rudy said in his soft voice. "That's what took so long. Hard to change a prop in the middle of the sound in this chop."

"Boat left on one engine," Hunter added. "Won't come back today, maybe not tomorrow. They're going to have to fetch a diver from Beaufort to fix it."

"We'd like to hear what exactly took place last night, if you don't mind, ma'am," the big ranger said, giving her a cheerful smile. His plump cheeks were pink from the wind, making him look more like Santa Claus than ever.

"Any particular part?" Bert took them inside the cabin. Outside, the wind howled, the air developing a distinct nip. "What did Jimmy tell you?"

"Rudy didn't get a chance to talk at Jimmy," Hunter said. "Ferry didn't get in till noon."

"Like ships in the night, we were," Rudy explained. "Range and Source loaded Luna Mae's body on the boat while I got off.

Captain was pushing to get the boat back, and Hunter was expecting me at the fishing camp."

"Hunter, you didn't come over with Rudy? When did you get here?" If he'd been at the fishing camp earlier, that meant she could have reached him by phone in time to catch the boat. She hoped he didn't find out.

Not looking at her, he said casually, "I came over on the three o'clock ferry yesterday."

At first, the significance of what he said didn't sink in. Bert was just disappointed he'd been so close but hadn't bothered to come up. Then suspicion dawned. "Did you drive up last night? I heard a motor, late." No. It couldn't have been Hunter. She was sure of that.

His answer was cold, almost formal. "Jimmy was here. I didn't want to disturb you or anything. Now, if I'd known about Luna Mae . . ."

Disturb her. What did he think they were doing? She'd get him on that later, but not in front of Rudy.

Rudy had not missed the exchange. His expression remained cherubic, but his blue eyes narrowed slightly as he darted a glance first at Hunter, then at Bert. Oh, shit. The grapevine would be humming. Wait until Hunter found out why Olin went back to bed. She stifled a giggle. Served him right.

"Why don't you tell us what happened from the time Hunter left here yesterday? Take your time, ma'am."

Bert went through it all, trying to keep it in order and clear. Rudy interrupted her only a few times.

"You're sure that when you first woke up, you didn't hear running?" he asked when she stopped.

Bert shook her head. "I thought Jimmy was at the shed, fixing something."

"Could it have been Olin, looking for Jimmy?"

"I never thought of that." He was good.

"But why didn't he answer?" Hunter broke in. "Even without his hearing aid, he's not stone deaf."

"Did you call for Olin or Jimmy?"

Bert had to think back. "Jimmy, I'm pretty sure."

"And you were still inside the cabin and not real concerned yet, is that right?" Rudy asked.

Bert nodded, her eyes widening. "You think Olin thought Jimmy and I were both inside?"

Rudy shrugged. "Doesn't explain why he didn't hear you hollering from the station. Be interesting to hear his account."

"Be more interesting to hear Jimmy's account," Hunter growled. "He had no call to leave her alone."

"Let me get this straight," Rudy said, ignoring Hunter. "When you found Luna Mae in the marsh, you called for help. Jimmy answered, and then you thought you heard someone else?"

"Not exactly. I heard someone near me. I yelled for them to come and help. That's when Jimmy answered, but from the other side, far away."

"Sound can play tricks over water. Did you hear anything that could identify what you heard as a person—metal clinking, footsteps, a scent? Think a minute."

Bert closed her eyes, remembering. "Just some rustling in the weeds. I don't think it was an animal. Sounded too big."

"What makes you say that?"

She shook her head. "What about the motor?" She had a feeling they didn't consider it important.

"That could have been anything, Miss Bert," Rudy told her. "A fisherman gigging flounder, a shrimper, kids in a boat."

"You know who it was. It was Donny Southard," Hunter growled. "Stands to reason that's who Jimmy saw. Reckon he parked his ATV on the other side of the fuel dump and walked in."

"But Donny would have helped me," Bert protested.

The men paid her no attention.

"Makes sense," Rudy said. "He could have lost Jimmy easy enough."

"Probably frightened poor Luna Mae so bad her heart gave out," Hunter added.

"Now, you don't know that," Bert broke in. "Why would he

be in the marsh at that hour? Maybe it was a fisherman getting an early start."

"Couldn't be from Long Point," Hunter said flatly. "There were only two groups there, and they weren't out after supper."

"How can you be sure of that?" Bert snapped. "Were you up all night watching?"

He had a strange expression on his face when he answered. "I had trouble sleeping. I think I would have heard a car start up."

They were silent for a moment. Then Bert said, "It might have nothing to do with Luna Mae or Donny. Don't you have problems with drugs around here? Smugglers? I mean, suppose someone's been using the island for something illegal. That would account for a lot of this, including them trying to scare us off."

Both Hunter and Rudy were nodding.

"We were talking about that on the way up," Hunter said. "Only they use planes for drugs these days, mostly."

"And the only place a plane could land would be on the airstrip right next to you. Or on the beach at low tide, unless it was a helicopter," Rudy added.

"It's right easy to tell a copter by the sound, don't you think?" Hunter was looking directly at Bert, his eyes a soft gray.

"It didn't sound like a helicopter," she said.

Rudy rose. "I need to inventory and lock up Miss Luna Mae's house before I leave. I hear she's got some nieces and nephews. They'll probably be up." He turned to Hunter. "Why don't you come along and give me a hand?"

Bert looked at the two men hopefully. She was dying to see inside the house again, but they ignored her and left. Having nothing else to do, she made some tuna fish sandwiches, feeling like a traitor to her sex. I am not catering to them, she told herself. I'm just low man on the totem pole here.

"How about something to eat?" She asked when they returned.

"Thank you kindly, Miss Bert, but I'll be taking the truck back now. Justin's making ribs." Rudy smiled at her and nodded toward Hunter. "This worthless man might be happy to oblige you. I don't believe he stopped to pick up any supplies."

Bert's stomach did a flip-flop. She struggled not to show any emotion. "You're not going back?"

Hunter's eyes met hers as he picked up one of the sandwiches. He gave her a lopsided smile. "We talked it over. It doesn't seem like a good idea to leave you here alone, not with all this going on."

"What's going to happen next?" Bert asked Hunter as they watched Rudy drive away in Hunter's truck.

"What do you mean?"

"They're not going to let me stay here, are they?"

Hunter sighed. "Rudy has to report to Crissie. Then she'll talk it over with the supervisor and me."

"And I'll be out."

"I don't want to see you go, believe me," Hunter said with flattering sincerity. "But it's for your own good." Their eyes met. With a slight turn of his head, he rose from the table and motioned her to join him outside.

They ambled slowly up the old landing strip. It was about two hundred feet wide and ten times as long. Both sides were lined with huge wax myrtles, ashes, and cedars. A flock of pink-beaked ibises were stalking mole crickets in the grass about halfway up.

"There's going to be a fuss at the park when this gets out. It's too close to the other one," Hunter said.

"Anne Source's death was an accident, wasn't it?"

Hunter scowled, his bushy brows meeting over his deep-set eyes. "Not if Miss Anne was frightened into setting that fire."

"How long do I have?"

"On the island, you mean?"

Bert nodded.

"That's yet to be seen. Report won't be ready until tomorrow, Friday. Reckon it'll be Monday, maybe Tuesday, before they get round to making decisions."

She didn't want to leave, yet she was definitely relieved Hunter was here. Now, it was Bert's turn to sigh. "Well, at least I have the weekend. Maybe we can find out who's behind this before then."

"That's what I'm fixing to do right now. Let's see if we can tell what happened in the marsh last night."

The clouds were still building, but Hunter said it wasn't supposed to rain until evening. They walked past the shed and the hospital cistern. As they reached the arm of the runway, Hunter turned left. The cross arm ended at a road by the gas pumps.

It was Bert's first time on this road. "Is this where you figure Donny parked?" she asked. "What's at the other end?"

"This is the back way to the mud flats from the village." Hunter was inspecting the ground. "You can also get to Sheep Island this way. You been there yet?"

"When? You guys have kept me busy every second." She stared at the packed, grassy lane. "How can you tell one track from another?"

"Can't. Not around here."

Bert followed Hunter across the fuel-storage area to an intersecting overgrown lane. So this was where the trail from the shed ended. The sand and grass showed a few tracks—some old tire marks and footprints. They could have been made by anyone anytime since the last big rain.

"It all seems to come back to here," Bert said, eyeing the area.

They were approaching the ruins of the burned shed, where the path widened out. The hospital cistern was to their left bordering the runway, barely visible over the marsh grass that surrounded the raised path. Here and there, elevated wooded hummocks ridged the marsh. Once, most of this had been underwater, part of Coast Guard Creek. The Atlantic was to the south, less than a mile away. The village lay to the north. Ocracoke was northeast. To the west, behind all the marshes, was the Pamlico. There was nothing here except the cinders of the old shed, the brick cistern, and the . . .

"Hunter, would anyone have reason to be interested in the ruins of the hospital?"

"The archaeologists say there was another hospital here, before they put this one up in—"

"Eighteen forty-six," Bert said.

He smiled. "You been doing your studying. Want to go back now? Got some tall weather moving in."

Bert shook her head. "No. Let's sit here a moment. It's nice and open, and the wind's blowing the bugs away." As Hunter eyed the sky, she added, "Just for a minute. I have this feeling."

He gave her a sharp look. "Don't want to argue with the feeling of no sea-born woman."

"That again. Do tell, exactly what powers am I supposed to have?"

Hunter found a sandy spot, smoothed it out with his feet, and plopped down. "Don't rightly know if it's up to me to say." Eyes dancing, he pulled her down next to him. "Might spoil things somehow."

"Hunter!"

"All right." He dropped his voice to a dramatic pitch and gestured with his long hands. "The ocean is a mother, birthplace of all, so women born on the ocean have a closer connection with her than the rest of us."

"That's it?"

"What more you want?"

"What's the power?"

He hesitated. "There's some that say sea-born women can influence the weather."

"Make storms?"

"No, more like help sailors at sea, open a window in the fog, lead them to safety."

"That's nice. Wouldn't work for me, though. I'm no boatman. I wouldn't know where to lead them."

Hunter grinned, but his brows were pulled together. "Part of the legend is that the sea creatures did Jerushia's bidding. She'd send dolphins and birds to help guide ships to shore."

"Neat. I'd like that. What happened to her, anyhow?"

"Let me see. Jerushia drowned and . . ."

"You stop that. What happened after Spriggs let the *Celestial Harp* go free?"

"They settled in New Bedford, Massachusetts. Jerushia grew

into a fine woman and made up her cloth of gold—"

"What cloth?"

"Didn't I tell you? Spriggs sent his men back to his ship for a bolt of gold cloth. A present for the babe to make her a wedding dress. When she married, that is."

"Did she?" Bert laughed. "She must have. You're here."

"I may not be directly related. Jerushia never had any grandchildren, that I heard tell. Her son adopted a child, although some said it was really his bastard. Our family was descended from that adopted child." He dribbled some sand through his fingers, stretching out. "Now, I'm getting ahead of myself. According to what they say, John and Mary O'Hagan went on to settle in New Bedford with their baby girl. Every year after that, on her birthday, Jerushia would receive a bolt of fine cloth. Except for her fortieth birthday, when Jerushia really needed it." ∽

Chapter 10

ALL DAY, JERUSHIA WAITED, but the package did not arrive. Nor did it the next day, or the third.

The messenger could have been delayed, she told herself. The captain must be getting old. Perhaps he forgot, or remembered too late, or—this she did not want to consider—was dead.

She didn't really think so. Some instinct told her he still lived, and that this year it was vital she be here to receive her gift.

Jerushia stared grimly out the one small window of her boardinghouse bedchamber, where she'd waited for the last three days. She was counting on that bolt of cloth, but not to make herself a dress. She had not used the cloth for herself since the sea had taken her husband. No, for the last two years, she'd sold it. The proceeds augmented the pittance she received from the business and provided a few small luxuries—a visit to her sister, a few baubles for her nieces, an evening at the Carter House, new trimmings for her bonnet.

Gloom settled even more heavily on Jerushia. If she had to stay in this small, dark room day after day, she would surely go mad. But what else was a widow to do? She could seek employment in one of the big houses. Oh, how her daughter-in-law would like that. Jerushia, a common maid. But her son would never permit it. He would force her to come to his house, and then she would be at the mercy of that witch.

Never. Jerushia paced back and forth. She had to find some release for her energy. At forty, she was well advanced in years but surely still too young to sit around waiting to die. If only Nathaniel were still alive, she would go and live with him in a hen's breath.

Outside, hooves clattered and the rumble of a carriage rose to her ears. She peered out the foggy glass. Carriages were rare in this section of New Bedford. It was a hired cab pulled by a handsome pair of Chapmans, and it stopped in front of the boarding-house.

Sudden hope flared in her heart. There was no one here of sufficient stature to be visited by a carriage. It must be her package. Perhaps he sent it by special messenger.

Jerushia skipped down the narrow flight of stairs. Already, the coachman hammered on the door. She threw it open as Mrs. Boil came from the kitchen, wiping her hands on her apron.

It was her package. A tall, smartly attired older man stood on the stoop, holding a carefully wrapped bolt of cloth under his arm. Doffing his hat, he inquired, "Jerushia Spriggs O'Hagan?"

"At your service, sir." This was no ordinary messenger. She dropped a curtsey. "Whom do I . . . ?"

The stranger stared at her, frowning. A bald, brown scalp showed under an ill-fitting white wig. His face was deeply tanned. His royal blue weskit was longer than the cut commonly worn in Massachusetts, his breeches and ornate buckles of a mode she'd seen on seafaring men, the wealthier ones. Seafaring men? No, it could not be.

Just then, the stranger lifted a brow.

"Godfather Spriggs!" Jerushia launched herself into his arms. " 'Tis you. I never thought, after all these years . . . Oh, Godfather Spriggs."

Then she found herself lifted off her feet and swung around—

no mean feat, for she was almost as tall as he. When he put her down, she was breathless and laughing.

"Hold still, lass. Let me fill me eyes." He held her at arm's length, and she did not miss his astonishment, and something else—pride? "My, but ye have grown into a large, handsome woman, me girl."

"Some are not so polite," she laughed, wishing her hair were pinned. "I have grown like a Cherokee squaw. Six foot be too tall for a woman."

He frowned again, turning her around. Jerushia would not have permitted such liberties from many, but this was her legendary godfather.

"Nay, 'tis like a willow ye are, slim and graceful, a head above the others, and that red hair . . ."

Mrs. Boil cleared her throat loudly.

Jerushia blushed, both from Spriggs's extravagant compliment and for forgetting the woman's presence. "My dear Mrs. Boil, please forgive me. May I present my beloved godfather, Francis Harrington Spriggs. Mrs. Boil, my landlady."

The introductions complete, Jerushia searched for a place to take her godfather. There was so much she wanted to ask him. The only public room was a hall containing two straight chairs and a rough table. It was a dreary, drafty place. Instead, she led him into the dining room. Since no meal was being served at the moment, it afforded privacy, if not comfort.

Spriggs glanced around the shabby room, which reeked of rutabagas. Waiting until Mrs. Boil took her leave, he said quietly, "I do not want to offend you, my dear, but I must confess to being shocked to find you in such modest circumstances." He eyed her black garments. "I assume from your dress you are in mourning. Your husband?"

"My youngest son, too. Their ship was lost in the storm of fifty-eight."

"But your father?"

"There was an accident the same year," she answered woodenly.

Spriggs bowed his head. "My heart goes out to you. I never met your husband, but your father was an uncommon man." He stroked his beard. "But surely, there is something left. Your father's shipyard, the house, your other sons?"

"Nathaniel became a preacher and went out west to live with the Indians."

Spriggs sat back. "How extraordinary."

Jerushia permitted herself a smile. "You never met him. He was so like his grandfather, always eager to see what lay on the other side. Only preachers and soldiers are commissioned to the new territory, so . . ." Her shrug was resigned. "I fear he is dead, too."

"Whatever makes you say that?"

"It has been five years now, and I have heard nothing from him."

Waving his hand impatiently, Spriggs said, "He is in a wilderness, my dear. That does not mean he is dead." He stretched his long legs uncomfortably.

The chair certainly did not fit a man of his proportions. Jumping up, Jerushia fetched a footstool from the front hall. "If Nathaniel were alive, he would have found some way to send word to me by now," she said, placing the stool.

With a sigh of relief, Spriggs elevated his feet. "I see that even in a place like this, you manage to make a man comfortable."

They spoke of other things for a time. Then Captain Spriggs took his leave.

"I plan to be in New Bedford for five days yet," he said. "On business, I am. It would give me much pleasure if you would allow me to call on you again. Perhaps tomorrow at this time?"

Jerushia inclined her head gracefully, hiding her delight.

"Please, I am remiss." Spriggs thrust the bolt of cloth at her.

Jerushia took it, clutching it to her body. "I shall treasure this always, for it has brought me a birthday never to forget."

"As I treasure the memories of another birthday, forty years ago." He leaned over and kissed her forehead. "Until tomorrow, my dear."

Two days later, Jerushia sat in the shipyard office confronting an angry young man.

"No. It's out of the question. It is too far away. You cannot go." Edward, Jerushia's son, thumped a fist on the table.

"Be reasonable, Edward." Jerushia fought to keep her voice even. " 'Tis a struggle for you to keep me here. Do not deny it." It would not be such a struggle if he let her help him with the business. She'd all but run it while her husband lived, and more profitably than Edward yet. That, she knew, was his problem. He was afraid to be bested by his mother.

"The burden would be eased if you took lodging with us," he threw back.

"You would have bloodshed?"

"Eleanor is willing to have you, if you, madam, will agree to keep the peace."

"I, why, it's she that . . ." Jerushia made herself be still. No matter what she said, her son would not hear. To him, his wife was all smiles and sweetness. It was only that pointy chin that gave Eleanor away. She never raised her voice, but her revenge was swift and deadly. Messages would not be given, food would be oversalted, a favorite shirtwaist scorched, a bedchamber plagued with mice.

"Eleanor loves you, Mother. If you could but curb your temper . . ."

Jerushia clenched her teeth. He was right. She did have a temper, and Eleanor brought out the worst. Just last week, her daughter-in-law had delivered Jerushia's stipend along with her usual biting comment: "Poor Edward, it pains him so to have his mother refuse his hospitality. Why, he went without a new top hat so he could afford your board." Eleanor never went without, Jerushia had noted grimly.

"It is not as if you have children I could care for, Edward." This Jerushia knew was a sore subject with him. "I cannot be idle for the rest of my days. I will be housekeeper for Captain Spriggs. And not only that, Edward. He promises to deed the house at Portsmouth to me after he is gone." Jerushia did not miss the spark of interest in her son's eyes and was quick to take advantage. "I will no longer be a burden to you."

For a moment, she thought she had prevailed, but then Edward sighed deeply and pushed himself back from the desk. "No, it is not fitting. You cannot live with a man to whom you are not married. You know nothing about him except that he was a notorious pirate, a cruel man."

"Do say," she snapped. "He is my godfather and twenty years older than I, and there will be others in the house. A cook and a housemaid." But that tiny inner voice of hers acknowledged her son's warning. As courteous and debonair as Captain Spriggs was, he frightened her, too. He was a powerful, domineering man accustomed to instant obedience. Indeed, she had broached her need for freedom with the captain. He had assured her that once her household duties were completed, she would be free to follow her own pursuits.

"There would be a scandal." Edward paced the room. "The gossip mongers would be at work. They would say that I forced you to leave, and that you are living . . ." He shook his head. "I cannot permit this."

Jerushia gazed at her middle son with distaste. Already, his hair thinned on top and his weskit was tight over an incipient paunch. "They gossip now. They say you are running the shipyard to the ground. Old John was here but a week ago to beg me to intercede in that affair with the—"

"Enough!" he shouted. "That is not your concern."

"It is my concern that soon there will be insufficient funds to keep me even in my reduced circumstances."

"Then move in with us, where you belong, and stop this nonsense."

"Move in with that simpering hypocrite? Never."

Edward blanched. "Mother," he said very slowly, "if you go to live with that man, I will disown you."

She would not have this posturing fool dictate to her. "So be it, then." Jerushia stood, tossing her mane of hair. She was glad her words did not betray her anxiety. She had not thought to go this far. There would be no safe harbor for her if this venture did not succeed.

Edward made one last attempt to dissuade her. "If you do this thing, you will spoil Eleanor's chance to join the Circle of Friends."

Suddenly, everything was clear to Jerushia. "It is not myself you are concerned about, or even the business. It is she." Fury charged her voice. "You spineless worm. You are afraid of that woman."

Edward said nothing. He turned on his heel and stormed out the door—the door of his own office. Jerushia smiled bitterly as she tied on her bonnet. She had no choice. She had made her bed and now must lie in it.

Outside, even the weather was against her. The wind had risen, bringing an icy rain from the east. She hoped it was not a storm brewing. Clutching her cloak tightly about her, she bowed her head to the wind and hurried back to the boardinghouse. 'Tis a pity that you could not bow a little more to Edward, she berated herself. He felt incompetent both in the shipyard and in his wife's childless state. And yet she could not stand silent and let him dictate her future just so he could bed his wife this night.

She tossed her head, spraying water. Regrets be damned. She would venture to Portsmouth Town with Captain Spriggs and see what new things life had to offer. And if she made a mistake in judgment, she would pay the price. Surely, anything would be better than the years of penny-pinching boredom that stretched in front of her now. ⌒⌒

Chapter 11

"I'VE ALWAYS WONDERED what Jerushia's decision would have been, if she listened to her inner voice," Hunter said slowly.

"You mean she wasn't happy?" Bert swatted another fly. There was a regular cloud of them droning overhead. "But tell me, did she regret her decision?"

They started back toward the lifesaving station.

"Is there anyone over forty that hasn't regretted a decision." It was more a statement than a question.

Did that mean he was over forty? How much over? "What do you regret?" Bert asked.

"You first," he countered lightly.

It was her fault. She hadn't really meant to get so personal. "It was a decision I didn't make. I stayed with my husband years after I should have left him."

"Why?"

Bert exhaled. "Sheer cowardice. We lived in upstate New York. I'd never held a real job. I had two small kids. I was afraid."

"Jerushia was afraid to leave, too, but she did."

"Don't change the subject." She was beginning to notice how

the thickness of Hunter's dialect fluctuated. Did he use it to hide his feelings, like he hid behind that hair? "What do you regret?"

He winced. "Look, could we do this some other time? It's getting late."

Bert frowned.

Hunter took her hand. "Let's get dinner started. I'll tell you on the way."

By the time they reached the cabin, the warmth of his palm had Bert's blood thrumming all the way to the top of her head. She could barely hear what he was saying. She wanted his arms around her shoulders, holding her, bringing her close.

"—decision I didn't make either. We were out trolling." Hunter spoke slowly and with difficulty.

Was he feeling the current? Or was it what he was saying? Her sexual awareness died as the seriousness of what he told her sank in.

"The wind came up. I should have gone in then, but she was having such a good time."

She—his wife? Bert hadn't been listening.

"We didn't get out too often, but that's no call to act like a fool." His voice was angry. "To make a long story short, the seas came up and the boat broached when I came by the bar at the cape. They fished me out, but they never found her." He dropped her hand. "Best wife a man could have, and I killed her, just because I didn't want our good time to end."

What could she say? Her regrets were for opportunities lost. His were irrevocable.

Then, to Bert's total surprise, he leaned over and brushed his lips to hers. "Thanks for listening." He reverted to his drawl. "This done me good, tonight."

Bert touched her hand to her lips. This couldn't be. He was too young for her, but it was nice anyhow. She almost ran into the cabin to start dinner.

Hunter whistled through his teeth as he hosed off behind the boathouse. Things were going just the way he'd planned.

Still . . . He shrugged. Nothing he could do about that except bide his time.

Rummaging through his backpack, he found a clean T-shirt. Best he could do. He pulled it over his wet head, ran a comb through his hair, and started for the cabin. As he came around the corner, the wind whipped his hair into his eyes. He glanced toward Ocracoke. Thunderheads towered over the island, rising high into the sky. Tall weather was moving in, all right.

He tapped on the screen door. "You looking for company?"

She was at the stove, an outline in the dark room. "Help yourself to a beer or iced tea," she said, her back still to him.

"You want one?"

"I'll have mine with dinner."

Popping the tab on a beer can, Hunter peeked over her shoulder. A pair of Delmonicos sizzled in a cast-iron pan. They smelled good, but the scent that rose from her—fresh shampoo and soap—was even better. Her newly washed hair fell softly, hugging her head and flipping up in soft curls where it met the tan skin of her shoulders. He had an overwhelming urge to lick her bare neck, to slide his arms around her waist and under her shirt and hold her against his . . .

Hunter pulled out a chair and sat down noisily. Damn, he was going to have to keep his distance. But it was good fun anyhow.

"How do you like your steak? Well done?" she asked.

There she was being a Northerner again, assuming they all liked their beef overdone. "Rare, iffen yuh don't mind any," he answered, exaggerating his drawl. Actually, he liked it medium, but damned if he'd say so.

Then he noticed she'd set their places as far apart as she could on the oblong table. What was eating her? Well, she didn't have to worry. He wasn't one to hit on a woman if he wasn't wanted. Besides, there was that other matter. He best eat up quick and get about his business.

"Hope it's all right," she said, setting their plates down.

A bowl of steaming mashed potatoes was already on the table. He picked up his fork and was about to start in on his steak when he noticed she was still puttering around. He waited, though his mouth watered from the savory smell.

Now, she placed a dish of green and red vegetables near him—tomatoes and some kind of squash. "How's your beer? Ready for another?" She bent over the fridge door.

He pushed his chair back. "I'm sorry. I clean forgot to get one for you."

"No big deal," she said, plunking a can on the table. "Use ketchup or anything?"

He shook his head, rising to hold her chair. She waved him off. He wished she'd sit down and stop fussing. It made him feel right useless.

Finally, Bert sat. She flushed when she noticed he hadn't eaten. "Oh, I'm sorry. Please start." She picked up her knife and fork, cut a big chunk off her meat, and stuffed it in her mouth.

She was uptight about something, all right, but what? She'd been all relaxed this afternoon, easy to talk to. To tell the truth, he hadn't run his mouth like that in a long time, talking about Rhoda and all. Still, she hadn't made out like she minded. She'd let him . . .

That was it. It had nothing to do with his unloading on her. It was that kiss. Not a kiss, really—just a friendly peck. But she'd been making like a skittish mare since.

All of a sudden, he was hungry, and the smell of that steak was more than he could stand. He picked up his knife and fork and dove in. Even though she'd pan-fried it, his steak was brown on the outside and juicy inside. She cooked like a pro, all right. Probably ran a great restaurant.

He didn't realize he'd sighed until she asked, "What's the matter? Too done?" Those big eyes of hers were more hazel to-night. Yesterday, by the water, they'd been green as could be.

"No way," he answered, feeling better. Damned if he knew what was making her so jumpy, but she wasn't indifferent to him, that was for sure. "Steak's done just right." He speared a zucchini slice and popped it into his mouth.

Her eyes lit up, changing back to clear green. That's another thing he admired about her. All her emotions were plain on her face. And that grin made him feel warm right down to his toes. He remembered the way her eyes had gotten big when she found that Scotch bonnet. You'd have thought it was a piece-o'-eight. What would she look like when she made love? Serious, or was she the open-mouthed . . . ? Better pay attention. She was saying something about supplies.

"—going to have to get some more food."

"Don't you get a thing," he told her quickly. "It's my turn to buy. I'm fixing to be back this weekend." That way, he could keep an eye on her and make sure she wasn't nosing about where she shouldn't. "You'll be going off Monday or Tuesday anyhow. Storm'll be over by then."

She leaned across the table. "That would be great. Look, if it turns out Luna Mae died of natural causes, maybe they won't kick me out. If you can pick up a couple of things, then I won't have to go shopping. To tell the truth, I'm afraid they won't let me back on if I leave."

She'd read that right. He was going to have to get her off the island, no matter what. His desk was buried under papers, and the annual week of law-enforcement training was coming up. They'd be real short-handed. "You can come back when things get more settled," he said, trying to prepare her.

She made a face and pushed her chair back. "That would be nice, but I don't think what's going on here is going to get fixed that easily."

She'd finished already? He better stop running his mouth.

"Don't rush," she said. "I'm a fast eater. Too fast."

He smiled at her. Pity she wasn't so quick to read a man's mind in other matters. "That's the truth. Never seen anyone finish a plate so quick."

"Hunter?" She leaned across the table, her gold hair swinging across her cheek.

He paused, a piece of steak halfway to his mouth. "Yeah?"

She sat back, color flooding her face. Her eyes dropped, and she reached for her beer.

He put his fork down. "You were going to say something?"

"What's the weather report?"

He knew that wasn't what she'd planned to ask. His eyes still on her face, willing her to look at him, he answered slowly, "Thunderstorms tonight. And there's a disturbance in the eastern Caribbean."

"Hurricane?"

"Don't you worry. We'll get you off the island in plenty of time if it starts looking bad." He took another mouthful of steak. "Weather don't usually amount to much, this time of the year," he mumbled.

He helped her clean up the dishes, standing close to wipe them dry. Every once in a while, he let his hand brush hers when she handed him a dripping plate. It seemed to him she was more relaxed, maybe because he hadn't been pushing her any. As he turned to set the frying pan on the counter, his bare arm jostled hers. It felt like he'd hit a live wire. The jolt ran up his spine and down to his groin. He darted a glance at her, willing her to lean into him and at the same time praying she wouldn't. Things were complicated enough already. She just went right on wiping the sink. But something about her jaw made him wonder if she was as unaware as she made out. The way he felt right now, he'd probably read too much into any reaction. Better get out quick, before he did something stupid.

Sucking in air, he muttered the first thing that came into his head: "I'll be sleeping downstairs tonight." Now, what made him go and say that, like he was expecting her or something? He just wanted to let her know he could come quickly if she called.

"Yeah, well, don't forget your backpack," she answered.

"You yell if you need anything." He stood close, her scent in his nose, unable to turn away. He willed her to look up, to smile and meet his eyes, but she kept her lids hooded, her body tense like a frightened doe. Dammit. He hadn't meant to scare her. "There'll be rain coming," he said, fighting the urge to take her in his arms. "You close up tight behind me, you hear, gal?" He went out the door, hoping she'd follow. She stayed inside, behind the screen.

Hunter was right about the weather, Bert thought two hours later as she ran around making sure all the doors and windows were tightly closed. It was thundering like nothing she'd ever heard before—one crack after another, so close together that it was like one continuous thunderbolt rattling the windows and making the floor shake.

Was there a lightning rod on this cabin?

The windows as secure as she could make them, Bert ran for her bed, wanting for some reason to get her feet off the floor. What was the highest point around here, the lifesaving station? Yes, but it wasn't close enough to take any bolts in her immediate vicinity. Besides, she wouldn't really wish them on Hunter.

The sky was flashing white. Both the radio and the cell phone were squealing. She pulled the plugs as fast as she could. Now, the rain came down in a solid sheet, slamming against the windows, some leaking in. Bert sat cross-legged in the middle of her bed, the blanket wrapped around her shoulders, watching wide-eyed and terrified as the bolts lit up the marsh brighter than the sun. Hunter was up, too. A light moved through the station. Even as she watched, the door opened and a slim figure holding a pack dashed out.

He'd get killed.

Bert was on her feet and over to the screen door, holding it open. Adrenaline pumping, she watched Hunter lope through ankle-deep water while lightning dropped about him.

Sleek with water, he bounced onto the deck wearing only a pair of shorts.

"You're crazy." Bert pulled him off the porch. "Come into the cabin."

"Don't want to mess up your floor. I've got a towel in my . . ." He lifted the backpack. Wind was blowing rain right through the screen.

"No, wait." Bert ran in and snatched a towel from the bath.

Hunter already had his out. She began to rub his back as he toweled off his head. Oh, God, he had a gorgeous back—silky gold skin and big muscles that rippled over his shoulder blades and down his arms. He must work out. She rubbed down to where his back narrowed and curved, the long, smooth muscles disappearing into the low waistline of his shorts. She swiped at the wet shorts, knowing he'd have to change, then knelt to wipe his legs, enjoying herself thoroughly.

He swung around. "Don't do that."

She looked up—and could not look away. Taking his hands, she let him pull her up into his arms. All the while, their eyes held each other, looking into the depths, meeting. She could feel his gaze in the pit of her stomach. Still looking at him, she unbuttoned her silk chemise and let it drop to the ground behind her. She hoped he didn't mind. Some men liked to do the undressing.

Then she was in his arms, straining against his bare, damp chest, her arms around his back, his hands on her breasts, both their mouths open, meeting, melding into each other as if there were nothing else in the world.

It was a short step to the bed.

Flesh meeting flesh, legs touching.

Him over her, awkward but sweet, stopping long enough to pull a condom out of his shorts on the floor.

She somewhat relieved he'd thought of it but also wondering at his efficiency. Had he planned this?

The pace escalating, his hands stroking, moving, knowing.

The joining. Movements becoming rapid, each unsure of the other yet driven by the excitement. Mindless rhythm, no longer awkward, one with the other, and then—the warm waves of release.

"Ohh," she moaned much later as he lay collapsed over her again. "That was wonderful. Both times, it was wonderful."

He chuckled. "Guess we made the earth move, all right."

Bert poked him hard. "And that wasn't thunder but our hearts beating, right? Any more cliches?"

He propped himself on one elbow. "Suppose I tell you that's the best time that's been for a while."

In the dark, she could see the white of his teeth and his shining eyes. She reached up and stroked his beard. "It didn't feel bad at all," she whispered.

"I take it you're not planning to have me up for sexual harassment?"

"Don't worry, Hunter. No matter what, I'm not the type."

"My job is in your hands," he said simply.

They lay quietly for a while, Bert's hand lazily exploring his body.

Hunter stretched out. "Let me ask you something, if you don't mind."

"Sure."

"Why were you so distant this evening?"

She wouldn't have put it that way, but she knew what he meant. "I don't want to be one of those older women that . . ." She wasn't really sure herself. "You know, that goes after younger men."

"Never." His arms went back around her. "You got one hell of a body, you know."

"But I'm a lot older than you."

"That don't much matter to me," he said softly, lying back and pulling her close.

"It might later, to others."

"You got a lot to learn, gal. Don't let worry about what's going to happen later spoil what's happening here and now."

Bert smiled in the dark. He was a nice guy. "Not to spoil this here and now, but what are we doing tomorrow?"

"I know what I'd like to be doing tomorrow. I'd like to be fishing, the both of us bare naked." He rolled over so he was looking down at her. "I want to be watching you in the sunlight, with all that water around and you working the pole and a big fish on the other end."

Bert felt herself grow warm. "And then you'll come up behind me and help me pull it in."

"Put it in, more likely," he laughed. "In a minute, I'm going to do it to you again, but first . . ." He turned toward her. "Like I just told you, what I'd rather do is be here with you, but what I got to do is go to Beaufort." He exhaled. "It's important. Park's got some sick horses." He was propped on his elbow, his head up so he could look down at her. "I have to be there to explain."

"You mean those wild horses on the islands? Wasn't there a fuss about the park wanting to get rid of them?"

Hunter winced. "That's exactly the problem. There's a group that wants to help take care of the horses. We need to work together. I have to be sure they understand."

"What if the weather's too rough?"

"Isn't supposed to be. You going to be all right, or do you want to come to Beaufort with me?"

"You'll be back tomorrow night?"

"You promise not to hit me again?" he asked. "Wild horses couldn't keep me away, equine fever or not." Then, still chuckling, he began making love to her all over again.

Bert dreamt about horses that night. Wild horses rearing up, neighing black horses. ∞

Chapter 12

EVEN THOUGH THEY DIDN'T FALL ASLEEP until very late, Bert woke up rested and content. Must be something about making love, she thought. It seemed to fill her with energy. Hunter apparently felt the same, for his cheery whistling filled the cabin.

"Do you want some eggs?" she asked. "That's about all I have. No cereal or rolls. How about bacon?"

"I wouldn't turn down bacon and eggs, if that doesn't put you out too much."

Bert smiled. He was so polite.

"You going to wear that on the ATV?" he asked twenty min-utes later as they cleaned up the dishes.

Bert looked down at her chemise. "I was going to shower after you left."

"Rudy took the truck back to Long Point. You're going to have to give me a ride down." He raised a wicked brow. "Reckon he won't mind if you take me over in that."

She laughed. "I forgot. Guess I'd better get dressed."

Soon, they were both on Bert's four-wheeler. The winds were still strong, the sky gray under a mist of high clouds. The water was deep in the flats, so the crossing was slow. They propped their feet on top of the front fenders; still, both were splashed with salt water before they were across.

"If that water isn't down some before you get back, don't try to get across," he told her as they stopped to wipe themselves off. "You wait for me at Long Point, you hear, Bert?"

She liked the way Hunter's voice softened and warmed when he said her name. It made her feel special. "What about the visitors? I can't leave them here alone."

"You'll have the place to yourself!" Hunter yelled over the roar of the engine as they took off down the beach. "Won't be anyone coming from Ocracoke till the jellyfish and eelgrass clear out, that's for sure." While she'd showered and dressed, he'd made a quick inspection of the village. "North end's a mess."

"Jimmy said the storm would blow them out." She leaned against him. There was a lot to be said for riding double on an ATV.

He pressed back. "Blowed them in, more likely. They're thicker than ever."

Bert wasn't sure whether to be relieved or not. She wouldn't have to worry about visitors—or worse, reporters—if the word got out about Luna Mae. On the other hand, after all the strange events, she wasn't sure she wanted to be here by herself.

The ferry wasn't in sight when they arrived at Long Point. Rudy was on the deck of the one-room ranger cabin, waiting for them. "Ferry won't be in for another hour," he told Hunter. "Call just come. One of the props still isn't running right. Had to take it off again."

"Son of a bitch," Hunter murmured, looking at his watch. "I got to make that meeting."

"Crissie knows it. She's going to meet you with a change of clothes at the museum. That way, you won't have to make an extra stop."

Hunter looked relieved. "That's right thoughtful of her. You give her the combination to my locker?"

Rudy nodded. "Got some more news, too."

The two men went ahead to the ferry landing. Rudy was

chubby in the slim-cut uniform shorts. Hunter's park trousers were streaked with sand and salt. Bert watched Hunter shake his head, then stop. He waved her over. "She's fixing to go back after we leave," he told Rudy, "so I reckon she's got a right to hear what's going on."

Rudy nodded, propping himself on the edge of the dock. Hunter sat next to him. Bert went over to the side so she could watch the water.

"So what's the news?" Hunter asked.

Rudy looked at Bert, then said slowly, "This is confidential. I'm treating you like park personnel, you understand. It's about Luna Mae." He turned back to Hunter. "They took her to Beaufort. That's a story in itself. Called in the medical examiner, on account of it being an unattended death. Beaufort doesn't have a county coroner, you know. Anyhow, seems he didn't like what he saw, so he sent her to that Indian doctor at the hospital for a consult."

From the tone of his voice, Bert figured it wasn't just a heart attack, so she wasn't surprised at what came next: "Like Jimmy Range said, there was water in her lungs. Muddy water."

"A stroke?" Bert asked.

Rudy threw out his hands, palms up. "They don't want to say, not for sure, but it seems there were other things. For one, her fingertips were all torn up, nails ripped, like she was struggling."

"They think someone killed her?"

"Now, they're not saying that," Rudy was quick to answer. "Could have been she was clawing, trying to get out of the ditch, if she was partially paralyzed or something. A person being drowned will fight like crazy, even a little old lady like her. Her face was bruised, too. They still have to do more tests." He glanced at Hunter. "May take awhile."

Hunter scowled. "I don't care for the sound of that. You'd better come off with us, Bert."

Her stomach dropped. "What are you going to do after your meeting?" She didn't want to leave, but she wasn't sure she wanted to stay either.

Hunter shrugged. "Come back here. What you getting at?"

"Up to the village?" As long as he was around, she wouldn't be scared. Besides, there would be compensations.

He nodded. "That's my—"

"What time are you coming back?" Bert interrupted.

Hunter thought a minute. "Meeting'll be over by two. No reason I can't catch the afternoon boat."

"Suppose I wait here for you? Then we can go back to the village together. I can't leave. Everything I own is up there. I don't even have my driver's license with me."

Hunter and Rudy looked at each other. "Your call," Rudy told him.

"Justin can let you know if any boats put in," Hunter said to Rudy. "Should be safe enough."

Bert swung around. "What's going on? Who do you expect to land?"

Rudy hesitated a moment, then shrugged. "That's the problem. We don't know for sure, but someone's been doing some digging."

"As in digging up artifacts?"

"Could be. Olin Source reported disturbed ground. So did Jimmy. And Hunter found a burnt-up metal detector in the ruins of the old shed."

"Why didn't you tell me?"

"We thought Donny Southard was doing the digging," Rudy answered. "But then Donny was out to see the superintendent Wednesday morning."

"Son of a bitch. I told you he was no good," Hunter interjected.

"Came in to complain he was being harassed by Hunter," Rudy said, ignoring the interruption. "Said it wasn't him taking artifacts. Told the superintendent he could get proof it wasn't him."

"That Donny can fool you good."

"You want to tell the story?" Rudy asked. "Go ahead."

"Sorry, buddy, but how'd you like to lose a night's sleep over a turd like him?"

"What are you two talking about?" Bert glanced from one to the other.

"The superintendent sent Hunter back over to Long Point Wednesday evening," Rudy explained. "Arranged for Donny to meet Hunter and give him the film."

"Set there all night, but Donny never showed."

"So that's why you were so sure no one came from Long Point," Bert said. "Was that your truck I heard?"

Hunter shook his head. "Don't reckon you could hear that far. I'm thinking you heard Donny's ATV." He turned to Rudy. "I say he was lying about that proof. Just wanted a clear field for his mischief."

"We stopped by Evergreen Slew on our way in yesterday," Rudy explained to Bert. "His cabin was shuttered up tight. No boat. You seen any sign of him today, Hunter?"

"No tracks in the flats. None on the beach either."

So Hunter hadn't just pulled over to wipe off. He'd been checking the trailhead for tracks.

"Justin said Donny's boat was over to Atlantic yesterday," Rudy told him.

Hunter nodded. "Keeps his truck there. I'm fixing to check with Lettie soon as we cross over. Don't want him bad-mouthing me again. Next thing, he'll be telling the superintendent I never showed."

Bert's mind jumped ahead. "Did Donny say who was digging? What was in the photos?"

Both men shook their heads.

"Said he'd let us be the judge," Rudy told her.

"It's his nature to act cagey," Hunter said.

Bert tipped her head, thinking. "It must be Source, then."

Both men stared at her. Hunter's brows were raised in a question.

"Well, you had Jimmy following Luna Mae, right? So he would have known if she'd been digging."

"Jimmy wasn't spying on Luna Mae, not to my knowledge. Was he, Rudy?" Hunter asked.

Rudy shook his head. "Jimmy Range got nothing to do with security. Did he tell you he did?"

It wasn't true? She'd been so sure. Bert felt herself flushing. "No, Jimmy never said so, but Luna Mae told me how Jimmy was always spying. She figured the park sent him after her."

"You know anything about this?" Rudy asked Hunter.

"No, but I reckon Jimmy could have taken it upon himself. He didn't cotton much to the old lady." Hunter sighed. "I'd better have a word with Mr. Range when I get back."

"Not today, you won't," Rudy told him. "He took the day off, to make up for yesterday. I understand he won't be back until Monday."

Hunter cocked an eyebrow in Rudy's direction.

The chubby ranger glanced at his watch. "Be awhile before that ferry gets here. Got a story you'll enjoy. Seems the sheriff's office was supposed to meet Jimmy to pick up Luna Mae's body yesterday, but when they found the ferry was on a four-hour delay, they left. So when Jimmy got to Atlantic, no ambulance.

"The way I heard the story, Jimmy didn't want to take time to fetch the park van all the way from Harkers, so he loads Luna Mae into his car. Now, he's driving that Shelby—fancy two-door sports car—and he puts her in the backseat. Not much room there."

Rudy's voice rose. "Jimmy phones for the ambulance as soon as he gets to Harkers, but there's a big accident on Route 70, and everyone's tied up. Crissie won't let him bring the body inside the building, so he leaves Luna Mae in his car.

"Then the superintendent gets back from Morehead City. Well, he tells Jimmy to take the body to the medical examiner right away. Now, she's been sitting in the back of a hot car for two, three hours." Rudy's eyes were almost lost in creases of amusement. "So when Jimmy goes to move Luna Mae into a park van, he finds rigor has set in but good. Heat does that, you know. There's no way they can get her out, short of using a sledgehammer."

Hunter chuckled. Bert felt guilty for her amusement, then

decided Luna Mae would have been the first to enjoy a good story, especially if it was on Jimmy.

"The superintendent tells Jimmy to take her down to the emergency room and let them get her out of the car. Says Jimmy should have followed regulations and used a park van in the first place.

"To make a long story short, the medical examiner couldn't get her out either, but he did cut the tarp open. That's when he decides he wants another doctor to take a look. Now, instead of unattended death, we got suspicious death, so the hospital people don't want to compromise the body. It's getting toward quitting time, and Range lives at Cedar Island. That's over an hour from Morehead. He's determined Luna Mae is coming out, so he takes his precious car to a body shop to get the seat removed. Keep in mind, the tarp's been cut open and you can tell it's a stiff. Next thing Jimmy knows, he's got the police there. Had to call the park and the hospital before they believed his story. I understand it was after eight before Jimmy had his car cleaned and back together.

"He called in last night and said he was taking the next two days off. Didn't ask, mind you. Crissie said he sounded real put out." Rudy brought his fingertips together. "Just lucky for the park the newspaper didn't get wind of all this. Can't you see the headline? 'Body Stuck in Ranger's Car.' "

They were quiet for a moment. Then Bert asked, "Jimmy drives an antique Shelby? Isn't that an expensive car?"

"He was a dentist, you know. Reckon he's got money," Hunter told her.

"Was he really spying on Luna Mae?" she asked Rudy. "Or was she paranoid?"

"I wouldn't call her paranoid. We're pretty sure she was doing some scavenging. There's a rumor she took some silver plate. No proof, though. The superintendent sent her a letter warning he could cancel her lease if she was caught digging or even probing again. So she had good cause to be jumpy."

"Olin Source turned her in, right? Was this silver worth anything? Besides historical value, I mean."

This time, it was Hunter who answered. "It was supposed to

131

be a silver bowl, not all that old, corroded pretty bad. No monetary value, the way I heard."

"So what's out there that's worth killing for? And don't tell me it's Blackbeard's treasure."

Hunter grinned. "Told you she was smart," he said to Rudy. "Bert, I figure if they're not hunting something old, maybe they're looking for something new."

"Like drugs or money?"

"We don't know," Rudy said. "And we may never know. Once it's gone, we'll never get to the bottom of this."

"But who? It has to be someone that's been around, unless they're sneaking on to the island at night. That boat I heard . . . Do you think there's a gang of smugglers or something?"

"A gang by the name of Donny Southard, more likely."

Rudy waved Hunter's remark aside. "A gang would explain the organ and some of the other things, if they're trying to frighten people away. The only problem is—"

"There aren't any reports of strange boats around," Hunter said. He gestured toward the horizon. "All of this may look like there isn't anyone around, but there's people here, and they know who's about, and who don't belong. It's got to be Donny or someone like him that wouldn't be noticed."

"What about Jimmy and Source? Any drug history?" Bert asked.

"Rudy and me checked their resumes when this all started." He grinned at her. "Yours, too."

"Oh?" They weren't as blasé as they seemed. "Resumes don't tell the kinds of things you need to know here. When you apply for a job, does the park follow up and do any checks?"

"Like background, you mean? That's a right good thought." Hunter turned to Rudy. "Jimmy and Source, right?"

"Luna Mae, too," Bert suggested. "Where does . . . Did she live on the mainland?"

"The park should have most of that information. What they don't have, we can get." Rudy stood. "Let me call in and get someone working on it."

Bert watched him walk across the sand road and past the gas pumps and sewage disposal site toward the ranger camp. She sat down next to Hunter. "Thanks for letting me stay."

"I'm hoping I won't regret it," he said quietly.

Bert was afraid he was referring to that other decision he'd made, with his wife. She wriggled closer. "You won't. I'm looking forward to spending another night with you."

Hunter chuckled, leaning against her arm. "Why do you think I agreed?" Then he got serious. "Don't you move until I get back, and then you do exactly as I say, you understand?"

"I promise," Bert said.

"I'll pick up a six-pack. You need anything else?"

"Milk and bread would be great. Oh, yes, a head of lettuce, if you can. Jimmy ate mine. And potato chips. If you like chicken, I make a killer paella."

Hunter smiled and put his hand discreetly over Bert's, glancing back toward the cabins. Not a soul was in sight. Pleasure flowed from Bert's hand up her arm to her spine and deep inside. This was the way things should be. She took a deep breath. The sound was at its narrowest here, so she could see the wavy outline of the distant mainland but no buildings, as if man and his greed had never touched these waters.

"Was the island like this when Jerushia was here?" she asked, deliberately changing the subject. She didn't want him having second thoughts about her staying. "Not the fishing camp, of course, but the rest. Was there a pier?"

Hunter glanced around before answering. "Two hundred and fifty years ago, when Jerushia came, this end of the island wasn't even connected to Portsmouth." He smiled at Bert's inquiring glance. "Swash Inlet cut clean across the island. It took a boat to cross over. Portsmouth Island was only about nine miles long, from Swash Inlet to Haulover Point. There was more land by Haulover then, too, and Sheep Island was connected to the village." His hand swept across the landscape. "This bank here was called North Core. Still is."

They were sitting on the pier, their feet dangling over the

water. A school of silversides, spooked by their movement, split the surface in a glinting shower. Something Hunter said triggered another thought. "Do you think Jerushia's house was by Haulover, the part that washed away?"

"Doesn't seem likely. They tell it was out a ways, on high ground, surrounded by yaupon and cedar and wax myrtle. Fine two-story building. I wouldn't think he'd build it by the warehouses at Haulover. And Sheep Island was where the fishermen lived."

"She must have loved this place," Bert said, longing in her voice. "Imagine getting paid to live here."

"It wasn't all roses, especially in those days." Hunter edged over so his thigh touched hers. "She had a time getting here, she did." He glanced at her mischievously. "Had some spring storms blow in, one after the other. She was almost drowned getting from Beaufort to Portsmouth. But that's how the news got around— about her having the gift." ∞

Chapter 13

JERUSHIA LEANED WEARILY ON THE RAIL. It seemed as if the world, or rather the sea, was against her reaching Portsmouth Island. First, the ship taking her to Hongry Town had been delayed two days in New Bedford waiting for an unusually late nor'easter to abate. When it did sail, heavy seas forced the passengers below into a pitching, semidark hold that was soon fetid with the stench of their misery. The sails close-hauled against heavy waves and a strong southerly wind, the sloop finally reached the shore of the Carolinas, only to have the wind change to an offshore flow. All day, they lay outside Hongry Town Harbor, until the captain, not wanting to be caught by the dark, braved the narrow channel on a beat with light sails.

Jerushia strained to see land. Would her passage to Portsmouth still be waiting?

When she finally disembarked, she discovered the island ferry had indeed sailed and would not return for seven days. Although Jerushia was grateful for this respite, seven days did seem overlong.

Captain Spriggs had made arrangements for Jerushia to stay in a room in the Taylor House and had left a letter of credit. He had also left a message with the landlady that Jerushia was to lay in supplies, as she would need to sew bedding, gowns, and aprons for herself. However, she would not need the cloth itself, as these were already on hand. He hoped they would meet with her approval. She was also to provide herself with such personal items as she would need. Another note, sent from Portsmouth just a few days earlier, asked her to add to her purchases a barrel of sugar, two gallons of varnish, and apples, if they were to be had.

The next morning, she set out to explore Hongry Town—or Beaufort, as the people now preferred it to be called. Named after its benefactor, Henry Somerset, duke of Beaufort, the town was not as large as New Bedford, having a mere sixty families.

Despite the town's size, Jerushia managed to find all the items Captain Spriggs had listed. After two days of shopping, she carefully laid out her purchases, examined each, and totaled her chits. Her instructions had been not to stint, yet at the same time, she was proud she'd been frugal in her purchases.

The provisions carefully stored, Jerushia grew impatient to end her journey. Mrs. Guthrie, her kind landlady, told her that travelers often hired a perriauger to take them to Portsmouth. Jerushia was quick to follow her advice.

The boat, which to Jerushia's dismay turned out to be little more than a large split-log canoe with a sail, left the following morning on the incoming tide. The inlet was at its calmest then. Jerushia was the only passenger.

They were not long out of Hongry Town when the captain, a sickly looking, meager man, began glancing anxiously to the southwest. Although the sky was fair and blue overhead, a dark line of squalls rolled toward them. The boat did not even possess a cabin. Grimly, Jerushia donned the oils the captain offered, thankful her trunks and purchases were carefully wrapped and tied to the deck chocks. The wind freshened. Dark thunderclouds spread out until they made an ominous angle in the sky, stretching wide overhead and coming to a point where they met the ocean. Already, the first cold drops pelted down.

The captain and the mate reefed the sail and checked their

lashings. There was nothing Jerushia could do save watch the squall come in. The thunderheads grew longer, the edges ragged, like combed cotton. A band of silver light still showed between the clouds and the water, but soon this, too, darkened and disappeared. The sea was building. Jerushia watched in horror as the black line advanced with fearful speed, the sea and sky disappearing, the ocean flattened by the heavy rain.

Wind and rain struck at the same moment, heeling the boat over until the sail was in the water. Had the captain not strung some lines for her to hold, Jerushia would have found herself in the sound, too. The boat rounded slightly before another gust knocked her back down. Water shipped in over the rail, flooding the scuppers.

Suddenly, Jerushia knew fear. Was she going to die here, in this insignificant backwater? Fate could not be that cruel, not when she was just beginning a new life. "Nay!" she raged at the storm. "You shall not have me!" Water up to her hips, she leaned against the high side, raising her face to the wind. "Enough! I have too much to do yet!"

As she shouted, there was a sharp crack, and the mast snapped off. Freed of the weight of the water-filled sail, the perriauger slowly righted herself.

Then, almost as quickly as it was upon them, the squall passed, leaving in its wake a cold drizzle and a white-capped sea.

The men were silent. They would not gaze directly upon Jerushia as they quickly set to bailing the boat. Abashed because she had cried out so strongly in her terror, Jerushia huddled on the seat, saying nothing. It wasn't until the mate shipped the oars and the captain turned the boat in the direction of the nearest land that she asked, "We return to Hongry Town?"

"We canna, me lady," the captain protested in a trembling voice. "We must make repairs, unless ye can . . ." He pointed at the broken mast.

Jerushia's brows lifted. "Surely, you don't expect me to cut you a new mast."

The captain backed away, practically falling over the seat. "No, me lady, indeed not. Forgive me. Ye have done enough for us this day."

Puzzled, Jerushia watched. Sailors were an ignorant, superstitious lot, as she well knew from her shipyard upbringing. She'd feared they would blame the storm on her because she was a woman, but instead they appeared to be afraid of her. It was nothing more than a fortuitous coincidence that the storm had ended when she called out, but the captain obviously believed otherwise. For a moment, Jerushia thought to disillusion him, then sat back. She was alone and unprotected with two rough seamen. It was to her advantage to let them believe she possessed unusual powers.

It was not long before she had an opportunity to bolster her new status. The captain found a sheltered bay in which to anchor. As the men waded to shore in search of wood to mend the mast, a plague of flying pests rose about them. The sailors cursed vociferously, swatting at the pests and dabbing themselves with sandy mud. In dire need to relieve herself, Jerushia joined them ashore. Pests had never bothered her as much as they did her sister or brothers. Now, except for a few, they left her alone, but the two men were in misery. Already, they had started a smudge fire.

As they searched the woods for a suitable mast tree, Jerushia surveyed the beach and marsh. Her mother had been adept in the use of herbs. Together, they had explored many a New England rocky cove in search of her mother's favorite plants. Wax myrtles grew like weeds here. Feeling pity for the men, whose curses echoed from the forest, Jerushia peeled some bark from a bush and set it to simmer in seawater over the smudge fire. She also cut switches from the fragrant plant and crushed some of the leaves to rub over her hands and face. A flick of a myrtle branch across an arm or leg was not only more effective than a hand in swatting a fly, but the aromatic oil from the leaves further discouraged the pests.

When the men returned, sweaty and bitten, she offered them her infusion of bayberries, an astringent and repellent. The mate, a short, fair-skinned fellow whose bites were already swollen like boils over his arms and neck, accepted first. The captain was more hesitant, but upon observing the mate's immediate relief, he followed suit.

After that, although they still treated her with great respect, they no longer appeared as fearful. Only when the mast was repaired did they begin to exchange information. The captain, whose name was Will Green, told Jerushia about Portsmouth. He was native to Crane Island and had sailed with the privateer Stede Bonnet as a lad. In turn, Jerushia shyly confessed to having been born on the *Celestial Harp* on her way to the promised land that was the New World.

The captain's eyes opened wide. "So that be why ye can command the wind and waves. Ye be a sea-born woman."

"Oh, my," was all Jerushia could say. She sat in a rough cart next to Captain Spriggs, gazing at the house that was to be her home—forever, she hoped.

A wide creek bisected the flat meadow. To one side was a small dock with a handsome white boat—no log canoe this, but a spry little sloop. Behind the dock was a raised grove of red cedars, yaupons, and myrtles. In the center, overlooking the creek and the inlet beyond, stood an imposing two-story home. The walls were golden heart-of-pine, the roof thick cedar shingles. The double porch was supported by four posts. To the rear, Jerushia glimpsed a summer kitchen and the necessary house. A roofed brick walk connected the latter to the main dwelling. Too overwhelmed to remember her manners, Jerushia raised her brows and pointed. "Is that . . .? It cannot be."

Captain Spriggs stroked his gray beard rather smugly. "You will find, my dear, this house is as well equipped as any in New Bedford. Neither you nor any guest of Spriggs Luck will ever have to set foot on the ground to attend to your needs."

The interior of the house was even more beautiful than the outside. Captain Spriggs stood proudly, one hand tucked in his jacket, as he watched Jerushia dash from room to room giving little shouts of joy. The floors were juniper planks polished to glowing, the walls whitewashed bead-board. Four rooms were on the main floor and four bedrooms on the second. The parlor contained the most magnificent fireplace Jerushia had ever seen outside the homes of the rich. It was tall and deep enough for a child to stand upright inside and even had a great black cooking hook.

In front of the fireplace, set into the ruddy juniper floor, was a magnificent marble slab. It ran the full breadth of the fireplace and was some four feet wide. Jerushia turned impudently to Spriggs, who stood watching her, his linen shirt open at the throat, showing several ornate gold chains and his emerald cross. "Pray, sir, with a hearthstone of these proportions, you must plan to roast a boar in this fireplace."

To her surprise, instead of laughing at her sally, Captain Spriggs growled fiercely, "I'll thank ye not to make light of me burial place."

Jerushia fell back, her hand on her heart. "Your burial place? Why, how?" Frantically, she collected herself. "Please forgive me, godfather. I did not understand. I have never been in so fine a house as this."

Mollified, Captain Spriggs stood on the hearthstone, one stockinged leg turned smartly, as fashion dictated, hand on hip. "I had not thought, when I began this house, that it would turn out so well." He wheeled about, inspecting the room—the windows with their panels of glass and brass fittings, the mirror that hung over his head, the painting of a brace of game birds, the Turkish rugs on the floor. "I will never leave this house, not during my life nor"—he paused—"after my death."

"But . . ." Jerushia quelled her protest even as angry thoughts sprang to her mind. He might not leave, but she would, she vowed silently, if the alternative was living with a corpse.

He must have seen some of this in her face, for he took her by the hand and sat her on a chair that faced the fireplace. "My dear, I had not thought to bring this up today, and I did not want to distress you." He strode over to the fireplace and gazed out the window to the bay. "I have chosen to live by the sea because this is where I am the most comfortable, but there are penalties. The water is a dangerous companion. Many times, I have seen storms wash graves out to sea. I do not wish this to happen to me." He placed one hand on the mahogany mantel, his bald, bewigged head bowed toward the marble hearth. "I chose this spot with great care. The house sits on high ground guarded from the sea by giant dunes. Under this slab is a brick vault that took four men to lay. 'Tis a great storm indeed that will ever penetrate the vault, much less float this grave away. Upon my death, I wish to be buried here." He fixed Jerushia with his strange gold eyes. "I will deed the house to you, but only on condition you give me your solemn promise you will abide with my desires."

Even as Jerushia nodded, she thought wildly, What does it matter? She could always close off the parlor and live in the rest of the house.

"Swear it before God," Captain Spriggs insisted.

When Jerushia had sworn to his satisfaction, he eased, almost smiling. "I promise you," he said as he led her to the second story, "that you will never know I'm there. After I am placed inside, the marble slab is to be mortared in place. I assure you, not even a worm could escape, or enter. There will be no putrefaction, nor will my body attract pests." He turned to her, his next words sending chills up her spine. "Quite the contrary. There I will remain, ensuring forever that no one disturb my resting place." ⌒

Chapter 14

BERT'S GAZE HAD BEEN FIXED on the approaching ferry for the last couple of minutes. Now, Hunter saw it and paused.

"Tell me quick, Hunter. What happened next?"

His eyes crinkled up at her interest, dark brows glistening in the light. "I understand that, for the next ten years, they had an ideal life. Captain Spriggs treated Jerushia like she was his daughter, not his housekeeper. He had a cook, a black man who sailed with him in the old days. And a maid came from the village every day. Jerushia planted a fig orchard behind the house, and in the middle of the orchard, Spriggs let her build a pergola. Summer days, she could laze there surrounded by blossoms, sewing or making lace."

"Making lace or sewing? That's not exactly lazing." Bert hated the needle. "What else?" Somehow, she knew there had to be more.

"You sure you haven't heard this before?" He gave that heart-tugging, lopsided smile he had. "Seems she did more than just make lace out there. Folks said all kinds of birds lived around that pergola. Said they'd sit on her hand and sing and follow her around the island. Like I told you, sea-born women have a way with animals. You ever noticed?"

"Come on. You know as well as I do that anyone can befriend a wild animal with food and patience. Causes a bunch of problems for the poor animals—and for you guys."

Hunter nodded. "You got that right. But there were other things. Jerushia's the one that brought over those nutria you're so fond of."

Bert lifted a menacing hand.

He ducked, grinning. "Seems there was a rumor, not true, that nutria got rid of rats, and she didn't cotton to all the rats around here. Got after the sea captains to bring her some nutria from down in South America. People said she kept them in cages and bred them before she let them go, and that every year, they'd come back to Spriggs Luck to breed. There's some that say the nutria came back when they needed doctoring, too."

"Ugh, I can just picture them following her around like the Pied Piper."

"You ever seen one?" Hunter asked. "Nutria don't look like rats. Play in the water like otters. They got shiny brown fur with long guard hairs, a pretty face with a white muzzle. More like a cross between a squirrel and a grinning groundhog."

Bert laughed. "This I have to see."

"She had a way with horses, too. Spriggs bought her a pair of matched Arabians, black ones. It must have taken some doing to bring them over here, if you figure how many times they had to change ships and all that. Had a buggy brought over, too, just for her. She'd ride that shiny black buggy all over the island, dressed in her black mourning clothes, red hair streaming out behind."

Bert ran a hand down Hunter's black beard, which showed traces of red. "Is that where you get your red from?"

"That's not red. I'll show you red when you meet my brothers. I'm what they call black Irish. There's one in each generation of O'Hagans—most likely the result of some slave or Indian blood, not the Spanish Armada, like my mother'd have you believe."

The South was certainly changing if he could so casually refer to a black ancestor. Bert smiled, standing up. She'd seen Justin's truck pull up to the ranger cabin. Rudy was loading in some gear. "Did they live happily ever after?"

"Not exactly." Hunter began putting his pack together. "Will Green, the captain of the perriauger, spread the news Jerushia was knowledgeable with herbs. Soon, folks—especially women—were looking to her when they were ailing or birthing. I heard tell Jerushia sent for books and taught herself doctoring, particularly on injuries. That was during the War of Independence, when she used Spriggs Luck as a hospital for the islanders. But I'm getting ahead of my story."

Jerushia had used her house as a hospital? Bert grabbed his arm. "Hunter, I just had a crazy thought. They built the new hospital by the old hospital. You don't suppose the old hospital was built where the Spriggs or O'Hagan house, or hospital, once was?" Bert grinned at her mixed-up sentence. "If you understand what I'm trying to say."

As always, Hunter paused to carefully consider. Sometimes, Bert thought, he was as slow and meticulous as an engineer.

"Don't know about that," he said. "She died in 1810, when she was ninety, and the house was left all boarded up. That's when she came back the first time."

"Came back? You mean haunted?" She'd expected Spriggs to be the ghost.

"It was during the War of 1812. Seems an English foraging party tried to loot the house. The story is they were set on by a woman dressed in black with a mane of whirling red hair. Took an oar to them. No English came near the place after that. Then, after the war, the place was sold. According to legend, if the owners kept the house in good order, there was no trouble. But if they let it run down, Jerushia would drive them away." Hunter looked up at her, his eyes a deep, ocean color. "From what I heard, the haunts went on till the storm of 1899, the San Ciriaco. That's when the house was washed away. A lot of places were washed away then." He made a wide, encompassing gesture.

"So the dates don't fit." Bert ticked them off on her fingers.

"The hospital was built fifty years earlier, in 1846, near what they said was a crude hospital built twenty years before that. According to you, the house was still standing then." She sank down next to him. For a moment, she'd thought she had discovered the location of Spriggs Luck. "Seems like everything is connected to the old hospital—the fire, Luna Mae, the digging. Like someone's looking for something."

"Can't imagine what. The sailors that went to the hospital were a poor lot. They were the homeless of those days."

She leaned against Hunter. "I just thought that maybe someone was trying to dig up Spriggs's grave."

"I don't reckon Spriggs would take kindly to that. I'm certain he'd come a-haunting if someone messed around his burial site."

To Bert's dismay, the ferry was turning into the channel. "What happened to Spriggs? I'm sorry I interrupted you."

Again, Hunter took his time collecting his thoughts. "Like I said, Jerushia took to doctoring the folks on Portsmouth. One evening, she was coming back from the village about sundown. As she turned into the lane on her buggy, the horses shied up. Took all the strength she had to calm them. Then she saw what frightened them. Seems the stable stood about fifty feet from the house, right next to the creek. And there, in the middle of the stable yard, was Captain Spriggs, face down, one of those Scottish knives—a dirk—sticking out of his back. He was dead." Hunter stood up, grinning fiendishly. "Guess it's time to say good-bye."

"Don't you dare." Bert didn't care that Justin had just pulled up to the landing, nor that the ferry was beginning to back in. "I won't let you leave now." She grabbed his hand.

He pulled her to her feet, turning around to the boat. "To be truthful, there's not much more to tell. There were no footprints about in the sand. Somebody erased them with a fig tree branch. The only thing left," he said, pausing for effect, "was a sheet of paper with a circle and a dot in the middle." Now, the ferry was in, the gate down. Hunter picked up his backpack. "That circle with a dot in the center was the pirate sign of revenge. That's all they ever found out."

Rudy came up and clapped Bert on the shoulder as he prepared to board. "Bye, Miss Bert. Don't you leave here until he comes back. You both need to be careful when you get to the village. Don't go out at night, on no account. You understand? You let this man here check out any disturbances." Rudy tapped Hunter's shoulder, then turned to Justin. "You keep a good eye on them pilings. Make sure no one moves them."

"Pilings?" Hunter asked.

Bert watched them, her mind still on Spriggs. Such a surprise ending, to be murdered by his own pirates. She had a million questions for Hunter, but Rudy was launching into an explanation of his labors. "While you and this lady was gabbing, we were working. Me and Justin set up a barricade, there by the dunes."

"Ain't no one taking a vehicle up the beach," Justin added. "It was all Rudy and me could do to pile them up."

Considering the size of both men, that was no idle boast, Bert thought.

Hunter frowned. But before he could say anything, Rudy spoke up. "Relax. We left your truck and the ATV on the other side."

Bert watched the ferry leave, feeling smaller and more lonely by the second.

Justin approached. "You is welcome to wait in my place." He pointed at a two-story camp. "I'm fixing to work on the roof, seeing we don't got no visitors coming over today."

Bert eyed his cabin dubiously. She really didn't want to spend the next four hours sitting around inside. "How are you going to stop them?" she asked.

"They got small-craft advisories out. Use that as an excuse. Hunter's fixing to close down the ferry, 'cept for park personnel."

"What's the weather forecast?" All she and Hunter had caught that morning was a radio quickie. She began carrying empty garbage cans to where Justin was loading them back on his truck.

He smiled his thanks. "They is calling for a hurricane to come up the coast. Give it a name already: Carlos."

Bert's eyes opened wide. "No! A hurricane watch?"

He shook his head. "They never said that. Carlos is headed out to sea, by Barbados."

"So it won't bother us here?" That's all they needed right now—first a death and now a hurricane.

Justin grinned. "Along with this front, it'll bring some high water and swells. Stir up the ocean some and wash a mess of shells up the beach for you."

Hunter had apparently been talking. Bert smiled back. "You know, it's almost low tide. I was thinking maybe I could do some clamming while I wait."

"You is welcome to my clam rake." Justin reached over the truck well and pulled it out from behind the garbage cans. He handed it to Bert. "I guess you ain't never used one like this before."

It was a wicked-looking weapon, make of stainless-steel knife blades welded to a crossbar like a garden rake. It was also the lightest, best clam rake Bert had ever used. But as the tide went out, she found she didn't even need the rake. The water was so still and clear she could actually see the tiny slits made by the clams where they barely breached the underwater sandy surface, feeding on the ebbing tide as they'd done for time immemorial.

As Bert waded along "signing" clams, as they called it Down East, she wondered again where Jerushia's house was located. It would be so much fun if she and Hunter could locate the ruins. Two hundred years was a long time, but surely the vault Hunter described would still be there. It was probably buried ten feet under a dune, or it could be ten feet under the ocean, covered by sand and water. If the park did send her back to the mainland, maybe she could do some research in the courthouse. She might find an old deed with enough description to locate the house.

Bert's mind skipped to another piece of the puzzle. What had Spriggs done to get himself murdered by vengeful pirates? He couldn't have double-crossed his mentor, Captain Ned Low, because he'd been living here quite openly. He'd never even changed his name from his pirating days, as had so many others. Why else would they kill him? And who were they? Bert had read enough to know the pirates had an organization that dispensed a sort of

workmen's compensation or retirement plan. Each ship put a por-
tion of its booty into a common fund, to be handed out if a pirate
was put out of business by injuries or old age. Spriggs had quit the
sea after a run-in with the Royal Navy. According to Hunter, no
one knew where he'd gone right after that. Had he run off with
the common fund and used it to finance his shipyards?

Bert shook her head. The tide was turning, and the wind was
picking up. She began working her way back toward the dock,
the net bag of clams heavy on her hip. Neither theory sat well
with her. Spriggs had lived too openly, in a seaport right across
the inlet from Ocracoke, an island settled at that time by pilots
and pirates. Surely, that wasn't something a wanted man would
do. His murder must have been revenge for some kind of private
quarrel, probably over a woman.

She was back at the landing now. Well, between these clams
and the ones Donny had given her, she had a nice supper—breakfast, too. She hoped Hunter liked steamed clams. Actually, she
didn't plan to steam them as much as to simmer them open in
garlic, hot peppers, and olive oil, her favorite recipe.

After packing the clams in the cooler she kept strapped to
the ATV, Bert wandered over to the beach. The wind was still
coming from the northeast, the surface of the ocean showing white,
the sky a washed gray. Finding a sheltering dune, Bert spread out
her jacket. As long as she wasn't in the wind, it was warm. Maybe
she could catch a little nap before Hunter came back. She was
dying to hear more details on Spriggs's murder.

She dozed, thinking about Spriggs. Why would a revenge killer,
a pirate passing through on a ship, bother sweeping away footprints in the sand? That seemed the act of a person who might be
identified by his footprints. Who would leave distinctive marks?
A man with one leg: Long John Silver, of course! She giggled at
herself. Then, suddenly, she knew the answer—and it wasn't funny,
not funny at all. Bert raised her head, staring blindly at the dune.
If the footprints were not of a man, but rather a woman . . .

She pounded the sand with a closed fist. Who had the most
to gain by Spriggs's death? Who did the police always look at first

when someone was killed? The immediate family—in this case, Jerushia herself.

"Beat up on the sand, why don't you?" A woman's giggle came from behind.

Bert jerked upright. Donny and a woman stood right behind her. Then she recognized the bleached hair and full figure—Lettie. Before she could say a word, Donny was down on the sand, his arm around her shoulder, giving her a big hug.

Her fear dissolved. No matter what Hunter said, she couldn't believe this good-natured, simple soul was a thief, much less a killer. "What on earth are you doing here?" she asked. "Hunter and Rudy have been looking for you."

"Have they now?" Donny grinned, his arm still about her. "Reckon they been looking in the wrong places. I ain't stuck in the back of no Shelby car, not hardly."

Bert struggled not to let her surprise show. How had they found out so soon?

Lettie guffawed. If anything, she had on less clothes than the other day. She wore the same cutoffs, or a close relative, but today she had on a silky bra top designed for someone much younger and less endowed than she.

Bert tore her eyes from the fold of breast caught under the cup. "Does Justin know you're here?"

"What's that got to do with anything?" Lettie plunked herself down on the other side of Bert. Her face was pink and shiny, and Bert could smell the fresh sweat. "We heard you was alone, so we come over to keep you company." She slapped Bert's thigh, laughing uproariously.

"You saw Hunter?"

"Bless you, gal, no. We was listening to Rudy and Hunter on the radio when they was talking to Crissie. So I said to Donny here, 'Let's go over and keep that gal company for a while.' " She leaned over, peering into Bert's face. "You don't mind, do you?"

Bert leaned back, trying to regain her space. "No, I'm just surprised. I know Hunter wanted to talk to you," she told Donny.

Donny sighed, dropping his arm from Bert. "I didn't mean to

make no trouble for him with the superintendent. Hunter's a good man. Knowed my father. Ain't his fault this place got him spooked."

"What do you mean?"

"Ask him why he never set foot in the village before Ben Willis done had his accident."

"Don't you pay him no mind." Lettie patted Bert's knee. "Ain't got nothing to do with ghosts. Hunter just don't take to all the momicking he gets about his relation."

They must be talking about Jerushia. Bert resisted the temptation to gossip about Hunter. Feeling noble, she changed the subject to the first thing that came into her head. "Weren't you supposed to meet Hunter on Wednesday night, Donny?"

Suddenly, Donny's face lost its geniality. His eyes changed to blue marbles; his mouth straightened into a stiff line. Again, Bert felt a stab of fear. How far would he go to protect his property?

"You Northerners think you know it all, don't you? Think you is better than us. Well, you ain't," Donny spit. "Now, you listen to me, missy. I weren't at Portsmouth Wednesday night." He turned to Lettie. "Tell her. She bear me out. Tell her."

Lettie straightened up and took a deep breath. "Donny stayed the night at my place, on Wednesday. He come over in his boat about, ah, eight." She darted a glance at Donny, who nodded. Encouraged, Lettie continued, this time a little more naturally. "I was over to the diner. That's our busy time. But I seen his boat. I seen him, too. He didn't go nowhere that night. Stayed with me, he did. Last night, too. We is cousins, you know." She leaned closer, jabbing Bert's ribs with an elbow. "I been married five times. I like my fun, if you take my meaning, but I don't mess around with no relatives." She licked her lips slowly and wiped the excess saliva off with a finger, obviously pleased with her performance.

And a performance it had been. So Hunter and Jimmy were right. Donny had been present the night Luna Mae died. And he was being very defensive about it. Bert stared at Lettie, who was fumbling in her pack. "No thanks." Bert refused the proffered Budweiser absently. Would Lettie still be willing to alibi her cousin if she thought . . . ? Bert took a deep breath and plunged in. "You sure he was there by eight? Because the police are going to want to know."

"You heard me, didn't you, girlfriend?"

She'd never get used to women calling each other that. Bert persisted. "Did you see Donny, or did someone tell you they saw his boat? You were probably real busy about that time." Bert leaned close and said softly, "They can put you in jail for perjury, you know. Even if it was an honest—"

"The park don't put you in jail," Donny cut in. "They just takes away your property and your livelihood."

"The park doesn't mess around with killings either. That's police business," Bert snapped back. She was tired of his constant slurs.

"Killings?" Lettie gave a little yelp. "You didn't say nothing about that, Donny."

"They saying Luna Mae were kilt?" Donny's blue eyes came together in an ugly squint. "How they tell that? I heard her heart give out." He shook his head, turning to Lettie. "Hunter'll be after me for sure. It ain't worth that, no ways."

Oh, damn. Too late, Bert remembered Rudy's plea for confidentiality. "I didn't say that. I'm just guessing. I don't know any more than you do," she babbled, but the damage was done.

Donny's face closed down. He jumped up, tugging at Lettie. "Time we get off."

"Damn," Bert cussed again under her breath as she gathered her pack.

She hadn't meant to blab, but just to stop Lettie from making a monstrous problem for herself. Even now, she heard the woman protesting to Donny: "I ain't fixing to get messed up in no court trial. Better believe I ain't. I knows I owes you one for taking him over, but . . ."

Taking him over? Bert tried to hear more, but their voices trailed off, lost in the echo of the surf. It wasn't until she was back at the pier waiting for the ferry that she remembered Donny's exclamation: "It ain't worth that, no ways." ∽

Chapter 15

THE SEAS WERE ROUGH. Bert could see the ferry pitching as it turned into the narrow channel. Hunter, the only passenger, was off before it even tied up. The boat stayed just long enough to unload ice and supplies for Justin. Then, engines still running, it headed back out to the sound.

"We did bring the cooler, right?" Hunter carried a plastic bag of groceries, another of ice.

"On the bike."

As they walked back to the ranger camp, Bert told Hunter about Donny's visit. "I'm sorry I let it slip about Luna Mae," she said, still annoyed at herself for her indiscretion. Telling Hunter didn't make it any better. "I just wanted to warn Lettie before—"

"I knew it was a mistake leaving you here."

Bert grabbed his arm. "It's not that big a deal, is it? They just came over to keep me company."

"You don't understand." Hunter shook off her hand. "It's everything put together. They been saying the hurricane might turn this way."

"I heard that. You know the media is going to milk Carlos for all it's worth. Look, there's no one here except us," she said. "Donny should be at Atlantic by now. He was taking Lettie back."

"I didn't give you Rudy's news yet. Source has a girlfriend." He paused. "Lettie!"

Bert did a double take, head jerking, mouth open—all the classic signs of surprise. "Lettie?" she repeated stupidly.

Hunter's eyes lightened at her reaction. "Fooled me, all right."

"How do you know? How did Rudy find out?" Bert's head was still reeling. Lettie and Olin?

It seemed forever before he answered. "Anne Source had a sister. Rudy met her after the accident, so he called her this afternoon while I was at the meeting. Gave him an earful, she did. Seems that two weeks ago, Olin had Lettie up to the house, and the sister caught them there."

"Maybe he was giving her some of Anne's things." Blowzy, overripe Lettie and the persnickety Olin? Hard to believe.

"That's not what the sister told Rudy. Said the car was there all night, and some other nights, too. Seems the sister never approved of Olin Source. Said he didn't come courting Miss Anne until after their father died and left them some property. Seems he never held a regular teaching job either, just substituted when the spirit took him."

Bert tried to imagine Lettie and Olin together. At first, it didn't fit, not until she visualized Olin in high school—gawky, bookish, a defensive show-off. He'd probably never been popular with the girls, and a woman like . . . She nodded slowly. "Lettie's so easygoing, so earthy. I'll bet she taught him a couple of things."

"That woman's worn out better men than him."

At least she had him making jokes. "Wish I was that uninhibited. She's definitely sexy."

"Can't lay a button to someone I know." Now, Hunter's eyes were warm, caressing her. "Still, it does make for complications."

"What do you mean?"

"Lettie's got a boat. She knows her way around the sound as well as I do, and the dark doesn't faze her any."

It took Bert a minute to catch on. "Oh, you mean she could

have been in the village Wednesday night. But why would she want to hurt Luna Mae?" Even as Hunter started to open his mouth, Bert knew. "You're thinking Anne Source's accident might not have been an accident."

Hunter nodded. "Luna Mae was always creeping up on a man before he noticed. Could be she saw something." He climbed into the truck. "It's time we got started. Hope you don't mind checking out Donny's camp on our way back."

Bert reached for the truck door, but he shook his head, pointing at the four-wheeler. "We better bring up the ATV. Need to keep at least one in the village."

That was right. She'd forgotten that she and Hunter had ridden her four-wheeler this morning, and that Jimmy had brought Luna Mae down on his bike, which left none at Portsmouth. What a nuisance! She'd been looking forward to telling Hunter her theory about Jerushia on the way up.

Bert followed the white pickup out to the beach. It was a nasty ride, the wind in her face, the high tide forcing her up to the soft sand. By the time they reached the flats, Bert's arms ached from holding steady in the ruts. She was dismayed to find the water in the flats as high as she'd seen it, a current clearly visible. There were even small whitecaps.

Hunter stopped and slid out. "You take the truck. I'll bring the ATV."

Bert opened her mouth to protest, but one look at his face stopped her. She'd rather be in the truck anyhow.

In the driver's seat, she looked at the controls for the first time. Standard shift. It had been a long time. At least the gears were clearly marked on the knob. Tentatively, she depressed the clutch and brake, then shifted into first. No problem. She went through the rest of the gears, turned on the engine, and put it into first again. Her crossing was uneventful. Hunter wasn't doing as well. He seemed to be weaving around, and his trousers were dark with water. She pulled up on the other side and got out just as he arrived.

"Best if we take the ATV to Evergreen, unless you want to

wait here." Before Bert could answer, Hunter shook his head. "No, that won't work. I don't want you alone. Can't tell who might be about."

"You think someone might be in the village?" Bert asked as she scrambled onto the wet passenger cushion.

Hunter ignored her question. Instead, he pointed at the flats. "Don't try to cross if the water gets any higher than that. You saw me floating, didn't you?"

It took them half an hour to get to Evergreen Slew, down a winding, overgrown path with deep potholes and long expanses of mud from last night's deluge. Donny's cabin turned out to be similar to many of the cottages at Portsmouth—an oblong box on pilings with an open porch in front. It was covered with brown asbestos shingles, many of them torn. And the trim had not been painted for years. The place was surrounded by junk—old barrels, tires, scraps of wood, rusty crab pots, broken foam buoys, tangled nets, bottles, cans, and other trash—but the location was lovely. The cabin sat right in the center of a clearing overlooking a creek lined by trees. Beyond the creek was Pamlico Sound.

"Oh, neat!" Bert exclaimed.

Hunter pulled up between a couple of rainwater barrels and two sheds, one obviously an outhouse. He yelled and rapped on the closed doors. Then he walked around the cabin toward a dock on the creek. Bert followed. No boats were tied to the dock. She breathed a sigh of relief. At least there would be no confrontation tonight.

"You didn't see him crossing when you came over?" Bert asked. Donny had left about the time the ferry put out from Atlantic.

"Nope. And he wasn't at Atlantic. Been trying to find him all day."

Hunter turned on his radio. Bert listened as he spoke to Rudy, careful to mention no names on the air. "No one here. Ain't been anyone around since the rain last night, that's for sure." Rudy came back with something unintelligible to Bert, but Hunter nodded gravely. "You need to talk to both of them. You leave word at the marina? Copy. Two forty-one clear."

Dropping the radio into his belt, Hunter headed back to the ATV. "Rudy's putting out the word to bring them both in," he told her with a satisfied smirk.

Bert ran to keep up with him. "I don't think Donny's any saint, and I'm sure he's taking illegal game and fish, but I honestly don't think he killed Luna Mae."

"He's got Lettie lying for him. That tells me plenty. Could be they're in this together."

"Then why would he say, 'It ain't worth that,' when he found out Luna Mae might have been killed?" Bert climbed back on the ATV. "Did Donny do something to you? I mean, you seem to have a thing against him."

"I'm telling you, that Donny's no good." Hunter twisted around so he was facing her. "Been in trouble since he was a little tyke. Stole cigarettes from the community store, played hooky from school, was sent up for burglary when he was eighteen. Been married a couple of times. Got two little boys, up for nonsupport. Says he can't pay on account of he can't get a job. Can't keep one is more like it. Only works when he needs cash for booze and gas." He gave her a lopsided half-smile. "Still, like you said, that doesn't make him a murderer."

Even as he agreed with her, Bert had a change of heart. A lack of responsibility often went hand in hand with difficulty distinguishing right from wrong. "Didn't he tell the supervisor he had proof of someone taking things? What if he had a picture of Luna Mae with the silver? Or maybe he was trying to get a picture of her. They could have struggled over the camera, and he killed her by accident. Maybe he didn't realize he'd killed her, and that's why he was so scared."

Hunter looked out toward the sound. "This whole mess is getting as tangled as a turtle in a pound net. First, we got no killers. Now, we got us too many killers." He gunned the motor and kicked the bike into gear, effectively putting an end to any more theorizing.

Two hours later, after dining on salad, spicy clams, and French bread, Hunter and Bert took their coffee to the deck of the lifesaving station. The hot gusts of wind coming from the ocean felt cool in the high humidity.

Once they were settled, Bert dove into her theories about Spriggs's death. "Don't you see?" she concluded. "It all makes sense. Jerushia killed Spriggs and spent the rest of her life trying to atone for it."

"Could be." Hunter sat propped against the station's brick cistern. "But why? She had no call to kill him." He stared at the dark clouds that scudded across the sky. "Spriggs gave her everything she wanted. And from all accounts, she wasn't a greedy woman."

"Yeah, but most crimes are committed by a family member. And it would explain why Spriggs's ghost is still around."

Hunter grinned. "I hear you. You trying to tell me that Spriggs's ghost is responsible for everything that's happening now?"

He'd changed into shorts and a worn T-shirt that showed every muscle in his upper body. Bert covertly admired his build— slim, no sign of a paunch.

"First, you have to believe in ghosts. Which reminds me, why haven't you been in the village until now? It wouldn't be because of a family spirit, would it?" Dinner had renewed her energy, and Bert was feeling good with the world.

Hunter guffawed. "People from Harkers got better things to do than get eat up by the meanest mosquitoes on the East Coast. Even the park leaves this village alone." Swinging away, he dangled his legs off the side of the deck. "It's not part of my job. Portsmouth is the furthest north point of the park. On account of the distance, it's managed separate from the rest of Cape Lookout." He paused, then added, "To tell the truth, I probably would never have come to this place if Ben Willis didn't get hurt. Nothing to do with ghosts."

Bert remembered what Lettie had said. "I'm sorry. Have I been embarrassing you?"

He shook his head. "Reckon I was a pretty stupid kid. I've been enjoying my time here, notoriety notwithstanding." He lifted a brow. "Might have something to do with the present company."

Bert flushed, looking away.

"To get back to my relation," Hunter continued, "why would Jerushia erase her footprints? I'd expect to find her footprints around the stable."

Bert had puzzled this out earlier. "Right, but only hers and Spriggs's. It's not what footprints would have been there, it's what wouldn't have been. There would have been no strange footprints belonging to an outsider if she killed him. That's why she had to wipe the area clean, to make it look as if a pirate did it."

He chuckled. "Got me on that one, you did."

Bert found herself liking him even more for the admission. At least he wasn't macho about being outsmarted.

"But I don't see what all this has to do with what's happening now," he said.

"Frankly, I'm not sure it does have any connection. I just feel that if we could find the house and the grave, it would help." Bert hesitated, staring across the inlet. "That cold fog the Sources noticed . . . Ghost stories always have cold as a manifestation—that and perfume, or music."

"You think it's Spriggs protecting his tomb? Next thing, you'll be telling me he played the organ."

"No, I still feel that was man making like ghost. But the other things—the nutria calling, the mosquitoes, the cold fog by the creek . . . I don't want to sound crazy, but don't you think there's something strange about all those jellyfish?"

"My family's made their living off the sea for three hundred years now. When Pa gets going, he tells stories a lot stranger than what you're talking, mostly about the O'Hagan men getting out of tight spots. You'd almost think we had nine lives." Hunter frowned, sliding off the deck onto the mowed grass. "Enough of that. I take it you're saying Jerushia's house was somewhere about the hospital." Hunter picked up the coffee mugs. "What say we take a look at the creek before it gets any darker? Yesterday, I was searching for tracks and all, not ruins."

They stopped at the cabin long enough to put on waders and arm themselves with bug spray. Hunter took along a shovel.

As they strolled down the path to the marsh, he said, "Hard to believe this was a waterway once. Used to bring the sick sailors in rowboats right from the ships, so they didn't contaminate the village." They reached the ruins of the old shed. Hunter backed up a little, looking for the spot where they'd left the path and found the site of Luna Mae's death. "This look like the place to you?"

Bert shrugged. Even though she and Hunter had searched the marsh yesterday, it looked pristine now—no trampled grass, no footprints. "I'm not sure. It all looks the same."

"Isn't, though. See that hummock over yonder? That's the beginning of high ground, over by the prickly ash. Fuel storage area is on the other side of those myrtles. You'll get used to it."

They were both knee deep in the marsh by the ditch, their feet protected by the waders. Bert shook her head. "If it's in here, we'll never see it."

"Let your feet do the looking," Hunter suggested. "They used ballast stones in those days for the foundations. Should still be some around—if the house was here, that is."

It was not pleasant work. They were disturbing the insects— particularly the mosquitoes, which rose in small clouds at every footstep, buzzing angrily around Bert's eyes and nose. She squirted on more bug spray, wishing she'd worn the mosquito mask. To distract herself, she continued theorizing. "If Olin had a thing for Lettie, that would give him a motive to get rid of Anne, wouldn't it? You don't suppose Anne had a bad heart or something, and he was deliberately doing all those things to scare—"

"She had high blood pressure, all right. It was on the papers they filled out."

"Really? What about that fire? Do you think he set it?"

Hunter frowned. "Now, if I ever saw a man in shock, that was Olin Source after the accident." He hesitated, then added, "If he was resenting his wife for keeping him from Lettie, I could see him being mean or scaring her, but I can't bring myself to believe he'd set the woman on fire."

Bert tended to agree with him. "I guess we'll never know."

She squashed a mosquito sucking on her arm. "But what about everything that's been going on since she died?"

Hunter thought a moment. "If Source was trying to scare Anne into a heart attack, could be he was afraid people would catch on if all the manifestations stopped with her death. Maybe she wrote about the hauntings in that log he was looking for."

"You think he's the one that played the organ the other night?" Bert kicked at the reeds. Something jumped away. "There's no snakes in here, are there?"

"Could be," he drawled. "Just keep your hands high." He shuffled toward her. "I don't know how Source would have gotten over to play the organ. Doesn't have a boat, that I know of."

"But Lettie does. So does Jimmy." Bert climbed out of the ditch.

"I've been wanting to tell you about that man since I got back. Can't believe it went clear out of my mind." He shook his head. "Must be getting old."

"You found out something about Jimmy?"

"You'll never believe . . ." Hunter looked around in disgust. "There's nothing in here, that's for sure. What say we give it a try over yonder?"

"Come on, Hunter, tell me."

"Give me a hand, will you? Be dark pretty soon."

Bert yanked him up, and they moved to the new spot.

"Seems Mister Range wasn't exactly truthful in his application," Hunter said quietly.

"Oh?" Bert tramped harder than necessary. This was a waste of time. There were no ballast stones in here. The only stones anywhere around were . . .

"Range give up dentistry twenty years ago," Hunter was saying.

Bert barely heard him. "Hunter, the old shed. There's all sorts of stones there. Are those ballast stones?"

Hunter swung around, his brows up, eyes wide. "Well, I'll be double screwed."

Without another word, they plowed their way back to the path. Bert tried to stomp off some of the mud clinging to her boots.

Hunter was already at the ruins, crouching, lifting one of the fire-blackened stones from the ground. He stood up as she approached. "You know, I get so used to seeing these everyplace that I didn't connect. You got a good head there, gal."

"Can we dig now?"

"Need to fetch some things first." He glanced at the sky, then at her. "You understand, if we find anything, that's where we stop. It'll be up to the park to decide how they want to excavate, and when."

Back at the lifesaving station, Hunter went directly to the boathouse and took some long poles out of the closet. They had three prongs, like Neptune's fork. "Flounder gigs, great to probe with. That's what they all use, Luna Mae and them, along with metal detectors. Didn't they tell you?"

Suddenly, Bert made the connection—Olin's attempt at humor, his remark about catching Luna Mae red-handed with a flounder gig in the latrine area. It had sounded so far-fetched Bert had brushed it out of her mind.

Hurrying back to the old shed, Bert and Hunter began driving the forks into the sandy soil. It was like clamming, Bert decided as she hit yet another ballast stone. That's all they were finding—stones and bricks, but no grave.

After forty-five minutes, Hunter stopped and leaned on his gig. "If that marble slab's here, it's buried deep. Want to call it a day? To tell the truth, I'm plumb give out."

Bert quelled her disappointment. After all, she'd had a nice nap while he argued with politicians and then made the two-hour return trip.

"It's not just that," he added. "Even if we find something, we'll just have to guard it until they get an archaeologist up here."

True, Bert thought. They probably couldn't get the tomb open anyhow—wouldn't want to either. And wouldn't it be awful if they got up in the morning and found it looted? The biggest problem right now would be getting to sleep tonight without knowing something either way.

Hunter strode ahead of her on the narrow path. His shorts

were damp, spotted with mud, and clinging to his butt. Sweat soaked through his shirt. Rather than repelling her, it was all Bert could do not to reach out and caress him. She hoped he wasn't too tired for a little loving.

She didn't have to worry. As she fumbled with the lock at the lifesaving station, he reached a hand around her waist and planted a wet kiss on her neck. "Damn," he said, backing away.

Bert frowned up at him. "What's the matter?"

"Bug spray. I just numbed my lips." He rubbed his mouth.

Bert giggled. "That's Portsmouth."

After they rinsed off the worst of the mud and removed their hip boots, Hunter put his arm around Bert. "You know what I'm fixing to do now?" he asked, pulling her to him. "I'm fixing to give you a bath."

Bert laughed again. "I don't know how. That's a small shower."

"I like tight holes."

It was indeed crowded, but Bert delighted in the feel of his naked, soapy body. Using both the washcloth and his slippery hands, Hunter caressed her in every spot he could, and she him in turn. They rubbed their bodies together, meeting and separating. Water dripped down Hunter's face, soaking his beard. His eyes were warm as they held hers. Their soapy lips touching and the water pouring down over their heads did nothing to dampen the rising fires. He tried to get inside her, but the curtain parted and water ran out on the floor. So, laughing, they rinsed off quickly. Hunter was breathing hard as he hurriedly toweled her off and pushed her out the bathroom door. "You as ready as I am?" he asked in a husky voice.

She could only nod as they headed for the bed, both stumbling in their passion.

A little later, when her breathing was back to normal and she could think again, Bert said sleepily, "You never did tell me about Jimmy."

He rolled over on his back and sighed. "You know, for a while there, I thought you were kind of sweet on him."

"I know you did. He's charming and, frankly, more of an age with me. What's the matter with him?"

"He isn't what he claimed he was," Hunter said with a touch of satisfaction.

"Okay, so what is he? A con man?"

"You listening? That son of a bitch is a treasure hunter."

"A treasure hunter? I don't believe it."

"Had trouble bringing myself to believe it," Hunter said. "Even Rudy doesn't know yet."

"What do you mean?"

He turned on his side, toying with her nipples. "I stopped by the park office to see what they could bring up on Range. Once you get a record with the federal government, it stays there forever, you know. They hit pay dirt. Seems like Jimmy has himself a hobby researching old letters and site maps. Got his hands slapped—couple of warnings—for digging in National Parks, mostly up north."

"That's illegal, isn't it?"

Hunter nodded grimly. "But it's hard to prove. Digging is just vandalism. You've got to catch them taking something, then it becomes a federal offense."

Bert nodded. It fit. Jimmy seemed the kind of easy-go-lucky character who would enjoy treasure hunting. "But it's not that bad, is it? I mean, he does all the work and research, probably has an investment in it. Like the divers that found Blackbeard's ship. They hit it big, and we got the benefits."

"There's lots of ways people try to justify wrongdoing," he snapped back.

She hadn't meant to sound as if she were defending Jimmy. It was just that she could understand his reluctance to go through government regulations. "I don't know what the answer is," Bert said tiredly, "but sometimes the government ruins things as much as individuals do. Yet I agree we need controls."

"This is a National Park. It belongs to everyone. You and me, we're here to protect and preserve coastal history," Hunter said. "People like Jimmy and Luna Mae got no call to do any digging. That's the same as stealing. Worse, even."

He'd stiffened, pulling away from her. She was learning not to defend Jimmy. Was it jealousy on Hunter's part, or real dislike? Bert hiked up on her elbow. "In other words, what you're saying is that Jimmy had a motive to scare Anne or me away. Especially if he wanted to dig around here." In the dark, Hunter's face looked young and carefree. She hoped the light was doing the same for her. "But surely, whatever he's looking for wouldn't be worth scaring someone to death, would it?" She ran her palm slowly down his chest to his flat belly.

Hunter covered her hand with his, stopping her caress. "No more, hon. I'm give out. I'm fixing to go to sleep and think on this in the morning. That all right with you?"

Not waiting for an answer, he rolled to his side, brought her close, and exhaled slowly. It wasn't long before he was asleep.

Bert lay still for a little while, conscious of a disappointment. It had been fun tonight—not much tenderness but a lot of sex. Well, that's all she was looking for, wasn't it, a summer romance? She pulled away gently, trying not to wake him. Really, what had she expected? The man was dead tired. They'd had about four hours of sleep last night, then he'd been running all day. And he'd been up the night before, too, waiting for Donny.

The next thing she knew, she awoke to the sound of wind rattling the windows and a man's voice coming from the kitchen. Bert leapt out of bed, pulling the sheets over Hunter. "There's someone here," she hissed as his eyes flew open. Then, grabbing her jacket, she hurried out of the bedroom, slamming the door shut. ⌒⌒

Chapter 16

"Five forty-three, Portsmouth Village. This is 422. How about it, Hunter or Bert? Come in."

It was the radio.

Bert heaved a sigh of relief, grabbed the handset, and flipped on a light. "Hello, Bert here!" she yelled into the mike. "What's the matter, Rudy?" She backed up to the bedroom, opening the door. Hunter had his pants on and was in the process of tying his shoes. She waved the radio, and he rolled his eyes up thankfully.

They could both hear Rudy's relief. "That's my gal. Hunter's still there, isn't he? Put him on, will you?"

Hunter pointed outside. Bert nodded. "He's over at the station. I'll get him." Hunter winked approval.

Still holding the radio, Bert glanced at the clock—almost five-thirty, but still dark outside. Must be quite a storm blowing in. Had Carlos come closer than expected? The wind tugged at the door as she opened it. Swirling sand blasted her face. Bert yelled as if she were calling Hunter at the lifesaving station, more for the benefit of electronic eavesdroppers and the park grapevine than for Rudy. The government usually stayed out of the personal lives of its employees. Besides, she was a volunteer, and Hunter was officially off duty.

Hunter waited a moment, the radio in his hand. Then, walking outside, he activated the mike. "What's up, buddy? Got a blow coming?" He listened, frowning, then came back inside and slammed the door behind him. "Say again?"

"—taken a forty-degree turn. Headed right at the cape. Hurricane warnings up."

"Carlos?" Bert mouthed.

Hunter nodded. "How soon?"

"Ocracoke cellular tower's out—" Static interrupted. "Ferry's leaving for Long Point now. Get down there while you can. Got high water already from that nor'easter. This is blowing more on top. Don't stop for anything. You know how the flats get."

Damn, Bert thought. They should have probed for Spriggs's grave last night. Then she was in the bedroom throwing on her clothes and tossing a jacket, credit cards, money, and keys into her fanny pack. She stopped only long enough to grab two Cokes from the refrigerator. Without another word, they ran out to the truck.

"Coca-Cola at this hour?" Hunter asked once they were on their way.

"Don't laugh." Bert braced herself as they went around a turn at full speed. "I need my caffeine in the morning, and Coke is the best substitute I've found for coffee."

He reached out a hand. "Don't mind trying some myself. What did you bring in place of bacon?" Before she could answer, he said, "Look in my pack. I keep a couple of candy bars on hand, to share with pretty ladies the morning after."

Bert giggled, hands smoothing her hair. "Thanks from someone who hasn't even brushed her teeth."

Hunter stroked his beard. "I was shaving dry in the truck a couple of times a week before I let this grow." He hunched over, peering through the windshield. "It's always something out here."

They were out of the sheltering trees now, approaching the mud flats. An invisible sun had lightened the sky, and Bert could see sand streaming across the road much like snow in a whiteout.

A real sandstorm, she thought. Ragged, dark clouds raced across the sky high overhead. "That's unreal," she said softly. "Looks like someone has the VCR on fast forward."

Hunter glanced up. "I'm just hoping we're not too late. It's important I get back to Harkers. We never got the hurricane plan switched about, so I'm island evacuation, plus I still have administration evacuation." He stepped on the gas, then slowed as sand blasted the windshield. A moment later, he skidded to a stop. "Motherfucker!" he snarled.

It was uncharacteristic of Hunter to swear like that, but Bert could understand why as she stared at the foaming river before them.

Hunter slammed out and strode to the edge. Then he climbed on the truck and sighted across. "The poles are gone," he said.

"Looks wild." The tidal stream was rushing by, rippling and tumbling. Wind whipped the surface into a cross chop. The water itself was full of sand and debris, the increased flow eating into the banks.

Hunter bent over the truck's toolbox. He extracted a towrope with two big hooks, one at each end. Bert watched him attach one end to his belt, the other to a hitch on the front of his truck. "You're not going to try to walk across, are you?" she asked.

"I'm going to see how deep it is first. This is my safety line." He removed his shirt and radio, then emptied his pockets.

"What about your shoes?"

He grimaced. "They'll just have to get wet. Don't know what's going to be on the bottom."

"What can I do?"

"Let you know in a minute."

Grabbing the rope in one hand, Hunter waded in. Although the water was below his knees, the current was so strong it pushed him sideways. Bert held her breath as he waded farther, his legs apart, braced against the water. To her relief, he soon turned back.

"Isn't all that bad!" he yelled, climbing into the truck.

As he closed the door against the roar of the wind and water, Bert leaned back in relief. "We're going back?"

"You wish." Hunter patted her knee. "Like I said, isn't all that bad. It's been blowing two days now, and Carlos is just aggravating the tide. This beast," he tapped the steering wheel, "has a high bed and good tires. We should be all right." He looked around. "Wish I had some life jackets. You can swim, can't you?"

Bert nodded. "I'm a good swimmer." She glanced at the water. "Does it get deeper?"

"We'll find out. If the truck stalls, we might have to wade. Should be able to get to shore all right. I'd just feel better if you had a life jacket." He leaned back against the seat, eyeing her. "Best be ready for a swim. Take off that pack and your shirt, but leave your shoes on, like me."

"You're just looking for an excuse to undress me." Bert pulled off her T-shirt, thankful she'd grabbed the same bra she'd worn last night for Hunter's benefit, a low-cut, lacy job.

Hunter scowled fiercely, but his eyes were bright. "Maybe you'd better keep your shirt on. If we walk into camp with you looking like that, Justin will never be the same again, I swear." Bert giggled, but Hunter was talking again. "I'll walk ahead. You stay in back of me and drive the truck. Try not to stop moving. That current will eat the sand out from under the wheels in no time. If you can't go forward, go back, but keep her moving, you understand?"

"What about you?" Bert's throat was tightening. She'd driven the truck through the water just yesterday, but she wasn't confident with it.

As if he'd read her mind, he said, "She's in four-wheel drive already. Just keep her in second gear. I'll go out front. That way, I can point you off any soft holes. The big thing is, keep moving. If you get too close to me, don't stop. I'll either climb on or get out of the way. You listening, gal?"

"What if I get stuck?"

He shrugged. "We go back to Portsmouth. It's been through more hurricanes than most places. Never been overwashed either."

"Then let's go back now." She really didn't want to do this. That water looked wild and terribly dangerous. "It would be fun to sit out a hurricane, just us two."

Hunter shook his head. "Hurricanes aren't fun. And if this thing hits, they're going to need me—you, too—to help clean up afterwards." He hesitated, then said slowly, "I'm not going to let my pleasure come first again."

Bert watched him get out and knew she could say nothing more.

He was out almost the full length of the rope before he signaled her forward. Bert clenched her teeth and put the truck into gear. She took the bank a little too fast. The truck bounced hard over the drop-off as Bert clung to the wheel, damning herself for her carelessness. Holding the steering wheel with a death grip, she concentrated on moving forward slowly but steadily. The water was up to the edge of the body, pushing the vehicle sideways. Then, to Bert's horror, she felt the wheels slipping over the sand.

Hunter plowed on, the rope over his shoulder, bent forward, braced against the current. Bert inched behind him, turning on the wipers. The roar of the tidal river filled her ears, and windblown spray clouded the windshield. It was easier to see with her head outside the truck. Hunter had opened both windows so she could climb out quickly if the truck tipped over, and also so she could hear him. "Don't leave the truck!" he yelled back. "If it gets stuck, you just wait for me, you hear?"

Hunter suddenly stumbled and went down in the water. Then he was gone.

Bert screamed, automatically putting her foot on the brake. Then she remembered his instructions and took it off. To her relief, Hunter emerged from the water, staggering and pointing upstream.

A hole, she figured. She slowed as much as she dared while he continued to fight his way forward. Again, the water deepened. It swirled around his hips. Even as she watched, Hunter lost his footing. In an instant, the water tumbled him the full length of his rope, almost fifty feet downstream. Automatically, Bert threw the truck into reverse, backing up slightly. "I want to go back!" she wailed. "Please, please, let me get back."

Almost immediately, Hunter's head reappeared. He was pulling himself out with the rope.

Something upstream caught Bert's eyes. Oh, my God. A bush was bearing down on them, tumbling over and over, the branches protruding. "Hunter!" she screamed, pointing, but he didn't notice. Frantic, Bert leaned on the horn, half out the window.

The bush was on him.

Horrified, she watched it roll between Hunter and herself. He disappeared from view, lost somewhere beneath. Then the truck jerked, knocking Bert against the window, cracking her head on the post. She screamed again, putting her foot on the gas. The truck shuddered and slipped. She glanced at the gearshift—still in reverse. She slammed it into neutral and pulled on the emergency brake.

Where was Hunter? He'd drown under all that stuff.

Bert was out the window of the pickup, onto the roof. Somehow, in the back of her mind, she thought she could follow the rope and find him. But that was a bad idea. A knife, she needed a knife to cut him free—Hunter's fillet knife, in the truck's toolbox. Grabbing the sheathed knife and jamming it into her pocket, Bert crawled back onto the roof. The truck bounced along as the bush pulled it downstream. Just then, she saw something, someone, Hunter? Oh, thank God. He was out in the middle, free of the rope, being carried rapidly downstream. She saw his hand rise from the water, pointing back toward shore.

He was alive.

Oh, Lord. Tears came into her eyes. Here he was being swept out to sea, and he was thinking of her, for there was no doubt in her mind he was telling her to go back.

The truck was bouncing downstream, tugged inexorably by the bush. Bert knew what she had to do: cut the truck free. She slid over the windshield, wishing the vehicle were a Cadillac or something that had a hood ornament she could grab. The water was over the front bumper. Holding on to the grill as best she could, Bert began sawing at the rope. The fact that it was stretched so tightly helped. But as the line parted, the truck reared up, throwing Bert into the water. For a moment, her feet were swept out from under her, and she thought she was gone. Then the water slammed her against the truck. She'd fallen backwards, to the upstream side. She grabbed the tailgate and used it to pull herself back on her feet and into the bed. From there, she slid through the window inside the cab.

The engine was still running. Bert put it in first and cautiously stepped on the gas. The wheels seemed to catch. Crying in relief, she patted the steering wheel. "Good boy," she said aloud. "Come on, boy. Let's turn around, back to shore." Slowly, she inched toward the Portsmouth side.

Where was Hunter? She scanned both banks downstream but saw nothing. Then, finally, after what seemed forever, she was back next to land.

Now, she had a new problem. The rising, rushing water had cut a huge swath in the sand. The bank was a good four feet higher than the bottom, and more sand was being cut out every moment. Not only that, but the water was getting noticeably deeper.

Damn, she couldn't go on like this. The truck would stall any minute. She could pull up close and jump to shore, abandoning the truck. But as she tried to approach, another huge chunk of sand slid into the water. If she jumped and didn't make it, or if the bank collapsed under her, she'd be swept away. Bert knew there was no way she'd be able to keep on her feet at this depth. But up ahead, the inlet widened. It had broken through some kind of low area.

"Come on, truck, don't give out now," she pleaded as the engine coughed. Bert slowed even more, barely moving. The water must be up to the bottom of the motor. "Just a little farther," she begged.

Then she was there.

Slowly, carefully, Bert turned the truck into the breach. Almost immediately, the current slowed, the water level dropped. Soon, she was back on dry sand.

Hunter, she had to find Hunter. Bert put the truck into third gear and drove as fast as she dared along the bank. Careful, she warned herself. Don't get stuck way out here. Pulling up beside a ridge of dunes, Bert jumped out and ran to the top. All she could see downstream was water. That's all she could see across the tidal plain, too. Had the flooded flats run into Swash Inlet and cut a path to the sea? That's what it looked like. No way, she told herself. It's an optical illusion. Too much wind and sand for good visibility. But in any case, there was no sign of Hunter.

Coming down from the dunes, she continued following the water until she reached another breach and could go no farther.

There was nothing more she could do for Hunter now. She sighed, sitting back. She hurt all over. Her breath was coming hard, and her hands were trembling so she could barely hold the wheel. She wondered if she'd be able to get back to the Portsmouth Village side.

She almost didn't. One of the hardest things she'd ever had to do was drive the truck back into the water to cross over the first breach, the one that had saved her. The level had risen already. If she'd hesitated any longer, she might not have been able to cross at all.

Suddenly, the radio squawked.

The radio. She'd forgotten the radio. Maybe they could send out a rescue party for Hunter. Bert stopped the truck and reached for the receiver.

No one answered her call.

The flats were not a good spot for reception even in ideal weather. The lifesaving station tower—that's where they'd told her to go when reception was poor.

She put the receiver down and began driving toward Portsmouth. Somehow, it seemed like desertion, leaving Hunter, but what else could she do? As she drove, she calmed. He was probably all right. He might even be in the village, though she suspected he'd come out on the ocean side of the flats—that's the way he'd been going. Still, she kept looking out the passenger window, hoping he would appear.

When she reached the road that led to Portsmouth from the

flats, she stopped and tried the radio again. Nothing but loud static. Revving up the truck, she drove as fast as she could. As she reached the edge of the village, the squawking from the radio became louder. She had just sighted the entrance gate when she heard a voice calling her. ∞

Chapter 17

BERT GRABBED THE RADIO and began speaking. "Justin, Hunter, come in. This is 543, Bert, at Portsmouth Village."

"Bert," the radio squawked. "We get you. Where are—"

A burst of static interrupted. Bert glanced at the sky. The high ceiling of gray clouds rolled rapidly overhead, tinged mustard here and there by an invisible sun.

"Justin?" she asked.

"Can't wait much longer. Tearing up the—"

"Justin, I'm at Portsmouth, on the beach road. Hunter's over there somewhere. He got washed over, I think. You have to go get him."

"—breaking up bad. Portsmouth—"

"I'm at Portsmouth, but Hunter's in trouble. Hunter needs help!" she screamed into the mike.

"Didn't read— " The radio buzzed fiercely.

Bert floored the gas pedal. The lookout tower—from there, the radio would carry even without the repeater. She tore through the gate she and Hunter had left open in their earlier rush. Occasional garbled words came over the radio. They were about to leave and thought she and Hunter had remained at Portsmouth.

Flying out of the woods, she pulled up in front of the lifesaving station and, grabbing the radio, rushed to the tower and up the ladder in record time.

"Justin, Justin, Hunter is caught!" she yelled into the mike as her head emerged through the trapdoor. "Justin. Come in, Justin." She pulled herself up the rest of the way, waiting for a response.

Then it came. "This is Elmo Smith, on the *Green Grass*. We read you, only it don't make sense. You got problems?"

Elmo, the ferryboat captain. Bert almost wept. "Elmo, Hunter was caught crossing the flats. A tree hit him. I think he made it to the other side. He may be hurt."

"Where you at?"

"I'm at Portsmouth. I'm okay. It's Hunter."

"—be here by now. Truck—"

Damn, she was losing them again. "Hunter!" she screamed. "He's on foot. I have the truck. Don't leave without him."

The deep voice came back. "Now, you just take it easy, Miss Bert. We'll take care of our man. Don't you worry."

Somehow, the casualness of his response eased Bert more than anything else so far. They had trucks. They'd pick up Hunter and tell her what to do—if he'd made it across. Of course, he'd made it across. Don't even think that way. "Thanks Elmo," she breathed.

"—left already . . . call when pick . . . boat top-heavy . . . wind—"

That was the last Bert heard for an hour. Justin's hand radio wouldn't carry any better than hers, and they were probably in his truck driving up the beach. She didn't expect to hear until they got back to the boat and the built-in radio. Meanwhile, the wind slowly increased.

While she waited, she paced, peering out the tower windows, still hoping to see a moving figure. Visibility was poor and worsening. The wind had whipped the ocean into whitecaps, blowing off the tops and filling the air with a mist so dense Ocracoke was invisible. Bert could see as far as the swollen flats—now a river—

and a rim of the beach beyond. And that was all. About one mile, she figured. Already, the tide was creeping into the village. Doctor's Creek and Coast Guard Creek were spreading over their banks and seeping into the low spots. How high would the water get? Suppose the hurricane got stronger?

Bert's stomach tightened in panic. Should she go the Washington Roberts House? That was the oldest home on the island, built on one of the high hummocks, but it was no longer in good shape. Bert doubted it would hold up to a lot of wind. Besides, it had been closed for a long time. It had no furniture and was probably full of bugs and spiders. What should she do? She glanced at her watch. It had been almost an hour. "Hunter," she moaned aloud. "Please come back."

As if in answer to her plea, the radio suddenly came alive. "Bert, Bert, you copy?" The voice was thin and weak, but it could only be—

"Hunter!" she screamed as the radio bounced around in her hands. "Hunter?" she said as she steadied it enough to press the mike.

"I'm fine."

It was him. Oh, thank God. Bert's legs felt weak. She clutched the radio with a desperate grip. "Where are you?"

"You copy?" The transmission was faint, as if coming from a great distance.

Bert tried again. "Where are you?"

"On the *Green Grass*. I tried . . . Look, we can't get back—"

Bert put the receiver to her ear. Nothing. "I lost you. Say again?"

"Bert, you copy?"

"Barely. You're very faint."

"Come again?"

"I copy."

"Can't get to Portsmouth. Elmo won't—"

Another voice came in—Elmo's. "Ain't no way I can get this old boat there, Miss Bert. Chop's coming right at me."

"I'm fine. I'll be fine, Hunter. Don't worry."

Despite the static, Bert picked up the relief in his voice. "That's my girl. We're headed back to . . . lose communications anytime. Go to the lifesaving . . . hear me? That building can stand up to anything. Don't you worry . . . scuttle holes . . . float off. It's been through worse—"

"What do you mean, float off?" Bert's voice rose. "How bad is it?"

Hunter's voice came back quickly. "Won't float off. Won't. Didn't mean to scare you." Her panic must have reached him. He began speaking again, his voice slow and casual—what she could hear over the frequent static. "Force two or three . . . landfall after midnight . . . plenty of time for preparations. You copy?"

"What should I do?"

"Fill all the water jugs, and run the generator so the batteries . . . Ain't going to be able to do that later. Might fill up the gas tanks on the truck and the . . . You copy?"

"Should I fill the gasoline containers?"

"Wouldn't hurt. How's the tide . . . over the road?"

"Not yet. It's over the bulkhead and up to the station ramp." Suddenly, that no longer worried her. This village had lived through plenty of storms.

"If you got time and the tide's not coming in too fast, wouldn't hurt to nail the church doors closed . . . button up the village some. That's a good road. You can drive it wet, but ain't nothing in . . . worth getting hurt for. You hear me?"

Bert smiled, feeling more confident by the second. He wasn't fooling her any. He'd picked up her relief at having something to do and was making sure she kept busy. "Ten-four, bossman. That's what we should have done in the first place."

"Come again? I didn't—"

"Hunter, are you there?"

"Elmo made the turn . . . losing you—"

Bert had the receiver to her ear. Suddenly, some of her panic returned. "Wait a minute!" she yelled.

"You take . . . now, gal. And don't go digging no treasure till I get back." His voice was barely audible.

Bert giggled. "That's where I'm going as soon as I get the village closed. Is landfall still Cape Lookout?"

This time, the radio stayed silent. Had the ferry traveled out of range, or were her batteries gone?

After fifteen minutes of dead air, Bert began closing up the tower. It was time to get herself and the island ready for the hurricane, and she needed to charge up the radio before Hunter reached Harkers. She was sure he would try to raise her with the park's main transmitter. The hurricane wasn't due for twelve hours. It was just the nor'easter in combination with the front-running winds that had the ocean so worked up.

Her decision made, Bert began working. First, she turned on the generator to build up the water and power supplies and to recharge the inverter batteries and her radio and cell phone. While they charged, she filled as many jugs as she could with water. Loading the truck with empty gas cans, she drove to the fuel compound area. After she filled both the truck and the cans, she turned off the fuel pump, tied down the extra propane tanks so they wouldn't float off, turned off the gas to her cabin, and tied that tank down. All the while, the wind swirled hot dust into her eyes and nose. Back at the shed, Bert shut down the generator, covered the motor and batteries with a plastic tarp, and nailed shut all the doors and windows. Then she went back to her cabin. She moved the throw rugs and cartons off the floor and checked to see what else might get wet if the water rose that high. The bottom of the bookcase was only a foot or so off the floor. She piled the books on the desk and pulled all the plugs from the sockets. Since the gas was off, her propane fridge had to be emptied into her cooler. It needed defrosting anyhow. She began to clean it, then stopped herself. There were more important things to do, and besides, the cabin might not even be here after Carlos. Shaking off that depressing thought, she carried her clothes, bedding, and cooler to the lifesaving station.

Then Bert decided it was time to run into the village and see what she could do there. Might as well keep busy in a constructive way, just like Hunter suggested. Besides, it was her job. She used the truck rather than the ATV, as it would shelter her against flying debris if the wind picked up. She just had to be careful the tide didn't float the small bridges and leave her stranded.

Closing up the church was easy. All she could do was nail a couple of boards across the double doors. The visitor center took a little longer. To her relief, the shutters worked. There were shutters upstairs, too, but the windows were painted shut and she couldn't get them open, not even with her pint-sized crowbar. She closed the bedroom doors so that if a window shattered, the wind would not funnel through and lift the roof. Before leaving, Bert took a minute to look around. The center had a great view of the sound and the Babbs and Potter properties, which were not visible from the lifesaving station. From the upstairs windows, Bert noticed that the Pamlico was not nearly as churned up as the ocean or the inlet, although whitecaps and waves were washing over Haulover Dock. As Jimmy had explained, Haulover could be impossible to access in rough weather, due to the extensive shoals that surrounded the dock and the narrow channel that didn't allow boats any leeway in meeting the waves. Past Potter's on the lee side of the island, a couple of crabbers were frantically dashing about retrieving crab pots and pound nets. They were probably out of Silver Lake, Ocracoke's sheltered anchorage. She switched on her radio, wondering if Donny was one of them. The radio was silent, which didn't surprise her. The park broadcast on a different frequency from the Coast Guard and fishermen. Besides, even if she did raise Donny or a fisherman, there was no way they could put into Haulover or any of the Portsmouth docks in that sea.

The tide was slowly rising, first filling the creeks, then spreading over the banks and creeping down the paths. By the time Bert finished closing up the village, part of Haulover Road was covered by water. Hunter had assured her that driving the road would not be a problem. Still, Bert was relieved when the lifesaving station came into sight. She drove the truck right up the ramp into the boathouse, where the mower and ATV were already parked.

Finally, satisfied the station was as secure as she could make

179

it, the boathouse doors braced and nailed, Bert wearily climbed the two sets of ladders to the tower. Propping herself against the railing, she tried to reach Hunter, Elmo, or even someone monitoring the park frequencies. But she heard nothing except static, even when she turned the squelch and volume way up. It looked as if, without the repeater, even the park transmitter wouldn't reach Portsmouth. She was on her own.

A strong gust of wind rattled the tower. Was it safe up here? Bert laughed at her sudden surge of adrenaline. This place was built to keep watch for ships during hurricanes. Still, it wouldn't hurt to put up the plywood shutters on the windward windows. Besides, she was in no rush to leave. Deep inside, she was still hoping she'd hear from Hunter.

All the windows boarded save two, Bert pressed her face to the glass and stared at the green-and-gray scene that fanned out below. Coast Guard Creek had spread over the sea walls. White-capped water covered the boat ramp and reached under the boathouse. Trees and reeds bent in the wind under the slate skies; darker slate marked the distant ocean. The inlet was a mass of pale foam. What would it be like to take a boat out in this? Bert took a last look. At least the surfmen had each other.

If only she could get hold of someone, find out the latest news. Was Carlos still headed at the cape? And exactly when was landfall expected? There was no rain yet, but it certainly was hot and humid, despite the leading winds that were churning up the ocean.

There was a marine radio at the summer kitchen. Maybe she could pick up NOAA—the National Oceanographic and Atmospheric Administration—in Newport, or even the Coast Guard.

Bert scrambled down the ladders, got her jacket, and went out on the porch. She held on to the door, careful to latch the screen on the outside so it wouldn't blow. As she came out of the shelter of the lifesaving station heading toward her cabin, she felt the brunt of the wind. About thirty-five miles per hour, she estimated, keeping a wary eye out for wind-driven trash.

The padlock on the cabin door gave her a hard time, as always. She wouldn't lock it again, she decided as she fumbled with her key. The hasp would secure it just as well. That way, she could get in quickly if she needed to.

The wind scattered the contents of the bookcase piled on the desk. Bert closed the door behind her and flipped on the VHF system. Nothing. She sat at the desk to check the controls. The display light was off, too.

She cursed. With all the goings-on, she hadn't plugged in and charged the reserve battery when she ran the generator. Hadn't done it since Tuesday. The only way she'd get it charged now was to turn the power back on. She'd have to pry open the shed and then nail it shut again, not to mention turning on all the fuel tanks. The question was whether it was worth it.

Bert leaned back in the chair, staring at the ceiling. Sounds were different in here than in the lifesaving station. The cabin was more fragile, closer to the outside. Metal trembled and vibrated. Something dripped. Wind whistled shrilly through the eaves and whirled the fan in the bedroom. Windows rattled; shingles thumped. The cabin shook slightly with each gust. It felt to Bert as if the tide already lapped at the foundation. The hurricane would pile up the water in the ocean. Then inland rains would flood the rivers, and northeast winds would blow all the water in the Pamlico to this end. How high a surge would the island get?

She stared out at the station. Something was flapping at one of the windows. For a moment, she thought she'd left a window open and a curtain was blowing. But the station had no curtains. Then she realized it was a torn screen whipping in the growing wind.

She sighed. No good trying to rationalize her way out of it. She needed to get that marine radio up and running, if not for now, then for after the hurricane. After all, it was her responsibility to have things ready in case of emergencies. There might be a boat in trouble, or even a shipwreck. It wouldn't be the first time.

Still strangely reluctant to go back to the shed, Bert began tidying up the papers and books. No sooner had she put them high on a bedroom shelf than she found herself reaching for her jacket. Her subconscious mind was directing her body to go out and start the generator. Bert peered through the window as she tied on her hat with the mosquito netting. The wind didn't seem any stronger, and there was still no rain. This wasn't her first hurricane. Sometimes, the weather stayed so nice beforehand that it was hard to believe a storm was coming. Besides, hurricanes weren't like tornadoes, when you had only minutes to take shelter. Landfall wasn't for hours yet. Even if the wind picked up or the rains started, she'd have plenty of time to get to the fuel compound, turn on the diesel pump, let the generator run for an hour or so, then turn it off again. It just meant she'd have to uncover and unnail everything, then do it all up again. Oh, well, as Hunter would say, "Pay's the same."

Tucking a hammer into her belt and grabbing the crowbar she'd used to close up the village, Bert set out toward the shed. The low spots on the cart path were wet, and Bert could see water gleaming through the reeds. She'd better keep her eye on the tide, though it was no big deal if it flooded the path. At least the wind had blown all the bugs away.

Now, to get the shed door open. The head came off one of the nails, and she ended up splintering the door, but finally she was in. When the generator was up and running, she headed toward the fuel dump to turn on the gas before the diesel in the lines ran out. It was a simple matter to flip the switch on the fuel pump.

There, that wasn't so hard, was it? Funny how the dread of a job was often worse than the job itself.

Feeling noble, Bert started back to her cabin along the cart path. There was not as much wind here as in the open area by Coast Guard Creek. In fact, it was rather pleasant back here, and she had an hour to kill while she waited for the battery to charge. As she reached the ruins of the burnt shed, the ground dropped, the sand, grass, and dwarf trees giving way to salt marsh. Beyond, she could glimpse part of Coast Guard Creek. To her side was a hummock covered with colorful orange, magenta, and gold Jobells. Bert paused, wishing she'd brought her camera. Behind the Jobells, a gnarled, stunted tree poked through the swaying myrtles. Funny-looking thing, Bert thought. She wandered over to have a closer look. Small green fruits hung off the branches—a fig tree?

A sense of deja vu crept over her. What had Hunter said about fig trees? Jerushia had lazed in a pergola surrounded by fig trees. Suppose this was what was left of that orchard?

Something she'd read her first night at Portsmouth sprang to mind. It had to do with deeds to the marine hospital. An estate had been divided. Eight acres with a stable had been purchased by a John Gillikin in 1814, then later sold to the government and used as a hospital.

Suddenly, everything came clear. Spriggs's stable, of course! A disgruntled would-be seller had sent a letter of complaint about the hospital, stating that it was a sorry shed with no windows and that it was large enough for only six cots. That description would fit a former stable. When the new hospital was built, the stable—or old hospital—was probably used as one of the outbuildings. Then, later, it became the generator shed.

Bert stared at the ruins of the old shed. It all fit. Jerushia died in 1810. Since the house was thought to be haunted, it was probably hard to sell, so they would have been glad to split the property to accommodate the buyer, Gillikin. Later, his heirs sold the stable and eight acres to the government for a hospital.

No wonder she and Hunter hadn't found the marble slab. They'd been probing the old shed—the stable area. What they had to do was probe the ground where the house had stood.

The main house, Spriggs Luck, couldn't have been far from the stable. Far enough to keep the smells and flies at bay, yet convenient in times of bad weather. What had Hunter said? The house was fifty feet from the stable and had a large, circular drive to the road. Assuming the cart path had once been the original road, that would put Spriggs's house fifty feet from the ruins of the old generator shed, close to where the lone fig tree now stood. She studied the area. Yes, the high ground toward the fuel compound side of the path would have been just the place to build.

Bert picked her way through the sparse cover of Jobells and

weeds. Thank goodness there weren't any trees here, just a prickly ash by the path. A large patch of dead weeds and bare ground caught her eye. At first, she thought it was just a spot where the nutria had been munching. But nutria ate weeds down to the roots. These looked as if someone had carefully spread them over the sandy earth. Had someone beaten her to Spriggs's tomb? Lips tight, Bert marched over and dropped to her knees. The sand was loose under her hands. Someone had definitely been digging here. She began to scrape out the soil, first using her hands, then scooping with the crowbar turned sideways, then, as the hole deepened, digging with the end of the crowbar and her hands again.

She was down almost eight inches, sand sticking to her sweaty face and arms, when she hit something solid. Spriggs's grave. It had to be. The feeling was entirely different from a brick or a ballast stone. The sound was different, lower. She tried to clear off some of the sand so she could see, but the sides kept caving in. She'd have to enlarge the hole.

Sweat poured down her face. The storm was raising the humidity to an unbearable level. She found it hard to breathe. She needed another tool. Yes, one of those large cockleshells would do fine. Bert bent back to her task, loosening the sand with the crowbar, then scooping it out with the shell. The swirling wind blew it back. She switched sides. Her vision blurred, and she felt sick to her stomach. It's too hot for this kind of work, she told herself. But nothing short of collapse could have made her stop digging.

Finally, she uncovered part of the slab. It was as pale as the sand and smooth to the touch—white marble. Sand flew in all directions as she scooped with renewed energy. Soon, she was into harder ground—ground that had never been dug before, she decided with a sense of relief. But why had they stopped? And who had been here? Not Hunter. Surely, he would have said something to her. A park archaeologist? No. Those uprooted Jobells had been recently and deliberately scattered to hide the digging. Luna Mae? Was this why she was killed?

Now, Bert actually crouched on the marble, which gave her

better leverage to remove the sand. Thank goodness the covering of dirt was not as deep at this end.

There, the entire six feet of marble lay exposed. Panting, sweat dripping into her eyes, Bert sank down, knees and forearms on the slab, like a Muslim saying his prayers. The marble was cool under her sweaty skin.

There really was a tomb.

Captain Spriggs had really existed. The stories were true, then, not legends that had evolved from a kernel of truth. That meant Jerushia was real, too. Once, she'd lived in this house, walked these paths, maybe even sat by the fire with her feet on this slab.

Chapter 18

JERUSHIA SMILED, DANCING A JIG. Today was her birthday—and the end of the first year of her new life. She threw a quick glance toward the house to make sure no one was watching. Goree, the captain's manservant and cook, would not approve of such levity, but there was no sign of the huge black man anywhere. In her apron, she had enough dewberries for the trifle she planned to make for the celebration, for she was sure her godfather had something special in mind. He'd risen early and left for the warehouse.

What kind of cloth would he give her this year? she wondered as she slowly made her way along the little path back to the house. Something light and cool, she hoped. But to be truthful, she had not found the heat oppressive. In fact, she'd taken to this latitude as if she'd been born to it, which she really had, for the *Celestial Harp* had taken the southern route to New Bedford.

Jerushia paused to lean against the bough of a giant, wind-bent cedar, kick off her moccasins, and dig her feet into the sand. She wore a loose, short-sleeved bodice over a single black muslin petticoat. The pleasant breeze coming from the beach whipped a loose tendril of hair from the red braid that hung down her back. In the creek, a huge white egret stood motionless, as if it were carved of wood. Behind it, the captain's sloop rocked softly at its mooring, and beyond that rose her stately house. Jerushia smiled. Already, she called it *her* house, because that was the way she felt. The captain was so kind. He made her feel more like a daughter than a housekeeper. Well, not exactly a daughter. Jerushia had been around too many men—both her husband and the other sailors and officers who had passed through the shipyard—not to recognize male admiration when she saw it. To be sure, he was a man, even if of an age. And to be entirely truthful, she thought as she slipped back into her shoes, she was a woman and not unaware of him. She wasn't certain she liked the idea. He would soon be an old man, while she again felt herself to be in her prime. Jerushia shrugged. Why worry over something that had not happened? Indeed, it would not be a bad match at all.

Jerushia found the kitchen deserted. The day maid had gone, and it sounded as if Goree was mucking out the stables. All the better. She could barely understand the Negro's patois, but he had nevertheless made it clear he didn't like her in his kitchen.

She dipped some water from the pail to rinse her dewberries, then left them to drain while she began building her trifle. First, she soaked the stale cake with a syrup of white sugar and rum. Then she spread it with grape preserves and added the berries. She had to go outside to the cool house, a tiny shed on legs, where Nansa, the maid, had left the rich egg custard to cool. She poured this over the top of the berries and the rum-soaked cake crumbs and topped the trifle with flakes of coconut, a special treat.

Covering it carefully with a dampened cloth, she set the trifle in the cool house and went to her bedroom to ready herself. Nansa had filled both her pitchers with water. Putting the washbowl on the floor, Jerushia half filled it with water. Then, making sure her door was securely latched, she unhooked her bodice and dropped her petticoat and shift, stepping into the water. Nansa had taught her this trick. If her feet were cool, then her body was, too. Jerushia then gave herself a sponge bath and finished by pouring the pitcher over herself. It was wonderful what a bath could do, she thought as she dressed herself for dinner. And all the years she had wasted, sponging herself off one part at a time, never entirely undressing. She threw the water out the open window so her basin would be ready for her bedtime ablutions. After making certain there were bayberry candles in each room and sprigs of myrtle on the sills to discourage the night pests, she hurried downstairs.

The table was set to her satisfaction with a bleached-white linen cloth and the heavy pewter candlesticks Spriggs had "collected" along with the pewter serving platters. A huge bouquet of orange irises decorated the marble sideboard, and a burgundy Turkish rug glowed softly under the table. The burgundy was repeated in the needlepoint chair seats and again on the wall tapestry that she'd created, weaving in the name of the house and its owner, along with symbols of the sea and sailing.

The house had been beautiful when she arrived, but she'd softened it and made it comfortable. Now, it was a place that made people welcome, which pleased her, as the captain often brought his friends or business partners home.

She went into the parlor, admiring the fireplace with its dark mantel but keeping her eyes from the hearth. She sat in the chair comfortably padded with cushions she and Nansa had wrought and looked toward the entrance. Light from the open windows lay paths on the polished floors, and a gentle breeze ruffled the curtains of tight lace, which kept out most pests but let in the air. It was almost too much. Jerushia looked across the shimmering creek. No one should be this happy. Something would go wrong— it always did.

She put away the unpleasant thought. Nothing would go wrong, nothing. This was her home now, and never would she leave it.

Hearing the thud of the captain's horse on the sand, she rose to greet him. Already, Goree had the reins and was leading the bay to the stable. Jerushia glanced at the sideboard. The captain's favorite beverage, bombo, stood ready to be mixed: rum, sugar syrup, freshly grated nutmeg, and water. That was one benefit of living in a port of entry—one had simple and economical access to many rare items.

Then Captain Spriggs himself stood at the door, a bolt of cloth under his arm. Had she not looked upon the white sand and emerald waters behind him, Jerushia would have thought she was back in New Bedford opening the door one year ago. She could see that the same thought crossed Spriggs's mind, for he smiled broadly and whirled her around. "Jerushia Spriggs O'Hagan, I take it," he said mockingly.

His hands circled her waist, spanning the small of her back. She felt them all the way up her spine. Carefully, she moved away, hoping he had not noticed. It would not do to have him think her a wanton.

"Open it." He thrust the bolt of cloth at her, his eyes flashing gold.

It was so light—what kind of cloth could it be? Carefully, Jerushia laid it on the side table and unpinned the wrap. "Oh" was all she could say. Inside lay a cloth of India, but it was unlike any she had seen before—a pure aquamarine silk, the weave so fine she could see through it. It was like looking at clear seawater over white sand. "Oh," she whispered again, stretching out a tentative hand.

Spriggs walked up next to her, his hand on her shoulder as she lifted a fold of the delicate silk and let it slip through her fingers. The edges were embroidered with silver and gold threads. "It's a sari," he whispered into her ear.

Too lost in her delight to be self-conscious, Jerushia looked into his eyes. "How does one wear it?"

He smiled at her. "Do you really want me to show you?"

Then Jerushia knew they were no longer talking about the cloth. Numbly, she nodded. This was what she wanted, she told herself as he led her upstairs to his bedroom. But as they got to his door, she hesitated.

"Do not be concerned," he crooned in her ear. "I will take good care of you. Have I not always done so?"

But when she was in his room, he was not so gentle. Indeed,

he ripped her bodice in his haste to open it. "Wait," she gasped, hastening to come to his aid.

He brushed her fingers aside. "A man likes to do his own unwrapping," he growled softly.

To Jerushia's surprise, she found his attitude exciting. The truth was, she and her husband had known each other since they were children. It had been assumed they would marry, and the marriage bed had been merely another one of their enjoyable games together. This was quite different.

Spriggs didn't seem to want her help or participation. His fingers pried open the hooks and eyes, exposing her stays. As her bodice fell away, he pulled down her shift, exposing her breasts. One large, brown palm enclosed her breast as he bent and put his mouth to her nipple. Now, he was pressing her down on the bed, half her clothes still on, her petticoats about her waist.

"No." She pushed at him. This was not proper, not proper at all.

But he didn't seem to hear her. His face was a hard mask, his yellow eyes gleaming like those of a lion intent on its prey, his hands grasping, kneading her. Then he had his knees between her legs, opening her, pressing against her. She could smell him, rancid, strong.

Jerushia braced herself, knowing what came next.

There was nothing soft and loving about this, she thought as he reared back and thrust hard. She moaned as he hammered, yet strangely, a warmth began to grow. "No." She tossed, trying to break away. She couldn't move. Instead, he brought her even closer until she felt he would penetrate through her body. The warmth built, rising to a crescendo. It had been a long time. She arched, shuddering, and heard his cry of triumph as he, too, exploded. Her heart pounded madly. They were both covered in sweat, their bodies making disgusting, wet noises as his effluvia soaked her inside and out.

Jerushia turned her head to one side and wept. Dimly, she heard him crowing. "Didn't I tell you? Spriggs knows how to please a woman."

In a moment, he was sitting up, buttoning his breeches.

Jerushia watched him numbly. He hadn't even undressed. She could have been a trollop in a tavern.

"Get up, woman." He patted her. "Goree will be bringing in supper any moment." Jerushia stared at him blankly as he finished dressing. He scowled. "Do not begin to take liberties because of this. I shall expect you at my table as always."

Numbly, Jerushia dressed, going into her room for another bodice. Suddenly, she knew the truth. He was not going to marry her, as somehow she'd supposed. No, this was what her son had feared. He would use his housekeeper in more ways than one.

Silently, she sat at his table and watched him eat the trifle she'd prepared with so many expectations. Then she sat up straighter. This was her house, too. They would reach an agreement.

She waited until he finished eating, then asked, "You do not plan to marry me?"

He frowned. "I have married twice, and both wives died within a fortnight. I shall never marry again."

His story was possible, but Jerushia thought it more likely a justification he'd invented to quell his strange conscience. "I will not be used as a trollop."

At that, he laughed, reaching across to pat her hand. "My dear, you have not been used. Did I not pleasure you? A man does not pleasure a whore."

She pulled her hand away, conscious of his touch. What was this, some devilish attraction?

Spriggs sighed. "A pox on you women and your prudishness." He leaned forward, his gold eyes intent on hers. "You are too old to marry again. I will give you a good home, provide you with all your needs and more. In return, you will keep my house in good order, act as hostess for my friends, and share my bed when I so desire."

Jerushia stared back, eyes cold. "And if I refuse?"

Spriggs guffawed. "You will not refuse. You are the same as I. You know what you want. You want this house, and I want you. Be a good woman and bow to the inevitable."

For a moment, Jerushia was so angry she could not see. She

reached for the flask of rum, thinking to throw it, but he grasped her hand with an iron grip. "No, my pretty. This is why you excite me. Now, I will strike another bargain with you. In return for my privileges, you may request a favor of me. What shall it be?" Still holding her hand, he smiled engagingly at her.

What manner of man is this? she wondered. One moment, he was a devil. The next, he was a small boy trying to please. She didn't have much choice, just as she'd never had much choice. But if she had learned one thing over her life, it was to make the best of what she had. And that was what she would do now.

"I want to be able to hold up my head in the village. No one is to know. You must be discreet when Goree and the maid are here."

"Agreed." He reached for the bottle. "Goree will not talk."

"There is more."

"Speak, woman."

"I want a pair of horses." Jerushia thought quickly to the most beautiful animals she'd ever seen. "A pair of black Arabians."

"And a carriage to match, no doubt."

"A two-wheeled buggy, like the one Beth Edenton has, so I can drive by myself."

Spriggs leaned back in his chair, a hint of admiration in his eyes. "Quite a sight you'll make on this island, in a rig fit for a queen. I'll have to sell my interest in one of my ships to provide what you ask."

"And you'll not question my comings and goings."

"I'll question anything I want. This is my house, and no one touches my woman."

Jerushia raised her chin. "I wish time to ride my horses and to visit with my women friends."

"You have that now," Spriggs growled. "Have I ever forbidden you to leave once your work is done?" He smiled at her. "It is good you make friends with the villagers. It keeps you from prattling when I am here." Then he fixed her with his strange eyes and added softly, "I will not countenance any other men, understand that." He leaned across and slapped her on her thigh. "Now, leave me to my thoughts, woman. I have other matters to consider."

Jerushia stood and began to climb the stairs, then paused. "One more thing."

"Take care you do not overvalue yourself," he warned coldly.

"This will not take gold from your coffers. You will wash yourself before you come to me."

His laughter rolled up the stairs behind her.

I have sold myself for a bolt of colored cloth, Jerushia thought as she entered her room. It was a weakness he'd understood. Indeed, he'd fostered it from the day of her birth. Well, it would never betray her again. She would dress in black for the rest of her days to remind herself—and him—of their wickedness and sin.

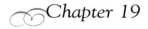Chapter 19

"HERE." JERUSHIA HANDED THE OLD MAN a carefully folded packet of leaves. "Chew on this. It will numb your gums until your jaw heals." She turned to his wife, a much younger woman. "And you, Mary. Your vapors are gone now?" The two women smiled at each other, knowing quite well Jerushia had not been called to attend to the wife, but rather as a pretext to bring relief to old Simon. Although Jerushia's reputation had grown during her five years on Portsmouth Island, men would still not admit to being treated by a woman, at least not openly.

Mary walked her out to the buggy. "I'm truly beholden to you," she whispered to Jerushia. "And not just for tending him." She touched her flat belly and handed Jerushia several packs of carefully dried herbs. " 'Tis such a blessing not to be in a family way again. If I can do anything else for you . . ."

Jerushia accepted them, hiding her bitterness. " 'Tis I who am in your debt for tending these herbs in your garden."

"There be other women using them?" Mary asked slyly.

Jerushia shook her head. "Just as I do not speak of you to them, I will not speak of them to you."

She placed the dried tansy into her satchel and climbed back into the buggy. Among many other things, it was useful in reducing fecundity. But unfortunately, like most of her remedies, it was effective only part of the time.

Wearily, she flicked the reins, sending the horses towards Spriggs Luck. However, as she neared, she changed her mind about returning just yet. It was early summer, and the heat was truly oppressive, worse than she'd ever felt it before. What she needed was a turn by the ocean. The breeze was always fresh there. Perhaps she could even wade in the water. That would cool her off, if anything could. She held the horses in tight check until they were well past the house, knowing they would try to turn into the stable.

As the horses reached the tidal mud flats, presently quite dry in the south winds of summer, Jerushia stopped them for a moment to loosen her bodice. Then she unlaced and removed her stays, breathing a sigh of relief. There was no one else in sight and would not be, she was quite sure. Mostly, the villagers stayed inside until the heat of the day had passed.

Skirts and petticoats up past her knees, stockings shamefully exposed, Jerushia leaned forward and flicked the reins over the horses' backs, clicking her tongue against the roof of her mouth. The Arabians had been waiting for this moment. They reared in delight and leapt ahead at full speed.

Jerushia let them run for several miles. The mud flats offered better footing than the softer sand of the beach, and they enjoyed it so. She was enjoying it, too, as their speed enveloped her body with a cooling breeze. She lifted her face to the wind, drinking in the air. It was heavy with salt and the fusty, strange scent of the flats, a smell neither repugnant nor pleasurable. Ahead, she could see dunes and trees reflected in what appeared to be a lake, but the flats were dry. This was a trompe l'oeil caused by the heat. Still, it gave Jerushia pleasure to look upon the cool stillness of this ghostly lake.

The flats merged into Swash Inlet, the southwest end of the island. She turned the horses toward the beach and pulled them to a halt in knee-deep water. The Arabians, Ahab and Moab, enjoyed a wetting as much as she did, and the buggy was light enough not to become mired in the wet sand. She walked with the horses along the surf until they came to where the inlet waters had no breakers. There, she removed her petticoat, lifted her skirt, and waded out deeper. But soon, that pleasure, too, grew old. Her back ached fearfully, as it always did when she was enceinte.

A pox on men, she thought. A pox on nature, too. Here she was, too old to marry but not too old to bear. She groaned aloud as she climbed heavily into the buggy. What was she to do after the child came? She had concealed her condition thus far with stays and extra petticoats, but soon it would be impossible to mask her growing belly. And what would happen after the babe was born? One could not hide a child. Jerushia turned the horses toward the house at a slow pace.

She would have to confront him again. Superstitious or not, he would have to marry her—if he ever returned. She was not deceived by Spriggs's protracted business trip, which had kept him away ever since her pregnancy had become an unequivocal fact. Even he could no longer insist it was her change. She feared he would not return until after the birth, and there was naught she could do about it.

She would need some excuse not to venture into the village until her time was done. Perhaps an illness—no, better, a broken bone. Jerushia sat up straighter, delighted with her idea. Excellent. A broken bone, a leg. That would give her a reason to remain in her room dressed in her robes or loose clothing. Even Nansa would not suspect if she did this properly.

The knowledge that she would not have to continue with the laces and stays and deception but would instead be able to pamper herself gave Jerushia new energy. Letting the reins hang loosely, for Moab and Ahab would not take advantage, she laced up her stays and put her clothes in order. Then she took off her stockings and bound them both tightly about her ankle, so tightly they would cause her foot to swell. Now, she had a plan.

Instead of pulling into the stable, she halted the buggy in front of the house and began calling for Nansa and Goree. Nansa appeared first.

"I have . . ." Jerushia made her voice tight with pretended pain. "I fear my foot is broken. Call Goree. I will need assistance to my room."

Nansa paled, lifting her apron and wringing her hands. "I not seen Goree, mistress."

Even as the maid whispered his name, the big Negro appeared from behind the stable. "You call, mistress?" he asked in his heavy brogue.

"I have injured myself, Goree." Jerushia kept her eyes away from the black man's. Sometimes, it seemed to her that those bronze orbs could see right through to her soul.

"Mistress wish I fetch the doctor?" There was a doctor in Portsmouth whose task was to tend to injured sailors and the men at Fort Granville, but mostly he tended to himself in Wade's Tavern.

Jerushia shuddered. "That besotted fool? Never. I will attend to it myself, but I need your help to reach my room."

Goree approached, his face impassive. He was a gigantic man, his eyes almost level with hers as she sat in the buggy. His skin was golden brown with a sheen to it, like the polished walnut of the imported desk. Now, he lifted his arms, indicating she should slide over.

Jerushia hesitated. She had never touched Goree. He was almost naked, wearing only the sailor's loose, knee-length skilts held up by a drawstring about his waist. A pleasant, spicy scent rose from the man—the clove-scented oil he used on his hair.

Well, if this deception were to work, she would have to continue her farce. Edging over, she slid into his arms, pretending a groan of pain as she did so.

Nansa leapt forward, little commiserating sounds coming from her throat.

Goree kept his eyes away from her. Indeed, the black was so strong he did not even hold her to his bare chest, but instead walked with her extended forward in his arms, as if she were a basket of gourds. Nansa pulled down Jerushia's petticoat so her bare feet would be covered.

Jerushia smothered a smile. Feigning weakness, she laid her head back against his arm, surprised at the warmth of his smooth skin. She peered at his chest through her lashes. He was heavily tattooed, although because of his color, it was hard to make out some of the designs. From close up, she could see the red-tinged horned snake that wound around his muscular breasts. Farther up, on his shoulder, a buxom Negress danced naked. Right in the center, below his nipples, were two birds, their necks twisted about each other, blood dripping from their open beaks. No, wait, that was not twisted necks; it was a cleverly disguised scar that wound its way across his chest.

He padded up the stairs soundlessly in his bare feet. She wondered how old he was. He'd been with Spriggs as a cabin boy, then as a pirate and later as a cook. He had to be at least ten years younger than the captain. There were no wrinkles on his copper skin, no gray in his black frizz.

Then she realized he'd stopped in the center of her room, waiting silently for her to tell him what he should do next. "On my bed." She motioned, suddenly feeling very tired. This was not pretense.

Goree set her down effortlessly. He backed away waiting, his eyes lowered respectfully. Still, he was at ease. Jerushia marveled at him. A Negro male, particularly an emancipated slave, did not touch a white woman no matter the provocation, much less enter her bedroom. Yet Goree had not hesitated. He remained aloof and dignified as always.

"Nansa," she called. The maid, unlike Goree, flitted nervously in the doorway. "I will need my bandages and four pine slats from the shed, about this big." Jerushia drew her hands apart. "And bring the bottle of laudanum from the pantry."

"Mistress wish me to pull on the ankle bone?" Goree asked.

A pox on him. He was too quick, Jerushia thought. "The bone has not come out of place, although it grates when moved." She winced, as if experiencing it again. "It will not be necessary to set it, but merely to immobilize it." He must have had experience with wounds and broken bones, which was not uncommon, considering his buccaneer upbringing. "You may leave, Goree. Nansa will be able to fulfill my needs from here."

Jerushia's plan worked even better than she'd hoped. The villagers came to call, but she left instructions she was not to be disturbed. Nansa was to tell the callers she was indisposed or sleeping. Privately, she confessed to Nansa that she was too hot and miserable cooped up in her room to try to dress herself and be polite to well-wishers.

She would look at the ocean from her window or watch the birds in the creek. Worried that her muscles would go to fat sitting around, she devised some forms of movement that would not betray her yet would keep her supple. Nansa brought her ribbons, silk, and wool from the captain's sheep, and Jerushia wove her first rug. She hummed to herself as she sewed a blanket for the child's crib.

The last two months passed quickly. The nights were cool again and the skies clear when she finally began her travail a few days before her birthday. However, as her labor progressed, she began to wonder if she would live to see her bolt of cloth this year. Would he give it to the child? she wondered as she stifled another groan.

Do not be a fool, she told herself. You have delivered five other times.

Yes, but you were not forty-five years of age. That is too old to bear easily.

Pshaw. You still have the body of a young woman and are strong. You will have no problems, other than not giving yourself away during the birthing.

But even if you conceal the birth, she argued with herself, how do you think to conceal the wail of a babe or the laughter of a growing child?

Deal with the present, she reminded herself. Let the future take care of itself.

When she began bearing down, Jerushia left her bed in favor of a litter she'd prepared on the floor—a straw mat lined with worn but clean linens. When her birthing was done, she would fold the clothes in among themselves, roll them up tight, and dispose of the signs of her labor deep in the dunes. A drawer was in readiness for the child, but beyond that, she knew not.

An hour later, Jerushia was mortally frightened. Her labor was not going as it should. The cramps were tearing her apart, but the babe was not advancing.

Another violent contraction wracked her. Jerushia felt herself convulsing and heard herself shrieking. When it passed, she wept. She no longer had control of herself or what she did. She groaned again. What did it matter, in any case? She was dying.

Dimly, she heard someone at her door. Horrified, she raised her head, not even breathing.

"Mistress?" came a low whisper, then silence.

Dear Lord, the contractions had begun again. Jerushia braced herself, the pillow over her mouth, willing herself not to make a sound. Her muscles cut her in half, arching her backwards, her legs stretching out in agony, her mouth open, shrieking. Then someone was there, someone large—Goree. His hands were on her body, lifting, holding. The pain.

"No!" she shrieked as his hands tore at her legs, opening her, hurting her. Screaming, she heaved up off the floor, trying to get away. He was pushing down on her, killing her and the child.

Then something happened. It moved, slipped, and Jerushia knew what he had done. He had turned the child in her womb, something she had read about but had never been able to do.

The birthing was done shortly. One last contraction and the baby was delivered. Jerushia lay back weakly, unable to do much except watch Goree as he wiped off the child.

"What is it?" she finally asked.

He hesitated a moment. She saw him look down. "A wee girl," he muttered in his melodic voice. Then his heavy lips opened, and a small gleam of white showed between them. Why, he was smiling, Jerushia realized in surprise. Goree never smiled, unlike some of the other blacks, who were pathetic in their eagerness to please.

"Thank God." Jerushia lay back. Spriggs, she was sure, would take more kindly to a girl child, and she'd always wanted a daughter. As Goree placed the child next to her, she asked him, "How did you know to turn the . . . ?" She blushed, regretting her question.

Goree stood impassive. "I mind the cows when I am boy in Martinique, mistress. Birthing baby not that much different."

She'd been likened to a cow. Jerushia bit her lips to hide her smile. This is what came of conversing with former slaves. Still, she could not quiet her curiosity. "You come from the West Indies, not Africa? Is that why you speak so differently from the other Negroes?" Goree had a singsong rhythm to his speech, a patois of English, Scottish, and French.

He frowned slightly. "Yes, mistress." After a heavy silence, he said, "I be sending word to the captain now."

Jerushia sat up, yelping as she stretched her tender flesh. "You have known all this time where he is? And you did not tell me?"

Goree said nothing, but his eyes glittered coldly.

Jerushia sank back slowly. She was as torn as she'd been with her first child. But if it hadn't been for him, she wouldn't even be feeling this pain. "I never asked you, did I?"

Goree was gathering up the birthing linens as if he did this every day. "Nansa come in the morning to do the wash."

Oh, he was sharp. "Thank you, Goree, for reminding me. It would be better if she did not come until after the master arrives. Could you see she gets word?"

The black man nodded, leaving.

The sun was just beginning to rise in the sky. Next to her, the bundle gurgled. "Yes, my little daughter," Jerushia said to her. "You will make me acknowledge your existence, but Lord God, I wish you were not here." To her surprise, the child was awake, staring at her silently with large blue eyes. Would they turn to that strange brown-gold of Spriggs's eyes, Jerushia wondered, or would she have the blue-gray of the O'Hagans?

"I will let him name you," she said to the babe. "After all, he named me."

Three days later, Jerushia woke from an afternoon nap, tired and aching, to the sound of a commotion downstairs. She knew immediately what it was: the captain had arrived. She wondered wearily if he would stop by her chambers this night. She hoped not, for her milk was just coming, her breasts engorged, and both she and the babe were worn out from trying to feed. Indeed, she had resorted to a rag dipped in sugar water to calm the poor child.

To Jerushia's relief, after about an hour, the captain mounted the stairs directly to his room. He'd apparently elected to visit her the next day.

In the morning, she rose hurriedly to make her ablutions and prepare to see him. She washed herself carefully and dressed in fresh garments and her most becoming blue bodice. Then she wiped off the child and tried to fluff up the pale fuzz on the girl's head. To be truthful, this was not a child to take a man's eye. As if the babe could hear her thoughts, she reached for Jerushia's hand, grasping a finger firmly. Jerushia smiled, bending to kiss the thin face. "Ugly child, beautiful woman," she whispered. "I will come for you soon."

She made her way painfully down the stairs to where Spriggs was taking his breakfast. He rose when she entered, kissing her hand and complimenting her on her dress. "Ye must be in league with the devil. No woman appears this handsome right after a difficult birth. Why, ye could be a filly of twenty, not forty-five this day."

She'd forgotten it was her birthday. "I have not named her yet," she said. "I thought mayhaps you would do this."

"I'll think upon it." He waved a hand magnanimously. "But first, you must come with me."

Jerushia followed him to the stable, walking softly. Her body was sore and tender, a sign that healing had begun, but an uncomfortable one nevertheless. However, rather than irritate the captain right now, she would have walked to the village. She hoped perhaps he'd brought something for the baby—a length of muslin, anything, as long as he acknowledged her existence.

The gift was not for the child. But as Jerushia reached the stable, she cried out in genuine pleasure. He'd brought her a new buggy, and what a handsome thing it was. The wheels were so large they would overshadow the driver, and the seat was so high she would be able to see beyond the dunes to the ocean. Oh, Ahab and Moab would fly pulling this magnificent conveyance! "Thank you," she cried, hugging Spriggs and caressing the gleaming leather. She pointed at some handworked curlicues. "What is the purpose of this, and this?"

"That is to hold the reins," he told her. "The other, I do not know." He helped her in, then turned away. "There is a packet under the seat. Do not rush to come back to the house. I will be at the books for the rest of the morning, I fear."

Perhaps this is for the babe, Jerushia thought, climbing up painfully. But the packet proved to be an intricately wrought silver locket with a likeness of herself inside. It was no doubt worth a fortune, but right now, some pink or white muslin would have been far more welcome.

She slid off slowly, wincing as her feet hit the ground. She would pay for this, she well knew. At least her breasts were easier now, her milk flow reaching normal. She hurried her steps to return to the child. She would be able to nurse her now.

The captain was in his office. She stopped long enough to thank him for the locket, then continued upstairs. To her surprise, the child was silent. Jerushia expected her to be mewing and grunting with hunger after the long night. She removed her bodice and unlaced her shift. As she bent over the improvised crib, she stiffened. The babe's face was slack, mouth open, eyes closed.

Just sleeping. A prickle ran up her spine. She slid her hand under the child's back, lifting. The child's head rolled to the side.

Jerushia froze, the baby half out of the crib, the lifeless head lolling.

"No, no. She was healthy," she said aloud. "She held my finger just a moment ago." Jerushia clutched the child to her shoulder, patting her back frantically. "Wake up, wake up. 'Tis I, your mother. I'm here. I'll never leave you again."

The body sagged limply against her.

Jerushia wailed. Her girl-child was dead. "Oh, God, no. Please, no. Not this one."

She was sobbing in choking gulps, still clutching the babe, when she felt someone at her shoulder. A hand touched her gently. At first, she thought it was Spriggs, but then she smelled the cloves. "She'd dead, she's dead," Jerushia wept as she let Goree take the child from her. Then she remembered he'd saved them before. "Make her breathe. You know how?" she begged.

Goree placed the child on the bed, opening the swaddling cloth, and lay his giant black head to her chest. Then he touched his fingers to the babe's neck, probing gently. Face stern, he shook his head silently as he drew the cloth over the tiny face.

Jerushia watched in frozen horror. She should never have left the babe alone to go look at the carriage.

Where was the captain?

She rushed down the stairs into the office. "Your child's dead!" she shrieked at him. "Now, are you content? You do not have to marry me," she spit at him.

He stood to face her. "I would not have married thee in any case."

"It was your present." She beat at his chest. "Your presents are all evil." She tore the locket from her neck and flung it out the open window.

"Control yourself, woman." He held her by her shoulders. "It was a sickly, weak babe, a breech birth delivered by a kitchen slave. I would have marveled had it lived."

He was right, she decided later from her bed, where Spriggs had taken her, weak with weeping. The babe had been a thin, small child, but so sweet, so uncomplaining. Then Jerushia groaned in new agony, for she was not able to stop that one terrible thought: now, her life could go on the way it had been.

Through the window, she could hear Goree opening ground

for the grave. Already, he'd nailed together a tiny coffin. Poor little thing. She hadn't even been named yet.

Slowly, with grim determination, Jerushia pushed herself from the bed. She would do one thing for this child: give her a name to be inscribed on the gravestone. She would call her Mary, after her own mother. Pleased that at least there was something she could do, she painfully made her way to the office to tell Spriggs.

"Are ye mad, woman? A tombstone? After keeping your secret all these months, ye now want to erect a monument for the whole island to see?"

Jerushia blinked. Then the truth of what he said flooded her. "You mean to bury her like a dog—no, like a maggoty ham?" She swung around toward the yard, where Goree bent with a shovel, his back gleaming with sweat. So this was her punishment for having sinned. After a few moments, she said quietly, "I cannot do this."

Spriggs must have understood some of what she felt, for he came closer, putting an arm about her shoulder. "Perhaps . . ." He hesitated, then began again. "There is another solution, not one that is to my liking, but a prudent captain runs before the wind."

Jerushia sighed heavily. There could be no solution to her baby's death.

"We shall bury it in my tomb."

"In your tomb?" Jerushia whirled to face him. For a moment, she was shocked. Then she realized his suggestion was the perfect solution. It would make an honorable grave site for her child. Not only that, but by placing the babe in his own tomb, Spriggs acknowledged the relationship. "Yes. You are right," she whispered. "It is the solution."

However, as Goree and Spriggs, together with the aid of a hoist, slowly lowered the marble lid back into place over the tiny coffin, Jerushia felt as if she were condemning her child to die a slow, eternal death in the airless tomb. It was too soon. Perhaps she was not really dead. "No, stop!" she cried, pulling at Spriggs's arm.

The lid slid into place with a dull thud.

"No!" she screamed, dropping to her knees and tugging at the slab. The room began to whirl. Jerushia sank dizzily to the floor, her cheek on the cold marble.

"I'll be here for you always," she promised as the world faded into darkness. ∽

Chapter 20

THE LID WAS HARD AND UNYIELDING. Her breathing slowed; her heart calmed its frantic beating; sweat mixed with sand dried like tears on her cheeks. Bert ran her hand over the cold white marble. This was no dream. She'd really found Spriggs's tomb.

Scrambling to her feet, she gripped a protruding edge and lifted. No way. Was it just heavy, or was it clamped in place? Retrieving the cockleshell she'd been using as a shovel, Bert settled back down to scrape yet more sand from the tomb. Sweat poured down her face, but she hardly noticed. As she threw the sand up in the air for the wind to blow away, part of the side wall was exposed. The vault was built of bricks held together by mortar. A thick layer of cracked mortar ran around the rim. Bert chopped at one of the cracks with her crowbar and hammer. If she could make a hole and pry the lid up, maybe it would slide off. The whole tomb lay at an angle, the ground under one side washed away, the bricks curving downward. There, the mortar was crumbling and came away easily. Soon, she had a good-sized hole.

Bert wedged the crowbar into the opening between the lid and the bricks. She used her foot to push down, hoping the lid would not slide back toward her. At first, it held firm. But as Bert bounced up and down on the lever, something cracked, and the marble lifted ever so slightly. Encouraged, she put one foot on the crowbar, balanced herself carefully, then brought the second foot up and jumped down hard with all her weight. Metal squealed, and the marble slab began to move. It slid two feet to the side before it stopped. A long, triangular slit gaped open into the grave.

Bert backed away, suddenly terrified. What had she done? Hunter wouldn't approve of this at all. Her first instinct was to quickly close it. But no, she couldn't do that.

Undecided, she stood staring, suddenly conscious that her nose was running, her eyes watering. Was it pollen in the wind? Maybe it was something coming from the tomb. She'd heard about grave fungus pollen before. It had killed some archaeologists in the 1920s. Don't be stupid, she told herself. It was just the mortar and sandy dust she'd raised.

Holding her breath, Bert forced herself to peer into the tomb. What she saw raised the hair on her neck. Two old wooden boxes were in the vault, one large, the other no bigger than would hold a newborn child.

Grief surged through her, driving all thought from her mind. Bert backed away. Calm down, she told herself, shivering as the wind cooled the sweat on her body. There was no reason to feel like someone she loved had just died. It was an old grave. Whoever lay in it had been dead for two hundred and fifty years. The big casket was probably Spriggs's, but what was in the small box— a child, Spriggs's treasure, Jerushia's ashes?

She crouched, staring for a long time, as if by doing so she could see into the caskets. Wait until she told Hunter she'd actually discovered the tomb. She was dying to know what was inside the caskets, but no way was she crawling down into that dark, damp vault full of God knew what. She hoped the park wouldn't be too upset at her for jumping the gun.

Bert tried to pull the slab back over the tomb, but it barely moved. Some of her earlier nausea returned. She tugged again, hating to leave the caskets exposed to the weather. But it was no use. There was a come-along—a hand winch—in the boathouse. That and a chain should do it. Suppose water ruined the contents now that she'd broken the seal? She'd better fetch a tarp, too, and shovel the sand back over. Damn, the generator was running. She still had all that to close up. She prayed there was enough time. Guilt churned coldly in her stomach as Bert grabbed the crowbar and headed back toward the generator shed.

The path in front of her heaved.

For a minute, she thought she'd gone mad. The ground was moving like a dark wave of water. Then she realized it was a solid mass of fur—brown fur and little black eyes and white muzzles. Nutria, dozens of them, were blocking the path.

Bert shook her head numbly, backing away until her ankle hit the marble slab. She screamed.

The nutria swung around to face her, whiskers flicking. Suddenly, they were no longer cute, bunny-like creatures with split lips. Even in the growing dusk, she could see the warning curl of the lips and the long incisors beneath. Now, they were all facing her, backs humped menacingly, snouts up, teeth bared. Oh, God, their teeth were elongated orange fangs!

Bert's stomach contracted. Her breath caught in her throat. She didn't believe in ghosts. Nutria couldn't think or act as a group to keep her here. Ridiculous!

They were edging up the rise, trying to force her back to the grave.

"I don't want to go there," she whispered inanely. "No." She stared back at them, growling deep in her throat, lifting the crowbar.

The foremost nutria crouched low.

Oh, shit, they looked like they were getting ready to charge.

Bert backed away, crooning, "I didn't mean a thing. Just kidding. I won't hurt you. See, I'm putting it down. You know me. Now, take it easy." She kept her eyes glued on them as she slowly placed the crowbar on the ground.

The solid mass of fur rippled. The nutria padded forward soundlessly, heads down, eyes fixed on her, lips twitching.

They backed her up to the slab. She now stood at the high point of the only dry land around. Behind her was the marsh. To her left, the path to the fuel dump and Sheep Island was already wet in spots. Did they want to back her into the water? She glanced fearfully at it, then moaned. The water was alive, too, but with snakes. Most of them were black ground snakes and racers, but there were others. A thick, mottled brown-and-cream snake caught her eye. God, that was a king snake. She'd read about them but didn't think there were any more around. And over there were banded water snakes and a couple of spiny lizards. Bert shuddered. But deep in her mind, she was relieved. That's why the nutria were backing her toward the grave. It wasn't some kind of response to a mystical command. They couldn't get into the water with the snakes, and the rising tide was forcing them to seek higher ground. The poor things were probably as scared of her as she was of them.

She glanced from the snakes back to the nutria. There was nothing pitiful about them as they circled her, faces up, whiskers trembling, sharp eyes fixed on her face, lips drawn to show their ugly, orange teeth. At least they'd stopped advancing. But she couldn't stay here. The hurricane was coming. The tide would probably get even higher than this. Bert glanced at the water, trying to estimate the height of the grave above sea level. About six feet, she guessed. The tide was already up two feet. An eight- to twelve-foot surge was nothing unusual during a storm like this. They'd all be standing in the water—with the snakes. And now that she'd opened the grave, there was a danger the coffins might float off.

She had to get back to the station. The question was how. Deciding she'd rather brave the nutria than the snakes, she took a deep breath, preparing herself to advance. If she moved very slowly and talked to them, would they let her through?

Something rustled behind her. She whirled. A shadow towered over her, rising from the grave. Bert shrieked, one scream after another. She backed up, into the nutria. They gave way, grunting and squealing as if her fright had infected them. Now,

Bert stood among them, staring at the apparition.

"Bert? What the hell is that around you?"

"Jimmy?" Bert choked, rushing toward him. "What are you doing here? I thought you were . . ."

He was wet and covered with mud. Jimmy's attention was directed toward the uncovered slab. Emotions twisted his handsome features. She could see suspicion narrow his eyes. "What the hell are you doing messing with my grave? And what have you got on your head? I couldn't tell who you were."

"What do you mean? You knew about the grave?"

"Don't tell me you're in on this, too."

"In on what?"

His lips were a tight line. "This." He kicked the marble. "You found it, I see."

This wasn't the Jimmy she knew. Something was wrong.

"Don't you pay any attention to evacuations? Or did you sneak back deliberately?" His eyes glinted green. "That's it, isn't it? You ditched him so you could dig. Who else is here? I saw Donny's boat. He in on this with you?"

"No one's here—that I know of." It might be smarter not to let him think she was alone. "Hunter's on his way back to get me."

"In these seas? I damn near didn't make it over to Evergreen. No one's getting on—or off—until the storm's over."

Bert was beginning to understand. "You're the one who dug it up. You came back in this weather to open up the tomb when no one was here."

He showed his teeth, like a cat about to pounce. "I planned to be in and out before the hurricane hit, but you messed me up. Had to beach the boat by the inlet where anyone could see it—goddamn jellyfish. When I heard the truck, I had to hide the boat quick. Took it over to the slew and hiked in. Now, I'm stuck until the hurricane's over."

That was Jimmy's boat she'd seen over by Potter's cabin when she closed the visitor center? Potter's was often used by boaters, since it had a little dock on the sound. Of course, the crabber.

Her eyes must have reflected her thoughts, as Jimmy suddenly stopped talking.

"Something's wrong here." Vertical furrows parted his brow. "You're no artifact hunter. Who are you, anyhow? Special investigator?" He grabbed her shoulders, shaking her.

Bert gasped.

Something darted forward. Jimmy yelled, kicking out. A black, furry object struck at his leg. Then another. "Stop them," he said, backing away, using her as a shield.

Bert held her breath, too frightened even to struggle, waiting for them to slash her. But the nutria seemed to hesitate. One began to edge to the side.

Jimmy countered quickly. "No way, you bloody bastards. You'll have to go through her to get at me." He glanced around. Behind him was the road to Sheep Island, mostly under water. Shadowy movement to the sides indicated the nutria were encircling him.

He made the decision Bert had promised herself to avoid. Still holding her as a shield, he shoved at the marble, enlarging the opening. "Get in." He pushed her down when she resisted. She slid inside, Jimmy right behind. It was deep in the vault, four feet at least. Jimmy crouched under the slab, half on a coffin, using Bert as cover.

"Please, Jimmy, no," Bert said, trying not to move. Her face was at a level with the animals. All they had to do was dart forward and slash. However, instead of advancing, they seemed to calm. She stared mesmerized into the tiny eyes. The orange teeth were no longer visible, the rapid muzzle movements slowing. Their fur smoothed. Suddenly, they looked like her friends again. "Thank you," she whispered soundlessly.

"Tell them to go away," Jimmy muttered into her ear.

"Don't be stupid," she hissed, trying not to move her lips. "They're not going to mind me."

"Tell them." He shook her slightly. Immediately, the animals' hackles rose. Bert held her breath, waiting for the attack. But the nutria fell back. However, when she tried to shift her weight, she found he had a firm grip on her belt. "Oh, no, babe. You stay right here until I'm done."

"The park will know you were here," Bert said. "They'll come after you."

"They need proof. They won't find any. It'll be my word against yours." He edged near what Bert assumed was Spriggs's coffin. "Unless you're a park detective. Of course, you uncovered the tomb, right?" He grunted, tugging at the lid. "My lawyer can call it entrapment." Using only one hand, the other still on her belt, he tried to open the coffin. Chunks of rotten wood came off, but the nails held. "I'd have been gone by now, if you hadn't come back."

"I'm not a detective, and I don't care what you take." Bert's voice shook.

Jimmy's grip loosened slightly. "Look, I'm not going to hurt you. I tried to keep you out of it, didn't I? Set up that recorder just to scare you into staying inside. Worked pretty well, didn't it? Anne gave me the idea. She kept going on about hearing a ghostly choir."

Bert barely heard him. "Just let me out of here." It was a nightmare, the whole thing. The tomb smelled moldy, rotten. Or was that coming from the nutria? The wind was full of rain and sand. Icy drops pelted the back of her neck and ran down the marble slab on to her wet jeans. Jimmy stunk like a swamp.

"Then don't move while I get this open, understand?" Jimmy hooked a foot inside Bert's thigh. Then he let go of her belt, twisting around so he could use both hands on the coffin.

Between Jimmy's body blocking off the interior and the marble cover partially over him, Bert couldn't see much. She heard him fumbling in his pack and saw the gleam of a hammer as he pried up the coffin lid. Of course. Very cautiously, she reached for the hammer in her belt. It wasn't there. She'd left it next to the hole she'd chopped in the mortar.

Jimmy grunted. Wood cracked and split. Dust rose thickly. Bert pulled the netting from her hat over her mouth. He crouched over the box, reaching in. She heard more cracking—bones? Her stomach contracted.

"Yes," Jimmy breathed. "Look what I got." He pulled Bert down inside the tomb, dangling a long chain with something bulky on it. It didn't look remotely like emeralds or anything valuable. "I knew it. The minute I saw Luna Mae pick up that locket, I knew it had to be here." He spoke triumphantly, as if they were partners. "But how did you figure out where to look?"

"You killed Luna Mae for that?" she asked, but Jimmy had already turned away, bent back over the coffin. Would he kill her next? If only she had some sort of weapon.

She heard the dull click of metal. He was probably removing Spriggs's gold chains. A trivial thought forced itself through her fear. Why would a woman as practical as Jerushia allow such valuables to be buried with the old pirate? Was it superstition? Was it meant to keep the dead man in his tomb?

Something slapped Bert in the small of the back, pushing her against the side of the vault. "Stop it," she moaned.

"Then move over." Roughly, he shoved her back by the tiny coffin. Then, very slowly, he raised his head through the opening, looking out.

Bert watched, hoping the nutria would let him depart. Maybe he wasn't going to kill her. Silently, she whispered an instruction to the animals: "Let him leave."

Jimmy ducked back down. He grabbed her by the neck and yanked her forward. "Get up there," he hissed. Hand on her butt, he pushed hard, forcing her head and shoulders through the opening.

She heard a quick intake of breath.

Instinctively, Bert jerked away.

Something slammed into the side of her head.

Blackness rushed in from all sides. She was falling, falling . . .

Chapter 21

"TAKE IT EASY, BUDDY," RUDY TOLD HUNTER. "It's not like she's in any real danger. Top winds are a hundred and twenty, and Carlos is still headed at Cape Lookout, not Portsmouth Village."

"Which means," Hunter said tightly, "Portsmouth will get the northeast side of the hurricane. Could bring twelve-foot tides."

"That lifesaving station's seen worse. Been through the '99 storm, and the '33, and the '44. And you know the policy: better to leave them there than have someone hurt in a late evacuation."

Hunter limped over to the plate-glass window of the park headquarters on Harkers Island. Wind screamed through the eaves as the first raindrops spattered the glass-fronted building. Across the parking lot, black sound water leapt in all directions. Low thunderheads churned and twisted, blocking the view of the Cape Lookout lighthouse on the distant barrier island. Hunter shook his head. "It just doesn't seem right to leave her alone in this."

Rudy sighed. "Can't say I like it much myself, but I don't know that we have much choice." He joined Hunter at the window. "If things change, the Coast Guard in Ocracoke can always pick her up. Trouble is, they got their hands full right now. Got a trawler aground on Hog Shoal and a big sailboat taking on water off Hatteras."

"I know. And it's just going to get worse. The state's already closed down the ferries. Anyway, there's nothing to say she'd be better off in some shelter at Ocracoke than at Portsmouth." Hunter counted on his fingers. "Shackleford and the cape's been evacuated. Crissie and Ben Willis took care of most of that before I got here. I'm not near as indispensable as I thought. This building is all that's left. Furniture's off the floor. Sandbags are out." He placed his palm against the window. "Nothing more for me to do here. Something's telling me to get back there."

"You can't, so put it out of your mind," Rudy said flatly. "You're plain lucky we got you out once."

"Yeah, right, lucky." Was history repeating itself? Hunter hadn't wanted to be rescued six years ago when his wife drowned, and now all he wanted was to get back to Portsmouth.

God knows, he'd tried to get back to Bert after they'd been separated. Was that only this morning? It seemed so much longer ago. When Bert backed up the truck with him on the other end of the rope, she'd pulled him right into that myrtle. He'd had a hard time getting to his knife, all tangled up in the bush the way he'd been, but he'd made it. He'd even managed to catch a glimpse of Bert on the hood of the truck just before the water swept him away. He was pretty sure she caught his signal to go back.

The swift current had carried him past Sheep Island. Once he made shore—on the wrong side—Hunter had scrambled up a ridge of sand. No sign of Bert or the truck. Damn, she was probably still at the crossing, stuck in the water. Well, there was only one thing to do. Sighting from the ridge, he picked out a spot where the river broadened and the current didn't seem so swift. If she was stuck in the truck, she might need help.

He'd expected it to be rough in the channel, but he underestimated the force and depth of the tidal river. He was only waist deep when it tossed him like a loose surfboard. He had to fight just to breathe as it swept him down the flats, then through the swash and into the new inlet the sea was carving for itself. For a moment, he thought he was dead. Never saw anything like it—white foam and spray. One moment, he'd been head over heels in a breaker. The next, he was slammed against the bottom, half a ton of water trying to squeeze what little air he had out of his lungs.

Finally, the ocean had spit him up on the beach. He heaved and coughed a spell before he was able to sit up. Sick to his stomach from the water he'd swallowed, he stared at the maelstrom. Now, he'd seen everything. The ocean had cut a new inlet, all right, and he was the first across—without a boat, yet.

He hoped Bert had hightailed it back to the village. If she got through on the radio, she could still get out. Could be the park boat was already headed that way to fetch her.

It wasn't until Hunter had started down the beach that he noticed the puncture wound in his thigh. He attributed the blood on his leg to minor scrapes from being buffeted in the surf. He must have gotten jabbed by a branch of that bush. At least the wound had been cleaned out good.

He'd walked about two miles down the shoreline when he saw a black speck coming up the beach. Hunter heaved a giant sigh of relief. Bert was safe, and she did get through to them.

It was Justin with his truck. "Miss Bert's doing just fine," he told Hunter. "Called us from the tower. She were all in a lather about you. I'd of been here sooner, but Elmo and me had to move them pilings blocking the beach." However, Justin had flatly refused to take Hunter back to the new cut. His orders were to return to the ferry. "Be better that way," he told Hunter. "Elmo can get you to the village with his boat. From what you is saying, there ain't no other way to get there nohow."

They had reached Long Point to find the *Green Grass* waiting offshore, chop breaking over her deck. The captain, Elmo Smith, was adamant about not navigating the sixteen miles to the village. "This boat ain't made to take that kind of a beating," he told Hunter. "Besides, even if she don't break up, she can only do about five knots into that nor'easter. We'd be out of gas and daylight before we got there." He clasped Hunter's shoulder. "That gal's a trouper, she is. She'll do all right, you hear? Now, why don't you go see if you can't raise her on the short wave?"

Hunter had tried the ferry's marine radio, hoping he could catch Bert in the cabin, where they kept the more powerful marine set. The traffic was heavy with fishermen organizing for the storm, but he could not raise Bert. Then he tried the park frequency. The repeater that amplified the signal was powered by electricity. Unfortunately, the power was already out on the islands. The signal would carry only a couple of miles without the repeater—slightly more if Bert was in the tower. He knew that, tower or not, there was no way he could reach her on her handheld once they left Long Point.

To his relief, Bert had answered almost immediately. He knew without asking that she had been waiting in the tower to hear from him. Her delight almost did him in. Elmo, who had been pacing the decks, cast off as soon as Hunter made contact.

And that was the last anyone had heard from Bert. Now, here he was at Harkers, with no power for the duration of the storm. The park's backup generator was worthless. He'd see to it that the system was upgraded when this was over, budget cuts and allocations be damned. He tried his marine radio band once again. Bert should be able to receive on the big set in the cabin—if she remembered to turn it on and if the antenna had not blown down. "I'm calling the Coast Guard," he told Rudy. "If anyone can get through to her, they can."

But the Coast Guard was unable to get a response from Bert either.

"She's probably out buttoning up the buildings like you told her," Rudy said.

Buttoning up or not, Bert should have been back in her cabin by now, or over to the lifesaving station, Hunter thought as he went through the local broadcast bands. It was almost four o'clock. He'd had time to change his clothes, have his thigh bandaged, and review the orders Crissie had given in his absence. "I'm standing here wishing I'd turned the truck back to Portsmouth, like she wanted me to," he said to Rudy.

"Ever notice it's only the decisions that don't turn out right we remember?" Rudy asked.

The remark surprised Hunter. Was it true? He regretted not bringing the boat in sooner with his wife, but nothing else. Not the fact that they had gone out in the first place. He didn't regret getting married or leaving the navy and making the park his career. He wasn't sorry he'd met Bert or slept with her. There were lots of decisions he'd made that were right, he thought as he watched the men attach towlines to the old barge.

The park offices were nearly deserted, the furniture raised several feet off the floor, the doors closed and bolstered with sandbags, the power off. Most of the residents of Harkers Island had been evacuated. Only he and Rudy were left inside the building. A few of the maintenance men were by the dock still working. All of the park boats had been taken out of the water or moved to the mainland except for the barge, the towboat, and the Downeaster—a small cabin cruiser. Right now, maintenance was backing a trailer into place to take the Downeaster out of the water. It would be stored here at Harkers, ready for immediate use after the hurricane.

Rudy clapped his friend across the shoulder. "Soon as she's out, we go."

Hunter brought himself back to the present. The germ of an idea was growing in his mind. "You go ahead now with the truck and take one last swing around the housing to make sure there ain't no one about and the gates are closed. I'll lock up and throw the mains as soon as maintenance is done." They had to be sure nothing was left on in case power was restored unexpectedly.

Hunter waited until Rudy was out of sight, then strode over to the men preparing the trailer. He waved one of them over. "Clyde, Coast Guard called. Got someone in trouble by the bar. Asked we leave the Mickey Mouse in the water in case they need an assist." Mickey Mouse was the men's nickname for the high-prowed Downeaster, whose squat cabin with two wooden-sided enclosures did indeed resemble the cartoon character.

Clyde glanced toward the cape. "Hell of a place to be right now. Poor bastards. You want us to wait?"

"No. You men go on home. They're sending over a crew."

Clyde breathed relief. His men had their own families and homes to prepare for the storm. "Should we leave the trailer here?"

Hunter started to tell him to park it and the truck in the maintenance building, then decided that might look suspicious. He nodded. "I'll make certain they take care of the trailer before Carlos makes landfall."

"That'll work," Clyde said with a grin. "Boss will have my ass if something happens to our new truck."

His boss would be even more unhappy if he knew what Hunter was planning to do with the park boat.

Hunter waited until maintenance left, towing the barge. Then he put away the truck and trailer. At least the truck would be safe. The boat was docked in the first slip, so getting out even in the growing chop was not a problem. Hunter lost no time donning rain gear and life vest. He did a quick check of the Mickey Mouse. Maintenance was the park's most efficient department. He would have been surprised if all were not in order and ready for immediate use. Five minutes later, he was out of the marina and into the choppy waters of Core Sound.

He looked at his watch. Twenty minutes after four. That gave him over four hours of daylight—more than enough time even against a headwind like this. The Mickey Mouse was built for weather and had a reliable four-fifty-four inboard. Visibility and chop would be his worst problems. The sounds averaged a depth of three to six feet, invisible shoals lying ready to capture those who strayed from the deepwater channels. If he didn't run her aground, he'd be fine.

And if he didn't get shaken to death, he amended an hour later. Hunter wondered if the Mickey Mouse—or any boat—was built to take a beating like this. It was slow going, even slower than he'd expected. Visibility was so bad he couldn't take the usual shortcuts, but was running on the compass from marker to marker. When he couldn't find a marker, he had to slow and peer through

the spitting rain and spray until he came upon some familiar landmark. Sometimes, it was a row of pound stakes, crab pots, or, best
of all, the red or green buoys of the Intracoastal Waterway.

Still, conditions were manageable until he passed the settlement of Atlantic and came out of the sheltered water of Core
Sound. The mouth of the Pamlico lay ahead. From the weather
reports, Hunter knew what he would be facing. Again, he looked
at his watch. Six-fifteen. Almost two hours, and he was little more
than halfway there. Beating or no beating, he was going to have
to make better time. He had a pretty good idea of what his speed
had been in Core Sound, and it would be even slower here. Carefully, Hunter made a notation on the chart, glancing toward the
west. It was hard to believe there was still a sun up there.

He could almost hear Rudy's voice in his ear: "Some people
got no sense. Taking off in the teeth of a storm in a park boat
without authorization. Even if you don't sink her, your career's in
the mud, boy."

But what kind of career would he have if he couldn't live
with himself? He couldn't have gone to the mainland to sit out
the storm in bed—or in some bar—knowing Bert was out here
alone. Besides, it wasn't just that. There was this sense of urgency,
as if he were running a race against time and someone was standing on the sidelines just out of sight, cheering him on.

He jury-rigged a harness and hooked it to the ceiling. Seas
like this could throw a man about and prevent him from being at
the controls at crucial moments.

Pamlico Sound was every bit as bad as he'd expected, perhaps
worse. It was a good thing he hadn't waited any longer. The hurricane wasn't supposed to make landfall until sometime in the wee
hours of the morning. Had the projection changed? he wondered
as the boat shuddered under a gust. His biggest danger in high
seas was a broach. Time after time, he fought the controls, playing with the speed of the boat as well as the direction, keeping
her bow at an angle to the racing swells, running neither too fast
nor too slow.

The Mickey Mouse pitched and rolled like a wild pony being

broken, Hunter decided tiredly an hour later. At least here in the Pamlico, he had more room to maneuver. But he had another problem. He peered anxiously toward the east. Between his speed and the compass settings he'd adjusted with every marker he'd found, he had a pretty good idea where he was, but how in blue thunder was he going to get to shore? The waves— eight to nine feet, he estimated—washed over the bow of the boat. Already, the glass had given way on the port side. The bilge pumps were running full blast, yet water was everywhere, running across the deck, slopping in the stern, whipping against the cabin. He couldn't tell if it was rain or spray. He couldn't steer much either, just enough to slide up the side of one wave and down the other.

No way would he be able to put in at Haulover. It was too exposed. Besides, the approach would put the waves at his stern, the worst possible course in these seas. No. He'd have to put into Evergreen Slew on Sheep Island. But how to find it in this mess? The approach into the creek was hard to locate even in full daylight and fair weather. His only hope was that the tide had built up enough water to get him over the shoals. If he ran aground there, it would be a matter of minutes before the boat broke up. He really didn't feel like another swim today.

Spray pelted his exposed skin like cold needles, coming in where the panes had broken out of the cabin. He fished a pair of goggles from the locker, but the water streamed over them, too, making it hard to see. Hunter waited until the boat was on top of a wave to sight again. Was that break in the tree line really a creek, or was it just airborne spray blocking out the trees?

For the first time, he felt his guts tighten. They'd called him a madman when he tried to go back into the water after his wife. Maybe they were right. He wasn't going to be able to help Bert. All he was going to do was embarrass the park when he was pulled out dead. It wasn't that he minded dying. Indeed, he'd always figured the sea would get him someday. He just hated the idea that people would say he died because he'd been stupid or foolhardy.

Come off it, he told himself. Things weren't that bad. It was just another challenge to be met. The thought made him feel better. He straightened up.

This time, when the Mickey Mouse fought to the peak of a wave, Hunter was ready. He sighted again toward that small break in the gray skyline of the island. Then, as the last of the sun vanished over the invisible horizon, he spun the wheel toward shore. Now, the waves hit him from the stern. He had to zigzag so as to take them from the quarter. As he came closer to shore, into the lee of the island, the size of the sea diminished, but the chop grew correspondingly fiercer. It was no longer a question of which way to take the waves—it was like riding a breaker, white foam everywhere. Frantically, he peered ahead, but the shore had disappeared. There was no twilight tonight. Darkness had closed in just minutes after sunset.

He slowed the boat as much as he dared. He had two choices: plow dead ahead and hope that by some miracle he was directly on course for Evergreen Slew, or take her in slowly, praying for some recognizable landmark he could use. He slowed the Mickey Mouse even more, clenching his teeth. It was like being in a mixer. He put his hand to the harness and checked his release. He might need to get out fast.

Hunter pulled at the wheel as another series of waves buffeted the boat. "Dammit, Bert, I'm sorry," he said aloud.

The wind roared, rising like a voice crying in the dark. A huge, breaking wave slammed the Mickey Mouse over on her side, practically jerking off Hunter's head. Water poured in. The boat righted herself slowly. Hunter raised a hand to his neck. He didn't know if something had hit him or if it was whiplash, but he was sick from the pain.

Another breaker beat the boat down. Automatically, he spun the wheel toward the wave, but the boat responded sluggishly. Chop and spray poured over the cabin. It was odd how it clung to the console, making strange designs in the glass as the high prow tossed in the surf.

He shook his head to clear his goggles, which made the pain

flare in his neck. He blinked. Was that someone out there, pointing?

He must be seeing trees—or flying debris. No matter. He throttled up, hauling the wheel around to where he'd seen the image. If he'd glimpsed a tree trunk—or a person—over yonder, then there had to be land there, high land.

The boat leapt forward. Suddenly, the sea calmed. He was in deep water—Evergreen Slew. This harbor had sheltered many a Portsmouth fisherman.

Though he still couldn't make out the shore, he took the Mickey Mouse ahead, steering by the feel of the water under the deck, going forward inch by inch. And inch by inch, the water quieted. Soon, he was in the creek itself. Although the boat still bounced in the chop, it was calm compared to what he'd left outside. The windblown rain reduced visibility to a few feet, but he could make out a gray line to the side—marsh grass. The dock would be straight ahead.

As he neared, to his complete surprise, he saw another boat tied to the pilings, a high-bowed skiff carrying several crab pots. Donny? Didn't look like his boat. A crabber caught short? Must have taken shelter at Donny's camp, Hunter thought wearily as he lashed the Mickey Mouse to the moorings. It took him awhile to add spring lines and make sure she was tied down as securely as possible, not an easy task in the conditions. Hopefully, she would ride out the storm.

He pulled his pack out of the locker and took a long swig of water. He hadn't realized how thirsty he was. One of the candy bars he and Bert hadn't eaten that morning completed his break. A little dry land, food, and water were all a man needed. He felt as rested as if he'd taken a two-hour nap.

Before he left, he took a closer look at the other boat, hoping to find some clue to its owner. He made note of the registration. There was little else to identify the boat—a couple of life vests, an oily orange rag, a metal gasoline tank.

Hunter began the four-mile hike to Portsmouth Village. As he limped along, he couldn't help wondering about the figure he'd seen at the mouth of the creek. Storms can cause strange illusions. A little edge of wind-swept phosphorescence, some eelgrass in a wave, who knew? He could swear it had been a woman pointing. Lucky for him.

The path was overgrown and sheltered by heavy scrub, but he'd be fully exposed once he reached the flats. At least the exercise was loosening up his aching puncture wound.

He stopped by Donny's camp. It was shuttered up and dark as the inside of a whale's belly. No one about, not even a crabber. But what if it wasn't a crabber caught by the storm? A boat like that wouldn't be noticed on the sound. That gas tank was just like the one they kept at the boathouse. Oh, Lord, how thick could he be?

Hunter broke into a jog. Now, he knew where that sense of urgency had come from. He just prayed he wasn't too late. ᴄᴏ

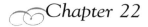Chapter 22

SOMETHING WAS ON TOP OF HER, crushing her chest. She couldn't breathe. Her head—a fiery pounding. What had she done? Drunk herself to oblivion. Driven into a tree? Bad nightmare? No, it hurt too much. It was so dark. Where was she?

Bert tried to push away the weight that constricted her lungs. The movement shot pain through her skull. She yelped, and her voice echoed. "Oh, God, no," she moaned. She shoved at the thing sprawled over her. "Let me out, Jimmy. Please let me out," she panted, gagging as the smell of hot blood flowed over her. It was a dream, the worst of nightmares. It couldn't be real. This couldn't happen to her.

What was holding her down? Warm, wet, and slimy, it sucked the breath from her. Arms. A person. She heaved it upward, ignoring the knives that slashed behind her eyes. She was blind. That's why it was so dark. She wasn't in the tomb. No way.

Squirming out from under the body, Bert shrieked as she came up against a rough brick wall. "No, no!" She fought to get to her feet. Her back and head slammed into a low ceiling, throwing her on top of the warm body. Something deep in her mind told her she might be hurting whatever was under her, but right now she didn't care. She had to get out.

Bert bumped against a wooden box. "Let me out. Let me out, Jimmy." She pummeled the coffin. Flailing, she threw herself against the ceiling, then against the caskets, clawing, hammering at the vault lid, shrieking. White-hot pain slashed through her head as she struck out, first against one wall, then another.

How can it hurt so much if you're asleep?

You're not asleep. It's real. You're making it worse. Stop banging around. There's someone in here with you. Maybe he isn't dead. Maybe you can wake him up. Try.

Bert's heart was pounding right through her chest, her breath coming in short gasps that didn't fill her lungs. She was about to pass out. She would die here, buried alive in the dark with a body. No, three bodies.

Again, the panic rose to choke her.

She fought it. Calm down, now. Count backwards. Breathe slowly. That's all you have to do. Just concentrate on breathing. Ninety-nine, ninety-eight, ninety- . . . She coughed, gagging again. What was in the air? Mold? Your fault. You stirred it up flailing around. Don't move. Cover your mouth until it settles down. What is that awful raw-meat smell?

Blood, blood all over you.

Her hands were wet and sticky, and something flowed down the side of her neck. Breathe slowly, she told herself. She sucked in air through her shirt, a little deeper this time. Ever so carefully, she touched the side of her head where it hurt. Pain flared.

She was bleeding to death.

Stop it, she told herself. If you're going to die, you're going to die. Don't make it any worse. Besides, scalp wounds always bleed like crazy.

Suppose it was a deep hole and something like brain fluid was leaking out? She didn't want to die, not yet, not here.

Oh, God, help me, she thought.

Help you? What about that other poor bastard in here? What about him?

How do you know it's a him?

It felt like a him. It wasn't Hunter either, she was quite sure.

Flinching every time she hit something mushy, she crawled to the lower side of the vault. She ran the tips of her fingers over his clothes. A belt, shorts. Slimy, fusty. Jimmy had smelled like a swamp. It couldn't be Jimmy. Jimmy was the one who left her here.

If only she had a light, matches, a candle. Her flashlight, on her belt, the little mini she carried all the time. She was almost afraid to check, afraid it wouldn't be there. It was. Sobbing with relief, Bert turned it on.

The air was thick with particles. Rotten wood? She blinked. Never had light—even light choked with dust and God knows what—seemed so wonderful. She flashed the beam on the body. His chest and face glistened wetly—blood. So much blood that at first she wasn't sure who it was. He wasn't in uniform. She bent closer, holding her breath. A small mustache. Jimmy, definitely Jimmy.

Even as she brought the light to the mangled chest, her mind reeled. If this was Jimmy, then who put them in here, and what did he do to Jimmy? Was Jimmy alive? It didn't seem possible with all the blood. She couldn't bring herself to touch the gory mess of muscle and bone, but she felt his wrist, then his throat. No pulse at all. She'd never seen a bullet wound except on television, but this looked like one.

Bert whimpered. Had she been shot, too? All she remembered was falling, no sounds. She probed gently. Her hair was stuck in a clump over the wound, but the bleeding had slowed. That calmed her.

Think, she told herself. There had to be a way out.

She pulled herself to her knees, head pounding. Waiting until she steadied, she let go of the coffin so she could push at the ceiling. It didn't even budge.

She needed both hands, but where to prop the flashlight? Reluctant to give it up even for a second, Bert tucked it back into her belt holder, still lit. How long would it last? She didn't need to worry about that now. She had to concentrate on getting out of here. Both hands on the lid, she pushed up.

Nothing.

She scrambled from her knees to her feet, crouching to avoid the ceiling. Swaying, she clung to Spriggs's coffin until her vision cleared. Just how badly was she hurt? Never mind. Even a slight blow to the head could make a person dizzy. Bert put her shoulders against the marble cover and heaved.

Damn. The lid was almost four feet off the ground. The height was wrong to get any power. She'd have to make some kind of lever or wedge and use it to pry off the slab. On her hands and knees, Bert scurried frantically, searching for something, anything. If only she had her crowbar or even her hammer, but she'd left them outside. She'd never get out.

Stop it.

She'd forgotten she had the flashlight. What else did she have? A quick search yielded her needle-nose pliers, her keys with the tiny pocketknife attachment, a comb, and her radio—for all the good those last two items would do. Wait. Maybe the radio would work. If it broadcast out of a building with walls, why not a vault?

She clicked it on.

Static. What a wonderful sound.

She shouted into the mike, "Anyone, answer me! I need help. This is Bert at Portsmouth. Mayday, Mayday."

Were you allowed to use Mayday on land? Who cared? Hunter had told her the Coast Guard and the sheriff monitored the park frequency. And half the people at Ocracoke and Harkers also listened in. She waited, holding her breath, but nothing broke the static.

Hands shaking, she checked the switches to make sure they were set right. The off button was forward. That was on, right? It had to be—the radio was making static. Then she remembered how Hunter had showed her to check the repeater. She keyed the mike and let it go, listening for the clicking echo to come back on the receiver. Nothing. She did it again, and again. Still nothing.

Bert sighed, crumpling against the side of the tomb. She'd been hoping they had miraculously fixed the repeater. Without it, her signal would carry only a couple of miles. It wouldn't even reach Ocracoke.

Keep trying, she told herself. Sometimes, there were fluke air-waves. Or perhaps a Coast Guard vessel or some other boat would pass near enough to catch her message.

Not likely, with a hurricane roaring up the coast.

The fear that had abated while she worked with the radio now rushed back. She broke out in a cold sweat, nauseated. It was so stuffy and humid. How long would the air last in here? Suddenly, she was gasping, bile rising in her throat.

Stop it, she scolded herself. In a minute, you'll be having another fit and use the air up even faster. That marble isn't sealed, not like it was in Jerushia's day. The mortar's long gone. Feel it—there's even a draft on this side, probably where you stuck in the crowbar. See if you can chip it out a little more, loosen a brick. Find something you can use. Didn't Jimmy have a hammer in here?

But Bert could find no hammer, not even when she forced herself to roll Jimmy over and look under him. He'd been carrying a pack, but it wasn't in the tomb. She tried to visualize what he'd done with it. He'd laid his pack on top of the open slab. It was probably still there, unless whoever shot him took it. He must have been hit from behind; she saw blood and what appeared to be a small entry wound there. She made herself turn him over again and check his clothes. In his bloody shirt pocket, she found a corroded metal object on a chain. An oval. It looked like a locket. Was it one of the chains Jimmy had taken from Spriggs's body? Didn't boaters carry a knife on them? Teeth clenched and hands shaking, she scrabbled through his shorts. His pockets were caked with mud and filth. She pulled out a sodden lump— a handkerchief— park and car keys, a limp wallet with his license, some credit cards, and about eight hundred dollars in big, wet bills. The last pocket she checked was full and heavy. Bert held her breath, hoping for a hammer or knife, but it was just the emeralds and other chains he'd removed from Spriggs. Fat lot of good they were.

Despair washed over her. She shook it off. You still have your pliers, she told herself. Use them.

Half crouching, half kneeling on the gritty brick floor, Bert began chipping away at the crumbling mortar. It wasn't hard to do, except for the ache behind her eyes. This wasn't real mortar—too coarse. However, it was thick. The flying grit stuck to the sweat on her face and got in her eyes. She tried to ease herself into a more comfortable position. Her head didn't hurt as much if she kept it upright.

The radio squawked.

She grabbed at it, yelling into the mike: "This is Bert, at Portsmouth Island! I need help. Anyone, come in, please. I'm trapped here, behind the hospital cistern."

She waited, praying for a response, but nothing came back except static.

Perhaps she shouldn't leave it on all the time. When had she last charged the battery? After she and Hunter were separated. Was that only this morning? She'd charged it for only an hour or so while she ran the generator. Usually, she charged it overnight. Maybe, just to be safe, she'd better turn it off between broadcasts.

But then she wouldn't hear if someone called her.

Better that than to have it run out of juice. After the storm was over, she'd still need to let someone know she was here. Better conserve the light, too.

Again, a chill of fear prickled her spine. Even if she didn't run out of air, she could still die here. They'd come looking and wouldn't find her. They'd assume she drowned and was washed out to sea. She'd starve to death or die of thirst.

Bert struggled for control. There was already a puddle on the low side of the tomb, and more water was dripping in. Was it rain or salt water? She tasted some seeping in from the crack between the lid and the side. It was brackish. Could be either. Rainwater floated on top of salt, didn't it?

She couldn't afford to be squeamish anymore. It was time to attack the coffin and see if she could salvage something that would do as a lever. A thighbone? Bert giggled hysterically. No way. She had deliberately avoided acknowledging who shared this space with her. She'd have to turn off the flashlight soon, too. Right after she made a lever, Bert promised herself, knowing she was postponing that moment.

It took her a half-hour to rip apart the lid of the coffin and free the crossbar, a thicker plank that didn't seem as rotten as the other wood. She paused to try the radio again. This time, she turned the set off when she was done. Somehow, the silence didn't seem so difficult to bear, now that she was doing something constructive.

Using a brick pried from under the rim, she hammered the plank into the hole until she was sure it was out the other side. Then she pulled down with all her might, hanging on, bouncing, ignoring the splinters that tore her palms. The lid grated, and a stream of cool water gushed over her sweaty face. She gasped, letting go. The slab cracked down, but water still streamed in.

Oh, God, the tide had risen over the level of the tomb. She'd be drowned.

No, think. If she opened the lid, the water would rush in, but she could get out. The creek wouldn't be terribly high out there, not yet. She could wade—or swim—back to the station. Anything was better than this.

Bert went back to her lever. Again, she hung on stubbornly, even when water roared in. But although the top gave, it would not slip off as it had before. Her plank was down as far as it would go. Meanwhile, water was accumulating at a frightening rate—a couple of inches where she knelt on the floor.

Sobbing, she let go. What was wrong? Why wouldn't it open?

Taking a deep breath, she forced herself to be still, to ignore the water running in like a tap into a bathtub. Stop a minute. Think it through. At least it's cooler now.

I'm going to drown.

The water's not coming in that fast. You have time. The weight of the water must be against you, and the fulcrum point is wrong.

She could lift a little at a time, placing planks from the coffin under the lever until she could get the lid up high enough to let her crawl out. But meanwhile, the water would be flowing in. How deep was it out there? Suppose it filled the vault before she opened it enough to escape? What was her alternative? Stop up the hole and stay here until the water receded? And pray it receded before the tomb was full?

What should she do? Her body began acting before her mind was reconciled to her decision. Bert wept as she wrapped the brick in part of her jacket and hammered it back into the hole she'd carved out. Was this the right thing to do? Maybe a quick death would be preferable to sitting here, letting the water creep up inch by inch.

The decision was made. Now, she had to pray the tide went down before the tomb was full. In the meantime, she might as well get out of the water. It wasn't cold, but getting waterlogged wasn't a good idea.

As Bert crawled to the high side of the tomb, something dug into her palm. She aimed her flashlight into the wet sand and saw the locket and chain she'd taken from Jimmy's shirt pocket. Strange thing for Spriggs to be wearing, she thought as she huddled back, trying to make herself comfortable.

Cold bricks pressed into her damp shoulders. Her head pounded in rhythm to the beat of her heart, and the relentless drip of water reverberated through her skull. She aimed her light at the hole. Was it coming in faster? What did it matter? The tide wasn't going to drop. The hurricane was coming. The water level would go up and up and up. Her whimpers echoed in the vault, mingling with the sound of trickling water. Bert shivered. Had the temperatures dropped, too?

Stop feeling sorry for yourself. Next thing you know, you'll blow another panic.

So what? I've been shot, and I'm going to drown.

Now, you're whining—and dramatizing. She knew better than to let things build up until they were overwhelming. Telling herself how miserable she was just made it worse. What she had to do was concentrate on something else, something constructive, while she waited.

Bert tore her eyes from the water gathering on the floor. The locket gleamed in a pinkish puddle at her feet. She stared blankly at it for a minute. Men didn't wear lockets. What had it been doing in Spriggs's casket?

Using the tips of two fingers and trying not to think of blood or moldering bodies, she lifted it from the water. The clasp was broken and swung open. With the pendant in her lap and the light right on it, she focused on the miniature inside. Someone had already wiped off the surface. Most of the painting was gone, but Bert could still make out the pale oval of a face and what might have been long, red hair.

Even as she turned her attention to the opposite side, she was aware already that she felt better. The other half was thick with dirt, even a piece of weed. No, wait, it was something else. Hair? A dark, tightly curled lock of hair? Two locks. One dark and coarse, the other fair and fine. Of course, that's what they carried in old lockets. And hair preserved well.

Was it Jerushia's locket and picture? Was this Jerushia's grave, not Spriggs's? Bert sat up straighter, turned the object over, ran her fingers over the gritty surface, felt and looked for initials. She wiped the locket on her shirt and tried again. Yes, something was there. She angled the light to illuminate the script. It was hard to decipher. Could be *J F B*. The *J* fit Jerushia, but *F B* did not stand for Spriggs O'Hagan. Anyhow, Spriggs's emeralds and gold chain had been around the skeleton's neck. It had to be Spriggs buried here, not Jerushia. Why was this locket in his casket? Wait, Jimmy had said something about Luna Mae finding a locket, hadn't he? It was hard to remember. She'd been so terrified he was going to kill her that she hadn't listened closely. That's when Jimmy had shot her.

Her muscles tightened. Jimmy killed himself? From behind? Impossible. Someone else must have shot them both and locked them in the vault. Why? So no one would ever find their bodies? Who was up there? If she escaped, would he shoot her again?

Bert sagged back, suddenly terribly tired. What did it matter? She was going to die in this nasty, dark hole.

You're whining again. Don't think about not getting out. Think about living. If you know who did this, then you can protect yourself when you get out. Concentrate on that locket. It's the key. Was it in the tomb or . . . ?

Bert sat back up. She was on the right track. Jimmy hadn't found the locket in the coffin. That locket had been in Jimmy's pocket all along. Jimmy had been following Luna Mae around. Now, she remembered what he said: Luna Mae had found the locket here, by the grave. Jimmy must have guessed it was Jerushia's.

Bert started to shake her head but stopped when the pain flared. Why didn't the initials fit? She looked closely at the miniature, hoping to find some clue. The letters were in a fanciful script. Wait, in the 1700s, Ss looked like Fs. J S B. Jerushia Spriggs something. What was Jerushia's married name? She'd have to ask Hunter. Bert squinted. Was it her imagination, or did the flashlight beam have more yellow in it than before? Heart in her throat, she turned it off.

Without the light, her headache seemed worse. Her fears closed in. Bert still clutched the locket. It felt warm in her hand, almost buttery. Concentrate on the locket, she told herself. Somehow, Jimmy had figured out it was Jerushia's. That's how he knew this was the location of the old homestead. He'd found the tomb and covered up the hole and was waiting for a chance to dig it all up. Then she spoiled his plan by returning to the village.

Why had he killed Luna Mae? Had they fought over the locket, or had he killed her to stop her from opening the tomb? But if Jimmy killed Luna Mae, then Bert was right back to where she started—namely, who had shot them and left them locked in the vault? No matter how many times she went over this, it just didn't make sense. Besides, how did the killer get on the island when no boats could land? Was he already here? What had Jimmy said about another boat?

She was too woozy to think straight. Bert turned the light back on to assure herself the water wasn't coming in faster. At least the dust from her panic had settled. She eased back against the side of the tomb, careful not to touch where she'd been shot. She was so tired.

A warning went off in the back of her mind. Concussions made you sleepy, didn't they? So what? There was no doctor to treat her anyhow. A nap might help her headache. And maybe when she woke, the hurricane would be done and she could get out.

Twice, she dozed off—or passed out—lapsing into a series of vivid nightmares. She woke shivering, her mouth dry, the echoes of her cries in her ears. It was so cold in the vault now. Everything was wet—the floor, the walls, her clothes. Bert checked the water level. It was up some, but not much. Then she tried the radio again. Nothing. She pulled the small coffin over and used it as a seat, curling into a ball. What she really needed was her jacket, but it was stopping up the hole. She thought about using Jimmy's clothes but discarded that idea.

Sleep returned, and the technicolor nightmares resumed. She dreamt of Hunter, water streaming from his back, then of Jimmy, his bloody face closing in above her as she screamed, "No, no, no!" She dreamt of a strange, cold fog surrounding her, soaking down to her bones, holding her with clammy tendrils. Then Jerushia was in the tomb with her, pleading for her help. "My baby, you call him Hunter," a soft voice whispered. "He's lost his way. He'll founder unless we help him."

Bert woke weeping, filled with fear for Hunter. Was he trying to reach her? The dream had been so real. She'd seen a boat tossing in the waves, Hunter's face—brows drawn, lips tightly clenched—peering though the spray.

"Please help him, Jerushia," she prayed aloud. "Lord, have mercy."

Chapter 23

"LORD, HAVE MERCY!" JERUSHIA CRIED. She threw the reins over the post and ran to the captain's crumpled body. A dagger protruded from his back. Dark, coagulated blood soaked his clothes and pooled in the sand. She fumbled down his neck for a pulse. None. She'd not expected to find any. The captain was dead.

Terror drove the air from her lungs and knotted her belly. She ran toward the house. "Goree! Jeremy! Dear Lord, no, please." She stumbled inside, afraid of what she would discover. Had he killed this baby, too?

The house was empty, silent.

"Goree!" The word tore from her throat, high and shrill, like the screech of a killdeer.

Goree's bulk filled the doorway to the study.

She couldn't speak. Her lips formed the question, her entire body shaking.

Pity filled his eyes, softening them. He stepped forward, opening his arms. "The baby safe."

Jerushia threw herself against his chest. She clung to him, dwarfed by his bulk, only the huge palms on her back keeping her on her feet as her knees gave way. For once, his warm embrace did not make her feel safe. "What have you done?" she moaned. "We are doomed."

He picked her up as if she were a child and carried her into the parlor. He set her on the long deacon's bench, carefully pulling her skirts back down over her legs.

She brushed his hand away. Her mouth opened to cry out again, but a look at Goree's face silenced her. Suddenly, she had a foresight of what he would look like when he was old. His lips hung open, jowls sagging. After taking several deep breaths, Jerushia said quietly, "He's quite dead, you know. You killed him?"

Goree sighed.

Jerushia met his eyes. They were mortally weary. "But how, why?"

He glanced out the window, then said in his deep, melodic tone, "I put the baby in his bed to sleep. Then I go down by the nets to fetch the catch." He fixed his eyes on the sound. "When I come back, I see the captain."

Jerushia followed his line of sight. The captain's white sloop was moored in the creek. She should have noticed the mast on her way back from the village, but she hadn't expected him. The last time she was enceinte, he had stayed away until after the baby's birth. This time, neither she nor Goree had let the captain—or anyone—know of the birth. They had been frantically trying to reach a decision. That was why she'd been to the village. "He tried to hurt Jeremy, like he smothered Mary, his own child," she said. It was not a question but a statement.

"He pick up that baby by the skin of his neck, like he a bitch-dog." Goree's eyes were glinting mahogany marbles. "Then he march around the courtyard, waving his pistol and shouting for you and for me. That baby be squealing like a rabbit. I come up from behind. I don't make no sound, aye? Then I knife him."

"Jeremy," Jerushia said, starting to rise. "You're certain he's not injured?"

"I catch the baby before he hit the ground. He get some bashes on his neck, that is all. Go look if you wish." Goree folded his arms.

"I believe you." Jerushia sank back. Although his face remained impassive, his thickening West Indian brogue betrayed his agitation. "We should have left before, as you wanted. Then this wouldn't have happened."

Goree turned to her. As always, whenever Jerushia looked into his eyes, his dark visage seemed unimportant. She felt the barriers she'd been raised to maintain fall away as skin from an onion. His warm, clear eyes shone with intelligence, humor, understanding, compassion, and even anger. Now, she saw pain and knew herself to be the cause. "It's not that I do not love you," she said, wanting the warmth back in his eyes. "I was afraid."

He stared past her, his gaze distant, as if he saw beyond what she said. "I take care of you and the baby, you know that." His voice was gruff.

Jerushia clenched her hands to keep from weeping. "I know you would, Goree." He would give his life for them, of that she had no doubt. "It's not that." She lifted her face to his. She knew she had to tell him the truth. "I fear what people will say," she choked out, watching his eyes darken until they were unreadable. "It's my pride. I would rather die than be an object of pity or scorn."

He said slowly, "You going to let that baby die to save your pride?"

Jerushia's mouth dropped open. "What do you mean?"

"When they find the captain hog-dead," he said, glancing toward the stable, "they hang me by the neck till I still, then they hang you also."

"Whatever for? I was not even here."

Goree took her hands, leaning forward. "You think they don't see that baby belong to me?" The pride was strong in his voice.

Jerushia barely noticed, fear filling her once again. "Oh," she said. "I did not think of that." She was silent a moment. "He's not so dark. Many whites have black hair, and the captain's complexion is just as dark as his. Did you not tell me there is white blood in your veins?"

"Aye, Indian also. He mulatto baby, just like me."

"No one need know."

"Open your eyes, lassie."

He was right, Jerushia knew with an icy finality. If they found Spriggs murdered and her with a dark child, they would reach the obvious conclusion: she and Goree had killed Spriggs to keep from being killed by him.

"In Martinique, they stone white gal when she have black baby."

Fear flushed her face and made her breathing hard. "What can we do?"

"Come away with me, aye?" His eyes held her, not begging but asking. Seeing her hesitation, the lines in his face softened. "I build you good house on hill by Teach's Hole. Ocracoke be safe place for rogue pilots and mariners."

Jerushia shook her head. "No. Too near and . . ." She eyed Goree from the top of his six and a half feet down to his scarred and tattooed body. "You be too outstanding. They will find the captain's body and come after us."

"Then we go west to the mountains."

Jerushia hesitated as hope flared in Goree's eyes. Suddenly, she felt old. "A woman, a Negro, and a child. We would be noticed. There would be talk."

"You say your husband dead and I be your slave. I keep cows and break horses."

"And live together?" It had to be said.

Goree sagged. "If that be what troubling you, then hire me out for wages."

He would turn himself back into a slave, for her? Jerushia turned to the window. To be somewhere far away, where no one knew them, where the three of them could be together. A small cottage by the water, perhaps in New Orleans. She'd heard they were friendly toward such unions. The word stopped her. No. She could not do it. She could sleep with Goree and love him, but she could not live with him. She would be a curiosity, a person to be singled out. The child would suffer, too. There was no place for them, not in this world.

He read the denial in her face. The gold sunburst in his eyes changed back to dull brown.

It brought tears to Jerushia's throat. She threw herself on his chest. "I love you, Goree. Truly, I do. I am just not strong enough to live like that."

He held her to his hairless chest, stroking her back gently, his familiar spicy scent rising about her. As always, he wore nothing save his sailcloth trousers tied at the waist with a rope. "Then leave me now. You take the baby and go far away from this place, quickly."

"And you?"

"I shall say you go away. I don't know where you go. Not my place to ask. I say that when the captain come back and discover you gone, he fly into big rage. He put his pistol to my head and say he cut out my tongue if I don't tell. I try to stop the man but he is gone mad. I kill by accident." His chest rumbled under her ear.

Hope flared for an instant. Then reality returned. "You will hang. A Negro cannot kill, even in defense."

He shrugged. "Be better that way for me."

His meaning did not escape Jerushia. If they could not be together, then he would rather die. "I will not let you do that. Besides, how would the baby and I live?" There had to be something they could do. If only they could stay here . . . She sat up, rubbing the tears from her face. "We forget. This house is now mine, as are all his investments." She shook out her skirt, smoothing it. "After enduring so much, 'twould be a pity to give it all up."

Goree leaned back against the bench, his legs stretched across the floor. The slit in the front of his skilts gaped slightly. Jerushia had an unreasoning urge to slide her hand inside, to hold him, to make love and pretend everything was still the same.

She sighed. There was no time. Someone might come by any moment. Why hadn't Spriggs just died at sea, or wherever he'd been? Surely, he had enemies. A man that rich always had enemies.

Of course!

She lifted her braid from her neck, swinging it forward. "What if they had no reason to suspect us? What if they thought the captain was stabbed by someone else?" Goree's eyes fixed on her. She began to undo the braid, combing the hair with her fingers. "Someone who owed him money, perhaps? Like Simon Green."

"You would let that poor man hang in place of us?"

"No, no. I didn't mean him. Someone like him they can't find. Help me think, Goree."

He reached for her hair, speaking slowly as he played with the deep red tresses. "That sailor that kill Will Brown, he ship out on the *Sea Vane* long time past. Will Brown serve on that same ship with Captain Ned Low."

"Of course," said Jerushia. There had been a murder in the village last winter. An old man, Will Brown, had been found dead by the warehouses. A shipmate had been accused of the crime. "We will make it seem like someone wanting revenge, from Spriggs's pirating days."

"That sailor left the mark next to the body."

"What mark?"

"The mark of the brotherhood. We be all one family. I am proud to—"

She lifted her hand. This was not the time for tales of his past. "Can you make it?"

Goree's brow furrowed. Finally, he answered, "I need clean piece of white paper, big like this, and India ink, too."

"In the office." Jerushia jumped up, grabbed Goree by the hand, and pulled him with her. "Here." She sat at the walnut desk Spriggs had imported from London and lifted a sheet of fine paper from its wrappings in the drawer. Then she pulled the stopper from the ink jar. "Wait." She rummaged until she found an old inventory sheet, which she turned over. "Practice on this first." Jerushia rose, giving him the chair.

Goree eased his bulk into the wooden armchair. He curled over the paper while she leaned above his shoulder. "You need a thicker nib." She showed him how to dip the quill in the ink, then how to drain the excess on the side of the pot, then how to use sand to blot.

Goree made three circles with a dot in the middle before he was satisfied. Then, tongue licking his lips in concentration, he drew the mark of the brotherhood in the exact center of the clean sheet.

While it dried, Jerushia started up the stairs to check on Jeremy, her mind whirling with plans. Goree followed her up the steps. The babe slept peacefully, his thumb in his mouth. Jerushia brushed the thick mahogany hair from his brow, trying to see him as others would. He was a beautiful child, strong, large, clear-eyed. He brought to mind a darker version of her Nathaniel. Jeremy's skin was a rich olive, his brows and eyelashes thick, his features heavier than those of her firstborn. Jerushia had not been sure, until the child was born, whether he was Spriggs's or Goree's. Spriggs had apparently known at first sight. What if Goree's return had not been so timely?

Feeling faint, she clutched Goree's arm. "The dirk that you used on . . . It's yours?"

"It once belong to the captain." Goree waited until they were out of the room to continue. "He use it to cut this, his mark." His finger traced the winding scar that ran from his breastbone to his navel. "I am small boy when he take me from my people," he added, his voice thick.

"Oh, Goree." Jerushia touched his arm, staring at the scar disguised by the tattoo of the two fighting cocks. The scar split both at top and bottom, like a stick figure holding something in each hand. Oh, dear Lord, Spriggs's dancing skeleton. "He branded you—with that?" So Goree had more bones to pick with Spriggs than the death of baby Mary and the attempted murder of Jeremy.

They reached the front door. At any moment, someone might come by and find Spriggs's body in the courtyard, and they would be undone. "If that is the captain's own dirk in his back, will that not raise suspicions?" she asked.

"How anybody know? I keep it hidden all this time."

"And now," Jerushia said, "it is where it belongs." She took his arm, holding it close to her, letting it fill her with warmth and ease her fears. His skin was so soft, so vibrant and alive.

The horses whinnied. She'd been so terrified upon discovering Spriggs that she'd just tossed the reins over the post and rushed to the house, fully expecting to find Jeremy smothered, as she'd discovered baby Mary five years ago. Now, Goree leapt forward to unhitch and attend to the Arabians. "The mark," he said, handing the paper to her. "Take care it stay clean white."

While Goree stabled the horses, Jerushia studied Spriggs's body. He lay face down in the sand, the large brass-and-ivory dirk protruding from his back, his pistol in his hand. As was the way with many old pirates, Spriggs was seldom unarmed, a fact that would help people accept that this was an act of the brotherhood. Jerushia deftly tucked the parchment under Spriggs's pistol. Then she stepped back and surveyed the scene.

It wasn't until Goree strode across the carriage ruts and hoof marks that Jerushia read the story their footprints told—or rather did not tell. He understood the moment she pointed it out. Using a branch Goree tore from one of the fig trees, Jerushia erased all the footprints about the body. Goree began to erase the ones around the stable, too, but Jerushia shook her head. "No, a stranger would come by road, and would return by road." She backed up to the lane, sweeping the sand as she went. Again, she paused, frowning in concentration. "We forget. My footsteps must be there, from when I found him." She walked over to Spriggs, then ran to the house. Then, dusting her hands on her apron, she glanced toward the road. "Now, I will raise the alarm at the neigh—"

"What we do with the boy?"

"Oh." Jerushia clasped her hand over her mouth. "We must hide him. Where?"

There was a long silence. Finally, Goree said slowly, "There be no place here to hide a Negro baby." He looked directly at her. "Best if I take him away."

"No, no." Jerushia shook her head violently. "I cannot let you. How would you feed him? He needs me." Her face contorted as she perceived the inevitability of what he said.

Goree took her gently by the hand and led her back inside.

There, he set her down again on the deacon's bench. "That be the only way."

"I'll leave," she babbled. "I'll go away with the baby. You tell them the pirates took me."

"How you going to eat? Where you going to sleep? The soldiers find you if you go to your son up north."

Goree was correct. They would surely write Edward, and he would feel obliged to turn her in. No, she couldn't go to her son. But how could she support herself elsewhere with a child? There was nowhere for her, not outside this island, and no future for her child. Spriggs Luck rightfully belonged to her—and Jeremy. No, hard as it seemed, Goree was right. She would stay here and preserve it for Jeremy. But what of Goree and the babe? "Where would you keep him?"

"I take Jeremy to your son, up in New Bedford."

"But if I can't go, how can you?"

"He want children, yes? I leave the boy with him, but I take care he don't see me. He be blood kin, and that be good."

"If the soldiers . . . He will know."

Goree chuckled. "I hear tell white folks leave their baby at door all the time, like they peck o' oysters."

"A foundling, yes." That might be the answer. Edward would have no cause to know the babe was hers. "But if they guess he's . . . of color?" The phrase came hard to Jerushia.

"I stay close by and keep watch over Jeremy," Goree growled deep in his throat. "I keep him safe, same as today."

Jerushia sighed. "That was a foolish question. I know you will watch over him. It's merely that I do not want . . . " She waved her hands. "I cannot do it. I cannot send my baby away."

"Not for always, lass. I bring him back."

Jerushia raised her head. "How long?"

"I wait till the commotion stop. By and by, people forget. Then you say your son Edward be sickly. Say his wife not want foundling baby. Say she jealous because she think he be true father. Then I bring baby to you."

"Very clever." It would not be the first time a bastard had

been passed off as a foundling. "How long?"

He shrugged his massive shoulders and glanced pointedly toward the stable. "First, see how good they believe about the mark."

"They'll believe me." Then new doubts came into Jerushia's mind. "How will you know when it is safe?"

"I know these things." He spread out one hand. "I come back in this many years."

"Five years? Why, he won't even know me."

Goree's brown eyes were warm. "There be another way. You come with me. We three go away together."

She could be with him, have him close, watch him curry a horse or play with the child. They would laugh together. Jerushia shook her head. Even if they were not brought up for Spriggs's murder, even if they went far away and pretended Goree was her slave, there would be talk. People would point her out. It would be even worse for Goree. She shook her head, tears seeping down her cheeks. "I want to, Goree." She leaned against him. "I want to, but I am too weak. I am afraid of what people will say."

Goree grunted high in his throat, as if he'd been hit.

Jerushia sobbed. After a moment, she felt his arm about her shoulder. He drew her to him, letting her weep on his chest, patting her back as a mother would a babe. He waited until she cried herself out, then detached himself from her. Walking over to the window, he spoke with forced casualness. "Already, the flies come. Soon, they bring the gulls, and the gulls be alerting the people."

He was right. The crabs would be at the body, too. Jerushia forced herself to her feet. "I will prepare Jeremy."

What would Edward name him? Tears flowed as she bathed the babe for the last time. From her leather trunk, she pulled out his garments, choosing and discarding. Finally, she packed all the boy's clothes, using them as lining for the basket. She would have to dispose of everything that might tell of a child here, in any case. Carefully, she added her sealskin wrap to keep him dry.

Goree was waiting when she came down. He reached for the squirming child, but she waved him off. "He's hungry." She unlaced her bodice. "Oh, Goree, how will you feed him?"

"You feed him good now, then fix some sugar water. Later, I find a woman—or a goat."

Jerushia sat and put the babe to her breast. He gulped eagerly. For a moment, both she and Goree were silent, watching. Never in her life had she felt so much pain, not even during Mary's birth—or burial. Jerushia tore her gaze away, staring out the window to the sloop bouncing in the water.

Goree pressed something hard and cold into her hand. It was the locket Spriggs had given her—the bribe. She recoiled. "How could you?"

He stretched out his palm. "I find the charm in the yard when I dig the grave for the wee girl. I clean and . . ." He snapped it open.

"Oh." Inside the locket, opposite the miniature, were two locks of hair, one fine and wispy, the other a tight mahogany curl. She touched the fair strand. "Mary?" Her eyes were brimming.

Goree nodded. "Jeremy also." He lay a finger on the cheek of the nursing child.

She pressed the locket to her bosom. "There is nothing you could have given me I would value more." Outside, water slapped against the sides of the sloop. Soon, that, too, would be gone. "How will you travel, in yonder boat?" Jerushia spoke to stop herself from thinking.

Goree tore his gaze from her breast. His throat worked. Finally, he said gruffly, "No. They say I steal the boat, and then they come after me. Best if I take the canoe." Goree kept a canoe, made by him, in Evergreen Slew. "When they find the captain dead, there be much commotion. Nobody see I am gone for one, maybe two days. When they ask, you say you afraid to keep me here with the captain dead." The hint of a smile appeared on his lips. "Dey believe dat." He exaggerated his brogue.

Jerushia nodded, unable to speak. Yes, they would believe that.

Goree leaned forward, took the sleeping child from her arms, and nestled him in the basket. "Wait a spell, then call the neighbors." He paused to search her tearful face. "Good if you red-eyed. Make it look like you weep for the captain."

"Not yet," Jerushia pleaded, lacing her bodice. "Wait, Goree."

"Waiting not change anything, you know. Hurt less when you cut fast." Hitching his roll over his shoulder, the basket on his forearm, he strode out the door with his easy, leopard-like movements.

"Here." Jerushia ran after him and thrust out a purse. This was why she'd gone to the village earlier, knowing they had to do something before Spriggs's return.

He pushed it away. "I have gold. I save for long time."

"Please. For your passage."

Goree accepted the purse, stuffing it into his belt.

While she was packing for the child, he'd changed into his town clothes—the leather breeches and cloth coat with pewter buttons. Jerushia watched him lope down the sandy road between the shadowing cedars, the child in one hand, his roll in the other.

"You will come back?"

He turned around, holding the basket before him. "I bring your son back to you. I give you my word." ⚭

Chapter 24

BERT WOKE TO THE SOUND OF HER OWN LOUD MOANS. As she fought her way back to consciousness, the vivid image of Hunter in the surf faded. It was only a dream, thank heaven. Slowly, she became aware of her clammy clothes. No wonder she was having such weird dreams. Her bed was sopping and her head hurt to beat all . . . A shot of fear-driven adrenaline spiked though her body. She lay wedged against a brick wall. Grit dug into her hip, and water dripped relentlessly all about her. This was no dream. She was still in the tomb.

Turning on her flashlight, Bert edged backward to the highest corner of the vault, head throbbing, body stiff with cold. Water covered the floor there, too. The tomb was filling up. Oh, God.

Stop it. Panic and you'll drown for sure. Besides, Hunter's on his way.

Don't be stupid. That was just a dream, a wish dream.

Bert ran the fading beam of her mini-light along the rim. Water was definitely leaking in where the lid met the side. And the mortar lining the walls was weeping moisture.

She checked her watch. She'd been out only forty-five minutes. That meant the hurricane—and the tide—were still coming in. She had to get help quickly. If only there was some way she . . .

The radio. How stupid could she be? She'd forgotten all about her radio. She'd planned to call every fifteen minutes. Better turn off that flashlight. Save it.

Careful not to splash, Bert edged toward the baby's coffin, where she'd left the radio. It was there, high and dry. She exhaled in relief as she flicked the switch. "Mayday, Mayday. I need help on Portsmouth," she called into the mike.

She waited, holding her breath until her lungs ached, but no one answered.

Her voice trembled the second time. "This is Bert at Portsmouth. I need help. Hunter, anyone, please answer."

The radio was silent.

Why had she called for Hunter? Hunter wasn't here. He was probably asleep in his bed at Harkers. Bert wished she were there. She wished she'd left with him and Rudy on the ferry.

Her heart pounded. She shook her head, wincing as pain stabbed her back to reality. She had enough problems without starting to play what-if. Right now, she had two choices. She could try to raise someone on the radio, or—Bert's chest tightened— she could start wedging that lid open and hope she got out before she drowned.

Maybe whoever left her here would have second thoughts if he heard her on the radio. Oh, God, suppose he didn't know she was alive. Suppose he heard her and came back to kill her.

She shrugged. What was the difference? If she didn't try, she'd drown for sure.

Taking a couple of deep breaths to calm herself, Bert called again. This time, she positioned the antenna as close as she could to the lid of the tomb and spoke very slowly.

Maybe there was something wrong with the radio. It wasn't even making static. Suddenly, Hunter's words came back to her: "It's supposed to make static. That's how you know it's receiving."

Idiot, she told herself. She fumbled with the dial. She'd turned on the switch but forgotten to adjust the squelch. There, now it was receiving—static.

Try again. If no one hears you, you're dead.

No, she told herself. If this didn't work, she'd find another way. "This is Portsmouth, Bert," she choked into the mike. "Someone, anyone, please come in."

Suddenly, the air exploded into noise and static. "—Bert!"

She screamed. The radio did a crazy jig as it bounced around in her hands. "Hunter!" she shouted, then pressed down on the mike, cutting him off. She let go and heard only silence. "Hunter?" No, impossible. It couldn't be him.

The voice came back, weak, faint, "Bert, Bert, been trying to raise you. I'm . . . should be there—" Static interrupted.

It was Hunter. Oh, thank God. "Where are you?" Bert could hardly speak. Hunter was here. She'd be all right.

"On the flats . . . mile . . . be there—"

"Oh, hurry. Please hurry, Hunter."

"Bert, are you—"

He was fading out. The battery? No, please. She could hardly hold on to the radio. Bert took a deep breath. She'd die if she couldn't calm down. She willed herself to breathe, to swallow, to think. Slowly, she contained her terror under a thin veneer of control. "Hunter, listen to me." She paused painfully after each word, ignoring the tremor in her voice. "I'm afraid the radio will give out any minute. I'm locked in the tomb, Spriggs's tomb."

"Say again?"

The incredulity in his tone calmed her even more. "You heard me right." She added quickly, "Oh, Hunter, be careful. Someone's out there with a gun. He shot Jimmy."

"You're going to have to talk slower. We got a hurricane out here, you know."

"I'm locked in Spriggs's vault. It's not by the old stable. It's about fifty feet to the right, toward the fuel dump. There's a little rise there. Hurry, Hunter. Please hurry."

"You're in the vault? Inside? Why?"

"There's water coming in. It must be covered." Again, fear rushed up Bert's spine. "You'll never find me. Everything's underwater."

"I'll find you."

His tone was low, calm, and full of assurance. Even though Bert knew he was trained to keep cool in emergencies, his confidence filled her with warmth. He'd know what to do.

Then his voice came over the radio again. "I'll be there shortly. You just take it easy, you hear?"

She sighed relief and leaned back, trying to form a mental picture of the grave's location. There was a clump of myrtle on the runway side of the slab, about ten feet away, below the grave. She called Hunter.

He didn't answer.

Where was he? How did he get here? Suddenly, Bert remembered her earlier thought. The person who shot her and Jimmy might still be on the island. Hunter? No, never.

That first doubt gave birth to darker ones. Hunter had been on the island the night Luna Mae drowned. Instead of waiting for Donny, he could have driven the truck to the village and hidden in the dunes, watching. Maybe Hunter killed Luna Mae. Maybe he felt the emeralds rightfully belonged to him. After all, he was Jerushia's closest living relative.

No. Whatever Hunter had been doing on Portsmouth that night, and whatever reason he had for being here now, Bert was sure it was not for personal gain. If money were important, one didn't take up a career with the National Park Service. Besides, although she could imagine Hunter killing in the line of duty or if someone was threatened, she could not see him sneaking up and shooting from behind.

She called again, and again.

Finally he answered. He sounded winded. "I just passed the compost toilets. Road's flooded, slowing me up some." Bert heard static. "Can't talk and run. Might drop the radio. Call you in a few minutes."

They were long minutes. To stop herself from losing control,

Bert began a countdown: sixty, fifty-nine, fifty-eight . . . Then, at last, the radio squawked.

"Bert, you copy?"

"You sound like a train."

"The wind. I'm having a hell of a . . . Not sure I'm on the path. Whole . . . underwater."

"Look for a rise past the ruins of the old shed, toward the fuel compound."

All Bert could hear was the water running into the grave. Then, finally, Hunter's voice, fuzzy, distorted: "Say again. I can't see a thing. Can't hear too good either."

"Past the old shed. Look for a big clump of myrtle taller than the other brush, toward the gas pumps."

Wind roared in the mike. "Shed ruins are underwater."

Of course. How stupid of her. If water was leaking into the tomb, which occupied the highest spot in the area, then everything else had to be covered, too. What else was around there, what landmark? Out of nowhere, it came to her. The toothache tree was close to the stable. "Hunter, look for the toothache tree."

"The what?"

For a moment, Bert's mind went blank. Where on earth had she gotten that from? "The prickly ash. Between the path and the ruins, remember? And a fig tree up top."

"Right." More static followed, then a curse. "Damn." He must have walked into the ash. "I'm here."

Funny, hurricane and all, as long as Hunter was near, she felt safe.

Then he was back on the air. "Hard to see. It's dark, and the wind's got the water all riled up. I'm by some myrtles—couple of big clumps here."

"You're close. I'm getting an echo on the mike."

He grunted. "That's good. Where are you, exactly?"

"In the tomb."

"Underground?"

"Yeah." Bert bit her lip. "There's water coming in."

"Can't you get out? What's holding you back?"

"The slab. Someone closed it. When I tried to raise it, the water came in, but it wouldn't open."

"I've got to be just about over you."

Bert's mind was racing. If she tried to pry the lid open again, would he see the movement? And how much water would she let in? "Hunter, can you see if I jiggle the top? I can't open it—at least I couldn't before."

"I've got a good flashlight, but the wind's got the water choppy, like I was in the sound."

"When I try to open it, it lets the water in."

"How deep is the water inside? Are you in any danger?"

"Not yet. It's about half full. Still have a good two feet left."

"You said something about a slab. Does it really have a slab of marble on top?"

"Yes, just like you said."

"Then I should be able to feel it."

"Watch out for the snakes," Bert warned, knowing without seeing that he was taking off his boots. "Be careful."

"Don't you worry none. These critters have other things on their minds right now."

Bert held her breath. Then she heard a tap. Simultaneously, his voice came over the radio. "Hear that?"

"Yes. Oh, Hunter, get me out."

There was silence for a moment, then a rumble. Water poured in, but the lid did not open. Another pause, another rumble, more water.

"Hunter, wait," Bert called, then remembered to key the mike. "Hunter."

"You all right?"

"Fine."

"It's a heavy sucker. Can't get a grip. Wish I had a crowbar."

"There's one out there somewhere, but . . ." The lever. Of course. Bert reached for her stick. "I'll pry it up from inside, get it started, then maybe you can grab it."

"Try it."

"Get off the top."

"Yes, ma'am."

To Bert's surprise, she found her hands were shaking. She'd felt so calm since Hunter's arrival. Forcing herself to slow down, she picked up the crossbar and tugged at the jacket she'd stuffed in the hole. It was wedged tight. She pulled harder. The brick went flying, splashing down behind the coffins.

"Something wrong?" Hunter's voice was still low and quiet, but Bert caught the slight note of worry.

"I lost the brick. Trying to find something to use as a hammer. It's hard to get around. Jimmy's in the way."

"Jimmy?" His voice rose. "What the hell's going on?" The slab rocked as he yanked. More water poured in.

"Do that again!" Bert yelled.

This time, she was ready. As he lifted, she slipped in the crossbar, then pulled down. Water gushed in. It was like being under a waterfall. Bert paid no attention, holding her breath and rocking up and down as hard as she could. She saw the top lift and knew Hunter was pulling on the other side. Then, suddenly, her head was through the water, up into the wind. It was dark, and it smelled so good. "I'm out, I'm out!"

His hands were under her armpits, lifting her all the way out, holding her to his big, wet chest. Good thing, too, Bert decided. Her knees wouldn't lock.

"You're wet," he said.

"So are you."

Even in the dark, Bert could see the gleam of his teeth through the sodden mass of beard. They broke into peals of laughter. Must be a touch of hysteria on both their parts, Bert thought. The laughter warmed her. She looked around curiously. They were standing in about a foot and a half of water. The roar of the wind drowned out nearly everything. Just as Hunter had said, it was as if the sound had moved and they were in it—which they were. What really surprised her was how much she could see. Despite the high cloud cover, the hurricane was not blocking out all the light.

"You okay? He didn't—" The wind blew away his words.

"I am now."

"Where's Jimmy? What happened?"

Bert pointed. "Got to get him out."

"Jimmy's in there?"

"He's dead," Bert tried to explain. "Someone shot him."

He threw up his hands. "Who, why? I was thinking it was Jimmy that—"

Bert couldn't hear his last words. "When I woke up, he was there!" she yelled.

"Who shot him?"

"I don't know."

"You sure he's dead?"

Bert nodded. "No pulse." Hunter bent closer to her. "He was cold!" she yelled. "And he's been cold for a couple of hours now."

"We can't leave him." Hunter carefully let himself down into the tomb, sitting at the side of the vault with water up to his chest. Then he had Jimmy by his arms and was dragging him out.

"What are you going to do with him?"

Hunter pushed Jimmy's body toward her. "Hang on."

Reluctantly, Bert grabbed hold of Jimmy's shirt. He was neither floating nor sinking. The current was running the same direction as the wind, tugging the body away from her as Hunter fished in his pack for a rope. He tied it around Jimmy's chest, then to himself. Bert couldn't help wondering if he remembered what happened the last time he'd been attached to a rope.

Hunter took her arm, and together they turned away from the grave. They began descending toward the station. Soon, the water was up to Bert's waist. It was a nightmare in slow motion, the wind sweeping down from their left, the current pushing them sideways, the water impeding their forward motion. Hunter had a hand firmly hooked into her belt, quick to steady her if she lost her footing. He stopped and bent to her ear. "Might be better if I go in front. Can you hang on to my belt?"

She nodded, stepping around Jimmy, who trailed along, partly submerged.

The wind seemed to rise, bringing with it more water. It was hard to see. A dark fog was moving in, covering the whipped-up surface of the water around them.

A fog in a hurricane, in this wind? Impossible. Bert stared in horror as it spread. The wind was tearing at it, shredding it, but still it rose about them, colder than the water in which they stood.

She pounded on Hunter's back. "Stop, stop! The fog." She pointed.

He shook his head. "Never saw nothing like this. Cold, too."

He plowed forward, tugging at Jimmy's rope. The fog swirled up like a living entity. Then Bert knew.

"It's—" She choked, swallowing water. "Oh, God, Hunter, I think it's Spriggs." She clung to him.

He said something, but the wind tore the words from his mouth. He bent back to his task, forcing his way through the water, pulling her and the body.

It was now dark, as dark as it had been inside the tomb, and colder than a January night. Bert's fingers were numb. Only the part of her under the water was warm. She couldn't feel Hunter's arm and could barely see him. Soon, she would be alone with Spriggs and Jimmy. What did the old pirate want? What was the matter?

He was protecting his tomb. Isn't that what ghosts did?

"The emeralds," she gasped, poking at Hunter.

He didn't seem to feel her, intent on driving forward.

The fog was up to their shoulders, tendrils rising, whipped away by the wind, then rising again, swirling madly. Frantically, Bert grabbed at the rope that held Jimmy, tugging with all her might.

That stopped Hunter. "What, what?" he mouthed at her.

"It's Spriggs!" Bert shouted so loud that the words rasped in her throat. "Jimmy took his emerald cross. He wants it back." She tried to unhook the rope from Hunter's belt, but she couldn't see the knot, and nothing could have made her lean into that deadly mist.

"What do you want me to do?"

"Let Jimmy go."

She could feel Hunter's resistance. "I can't do that. He's evidence."

The wind rose to a shriek. A bank of fog bore down on them, a six-foot wave of gray over the water.

"Hunter, please. He's coming after us." His hands reached ever so slowly for the rope. "Hurry!" Bert screamed, pointing.

Hunter fumbled, muttering curses. Then Jimmy was floating away. Bert had one last glimpse of the body, half submerged, the current taking it with amazing speed back toward the tomb. Then the gray haze billowed over them. For an instant, the wind seemed to cease. Cold crept through Bert as if it were acid eating right down to her core. Just when she thought she was dead, they were suddenly in the open again. She gasped for breath and realized Hunter was doing the same.

He shook himself like a dog. "What in the hell was that?"

"Spriggs!" Bert yelled, clutching him. The wind seemed a little less. "Jimmy had his emeralds and gold chains."

"Park's not going to like this." He shrugged. "Well, they're gone now. Doubt we'll ever see them again—or Jimmy Range."

Or Spriggs, Bert thought. No doubt, the water would float the coffins out of the tomb. For a moment, she felt ridiculously sorry for the old brigand.

They splashed on in silence. It was easier now, without Jimmy's weight holding them back. The wind still howled. The surface of the water was full of foam, as if they were in a mixer. Branches, rafts of grass, and other things Bert was glad she couldn't see washed by. But the fog was gone, and the thick shrubs by the runway protected them from the larger pieces of flotsam. Finally, she recognized the new shed. The water was over the threshold. That meant the tide was almost three feet above ground level here—nine feet over sea level.

"The generator," she groaned. She never had turned it off or secured the door. It wasn't running. The tide must have shorted it out.

"Something wrong?" Hunter shouted over his shoulder.

"No, not anymore."

They moved past the shed and circled Bert's cabin. A light shone from a window at the lifesaving station. Its warm beam sent a cold shaft into Bert's heart.

"Wait, Hunter!" Bert yanked on his belt.

"What's the matter now?"

"Someone's there." The wind sucked the words from her mouth. She pointed. "I didn't have any lights on."

Fighting the wind and the current, he pushed her around the corner of the cabin, to the lee side. There, he backed her up to the wall, his face practically in hers. "I guess it's time to talk. Want to tell me exactly how you happened to get locked up in the vault? And how did Jimmy get shot? Take it from the beginning."

Bert laid out the story, glad that at last, here in the shelter of the cabin, she could make herself understood. She told Hunter about finding the tomb, about the nutria, about Jimmy forcing her into the vault. "I think both Luna Mae and Jimmy were searching for it all summer. That's what woke up Spriggs and his fog. When Jimmy saw Luna Mae find the locket—which he knew was Jerushia's from his research—he figured out the location of the grave and came back to rob it."

When Bert got to the part where she woke up bleeding, Hunter grabbed her shoulders. "Why didn't you tell me you were hurt? How bad?" He got the flashlight out of his pack and shone it on Bert's head. Then he started swearing. "Godammit to hell, why didn't you say something? I took all that blood for mud and dirt. Hold still, now. Let me look." He bent her head forward. "Does that hurt? Bullet hit you or what?"

"I don't know," Bert mumbled, not moving as he dabbed at her gently. The last thing she wanted to do was start it bleeding again. "I had a real bad headache for a while, but it's almost gone now."

"Nausea? How's your eyesight? Seeing double?"

"I'm okay, as far as I know. Ouch." He'd just probed a tender spot. "I won't be able to brush my hair for a week."

"Won't have to. I'm fixing to cut it off just as soon as we get you inside." He grunted, turning her neck slightly. "Don't see any bone showing, but you got yourself a two-inch gouge there. Must have bled to beat all hell." He put an arm around her, cradling her gently. "I'm sorry I wasn't here."

"It's not your fault." Tears were close.

His next words snapped her out of the sudden self-pity: "You sure it wasn't Jimmy that shot at you?"

"I don't think so. No, it couldn't have been." She started to shake her head but quickly stopped. That still hurt. "When Jimmy pushed me out, there was someone in the marsh. He made a sound, like he was scared. Then something hit me, and I remember falling."

"Did you hear a sound like a gun clicking?"

"No. Like a person sucking in his breath—real soft. Anyhow, how did the cover get back over the vault if it was Jimmy?"

"Wish I hadn't let go of him," Hunter muttered. "Don't suppose you'd know the difference between a shotgun wound and a thirty-eight, would you?"

"Nope. His chest was a mess. I could see bone and . . ." Bert winced as she understood the significance of the question. Donny hunted ducks.

"Any idea who's inside?"

She was sure whoever was in the lifesaving station was the same person who'd killed Jimmy. "There was a boat offshore by Potter's when I closed up."

"Carolina skiff with pots? I found a crabber's skiff over by Evergreen. Reckon it was Jimmy's. Had a Park Service gas can inside." The wind was picking up again.

"It looked more like Donny's boat, and Jimmy said he saw Donny over here. Doesn't Lettie have a skiff, too?"

"Reckon it could be either of them, or both. Lettie could have brought Olin over, too. Could be all three." Hunter was silent. Then he slipped off his pack, dug inside, and removed a gun.

Bert watched him belt it on, then take a magazine from the holder and slip it into the gun. This was getting wilder by the moment. The last thing she wanted was a gunfight. Let the hurricane take care of whoever was in there. She tugged at Hunter's arm as a gust of air blasted them.

He bent and shouted in her ear, "We'll go round back! I'll head in through the boathouse and come up on him—or them—from there."

"No." Bert hung back, pointing toward the village. "The Washington Roberts House?"

Hunter shook his head. "Too much water. Doctor's Creek'll be flooded."

He pulled her out of the shelter of the cabin. Bert gasped, then choked. The wind was full of water, knives of icy horizontal drops. The storm was whipping the sound into froth, making it impossible to see. Blind, hitched to Hunter's belt like a trailer to a car, she followed him around the lifesaving station to the boathouse. There, in the lee again, Hunter opened a window and climbed in, gun in hand. After a moment, he motioned her to follow. Then he signaled her to close the window while he stood guard. Outside, the wind roared like a freight train. Bert knew, to her relief, that the person inside was not likely to have heard their entry.

A foot of water shimmered on the boathouse floor. It had oil in it, Bert guessed, and probably gasoline, too. No time to strike a match.

"How about that mini-light? You still got it?" Bert fished it out of her belt. "Flash it over yonder. That's it." One hand in the small of her back, Hunter steered her around a workbench to the door that connected the boathouse to the main building.

Adrenaline rushed through Bert's body. Something was on the other side of that door, waiting. She was certain. "Please, don't," she hissed.

Signaling her to be quiet, he reached for the doorknob. It turned easily.

"I left it locked," Bert mouthed. "From the other side."

"You stay here. If something happens . . ."

Bert stared at him wide-eyed, knowing they were thinking the same thing. There was nowhere she could go for help if someone shot him.

He frowned, then leaned over to whisper in her ear, "Just stay far enough back of me so I don't have to worry about you while I'm dealing with him. You read me?"

Relieved that at least she would know what was happening, she nodded, trying to smile.

Gun ready, Hunter pushed the door open.

261

Chapter 25

IN ONE QUICK MOVEMENT, Hunter was through the door. Bert held her breath, listening. Finally, he reappeared, waving her in.

They followed the gleam from the light to the front of the station. Gun at eye level, Hunter slid into the card room. Bert obediently stayed back until she was sure no one was inside. The Coleman lantern she had brought over stood in the center of one of the tables. A yellow slicker hung over the back of a chair. It was dripping.

Bert glanced around, half expecting something to come flying out of the deep shadows in the corners. There was a heap by the door—a backpack. She recognized it. "Hunter, look," she whispered. "That's Olin's pack. It wasn't here when I brought my things over." The significance sunk in. "Then Olin's the one who shot me. He's the one with the gun."

Hunter spoke quietly in her ear. "I'd say that slicker would fit Donny better than Olin. Reckon we'll find out soon enough."

Satisfied no one was in the lower rooms, he turned toward the stairs. Bert followed him up the winding flight, her back feeling vulnerable. The second-floor hall led to the surfmen's dormitory and two other rooms. A fixed ladder rose through a trap to the tower, two stories up. Hunter motioned her to remain in the hall by the ladder as he edged toward the dormitory.

A shower of sand dropped on her head. Startled, Bert jumped forward. Hunter was at her side in an instant. She pointed to the lookout tower above. Sand was ingrained in these old buildings, and any movement dislodged it.

He listened. Outside, the wind tore at the lifesaving station, flapping the shingles, rattling the windows. How could he hear anything in this? Just then, sand fell on Hunter.

Was it wind-generated? Apparently, Hunter didn't think so. Signaling Bert to stay back, he began to climb the ladder to the tower. He used his left hand to mount the rungs and clasped the gun in his right. Bert watched, barely breathing. If someone was up there with a gun, Hunter wouldn't stand much of a chance.

He'd just reached the landing halfway up the ladder when something caught Bert's eye. The darkness above him was shifting. Trouser legs, the edge of a shoe, something glinting—light reflecting on a narrow barrel. "Ah, ah, ah," Bert choked.

Hunter looked down at her.

She struggled to speak, pointing. Everything was in slow motion—Hunter's inquiring brow, the gunman's finger tightening on the trigger, the gun pointing at the back of Hunter's head. Suddenly, the arm twisted, bending back. A flash. The gun went off. "Hunter!" Bert screamed. The men yelled. The trapdoor crashed down, closing off the cupola. Agonized howls broke out from above. Sand filled the air. Someone was catapulted into a wall. More sand showered. Gunfire—three dull pops.

"Hunter!" she screamed again.

He was shouting, too.

The howls grew in intensity. "Go away! Go away!" a man's voice yelled.

Olin!

Above her, Hunter crouched on the ladder, both hands on the trap. He strained upward. Wind whistled through the cracks.

"No, Hunter!" Bert couldn't hear herself over the banging and hollering. Then came a prolonged, high scream. Now, the clamor seemed to be coming from out on the roof.

Hunter grunted, shoving. The trap opened. Sand and old plaster blasted down at Bert as the stairwell turned into a wind tunnel. Above her, Hunter clung to the ladder with both hands, head bent under the onslaught. Then his feet disappeared through the trap.

"No!" Bert yelled, starting up the ladder behind him. The wind shrieked. More sand blasted down.

To her enormous relief, she found him in the tower, shoulders hanging out the open window. Below, clinging to the peak of the roof, was a dark figure. "Olin?" she shouted.

Hunter nodded. He leaned out farther, cupping his mouth with one hand and pointing the gun at Olin. "Throw down that gun and come back inside! Move slowly or I'll shoot!"

Olin didn't even raise his head, his attention riveted to the roof behind him. Nothing was there. Even though the wind tore around the tower, Bert could hear his high-pitched, terrified howls. "No, no!" A gust threw the man backward, as if he'd been hit by an invisible fist. He landed in the valley between two sections of the roof. Rising to one knee, Olin lifted his gun.

Hunter grabbed Bert, ready to duck, but Olin wasn't aiming at them. He fired over the peak where he'd perched a moment ago. Then, as they watched, the gun flew out of his hand and over the side, lost in the frothy water below.

"Oh, God." Bert stared. Coast Guard Creek was right up to the boathouse walls, a seething, churning body of water. She watched, horrified, as Olin crawled backwards on all fours, looking for all the world like a giant black crab.

"No, please!" he wailed. "It was Luna Mae's fault, sneaking around. She wouldn't shut up. I had to stop her." Then his head snapped sideways. He screamed the high-pitched cry of a trapped animal.

Then, as Bert and Hunter stared, frozen, Olin scuttled rapidly backwards—and disappeared over the edge of the roof. There was no scream, no splash, just the shriek of the wind and the crash of the waves.

Hunter was hanging halfway out the window. "You see that?" he asked, disbelieving. "He went right over the side."

"Someone was out there," Bert said.

"I wouldn't have hurt him. You heard me tell him to come back."

"He wasn't running from you. There was something else out there, the same thing that spoiled his aim in the cupola." She drew away from the window with a shiver. "Olin tried to shoot you. He killed Luna Mae. But why—"

"He lost it altogether, went schizoid."

"You mean he's crazy?" Bert hesitated. "Or maybe . . ."

"You telling me that was a ghost on the roof?"

"You saw that fog when we were dragging Jimmy that was Spriggs."

Hunter's brows shot up. "Even if a man believed that, why would Spriggs go after Olin?"

"That wasn't Spriggs on the roof," Bert said. "It was something—or someone—else. And that scent. . ."

"Scent?"

"Like cloves. Don't you smell it?"

Hunter stuck his head back out the window. "All I'm smelling is gunpowder and salt spray. Wait, there is something." His eyes narrowed. "Puts me in mind of another time . . "

Suddenly, Bert knew. "When your boat broached and your wife drowned."

Hunter was silent.

"Someone saved you then, too, didn't they?"

"I thought it was . . .That's why . . .Ah, I'm running my mouth." Hunter slammed the shutter into place. Holding it against the wind, he turned the clips, all the while muttering to himself. "Hurricanes do strange things to a person. Atmosphere gets loaded with electrical particles, not to mention the pressure changes. Women go into premature labor. People start thinking stupid, seeing and smelling things that aren't there." Shaking his head, he took one last look outside as he closed the other window. It was dark, but the tossing, churning ocean glowed with white phosphorescence. "It's not the first time man's attributed something he couldn't explain to the supernatural. Got to believe the only ghosts out there were in Source's mind."

"Whatever." Let him cling to his logic. Deep down, he knew better. Bert stared at the maelstrom through the glass, wondering if anyone could survive it. "You don't think he'll come back?"

"Don't reckon he's got a chance. Even a Navy Seal would have a hard time in that ocean. Tide's going out, and this is just the leading edge of the hurricane." Hunter shuttered the last window. "At least it'll save the county from trying him for Luna Mae's murder."

"You think Olin shot Jimmy and me, too?"

"He had a gun. Lucky he missed me coming up that ladder."

"He didn't miss. Something grabbed his arm."

Hunter raised a brow, then dropped to a crouch by the floor trap. With a little grunt, he motioned Bert over, pointing his flashlight at the wooden pole he used to prop up the door. "There's your guardian angel. Olin bumped the post and brought the trap down on himself."

Bert stuck her arm through, as if she were aiming a gun down the stairwell. "That could be it," she admitted. "But guardian angel?" She wished she could cock a brow like he did.

Hunter cleared his throat. Bert could almost feel him flushing. "Family joke. My mama always said the O'Hagan guardian angel was the only thing that kept us boys alive."

"But you don't believe in it."

He signaled her to start down the ladder. "You got to understand us Down Easters. We been here two, three hundred years, some more than that. Before they built the roads and bridges, families stayed put, and so did the old legends." He lowered the trapdoor behind them. "Had a historian tell me they can trace some of the songs and the folk stories right back to London town."

Somewhere, from the dark around them, came a faint sound. Bert swung around. "Did you hear that? There's someone here."

Hunter slid down the rest of the ladder, landing hard. "Downstairs?"

"Back there." Bert pointed down the second-floor hall. Had Olin fallen onto a porch and made it back?

Hunter stood motionless, head tilted. "I don't hear anything. You stay back."

Bert followed him down the dark hallway into the dormitory—a large room with eight beds, four on each side, each with its own footlocker. Hunted panned his flashlight around. Two of the beds were heaped with the sleeping bags and pillows Bert had brought over earlier. One of the bags was unfolded.

Bert reached for Hunter. "Someone's here."

Hunter grabbed his gun. It stuck for an instant before he pulled it out of the holster.

How could Olin have gotten up here so quickly?

A closet door squealed. A voice floated out: "Don't shoot. It's me."

"Come out slowly, hands in the air," Hunter said.

"I'm a-coming. You got Olin?" A small, slight figure in shorts and a hooded sweatshirt jacket slid out of the closet.

"Donny?" Hunter and Bert exclaimed simultaneously.

"That you, Miss Bert?" Donny peered at her, rubbing his eyes. He cackled rather like a marsh hen.

"Don't you move, boy." Hunter had the gun aimed right at Donny's face.

He flinched. "Hey, man. I didn't do nothing."

"Over by the wall, slowly. That's it. Hands up, feet spread." Hunter patted him down. "Now, take off that shirt."

Mute and white-faced, Donny followed orders, peeling off the ragged sweatshirt.

"Check the pockets." Hunter handed it to Bert, then turned back to Donny. "Take off your pants."

"In front of her? I don't wear no underwear, you know. I'm a real man."

"Turn around, Bert."

Bert turned away. She had no desire to see how Donny was hung or how dirty he was under those filthy shorts. These jacket pockets were bad enough—cigarette butts, crumpled packs, a disposable lighter, loose tobacco, sand, nails, several Scotch bonnets, a lion's paw shell, a disgusting rag, a set of keys, and a disposable camera.

Shells. Did Donny leave that shell by the gate?

Hunter handed her Donny's shorts. The rear pocket held a battered leather wallet. She waved it at Hunter, then put it on a bed with the rest of the collection. The heavy item in the front pocket turned out to be a large knife in a worn leather case. "He has a knife here."

Hunter didn't seem to find that unusual. He glanced at it as she laid it on the bed. "No bullets? Any sign of a gun?"

"Nope. Want to give him back his pants?" She held them up with two fingers.

"Supervisor's going to hear about this," Donny muttered as he dressed. "Ain't got no right to come in and search a man like this."

"What are you doing here?" Hunter's voice was low, threatening.

"Is that what got you all riled up? Let me tell you. This is a public building, and in case you didn't notice, there's a hurricane outside. The public got a right to take shelter in a storm. Tell him, Miss Bert. I ain't done nothing wrong."

"Tell me about Olin," Hunter said. "You in this with him?"

"No way, man. I been hiding from him. You shot him, didn't you? I heard guns going off." He peered at Hunter and Bert. "He's crazy, you know." Something about the expression on their faces reached him. Donny sat on the bed. "I ain't sure what's going on, but I ain't done nothing. You got to believe me." He eyed Bert. "Ever since she told me Luna Mae were kilt, I been trying to help."

"The only way I'll believe you is if you tell me everything you know, right now. Let's start with Wednesday night. I know you were here. Why? What was that proof you told the supervisor you had? And don't lie."

"If you're a-wanting to hear, I'm a-wanting to tell you. Only I got to begin before Wednesday." Donny raised his eyes to Hunter's.

Hunter gave him a brief nod.

Donny took a deep breath. "The other day, I went to take a mess of clams to Luna Mae. She weren't there, and I didn't want to leave them outside—coons would take them for sure, you know. So I opened the window to leave them in her sink. Didn't have no extra container. I seen this round thing, silver. She had it soaking in some soapy water. It was one of them lockets that opens, all mud inside. I was fixing to bring a camera and get a picture of it for you. Proof it were Luna Mae taking things, not me." He glanced at the pile of his belongings. "When I come back Wednesday night with my camera, Luna Mae weren't around, and neither were the locket. House was open, and it was way late for her to be out—only two hours to sunup. Then I come upon this man walking sneaky-like. I seen it's Olin. Tell the truth, I never did care much for turning in Luna Mae." Donny grinned. "I'm thinking to get something on Olin instead, so I go after him into the marsh." He turned to Bert. "Then damned if I don't hear you hollering that Luna Mae were dead." Donny sucked in air. "I headed out right fast, I did. Ain't healthy to get mixed up in no police matters."

"That was you and Olin in the swamp, before Jimmy got there? Then who turned off the power, and why?" Bert asked.

"You wouldn't happen to know anything about that, would you?" Hunter asked. "Don't lie to me, boy."

Donny hesitated, then took a glance at Bert. "She left them porch lights on."

"And you couldn't get into the village without someone seeing you, right? So you turned the power off. Did you turn it off the night Miss Bert got here, too?"

Donny sighed, reaching for a cigarette, but Hunter's look stopped him. "I was out of gas. I knowed there were some in the boathouse. You never even missed it."

"Get in through the window?"

Donny nodded. "None of them windows have catches."

"And the music, the organ?"

"I didn't have nothing to do with music or any of them goings-on. You'd do better asking Source about them things. Lettie said—" Donny clapped a hand to his mouth.

"Lettie said what? Was she in this with Olin?"

"No way, man. Lettie didn't even know Olin were married when she took up with him. You-all knew him and Lettie had a thing going, right?"

Bert exhaled in relief. She liked Lettie.

"When she found out Olin were married, she dumped him right quick, she did. Told me Olin were real bust up, bawled and begged her to give him a chance. Told her Miss Anne's heart were real bad, that the doctor said it could go anytime. That's why he couldn't leave her." Donny shook his head. "Lettie never did have no sense about men. You hear Luna Mae caught them in the act?" He cackled at their expressions. "They was hard at it in the cabin when Lettie looked up, and there's Luna Mae's face mashed up against the screen, mosquito net and all. Lettie told me Olin near killed her. Picked up the old lady clean off her feet, shook her like a dog with a rat. Luna Mae's a-yelling she's going to Miss Anne—that's when Lettie found out he were married. Olin told the old lady if she says one word, he'll report her for having a metal detector. Lettie said that shut Luna Mae up fast. She knowed it meant her lease."

"You bring Olin over today?" Hunter's tone was stern.

"Brought him over yesterday and been chasing after him since."

"He pay you?"

"Like I said earlier, I was just trying to help. When Miss Bert let it slip on the beach about Luna Mae, I was fixing to tell Olin the trip were off. I owe Lettie, but it weren't worth getting mixed up with no killings. Then I'm thinking I could follow Olin, get pictures of what he were up to." He glanced at his camera. "I left Source off at Potter's. He said it were all right with you. Ain't my job to check."

"Go on."

"Pulled my boat in at Haulover and snuck back, but Olin never set foot out of the camp, so I went to Evergreen Slew. Woke up to three-foot seas out my door. Didn't take no weatherman to tell me we was fixing for a blow. I got to pull my crab pots. I tried to get hold of Olin to tell him I'd be by for him later, but the cellular were out."

"That was you I saw, over by Potter's around five?" Bert asked.

Donny shrugged. "There was boats out everyplace. Them waves was fierce. Weren't nobody at Potter's by the time I got there. I tied up and set awhile. That dock's protected good." He snickered. "I keep a jug in the boat. Man gets worn out this time of the year, so being there weren't nothing else to do . . ."

"How did you get here?" Hunter asked.

Donny scratched his head. "Fell asleep. I woke up with the tide real high. Reckoned Potter's were no place to be in the middle of a hurricane, so I headed on over."

"And you found Olin here."

Donny shook his head. "He never showed till later, not too sure exactly when. I set myself on that sofa and took a little nap. Next thing I knows, I got Source in my face, shaking like he's freezing. He's yelling at me to take him off the island right quick, running his mouth like a madman about ghosts and Luna Mae. Told me she popped right out of the ground wearing that mosquito hat of hers."

Hunter and Bert exchanged glances. Had Source mistaken her for Luna Mae's ghost?

"He scared two years' growth off of me. I do believe in my heart that man kilt Luna Mae and Miss Anne. He were going on about a timer, and how it weren't his music that scared Miss Anne into burning herself up. Gave me the willies, he did. Next, he starts in on Luna Mae. He's telling me how he didn't mean to kill her neither. Then he's giggling and says it don't matter nohow, on account of no one stays dead on this island."

"What the hell did he mean?" Hunter asked.

Donny shrugged. "He were still going on about Luna Mae. He told me he thought she were dead, but that she come back, popped out of the ground. Then he ducks his head, smiles up at me, and says, like it's good news, 'But Anne's the one that got toasted.' "

Chills ran up Bert's spine.

"Did he say what he was doing at the station?" Hunter asked.

Donny hung his head. "He were coming back from Evergreen, been hunting me. Reckon we was chasing each other all evening."

"So what happened then?"

"I seen Olin's losing it. One minute, he's smiling and saying he didn't kill no one. Next minute, he's shaking and sweating and telling me he got to get off the island." Donny sighed. "There's no way I'm taking a boat out in a hurricane, but I didn't want to rile him none. Told him to go outside and get an eyeful, and if he still wanted me to take him off, I would. That shut him up. Took to pacing around muttering and sweating. Wore me out watching him, so I headed up here to get away." He grinned. "I were hid in the closet when I spied Olin on the stairs with a gun. I ain't no dummy. I didn't plan to stick around till the storm let up. Figured I was a dead man soon as I got him off the island. Next thing I know, I hear shots and all that commotion. Then you come along with this gun and order me out." He fixed his gaze on Hunter's weapon. "You think you could put that away for a while? It's making me right nervous, it is."

For the first time, Hunter relaxed. He waved Donny back to the bed. "Go on back to sleep. We'll go over this again in the morning." He holstered the gun. "Meanwhile, I don't want you leaving this room, you hear? If I as much as see you out in the hall for one second, I'll handcuff you to the bed and lock the door."

"No problem, man." Donny reached for the sleeping bag. "My conscience is happy now."

"I was wearing mosquito netting. Did Olin really think I was Luna Mae's ghost and shoot me?" Bert asked as they started downstairs.

Hunter frowned in concentration. "She never went outside without the netting. From the path, he wouldn't have seen the opening into the tomb. Could have looked like you were materializing from the bare ground."

Bert remembered how frightened she'd been when Jimmy

popped up behind her on the path. "That's probably it, but what about Jimmy?" The water had risen while they were talking to Donny. They sloshed their way through several inches on the floor.

"If it had been me there and someone shot at you, I'd have gone after him," Hunter said as a particularly violent gust rattled the front of the station.

"Oh, you mean he got killed protecting me?"

"Running away, more likely. Didn't you say he was shot in the back?" He turned into the card room. "Source shot at you. Range thought he was after the emeralds, so he runs off. By that time, I reckon Source realized neither of you were ghosts. But he'd already shot you, so he had to shoot Jimmy. Couldn't leave any witnesses."

"Then he dumped Jimmy's body on top of me in the tomb. He thought I was dead, too." Bert sucked in a long breath. "It would make sense. The tide was rising. Olin must have figured it would wash the blood and all signs of excavation away, hide the tomb. That would be better than having our bodies show up on some beach a week later with gunshot wounds. I'll bet he didn't know about the emeralds. Were they really all that valuable?"

"Can't say for sure. From what I've heard, a lot of those old stones were flawed. Badly cut, too. Reckon the necklace was worth more as an artifact."

"Poor Jimmy." She stared absently at the water seeping under the door. "Shouldn't we pry up some floorboards or something?"

"Only if the tide rises faster outside than inside." Hunter glanced out one of the windows. "Doing about the same." He pulled out a chair. "Come here and sit down. Time we cleaned out that wound of yours." Slinging his pack onto the table, he removed his first-aid kit.

A few minutes later, Bert's hair had been clipped off behind her ear. The bandage felt cool and soothing.

"Time for a break." Hunter sat down and leaned back, his feet stretched out, his heels under the water. Bert shoved another chair over. "Thanks," he said, putting up his feet. "Now, all that's missing is a can of beer."

"Beer? With a hurricane about to float us away? And what about Olin?"

He glanced at her, his gray eyes bright. "Ain't much I can do about either right now, and worrying won't help none. Why don't you lay down for a while?"

Bert smiled. "I'm fine. Frankly, that beer sounded better than a nap."

She was conscious of his eyes following her as she went out to the front hall. She'd packed water and a thermos of coffee, as well as most of the contents of her fridge: beer, milk, cheese, bread, butter, hard-boiled eggs, ham, Polish sausage, lettuce, and mayonnaise. She unpacked the cooler and, with a flourish, spread the makings for sandwiches on the table.

Hunter reached over and patted her butt, then helped himself to a beer. "Knew you were my type of gal. From the first time I laid eyes on you, I said to myself, 'Now, there's a woman that knows how to care for a man.' " He ducked as Bert pitched the bread at him.

"Just for that, you get to make your own sandwich."

He hefted the Coors. "I'll make you one, too, soon as I'm done with this. Then we got to go through that backpack of Olin's."

She'd completely forgotten that. She brought it over, undoing some snaps.

Hunter swung around and placed his hand flat on the bag. "You know, this is probably evidence against the man. Don't reckon we should be messing with it."

Bert cleared her throat in exasperation. "You said you wanted it." Hunter's eyes shone with laughter. "Oh, you're such a tease. Do you think he found that journal?"

"I'm guessing that was a cover for what he was really after. Source hasn't been exactly truthful about a lot of things."

"Open it, then."

Hunter reached for the pack. "Going to have to make an inventory, note the order things come out." He glanced at the water covering the floor. "I'm thinking it might be smart of us to head on upstairs, where it's dry."

They took everything with them—Olin's pack, Hunter's first-aid kit, the food, and the lantern. Rather than moving into the dormitory with Donny, Hunter voted for one of the storage rooms. It had two beds, a dresser, and a desk. Metal filing cabinets lined the walls, and file boxes were stacked inside a set of floor-to-ceiling metal shelves. There was barely enough room to walk.

After they loaded their flashlights with fresh batteries from Hunter's pack, Bert cleared off the desk and set out their sandwiches. For a while, they ate in silence. Bert glanced at her watch. Two in the morning. Strange to be eating at this hour, but she wasn't in the least bit sleepy. Punchy, yes. Her headache was gone, but the low pressure was making her teeth ache, and her mind was definitely not running on all cylinders. It seemed hurricanes did make a person muddy-minded. Was it really a weather phenomenon that had led Olin to act as if someone were after him on that roof? She flinched as something banged into the wall near her. The card room was sheltered under the enormous porch. But up here, they were much more exposed.

"You know," Hunter said lazily, "I was trying to figure out how many hurricanes this station has seen." He ticked them off on his fingers. "There was the storm of 1894, when the keeper had just been hired. Had to call on the villagers to rescue the *Spofford* when she ran aground on a shoal by Ocracoke. Then there was the San Ciriaco in 1899. Now, that was a blow. Had to scuttle the floors to let the water in. Portsmouth's most famous shipwreck, the *Vera Cruz*, happened in 1903. And then there were the '33 and '44 hurricanes, Gloria in '56 ,and Dennis and Floyd in '99, then—"

"The San Ciriaco," Bert interrupted. "Wasn't that the hurricane that wrecked most of Portsmouth and took Jerushia's house? Did she stop haunting then?"

"Depends on what you call haunting. I told you, Sea-born Woman's supposed to send dolphins to meet all incoming boats."

Bert smiled. "I love that story. But why does she do it?"

Hunter turned thoughtful. "My daddy always said she was waiting for someone to come back to the island."

"That's what Luna Mae said. Maybe Jerushia had a lover—a

sailor—and Spriggs sent him away. She's waiting for him to come back."

Hunter dropped his voice dramatically, his eyes bright under his brows. "Or maybe she's waiting for Spriggs's killer to return, so she can take her revenge."

"Spriggs was murdered around 1770, right before the Revolutionary War, wasn't he? What if her lover couldn't get back? Suppose he was conscripted to fight, or was killed in the war?"

"Those were hard times, all right," Hunter said. "My great-great-great-granddaddy's boatyard failed. The family had to move from New Bedford to Boston. Later, his adopted son, my ancestor, bought property here in the Straits—that's near Harkers Island. Came down for the whaling, you know."

"Luna Mae said something about the O'Hagans having to return before Jerushia's man could come back. Did your whaler ever live here?"

"To the best of my knowledge, I'm the first O'Hagan to set foot on this island in two hundred years. Didn't even know we were connected to the Portsmouth O'Hagans until my mama's aunt got into genealogy." Hunter reached for Olin's pack. "Might as well get this over with—unless you'd rather take a nap, that is."

"Not while it's doing that." Bert nodded toward the window, where the panes rattled and the sash blew. She dragged her chair up to the desk and opened a notebook. "How should I do this?"

"I'll call each item out. You number and list them in order."

Right at the top of the pack was extra ammunition for a gun. "One ammo clip," Hunter called out. Work gloves and a folding camp shovel followed. Then, under some clothes, Hunter found a charred white box. They both stared at the melted, twisted piece of plastic. It still reeked of burnt synthetic. "So that's how he did it," Hunter said.

"What?"

"It's a timer. The Sources weren't having power failures at all. Olin was turning off the lights with this." Hunter used a handkerchief to pick it up. "Wager that's why he wouldn't come into the cabin with Jimmy and me. Left us to pack up Anne's belongings, while he checked out the ruins. Then when he couldn't find the timer, he used the log as an excuse to keep coming back. That man scared his wife to death. Probably had a whole bag full of nasty tricks."

"Jimmy said Anne talked about a ghostly choir. That's what gave Jimmy the idea of setting up a cassette to keep me inside while he searched for the tomb."

Hunter nodded. "Olin was after the timer the whole time. Reckon he was afraid if someone like Luna Mae found it, they might wonder if Miss Anne's death was truly accidental."

"Wouldn't Anne have noticed a timer?"

"Not necessarily." Hunter slapped the table. "That's it! Anne might not have noticed a timer, but you can bet the chief would have. I always questioned Ben Willis's accident. He said Olin acted real surprised to see him, didn't know Miss Anne had called to report the generator. Ben told me Source accidentally rocked the boat just as he was stepping off. He ended up doing a spread eagle between the dock and the boat. That was no accident. Olin had to stop Ben from checking out the shed."

"But there really was a cold fog. You felt it."

"There's always fog on the Outer Banks—and inversions. Source played dirty using his wife's fears, probably planned to bring on a stroke or heart attack. Instead, he set her on fire."

"You think he did it?"

"Directly or indirectly."

Suddenly, it was all clear to Bert. "Olin must have killed Luna Mae right after Jimmy and I saw him heading for the generator ruins."

"I'm thinking she spied him finding the timer."

Bert shook her head. "If Olin found it the other night, he wouldn't have it in his backpack now. I'll bet Luna Mae was out probing by the shed and hid when she heard him coming. Caught him digging in the ruins and thought he was looking for the tomb, too. They got into another fight. Olin drowned her and was coming back to dump her body in the ocean—except I found her first.

I told you it wasn't Donny."

"Rub it in, why don't you?"

Bert's giggle stopped abruptly as her temple throbbed.

"What's wrong?" Hunter asked. He turned the flashlight on her face, which made her flinch. "Head hurting? I thought so." He shone the light directly into her eyes, exhaling in relief. "Pupils are all right. Here." He led her to the bed. "Time for a nap." Hunter's hands were gentle but insistent.

"You, too." She pulled him down next to her. She inhaled as Hunter curled over her. "You smell good."

His fingertips stroked her forehead ever so gently. It sent prickles of pure pleasure rippling through her scalp. He was nice. They said you had to be with a person under stress to really know him. They'd had a bad day, both of them, but it had brought them together faster than years of dating. With his soothing hands still on her head, Bert drifted off to dream about giant waves, cold fog, and Hunter's ancestors—Outer Bankers whose lifetimes still echoed in the wind and waves.

Chapter 26

AFTER HOURS OF POUNDING WINDS and shaking floors, the storm gradually ceased, and with it went the last of Bert's headache. She awoke to find Hunter watching her, his face dark and haggard. "Did you sleep at all?" she asked, then turned to hide her face. She probably looked even worse than he did.

"Some, when you weren't tossing and turning. Never saw such a restless sleeper. You sure you're all right?"

"I'm fine, truly." She sat up, fishing for her comb. "You won't believe the dreams I had."

"Is that why you were hanging on to me so hard?"

"Guess I didn't want you to leave me." Bert looked down. "I dreamt you left and never came back."

"Don't think you have to worry about that." Hunter hugged her, glancing toward the window. Faint light gleamed in the sky.

Reassured by the dawning daylight and the diminishing wind, they woke Donny. The three made their way downstairs. The tide had receded from the first floor, leaving a ripple pattern of water, sand, and mud on the planks. While the men used the hole in the floor of the old bathroom as plumbing, Bert went to the boathouse to do some rudimentary cleaning. Then they breakfasted out of Bert's cooler. Thanks to her can of Sterno, they even managed instant coffee.

Hunter and Bert went outside to check for other survivors and damage. The floors in the summer kitchen were wet and buckled, but otherwise the cabin was miraculously in one piece. The generator shed had not fared as well. The little building had floated off its foundation and lay at an angle nearby, its roof and most of one wall gone. Bert confessed to leaving the motor running, but Hunter only shook his head, staring at the exposed machinery. "Once the tide got to it, it was history anyway."

Stepping carefully, they waded up the wet runway to the cistern, now full to the brim. Behind it, water gleamed among the deposits of sand, the wrack, and the uprooted trees. There was nothing left of the path and no trace of the tomb.

"I don't even see the prickly ash," Bert said, staring at a pile of downed cedars.

"Reckon it's going to take some doing to uncover that grave again."

"I shouldn't have opened it. Even if they find it, the water will have washed everything out."

"If you didn't open it, then Range would have. Some things are meant to happen."

Sharing an ATV, Bert and Hunter took a quick trip through the village. The roads were eighteen inches underwater in places. The bridge at Doctor's Creek had been partially washed out. Shingles by the hundreds cluttered the sodden grass in the village. They passed among fallen junipers, their root masses rising like dark walls, and bounced over heaps of wrack left by the high water. The church had lost two windows and looked to Bert as if it was listing. At the visitor center, the roof had leaked and brought down part of the ceiling. The water had floated the cool shed deep into the marsh. The dock at Haulover had fared the worst. Much of the decking was gone, and the entire **T** at the end, pilings and all, had vanished. They found no shipwrecked sailors in the village, nor did they see any sign of life along the shore.

Back at the cabin, Hunter hooked up the propane to the kitchen. Then he and Donny took the marine radio to the station tower to see if they could reach Harkers. Bert stayed in the cabin. The windows and doors had leaked, plus the tide had risen over the floor level. The linoleum was wet, marked with rims of sand left by the shrinking puddles, but the cabin was habitable. She had no desire to spend another night at the station.

Already, the experiences of the night before were taking on a dreamlike quality, Bert decided as she removed the nails and planks from her windows. Had something really chased Olin off the roof? Was it the wind, or had his guilt killed him? And that fog—how much had been real and how much a product of trauma and stress?

Bert swept most of the water from the cabin, then stretched out on the damp linoleum to light the pilot for the fridge and oven—but not the hot-water tank. They would conserve its contents carefully, as there would be no fresh water until they got one of the portable generators hooked up, and that could be awhile, according to Hunter.

"You doing good?" Hunter called from the door, his bulk shading what little light she had.

"Fine. How about opening the windows?" She continued loading the fridge with the food from her cooler.

Hunter nodded. "Might be here another couple of days yet."

"You got through?"

"Not to the park. The power at Harkers is still out. Going to be awhile before they get it back—least that's what the Coast Guard at Ocracoke tells me." He walked over and put his arm around her shoulder. "You got a problem if we stay here a few more days?"

"I'd love it. Can someone let my daughter know I'm okay?"

"She'll probably be calling Harkers, and they'll pass the word. If she doesn't, I'll get Rudy on it when they get power. But how's your head? Any more headaches or dizziness?"

They had been over this earlier. He'd changed her bandage and agreed her wound was healing and didn't need stitches. "I'm fine, really." Bert made the connection between her medical condition and the radio. "Why, does the park want us to stay?"

"Yep. At least that was the message the superintendent left with the Coast Guard. Park wanted to know who was here and if we had any injuries or reason for an emergency evacuation. I told them no, all right?"

Bert couldn't help smiling. "I'll bet you didn't say anything about Source or Jimmy."

Hunter banged on a window to loosen the seal. "Nothing the park can do for them anyhow. No bodies washed up, not yet. Park's got enough on its plate right now. Ocracoke's no better off than us. It's been evacuated. No water or electric, no doctor over there, no ferries running, not even the big ones. Three-foot seas in the sound, and lots of flotsam—not a good place for a boat." He slammed the window open. "We're better off here. It's not like we don't have enough drinking water."

"Food, too." Bert pointed at the array of canned goods and boxes on the shelves behind her.

"There should be whelks for the taking on the beach. Nothing tastier than North Carolina whelk chowder. We'll be better off than some. At least we've got water and cooking fuel."

"Won't they think it's odd if we don't tell them what happened right away?"

"I planned it out. Left a message to have Rudy call the Coast Guard. They can patch him to Ocracoke through Fort Macon. I'll give Rudy the news, and he can run with it. There's relatives to be informed and all that before we think of making it public."

"What about Donny?"

"He's off to check his boat, then his camp and the Mickey Mouse. If the park boat's not beat too bad, we can take her back to Harkers when it calms down some. Donny's fixing to stay at his camp till then."

"You're not afraid he'll leave?"

"I told him not to. Don't expect he'll cross me. He's right pleased to be on my good side for once."

Bert hoped Donny was smart enough to stay there, but somehow she doubted it. He was the type who would forever be in trouble with authority. "Let me get this place swept out and wiped down while I still have the energy, then maybe we can go out on the beach. I'd love to see what it looks like."

The beach was more spectacular than Bert had imagined. The sky was still overcast, the wind still blowing. The crossing over the flats was difficult, but the view made the trip worthwhile. Before them, the white sand stretched for miles, virginal, washed clean from the low-water line right to the back dunes. Hunter parked the ATV, reluctant to spoil the landscape with even a tire mark. Hand in hand, they strolled down to the water's edge, Bert speechless in pleasure. This was what beaches must have looked like millions of years ago, before the coming of man—wind-swept waves of sand mounded with shells, wrack, and, here and there, dark mounds that signaled a dead bird or fish. Beyond the beach, the dark ocean still roared, huge breakers sending powerful surges of water hissing up the shore.

Hunter bent to pick up a large whelk. For a moment, Bert thought he was shelling, then realized the living creature was still inside. Hunter was gathering food. They walked for an hour finding treasure: huge horse conchs, helmets and channel whelks by the hundreds, and a beautiful orange tulip shell. Pieces of lumber lay everywhere. Now, Bert understood how the original settlers had scavenged wood from the beaches for their homes and fires. There were even two crab traps torn from their moorings. Both had live blue crabs inside. Hunter gathered those, too, and carried the traps past the high-water line, to be salvaged later. Did they belong to Donny? Bert wondered. The only thing that marred her pleasure was the nagging fear that one of the big mounds of seaweed contained a body.

Hunter must have read her thoughts, as he said softly, "Bodies don't usually wash up for three, four days."

"How did you know what I was thinking?" He was getting much too good at reading her.

He chuckled. "You're a great one for taking the lead, but today you're letting me go first."

"I didn't mean to."

He turned, his slate eyes warm and bright as he drew her close. "All I know is you'll always be first with me."

The heat felt good through her thin shirt. Bert let herself flow into the curves of his warm, hard body, staring dreamily over his shoulder at the storm-tossed water. The wind blew in her face, heavy with the scent of salt, seaweed, and something else—decay. Reminded her of the jellyfish at the pier. She'd felt threatened by them, but they had stopped Olin from coming ashore, hadn't they? And the mosquitoes had sent her scurrying to the safety of her cabin. And the nutria had defended her from Jimmy.

Bert drew a deep breath and murmured into Hunter's ear, "You know, if it hadn't been for the nutria, Olin would have dumped Luna Mae into the ocean and gotten away with it."

"Guess I got a lot to thank them critters for—my sea-born woman most of all."

As Hunter's arms closed around her, Bert knew without a doubt that she belonged here. Age was not important. Neither was the opinion of others.

Overhead, a solitary pair of gulls called softly, as if approving her decision.